Smell

Smell

A Novel

RADHIKA JHA

SOHO

SOUTH BOSTON

First published in Viking by Penguin Books India in 1999

Copyright © Radhika Jha 1999

First published in the U.S. in 2001 by Soho Press, Inc. 853 Broadway
New York, NY 10003

Library of Congress Cataloging-in-Publication Data
Jha, Radhika.
    Smell : a novel / Radhika Jha.
        p. cm.
    ISBN 1-56947-241-6 (alk. paper)
    1. East Indians—France—Fiction. 2. East Indians—Africa—Fiction.
3. Paris (France)—Fiction. 4. Young women—Fiction. 5. Smell—
Fiction. I. Title.

PR9499.3.J489 S64 2001
823'.914—dc21
                                                                00-067100

10 9 8 7 6 5 4 3 2 1

To souls without borders

acknowledgments

First, I must thank everyone who read the manuscript in its raw form and whose remarks helped me cook it further—Nina Payne, Cheryl Slover-Linett, Ava Li, Helene Peu du Vallon, Ajay Agarwal, Fred Glick, Donna Bryson, David and Pat Specter.

Sudhir Kakar, for his encouragement, and for sending the manuscript on its way.

My editors at Penguin India—David Davidar, Karthika V.K. and Sayoni Basu, who taught me that less can also be more.

Melanie Fleishman, editor with a nose par excellence and a sense of humour.

My agent, Laura Susjin, for always telling me exactly what she thinks.

Prabuddha Das Gupta and Bena Sareen, for giving Leela an unforgettable face.

Sabine Thiriot and Sabine Gaudemare, who turned the shock of arrival into a welcome.

My father, Prem Jha, for being a mother as well. My family—flesh and soul.

PART
one

When the wind blew hard, as it did very often that spring, the smell of fresh baguette would fight its way into the Epicerie Madras to do battle with the prickly smell of pickles and masalas.

It would enter the store confidently, making light of the heavy-breasted, sari-wrapped mannequins, Chinese prayer wheels, and Indian video cassettes that were on display in the large window sill facing the street. Before the shelves of cooked foods—banana chips fried in coconut oil, samosas, gulab jamuns, and papads—it would pause, some of its strength diminished by the pungent foreign odours.

Another gust of cold April wind bursting through the open door would bring reinforcements, and the smell of baguette would venture farther into the store. It would pass over the vegetables undiminished, past the counter where my uncle sat reading his newspaper, past the magazine rack with its smell of ink and chemicals, and finally, turn the corner into the back room where I sat. There, hemmed in on all fronts by the heady perfume of cardamom, turmeric, cinnamon, and coriander, and cut off from reinforcements by the L-shaped configuration of the room, it would make its last stand, until overwhelmed by the alien hosts.

In those last moments of reckless courage it would invade my nostrils. I would hold my breath seeking to give it shelter till my traitorous lungs would betray me. With a whoosh of defeat, I would let my breath out and let the spices of my native land, the land I had never seen, reclaim me.

My uncle Krishenbhai Patel owned the *épicerie*. He had bought it thirteen months ago from the widow of its former Sri Lankan Tamil owner, M Gunashekharan, who was stabbed to death in this very shop. Everyone in the community knew that it was the Tamil mafia who had killed him. 'The man was a fool,' Aunty Latha told me, 'he cheated on the protection money. Now what man would cheat on his protection, you tell me?'

Aunty Latha was my uncle's Indian wife. Krishenbhai was my father's youngest brother, the baby of the family. He had stayed in Nairobi as long as he could, long after my grandfather died and my father inherited the store. But he had had to leave eventually. He left shortly after my father married my mother. I never found out why, but it was whispered amongst the servants that he had fallen in love with her. No one in the family ever spoke about it.

It was to this third uncle then that I was sent when the riots began again and they came swarming over the compound walls into our home in Parklands. My father was already dead and his beloved department store had perished with him. The rest of us had been in Mombassa at the time, at my second uncle's home, where we always went for our vacations. My father had stayed behind to supervise the remodelling of the store. He was going to turn part of it into a gallery for young African artists and he wanted the work finished before the rains, well in time for the tourist season. He was confident that the riots would not last more than a day or two, like they always did. He told the workers he'd pay them double if they finished the work. And so most of them had stayed. Only, one day, when he arrived at the store, he found it deserted. He got nervous and called the house for the car. But the car, he was told, had been sent to the chemist's to fetch my grandmother's laxatives. By the time the driver, Chege, arrived at the store, it was in flames. They found the charred skeleton inside the store the next day after the fire had died down. Overnight, I learnt to hate Chege and with him, all black men. But I was isolated in my hatred. The rest of the family accepted it dumbly as fate. Even my mother, who should have known better, blamed Papa for getting killed. 'He trusted them too much,' she said bitterly.

We returned to Nairobi for the cremation. It felt silly to burn his bones a second time. When I said as much to my mother, she slapped me. It was the first time she had ever done that. 'You are an unholy, ungrateful wretch.' She burst into tears. As I watched her and the stinging in my cheek subsided, a terrible curiosity filled me. What made the cremation so important when he was already dead and there was no body left to burn?

'Maa,' I said hesitantly, 'I'm sorry, don't cry.' She didn't reply. I began to pat her back gently, the way she did when the boys or I couldn't get to sleep. I felt terrible for having spoken without thinking. Finally her shoulders stopped shaking. She wiped her eyes with the corner of her white sari. I got up quietly and began to move towards the door.

'Leela.' Her voice made me stop. 'You have to guide the dead out of this world into the next. Otherwise they will haunt you.'

'How?' I challenged her, unable to believe that my father who loved us all would harm us just because he was dead.

'They will take away your memories,' she replied, 'because you have not created a dignified final memory for them in your mind.'

They cremated him with the full Hindu rites, with lots of ghee, flowers, rice, and a bed made of reeds. Five-year-old Sunil, the elder by ten minutes of my twin brothers, was made to light the pyre as he was now the head of the family. My mother had to hold his hand for him when he had to pour the ghee onto the wood, and repeat the words after the priest because Sunil could barely pronounce the strange syllables. Although girls were traditionally not allowed to go to the cremation grounds, she made me go with her and watch the pyre burn. I stood behind her and my brothers, watching the flames, dry-eyed. I can still remember the bitter smell of the smoke. When we returned to pick up the remains as ritual prescribed, my mother made me carry the urn with his ashes and bits of bone home.

The second riot brought them into our home, tearing the upholstery in their search for cash. They didn't find much, so they took the TV and VCR and my father's collection of wildlife videos instead. After that, my mother decided to leave Kenya altogether. She wrote to her brother who was settled in England and he reluctantly invited her to stay. 'It's a small house,' he wrote, 'and we have only one spare room.'

My mother became even more withdrawn than usual. At odd moments I would catch her looking at me. I could not read the expression on her face, but she made me feel uneasy.

One day, I found her waiting for me outside the college gate. 'Let's go for a drive,' she said in answer to my unspoken question. 'I thought we could go to the Park. There are some things I want to discuss, and we could talk while I drive.' My heart lifted. The Nairobi National Park was only twenty minutes from the heart of the city. It had been one of my father's favourite places. He had loved taking us there when he had finished doing the accounts on a Sunday afternoon. My mother always drove while my father told us about the animals. She liked to drive. But my spirits plummeted to depths I had not known when I heard what she had to say. She had decided to take only my two little brothers with her to England. I was to go to Krishenbhai and his wife in Paris.

'It is only till I find a job and get settled,' she said anxiously when she saw the anguish on my face.

'Why can't I come with you?' I asked angrily. 'It's so unfair. First Papa is taken away. I have to leave college and Nairobi and all my friends, and now I have to lose you and Sunil and Anil.' Bitter tears came flowing out of my eyes. 'Don't you love me at all, Maa?'

'Don't even think that, Leela,' my mother cried out, braking hard and pulling the car to the side of the road. A pair of bush bucks that had been hiding in the reeds crashed out in alarm and leaped away. 'Do you think this is easy for me? Have you not seen how distraught I have been since Atul's letter arrived? But I can't stay on in Nairobi. It holds too many memories and too much fear. Besides, we will starve. The store was insured, but the insurance will cover only a fraction of the damage.' Her hands tightened on the wheel, and the little frown that I had come to know well since my father's death appeared between her eyes. 'There were also debts. Business had been bad since the riots began. I can't even afford to repair the damage they did to our home. If we sell it, I will have something to start with in England.'

'But why can't I come to England, too?' I asked, fighting to control my tears.

My mother leaned across and gave me the corner of her sari to wipe my eyes. 'Because my brother is not a wealthy man; we cannot burden him with the four of us,' she said tenderly.

'Why does it have to be me? Why can't you send one of the boys to live with Aunt and Uncle?'

'They are too small, and besides, your Aunty Latha wants you, Leela.'

'But why me?'

'She wants a girl. Aunty Latha can't have children because of her condition. She desperately wants a girl to pet and spoil. It would be selfish of me to refuse.'

I knew at that moment that my mother had decided to give me up. 'Why?' I asked dully.

'Because Krishen is your father's baby brother. He is very much like your father too.'

'No. I mean why can't she have her own children?'

My mother looked embarrassed and stared down at her hands. 'We don't know,' she replied at last. 'There doesn't seem to be anything wrong with her medically, nor with Krishenbhai.'

I didn't quite understand what this 'condition' was, but the servants giggled whenever they spoke about it. I wanted to ask my mother, but from the way she avoided my eyes I knew she would not tell me the truth.

In the days that followed, as we made preparations to leave, this continued to bother me. Who was this person with whom I was going to live? Why was everyone so evasive when I asked them about her? As I was getting ready to leave for the airport, I tried one last time.

'What is Aunty Latha's "condition," Maa?' She did not reply. I tried to catch her eye in the mirror, but she kept them focused on a point roughly six inches above my head.

'Tell me, Maa, please,' I pleaded. 'No one tells me anything any-more.' The hand that was combing my long hair stilled for a second, then continued.

'You are a very, very lucky girl,' my mother said, changing the subject deftly. 'You will live in the most beautiful city in the world. You will be spoilt and petted by your aunt and uncle who will love you as their own daughter. You will grow more beautiful with every passing year, and one day the world will be at your feet.'

Her eyes met mine in the mirror and we both suddenly broke into a smile.

The smiles felt strange on our faces, and as we watched our reflections in the mirror, they faded. We looked away guiltily and didn't speak again till it was time to say goodbye.

But it is that image which comes to mind whenever I think of her now—my beautiful, loving, defenseless, but ultimately treacherous mother.

two

My uncle Krishenbhai came to pick me up at the airport. He recognized me almost as soon as I came through the automatic doors, and beckoned me to come his way. Seeing him, I felt stunned. He was much taller than my father, but looked so much like him that he could have been his twin. But he was much better dressed than my father had ever been. He wore a long overcoat of soft black wool. A black, red, and navy-blue scarf hung around his neck. I felt ugly in my shapeless blue overcoat with its schoolgirl hood, and my scuffed leather school shoes. I had always hated those shoes and had wanted to leave them. 'Please, Maa, they make me look like an African in cast-off mazungu clothes,' I had wailed. But my mother had not been moved. 'We are poor now,' she had said impatiently, and had added as an afterthought, 'but that is nothing to be ashamed of.' We had both smiled then, for she had used my father's oft-repeated words.

My uncle and I stared at each other, unable to think of anything to say. Finally he broke the silence. 'My God, how like your mother you are! Those same eyes . . .' His eyes became moist. He groped in his overcoat pocket for a handkerchief, and blew his nose. Almost un-willingly, his eyes moved back to my face. 'Your father was the lucky one. But look what happened to him in the end, poor man.'

His words sounded sympathetic, but with a sick feeling I realized that what he was expressing was an obscure guilty satisfaction. It ended whatever resemblance he had to my father. The man before me was a complete stranger. A terrible sadness engulfed me, depriving me of words. 'No luck, I tell you,' I heard him say.' And your poor mother a widow. So young too. The pundit must have mismatched their horoscopes.'

I stared at him in horror, unwilling to believe what I had just heard. 'But he's dead now,' I snapped. His face changed immediately and assumed an expression of sorrow. 'Of course, of course. Forgive me. I did not mean to make fun of the dead. But you see, to me Prembhai still feels alive.' He shook his head, and his mouth turned down even more, 'It will take some getting used to.'

I looked down at the ground, refusing to meet his eyes. I could not bear to see the easy sorrow on his face.

My uncle must have sensed my revulsion. 'Come. Where is your luggage? Is that all you have?' he asked gruffly, not looking at me.

'We could only bring twenty kilos on the plane, Uncle,' I lied. Actually Papa's will had still not been probated, and we had had to sell just about everything we owned to pay for the tickets to Paris and London. My uncle looked at my bag, then at me and patted my head. 'Don't worry, Aunty Latha will buy you lots and lots of clothes.' He picked up my bag and strode towards the exit.

I followed him outside. After Kenya, the wide pavement seemed strangely empty. The sky was grey and a bitterly cold wind was blowing. The few people around scurried away, their heads bent, their eyes refusing to meet anyone else's. Cars loitered beside the pavement, their exhausts emitting thin plumes of smoke. My uncle's black-clad back ploughed through the wind, seeming not to notice it. I tried to do the same, but my body bent before the wind and curled like a cup to conserve some of its heat. I had never experienced such cold. The wind whipped through my thin clothes, turning my body to glass.

My uncle strode across the car park to a battered blue station wagon and opened the passenger door. I climbed in gingerly. Inside, the car smelt of petrol, leather, and cigarette smoke. They were exciting smells and I drank them in eagerly. I turned towards the window and looked out. We were on a smooth grey road that curved around the airport. Huge billboards advertising familiar things with strange names blocked the view on either side. Then we were on a broad highway with six lanes and many cars. I watched the other people inside their cars.

Occasionally I would catch someone's eye, and sometimes the person would smile. But usually these were people who drove older, slower cars. The drivers of the powerful-looking new cars kept their eyes fixed firmly on the road before them.

After we had been driving for what felt like a long time, I asked, 'Where is the city? And where are all the buildings?' My uncle laughed. 'We are still a long way from it. The airport is more than fifty miles from Paris.'

'Do you like to live in the city, Uncle?' I asked him.

'In Paris?' He lifted an eyebrow in mock disbelief. 'It is the best city in the world.'

'The best,' I repeated. 'Why?'

'Why?' his voice became hoarse with excitement. 'Because it is a truly international city, filled with people from every corner of the world.'

'How wonderful!' I turned to him, thrilled by the passion in his voice. 'It must be like Muthaiga then.' He looked uncomprehending. 'Muthaiga in Nairobi, Uncle. It's where all the embassies are, and where the white people live. Surely you must have visited it when you lived in Kenya?'

He shook his head. 'Nope. I never went there. In those days it was strictly off-limits to non-whites. In any case,' he added dismissively, 'compared to Paris, all Nairobi is a village. People come from all over the world to become a part of this city. They come to take on the spirit of the city, because it is greater than all the people who live in it.'

His enthusiasm was infectious, and I warmed to him. 'I can't wait to see it,' I said and sat bolt upright, straining to look over the fences that now lined the highway. But there was nothing to see. Just huge empty fields, and hedges turned brown by winter. I turned to look at my uncle and asked, 'Which part of the city do you live in, Uncle?'

He shrugged impatiently. 'The name wouldn't mean anything to you.'

'But is it in the east or the west, the north or the south?'

He took his eyes off the road for a second and gave me a strangely defensive look. 'We don't exactly live inside the city.'

'But your letters were postmarked Paris!'

His hands gripped the steering wheel more firmly. 'It's too crowded in the city, too many people, too hot in summer. The houses are very small and close together. No one actually lives in the city anymore. They all live in the suburbs now. Like us.' He gave me a small triumphant smile and looked at the road again.

I kept quiet. But I felt strange, as if I had just been given bad news.

We left the highway, and began to wind through little streets. The narrow-fronted houses had miserly shuttered windows and nondescript doors. I suddenly felt homesick for the broad clean roads of Parklands, lined with jacaranda and coral trees. I wanted to be back just once more in our garden, and to thrill to the knowledge that the edge of the Park, with eland, gazelles, and rhinos, was only a stone's throw away. The tightly packed houses and alien architecture made Papa feel even more far away.

Then we were past the houses and driving between silently towering buildings, painted in impossible combinations of colours. The land in between was flat and drab. As at the airport, there was no one to be seen. The road came to an end before a large gate. We passed through and stopped before a group of buildings painted brown, red, and mauve. With a sinking feeling I realized that this was my new home.

Three

A creaking elevator with graffiti scrawled on the steel walls took us up to the fifth floor. It came to a jerky halt, and the door opened with a terrible slowness. I took a deep breath and stepped out quickly. We were in a silent grey corridor with steel doors leading off it. Almost immediately I could smell it—that smell of oil, pickle, and spices, which is the hallmark of the Indian home. Three generations of living among a people who smelt of woodsmoke, ash, and slightly rancid butter, in a land of wide-open spaces and wind had made recognition even easier. When I was a child, my nurse Mariamma once told me that Africans recognized Asians by their smell, long before they actually saw us. I had tried hard to smell myself, but could smell nothing. On that day, in that airless corridor closed off on all sides by thick concrete walls, the smell that Mariamma had spoken of took on a shape and form, and emerged shyly from the shadows like a jackal.

I stood still. I had never smelt anything so strong, and so utterly alien to its surroundings. A terrible sense of foreboding filled me. I wanted to run down and feel the wind sink its teeth into my body once again, and cleanse me of the memory of this smell. But it was too late. The lift had moved on. My uncle led the way down the hall, past three identical anonymous doors and stopped before the fourth. I trailed behind him slowly, the smell growing stronger and more insistent with each step.

A dried chili hung to ward off evil spirits dangled above the entrance to their apartment. He put down my bag, opened the three locks on the door and gave it a push. The steel door swung open. He picked up the bag and stepped inside. I hung back. From inside the small foyer my uncle shouted impatiently, 'Don't stand there, come inside quickly. I have to lock the doors.' His voice sounded far away. I took a deep breath and stepped in. The stale smell surrounded me, telling me I was as trapped as it was.

I looked around for an avenue of escape. Four doors gave off the hallway. But they were all shut. My uncle finished locking the door and picked up the bag again. He opened one of the doors and led the way down another corridor. Here the smell was less overpowering, but it continued to follow us.

My uncle stopped beside a door at the very end and waited for me to catch up. Making a gesture of welcome, he allowed me to enter first. I stepped into a small square room. It was bare except for two mattresses rolled up against two facing walls. At the far end of the room was a window with grey metal blinds drawn tightly over it. On the wall above one of the mattresses was stuck a picture, obviously cut out of a magazine, of a young Indian film star. She had a round plump face, a tiny nose, and a small pouty mouth. The image ended where her substantial cleavage began.

Krishenbhai placed the bag in a corner near the other mattress. 'This is your bed,' he said smiling, slightly embarrassed. 'Now rest here for some time, I will see what your Aunty Latha is doing.' He began to move towards the door.

Suddenly, I didn't want him to leave. The thought of being alone in that room scared me. 'Uncle,' I called to him, 'do you know who lives in this room?' Tiredness made the question come out all wrong.

He paused, his hand on the door. Without turning around, he said casually, 'Yes, of course. Amma lives here. She is a great help to us, looking after your aunt when she has her condition. She can look after you too.'

The room seemed even smaller. 'But . . . but I'm almost eighteen, I don't need any looking after,' I wailed. 'And I don't like people watching me all the time.'

He turned around and stared quite deliberately at my legs. I watched his eyes. They were wet and shiny like pebbles in a stream. Around the knees where my flesh was bare, I felt goose bumps begin. Then he looked up and smiled coldly, 'We didn't realize you'd be so grown up, Leela. That's a pity.' His voice sharpened, 'But apartments are small in this country and you'll have to learn to manage. You people in Africa are spoiled.'

I could not believe my ears. How could we in Africa have more than he had in Europe? Wasn't he the one living safely in Paris while his brother was killed in Nairobi?

He took advantage of my silence to leave. 'Good girl. Rest now. You will soon get used to things,' he said more calmly, and let himself out of the room.

The door shut behind him. I felt imprisoned. I looked desperately around the room and was lured to the window. But there were thick steel strips nailed to the window frame that prevented me from getting even a glimpse of what lay outside. I struggled to open the window, feeling the panic mount. Finally, I succeeded.

A gust of cold air in my face made me conscious once more of my surroundings. I leaned out eagerly, hungry for the sight of other human beings. But there were none. All I could see was row upon row of identical rectangular windows outlined in yellow against the lilac and blue walls of the building in front. I sat back, remembering in minute detail the view from my room in Nairobi—the red earth and the purple bougainvillea along the compound wall, and across it, the back street. There were always people there—little children kicking stones and sending up puffs of dust, the *bokamama* with her straw bag filled with greeny-purple *sukumawiki*, or Chege flirting and smoking with the maids.

The image didn't last long. The colours dimmed and flattened. And once more I was staring at the windows of the building opposite. They were like mirrors, and all I could see was myself reflected in one of their flat surfaces. My body slumped against the windowsill, unable to move.

I heard the thump and shuffle of approaching footsteps. They stopped outside the door. I waited. Suddenly, the door behind me flew open with a bang. I turned around hurriedly, feeling vaguely guilty.

A mountain of a woman stood framed in the narrow doorway, a

look of surprised horror on her face. Her arms were as wide as both my thighs put together. Her breasts could have fed an orphanage. Her stomach was vast like a sail filled to the brim with wind. This, I realized, torn between disgust and wonder, was Aunty Latha. Usually Gujarati women are small and, as they grow older, tend to dry up like bits of wood. My mother had shrivelled up in a night after my father died. But this woman had become a balloon.

While I remained frozen in front of the window, the mountain did not stay still. It moved swiftly and unsteadily across the room, dark-skinned and angry. With her came the aroma of mustard oil and masala and cheap talcum powder, making her seem too large for the room. 'Oh no. What are you doing opening that window? People will see you,' she squeaked in Gujarati. I pressed myself hard against the sill. 'You must never open the window or we will get robbed! You don't know how bad these people are!' She pushed me aside and shut the window, pulling down on the handle to lock it firmly. 'I told him glass windows were a bad idea. What we need in this place is bars, solid iron bars. But Krishen will insist on wasting money on clothes, and we still have to pay the mortgage on the shop!'

When at last she had got the window securely fastened, she turned and looked at me steadily. 'So you are my husband's niece,' she stated flatly, 'welcome.' But there was no softness in her voice, or in the lines of her body resting heavily against the window. She studied me carefully, noting my worn clothes and scuffed shoes. Her eyes settled once more on my face. 'Krishen tells me you are very much like your mother.' She nodded to herself. 'She was a nice girl from Saurashtra, no?'

'What?' I was surprised and slightly annoyed at her ignorance. 'My mother is from India, not Saura-whatever.'

She began to laugh, her cheeks shaking, and then her neck and arms quivering too. 'You silly, Saurashtra is in Gujarat.'

'Oh, of . . . of course,' I said, suddenly feeling very stupid.

I stared at her huge body and wished she would disappear. But she remained where she was, staring at me, the laughter dying out of her eyes. It was replaced by a more complicated look. 'Now you be a good girl,' she said, 'and there will be no problem, you understand?' She had a way of rolling her r's and exhaling as she spoke that left one feeling off-balance.

The halting breathless cadence of her speech resembled the uneven sound of her footsteps. Suddenly, I felt sorry for her, for the unwieldy bulk that she was forced to carry around day after day. I wondered how my uncle, so slim and elegant, had married this vast mound of flesh. I tried to imagine them making love, him bounding atop her.

She saw the look on my face and her expression hardened. 'Krishen has lied to me again. He said you were young, unspoilt. You Africans are all alike, spoiled rotten, with a taste for luxury.'

Furious, I took a step towards her, 'How dare you?' I shouted. 'I'm not African, no more than y . . .' The word died on my lips. She brought her face close to mine, and I was confronted by her black bead-like eyes. They gave a lie to the softness of the rest of her frame. 'You're not African?' she jeered softly. 'Then what are you? You're certainly not Indian. You were not born there, and our gods don't travel across the seas.' Those eyes dared me to prove her wrong. I glared back, full of hate, but unable to think of a suitable reply. She moved away hurriedly, as if what she had seen in me repelled her, and continued her harangue, 'You had better mend your ways, my girl. There is no luxury to be had here. You are living in my house now and you will have to follow my rules. Pray to God to help you.' With that, she turned and left.

At last I cried. I cried for my father, my mother, my brothers, my grandmother, the courtyard inside our house and the streets outside which were always so full of people, and animals in the Park. I cried because at last I could see everything that I had lost.

four

My uncle's voice calling me for dinner from the other end of the house reached my ears. Quickly I tidied my hair, removed my coat, and ventured out of the boxlike room. Next to it was a tiny bathroom. Without bothering to search for the light, I went inside and sat down on the pot. The bathroom was cool and smelt fresh and soapy. Seated on the pot in the darkness, I relaxed. Suddenly I heard the sound of an explosion somewhere above my head. I jumped up and stared wildly at the ceiling. Then I heard the reassuring sound of water rushing through a pipe. Someone in the apartment above us had just pulled the flush. I began to laugh, oddly comforted by the sound.

When I arrived in the living room after washing my face and hands, they were already seated. The dining table was placed right under the window, across which rose-coloured satin curtains were drawn tightly shut. The room itself seemed only slightly larger than mine, with the same set of windows along one wall. But it felt smaller because it contained a large carved velvet sofa and chairs, and a low glass table crammed with silver and brass gods and goddesses.

'Come on, come on. Sit down and eat,' my uncle commanded. Obediently I sat down at the empty place beside him.

'No, no, not there,' my aunt snapped, her mouth full of food. 'You'll only be in Amma's way. Go sit there.' The place she'd pointed to was at the foot of the long rectangular table, farthest away from the two of them.

I sat down quietly, staring at the food on the table. There were puris, pulao, chicken, meat, papads, kheer, srikhand, three kinds of vegetables, and dal. It was a feast—but a forbidden one. It shocked me to see the chicken and meat sitting brazenly amongst the vegetables. My father would have been horrified.

Just then, an old woman shuffled in from the kitchen, bringing more plates of food with her. I looked at her curiously. Despite the heat, she had on a sweater and a shawl which she wore wrapped around her head and pulled low over her forehead, leaving her face in darkness.

'This is Amma. She helps us in the house,' Aunty Latha introduced us. Amma shuffled up to where I sat and peered down at me.

'You are so pretty,' Amma smiled. I looked shyly up into her face, and went cold. Half of Amma's face was white and pink with leucoderma and the other half was dark brown. Seeing the look on my face, she backed away towards the other end of the table, muttering something beneath her breath. She put the dishes down clumsily and moved away, still talking to herself.

'I will be sleeping with her?' I whispered dully.

Neither of them responded. They were busy shovelling food into their mouths at a ferocious speed.

At last my uncle looked up at me, his cheeks swollen with food. 'Come, come. Don't be shy. You should eat. You are with family now.'

I looked at the food. The scent that arose from them was at once familiar and unfamiliar, the known aromas and the unknown ones so cunningly woven together that I couldn't separate them. The smells swamped my senses, making my head swim. Our vegetables never smelt so rich and heavy, I thought fuzzily. It must be the masalas, I decided, they probably couldn't get the right kinds here.

My hand moved resolutely towards the dal and then suddenly changed direction, hovering hesitantly over the bowl of chicken instead. My uncle noticed and smiled. 'Hahn, hahn, beti, take some. You are in a foreign country now, those old-fashioned rules don't apply here. You must take some or the cold will get to you.' I compromised and took some gravy but no chicken, feeling guilty but excited too.

Gingerly I tasted it. The food was delicious, the curry seemed to have absorbed the flesh of the chicken into itself, the basmati was cooked to perfection—each grain perfect and distinct. For a few seconds I let my face hang over my plate, absorbing the many aromas.

Then I wasted no more time, spooning it into my mouth as fast as I could.

Suddenly, my aunt broke the silence, 'Has Mme Gunashekharan paid up yet?'

My uncle's spoon jerked sharply just as it was about to reach his mouth. Some dal spilled onto his shirt and a few drops clung to the ends of his moustache. 'Not quite . . . almost . . . no really,' he faltered.

'Has she or has she not paid her bill? That is all I want to know.'

'We-ell . . .' my uncle seemed to grow smaller by the minute.

'Do you want us to be ruined? She still owes us 157.50 francs. Who will pay this money if you don't make her?

'But she is my boss's wife.'

'Your ex-boss—he's dead now. Now it's you who's the boss, so try to act like it.'

'It is not her fault that he is dead,' he shot back. 'It has only been thirteen months, Latha, she is still crazy with sorrow. Her husband's ghost is still in the store. Let him leave—then I will tell her to pay or get out.'

'Oh, you stupid men!' my aunt spat. 'There is no ghost. She is very clever and she knows you are a coward.'

'She is crazy. Poor thing,' my uncle replied.

'Huh, crazy. She is not crazy.'

We ate in silence after that. My uncle and aunt ate without pause, putting away huge quantities of food, fifteen or twenty puris, four helpings of the cardamom-scented pulao, and vast amounts of chicken and vegetables.

Finally, they turned to look at each other. 'I brought the new one,' my uncle said to her.

'What is the name?' she asked.

'*Tum Mere Ho*,' he said.

'Who's in it?'

'Aamir and Juhi,' he replied.

I didn't understand what they were talking about. But I decided not to ask them.

My uncle went out of the room and came back with a videocassette.

He handed me the case. 'I got this especially so that you don't feel homesick,' he said. 'You must have watched many Indian movies at home with your mother. She used to love them.'

I didn't reply. In our house, my father wouldn't allow them. 'They are rubbish,' he would say. 'Watch wildlife films instead. You'll learn more about humans that way.' When he was away, my mother sometimes sneaked them into the house. But I always stayed loyal to my father and refused to watch.

My uncle opened a cabinet that stood against the wall, and proudly stood back so I could see the large-screen TV. 'This video and TV set, it's a new item. I bought it only two months ago.'

'And you still haven't paid for it fully,' my aunt said dryly.

'The colours are so good—it is like being in the cinema,' he boasted, ignoring her words.

I tensed, expecting her to lash out at him again. But instead she smiled.

'Do you go to the cinema here, Uncle?' I asked, remembering how in Nairobi we skipped school on Saturdays and went to the Blackstone to watch the newest American film.

'Oh no. There is no point,' my uncle replied. 'Everything here is in French anyway.'

'Oh,' I replied, feeling the room shrink again.

I watched the movie for a while but it felt as alien as everything else. So I excused myself, mumbling something about being very tired. Neither of them turned their heads at my goodnight. I tiptoed out of the room. At the door, I paused and looked back. Their eyes were glued to the TV screen. I stood there and watched them for a while— the man who resembled but was not my father, his fat wife, and the maid with the patchwork face. My new family.

five

When I awoke the next morning the house was quiet. Amma had already left the room. Her mattress was neatly rolled up against the wall. The window which we had left open last night was shut tight and the heavy red curtains were drawn. The room was stifling and an eerie red light bathed everything. During the night I had thrown off my blanket and my nightgown had somehow entangled itself around my chest. Despite that I was sweating, the mattress beneath me damp. The light stained my body, from waist downwards, a dark red. I pulled the nightdress down and curled up into a tight little ball. Where was my mother now? She had promised she'd call when she reached England. I could hardly wait, already playing the conversation in my head.

Maa, I can't do it. I can't stay here.

Why, beti? He is your father's brother.

Because they're too different. They're not like us.

What do you mean 'different'?

They . . . she's fat. And . . . and they eat meat and chicken . . . and they watch Indian films every night . . . and she never goes out . . . and my uncle has strange hot eyes . . .

I wondered where the phone was. I thought I had seen it last night in the living room. But I wasn't sure. Suddenly, it struck me that if I waited beside it, then when Maa called I would be the one to pick it up and so I could tell her how I felt before my uncle and aunt got there. Before they could hear. Quickly I stood up and rolled my mattress up against the wall as Amma had done. I stepped tentatively into the dark corridor. In the next room I could hear Indian film music being piped out of tinny loudspeakers. In the kitchen someone was cooking lunch already.

I began to walk quickly down the passage. The door to my aunt's room was ajar. Just as I was about to go past, I heard her voice, 'Leela.'

I stopped. I looked desperately down the corridor. Could I pretend I hadn't heard? 'Leela,' she called again. 'Come here.' I could just about make out her vast form on the bed.

Reluctantly I pushed the door open a little farther and walked into her bedroom. Like mine, the room was a square box. But it had full-length windows that spanned the width of one wall. These windows were covered by heavy red curtains, just like the ones in my room, and everything in this room, too, was tinged by the strange light. A huge double bed dominated the room. Squeezed against the window was a low armchair, on top of which sat another TV.

'Come inside, Leela,' the mountain on the bed whispered. 'Did you sleep well?'

'Quite all right, thank you,' I replied politely.

'Come and sit here, child. I can hardly see you. You are so small and skinny.' A huge arm emerged from under the bedcovers and beckoned.

I walked forward slowly and sat down on the edge of the bed. 'Here I am, Aunt.'

But my aunt was no longer looking at me. Her eyes were on the little TV screen, watching yet another Hindi film. I stared at the screen dumbly, across which toy figures dashed.

Suddenly an advertisement flashed onto the TV screen. A young Indian couple, the lady in a sari and the man in a suit, stood in the middle of a group of dancing Masai with spears. The Masai were painted for war, their faces daubed an ochre red, their long hair plaited with mud of the same colour. They danced and stamped unconvincingly around the couple who stood unperturbed, smiling lovingly at each other. My lips curled in disgust. The Masai were merely stage props in this great new world of commerce. Their wars, their affinity with the animals among whom they lived, and their predator's view of the world, simply weren't real to the couple staring blindly at their own reflections in each other's eyes. It wouldn't matter, I thought wryly, until one of the Masai, fed up of remaining unseen, would lean in and chop off the Asian man's head. Then the woman would cry and flee to England.

But my father had been different. He had truly loved Kenya. He had believed passionately in Kenyatta and the freedom movement. So had my grandfather—he had even sheltered one of Kenyatta's aides in our house. Because of his love for the land, my father had understood that to be African one had to love the Africans, and love, according to my father, only came with understanding. But the Africans hadn't seen that. Abruptly, I turned away from the screen as unbidden tears came to my eyes and blurred my vision.

With my father's death, the Africa we thought we knew and loved had died too. As my mother sold off our life's accumulations and waited for someone to buy our house, we moved from the two-storeyed luxury of Parklands into a single bedroom suite, with walls painted a bilious yellow, at the Herald Court Hotel. This was famous mainly for its nightlife. It boasted one of the roughest bars in Nairobi, which drew hard-working secretaries, shop assistants, and nannies of easy virtue, who came there for the evening to make a little money for that new dress they simply had to have. Our room was in the wing of the hotel that housed the bar, and getting to our room in the evening was a form of torture I had never known existed. As I learned to sidestep the leering half-drunk customers and lay awake on Saturday nights terrified by the screams and curses of prostitutes whose clients refused to pay up, the grunts and thud of fists, and the whimpers of pain that followed, I realized that there had always been two Africas in Nairobi. We had simply crossed the boundary between the two.

Sitting on my aunt's bed, I looked around me at the red-tinged walls of her room. They were even more dreary than those of Herald Court. Where have I come, I wondered bleakly.

Suddenly the huge arm emerged again from under the bedcovers and patted my head. 'You poor thing,' she whispered softly, 'losing your father at the hands of those black savages.'

She lowered her voice dramatically and looked over her shoulder for a second. 'I must tell you the truth . . . I cannot hide it. They are even here, yes, in the building. Many, many of them . . .'

I was mystified. 'Who, Aunty? What are you talking about?'

'Them. Afrricans.'

My heart went cold. 'They're here?' I asked incredulously.

She nodded vigorously. 'It is terrible, they are like rats, everywhere.'

'You mean they have rats here in France also?' I asked, amazed and momentarily distracted.

'Yes, of course,' she said impatiently.

'But I thought rats only lived in poor countries.'

She began to laugh, her body shaking. 'Oh, you are a funny girl,' she said finally. 'Rats have no country.'

Her face became serious again. 'You must be very careful here. They are in the building—lots of them. They have no morals, no rules. They are like animals, animals.'

'But what about the French people, Aunty? Why don't you live with them?' I asked.

She looked away. 'Well,' she paused, 'we would but there is no use. They are everywhere.'

I shivered.

'You cannot be too careful here.' She looked at me sternly for what felt like a long time. At last I looked down. Then she said in the voice of a confessor, 'Amma told me what you did.'

I looked back at her, confused. 'What did I do?'

She looked annoyed. 'What do you mean? You don't know what you did?'

I lowered my eyes again, feeling inexplicably guilty.

'Didn't you open the window last night?' she said finally.

I looked up in surprise and then quickly averted my eyes, biting my lip.

'It was very stupid of you. Very dangerous. You could have got us robbed, or killed. I don't know if that's what you do in your country, but over here you cannot.'

'But Aunty, it was so hot,' I tried to defend myself, 'and there's no way anyone could climb these five floors up these walls.'

'You do not know these people,' she replied. 'They are very clever. They know just who to attack.'

'Do they rob and steal very often then? And do they murder as well?' I asked sceptically. 'I never saw a soul outside yesterday.'

'That is because everyone is too scared.'

'Really? But then why do you stay here, Aunty? It must be like a prison for you.' No wonder she's become so fat, I thought.

She sighed gustily. 'I'm saving every penny I can but there is the mortgage on the shop. This is a hard country, full of foreigners like us, struggling to survive. It is when you are most weak that bad things happen. Like your father. Poor man, he had no luck.'

'It wasn't a question of his luck,' I leapt to my father's defence. 'Maybe they didn't know Papa was still in there. He was a good person. He never hurt anyone.'

I buried my face in my hands and cried. She said nothing, but kept stroking my hair. Something in the rhythmic way in which she did it reminded me of my mother. 'It's the memories,' I whispered haltingly. 'I cannot forget the things he said, the way he made everything seem so big and yet so safe. Even in Nairobi National Park, you understand? Now all that is finished and I feel like I've lost everything: a family, a country, a big future that was all around and waiting for me to fill it.'

My aunt didn't respond. I looked up at her. She was watching the TV screen again. I shut my eyes and tried to bring back the dry, clean fragrance of the grasslands, the sharp aroma of the red earth mixed with the heavier odours of animals, smells that made me want to throw my arms out and embrace the huge blue sky, and run and run and run. I shut my eyes tight in an effort to remember, but I could no longer feel the wide-open space, the vaulted sky, or the motion in my feet. I was losing it. I buried my face in her lap, searching for total darkness, afraid of the strange red light bouncing off the walls, robbing my memories of their potency.

Finally, the tears stopped. I was exhausted. I lay still in her lap, suddenly aware of the stench of hot urine that came from it.

At last my aunt broke the silence.

'So what shall we do with you now?' she asked gruffly. I did not know what to say. Yesterday I had wanted to go and see Paris, the gardens, the shops. But today I could no longer think of such things.

'What would you like me to do, Aunty?' I asked obediently. My aunt was pleased by my reply, but she tried to hide it. 'We-ell, if you were a normal guest from India, I would have taken you shopping. But you don't have any money. And we can't spare any of ours—what with Krishen buying the shop.'

'I don't want any of your money, Aunt Latha,' I replied, stung.

She looked satisfied. 'Well, then, no reason to go out at all. Your uncle will bring back a movie from the shop this evening and we can watch it tonight.' Her eyes went back to the screen. I watched her miserably. Suddenly, she said, 'You know it was my idea to have videos from India. Your uncle was scared. But I just went ahead and wrote to a cousin of mine in Bombay asking him to send us a dozen. And now they are selling like hotcakes. All the Tamils and even the Arrabs are jealous.' Then her eyes came back to me.

'So what shall we do with you? Maybe you should help Amma with the cooking. Or if you like, I will let you cook the dinner tonight, yes? The Ramdhunes are coming for dinner with their daughter.' I looked down at the counterpane and didn't answer. I didn't know how to cook. In Nairobi, it was always my mother who cooked, or the servants. I found it a waste of time. When my mother tried to teach me, I ran to my father who always took my side.

'I c-can't,' I replied uneasily.

'You can't what?' my aunt asked.

'I can't cook,' I said defiantly. 'My father didn't think I needed to, either.'

Aunty Latha looked at me with distaste. Finally, she said, 'We'll have to teach you then. In France we don't have servants, and everyone has to do their share of the housework.'

My ears burned. After a few seconds I replied docilely, 'I promise I will learn, Aunty.'

'Go and help Amma then. The guests will be arriving at seven and there is a lot to be done.'

The kitchen was long and narrow with one large window at the end. The view outside was exactly the same as from the bed-rooms. The gas stove was ringed with dark brown grease that glowed in the yellow light from a bulb suspended above it. Next to the stove was a sink filled with dirty dishes in grey oily water. I moved quickly towards the window. Beneath it, there was an oasis of order. On a little wooden table painted yellow, there stood three bowls of vegetables—purple brinjals, red tomatoes, and creamy yellow potatoes.'

Amma was already sitting there, peeling and slicing vast quantities of potatoes. I sat down beside her and began to peel them too. They were slippery and twice the knife slipped out of my hands. I realized that the potato was not the benign vegetable I had imagined it to be. It gave off a white milky liquid as you cut it which gradually ate into your hands. After a while my hands began to burn and tremble. I turned to Amma. 'I can't peel anymore. My hands hurt.' She looked at me uncomprehendingly. I held out my hands so she could see how red they were. Slowly understanding dawned on her face. She began to laugh. 'Your hands hurt after just eight potatoes. Oh, maa, how will you look after a family? At your age I was already a mother.'

I stared at her mottled face in disgust. Suddenly it was no longer the face of a person, but that of a senseless fate. 'My mother taught me to read, not cook,' I snapped. But this made her laugh even harder. 'Well, you won't have much use for that here,' she said, wiping tears from her eyes.

After that we worked in silence. Amma sliced potatoes faster than I could peel them, and while she waited for me to finish, she sang old film songs. When I handed her a potato, the singing would stop for a while. Then it would begin again. My fingers burned, my wrists and neck began to ache, and my peeling got slower and slower. Finally, Amma took over the rest of the potatoes and let me go wash my hands.

The sink smelled of rotten food and stale spices. Little mustard-yellow and saffron globules of oil floated on the surface of the water. I averted my eyes and turned on the tap. The water gushed out and hit the dirty dishwater with a slap, causing some of it to splash onto my chest and face.

'Amma,' I burst out, 'these are yesterday's dishes, are they not?' She didn't reply. 'Why haven't you cleaned them?'

'I'm an old woman,' she replied sulkily. 'My fingers hurt in cold water.'

'But you could empty the sink and fill it with hot water,' I pointed out.

She gave me a look full of resentment, and muttered something in a language I couldn't understand.

'What did you say?' I asked in Gujarati.

'I said do it yourself,' she replied. 'You ate my food last night. So now you can help with the washing.'

I tried a last desperate tactic. 'I don't know how to wash dishes.'

'Anyone can wash dishes,' she scoffed. 'Come, hurry up and do it. Since you can't even chop potatoes, I'll finish them and the onions while you do the dishes. Then we'll do some cooking.' She gave me a sly smile, 'Be quick, or else your Aunty Latha will be angry.'

I knew I had lost. Reluctantly I went over to the sink and taking a deep breath, plunged my hands into the filthy water. Lumps of half-dissolved food brushed against my hands and disintegrated. The stench was horrible—the water had embalmed all of last night's flavours, but now they were rank and disordered, fighting with each other to stay alive. I felt my gorge rise.

The dishes were slippery. I pulled one out to get a better look. It was encrusted with congealed fat. As the hot water warmed the sludge in the sink, the fat began to melt. Soon my arms were covered in a patina of red-brown fat right up to my elbows. Embedded in the grease, the smell entered my traitorous pores with ease. Suddenly I remembered the old perfume from Zanzibar that my grandfather had given me when I was ten. It had smelt of wild roses and honey, with a touch of musk, and had come embedded in a pot of grease.

Taking refuge in the memory, I washed the dishes as fast as I could. I let the water out of the sink, scooped out the sodden, unrecognizable remains of the food, and scrubbed the sink vigorously with detergent, ignoring the pain as the chemicals ate into my chafed fingers. I felt soiled and longed for a bath, but my aunt stood blocking the kitchen door.

'I'll just go and wash. I've been washing last night's dishes.' I looked pointedly at Amma.

My aunt ignored my remark. 'I'm glad you're making yourself useful. Before one knows how to cook, one must know how to clean.' She looked at Amma, and the two women exchanged a smile.

I saw the smile and felt anger flare within me. 'Excuse me, Aunty,' I said as coldly as I could, 'I need to take a bath.'

She didn't budge. 'You can do that later, when you have finished. Now I will show you how to cook.'

'But I smell,' I stared at her rebelliously.

'No matter,' she replied.

Amma had finished cutting the vegetables. They were sitting on the table beneath the window sill. Aunty Latha pulled out a white ceramic bowl covered with a piece of gauze from the fridge. 'The first thing you must learn is to prepare the spices. You can either crush them into a fine paste, or you can fry them whole. If you crush them, then there is no problem; you can use them any way you like.' She pulled aside the cloth, and looked inside. 'Or else you can fry the spices in oil first and let the heat free the smell.' She handed me the bowl and reached into the cupboard. I looked into the bowl. There were finely chopped pieces of ginger and whole tear-shaped cloves of garlic, already peeled. The bowl almost fell from my suddenly nerveless fingers.

'Aunty Latha, you . . . you eat garlic?' I asked her tentatively, still unable to believe that what I was holding was in fact garlic. Her back stiffened and she turned around, 'In cold countries you need all the garlic you can get to keep you warm. At least we cook it. These barbarians,' she looked out of the window, 'eat it raw.' She pushed the bowl into my stomach. 'Now you crush,' she ordered, and turned her back to me once more.

I didn't have the courage to argue. Everything was different. My life had changed so fast: what did it matter if my aunt, or I for that matter, ate garlic? I remembered my father telling me about how food was divided into three types—*satvik*, which encouraged detachment and contemplation, *rajasik*, which promoted vigour and action, and *tamasik*, which generated heat or passion. Passion was what was most to be feared because it gave birth to anger and lust, which destroyed families. Garlic, my father used to tell us, was the epitome of *tamas*. That was why he, like other Gujaratis, wouldn't let us eat it. But suddenly I felt free of his disapproval. My father was dead. I had no family now. So of course I could eat garlic!

I looked around the kitchen for an implement to crush with. Not finding anything, I settled for the handle of a large heavy knife. *'Aiee,'* Amma screamed when she saw what I was doing. 'You stupid girl,' said my aunt. 'Amma, show her where the mortar stone is.' Amma went over to the large cupboard built into the wall, rummaged in a corner piled high with plastic bags, and pulled out a large stone with a bowl-shaped hollow in the centre. Inside this hollow was a heavy pestle of the same stone. She grabbed the bowl of spices from my hands and threw some into the hollow. Then she took the pestle and using the heavy end, began to pound away at the spices. In less than a minute the room was filled with the hot heavy odour of garlic and ginger, a velvet blanket that coated my senses, making my body feel heavy and languorous. I watched Amma's body quiver as she pounded on the stone. I wanted to do it myself, to feel the rhythm of the pestle in my hands beating into that smooth hollow, liberating the pungent essence of the ginger and garlic. In a daze, I took the stone from her and began pounding myself. The smell of the paste made me feel hungry and satisfied at the same time.

In the kitchen my aunt was a different person. Her movements were crisp, filled with sudden energy. I watched mesmerized as her hands opened like flowers and closed around the onions, not letting a single morsel drop in the process. She sniffed at the paste I handed her and shook her head. 'Not enough salt,' she said. Without looking up, she stretched her arm above her head. Her fingers closed around a plastic jar of salt. She took out a pinch between two huge fingers and sprinkled it over the paste. Then she added some green chilies and sesame seeds. She took the pestle and ground the spices a little more, no longer pounding away at them but moving the pestle around gently in the hollow. Subtly the smell of the spices sharpened and became tinged with a hint of lemon. Aunty Latha began to speak as she worked away at the spices, 'You know, Leela, each spice has a special smell. The challenge is to marry the spices together. As in life, some marriages last well—like your uncle's and mine. We are matched nicely. Other couples are not so lucky. My sister has got a horrible husband. He never listens to what she says.' She smiled, looking suddenly coy, 'Not like my Krishenbhai at all, her husband.' She shrugged her shoulders and her flesh rippled.

On the stove, the oil was hot. Aunty Latha walked over to it quickly and threw in the onions and the paste. The smell exploded into the air. I fell back against the little table by the window. My aunt, meanwhile, was peering into the pan, stirring vigorously. Her double chin was lit up from below by the blue-yellow flames. 'Come here, Leela, and stir this,' she called.

I went over to the stove and grasped the flat spoonlike implement she was using. 'Keep turning the onions till they become transparent,' she commanded and swam away to the other side of the room. I peered into the mist that arose from the pan. The steam wet my face like a warm kiss. I moved the little white cubes around gently in the frying pan. Suddenly a new odour hit me, completely different, an ugly death smell. I jumped away from the stove, as if I had been slapped in the face. The spoon slipped out of my hands and clattered to the floor. Within half a second my aunt had crossed the six feet of space between us and was upon me. 'What is the matter?' she asked. 'What happened? Did the oil burn you?'

'No. No it's . . . it's just the smell, that's all. I was surprised.' I felt a fool even before the words were out. Quickly I shut my mouth and looked nervously up into my aunt's face.

But instead of being angry, she smiled, genuinely amused this time. The smile transformed her face. 'I see now that your mother never did teach you to cook. I thought you were lying.' She grabbed another spoon and began to stir the onions vigorously. They had stopped making their hissing noise and were slowly turning brown. 'But no matter. Your instinct was right—listen to the smell, it will tell you things,' she said, stirring away. 'Onions give off smell with water. That is what stings the eyes and makes them cry. So we fry them to get rid of the water.' She paused and looked at me.

'To begin with, the onions fight back. They hold on to their water, afraid to die. They sing a song, they shout at you and curse you. And they give a terrible smell. Then the fire and the oil have their way and the onions give up. The smell leaves the onions like a dying breath leaves the body, and enters the rest of the food.' She paused dramatically, 'The onion's smell is the smell of dying.' I stared at her in surprise. Aunty Latha's face had become soft and her eyes glistened in the afterglow of her smile. 'You will be a good cook, my child,' she said.

Through the day, as we cooked, my aunt talked to me about the Ramdhunes. They were Aunty Latha's only friends in France. Every Saturday they came to her house for dinner, and every Sunday, Krishenbhai left the shop in the hands of a Sri Lankan boy called Arun and drove Aunty Latha to the Ramdhunes' for lunch.

'This place is not like England. There are very few good Indian families here. But the Ramdhunes are good people,' she said, as she mashed the tomatoes, 'even if they aren't Gujarati.'

She pronounced their name Ramdoon. 'Ramdoon—that's a strange name, isn't it, Aunty?'

She laughed. 'In India it would be Ramdhun. But they haven't lived in India—not for the last three generations.'

'Then where are they from?' I asked curiously.

'From an island somewhere in the middle of the sea. I forget its name. But there are many Hindus settled there. It used to belong to the French.'

'Oh,' I said, realizing which island she meant, 'Mauritius, Aunty? It's between India and Africa.'

'Yes, Mauritius.' She pushed away the bowl of tomatoes and looked at me briefly, 'But they don't live there any more. Now they live here in Paris.' My aunt told me that Mr Ramdhune worked at the post office and was a French national. When Mauritius became independent, the Ramdhunes had decided to shift to France. Within ten years of their arrival they had acquired their very own semidetached bungalow in Bobigny.

'Mr Ramdhune is a big man,' my aunt concluded. 'I see,' I said, not seeing at all. Postmen were not important men in Nairobi.

The Ramdhunes had one child, Clothilde Radha, whom they called Lotti. She had been born in France and was therefore French, not an immigrant like her parents—and like my aunt and uncle and even my mother. I was like Lotti, I reflected, born in Kenya. So was my father. That's why we were different, I thought proudly. I began to look forward to meeting the Ramdhunes—especially Lotti.

By six in the evening, we were finished. Five types of vegetables, two kinds of dal, three meat and chicken dishes, rice, papads and puris sat upon the little table by the window waiting to be eaten. Three types of sweets were unpacked and placed there as well. If last evening's meal had been rich, I thought wryly, this was three times as sumptuous. The house was afloat in the smells of almond, fried meat, pineapple raita, and other delights. My cooking-sensitized nostrils felt buffeted by the hordes of new and rich smells. 'That is good,' said Aunty Latha finally as she surveyed our work. 'Now go, bathe and get ready quickly. The Ramdhunes will be arriving at any moment.'

seven

At seven the bell rang. They had arrived. Hurriedly I finished changing into the clothes my aunt had ordered me to wear—a hideous red salwar kameez, a welcome-to-Paris gift that she had bought for me. But it was at least two sizes too large, and the kameez was too long and cut in such a way that it made me look lumpy. And the synthetic silk of the salwar stuck to my stocking-clad legs, making them look like sticks. I contemplated changing into something else, but did not have the courage to offend Aunt Latha. The contentment of the cooking lesson faded. I no longer wanted to meet the Ramdhunes.

'Leela.' My aunt's voice came whipping through the walls. 'Come here quickly. Our guests have arrived.'

'I'm coming, Aunty,' I called back.

As I walked unhappily down the grey corridor, I could hear their voices, and the mingled accents of Hindi, Gujarati, and English.

'It must be so lovely for you, Latha, to have your niece here,' a female voice trilled. 'At last you have a complete family.'

'She is lovely,' my uncle said suddenly.

'Our Indian girls,' another male voice agreed, 'are much more beautiful than French girls.'

'Because our girls are pure and innocent,' my aunt put in, 'unspoiled.'

I turned the corner and found myself face to face with the legendary Ramdhunes. The conversation stopped, and they all stared at me.

Mr Ramdhune was very like my uncle. He carried himself with the same slow-moving grace, but he had a small goatee. And his hair was white, which gave to his otherwise youthful face the dignity of age. Mrs Ramdhune was a softer, shorter version of my aunt. Her drooping flesh was wrapped tightly in a sari of peach and lemon-coloured chiffon so that she resembled a child's sweet in a multicoloured wrapper. I felt surprised at how dark they all were. Especially Lotti, whose skin was the reddish brown colour of polished copper. She did not look French at all. She was no more than five feet tall, with long black hair that fell to her knees. Her big brown eyes slanted upwards slightly at the ends. Her body was lush and feminine, tightly bound in black. Her nose was pierced, and in each ear she had no fewer than four earrings. Clinging to her like a transparent film was a feeling of excitement, of something terribly important left unsaid.

Lotti moved first. Coming fearlessly up to me and taking my hands into her own, she pulled me into their circle. 'Salut. Namaste,' she said in Hindi with a French accent. Her lipsticked lips parted in a smile and she kissed me on both cheeks.

I returned the greeting awkwardly in English, 'Hello, how are you?'

Her smile broadened. 'You have such a funny Engleesh accent,' she said, 'and you are so tall.' She was so bright and lovely. I fumbled for something interesting to say, but could think of nothing.

Her mother rescued me. 'Tiens, Lotti. What are you saying to embarrass her like that? You know that she has just arrived, she must be still tired.' She wrapped me in a soft scented embrace. 'Poor child, I'm so sorry about your father.'

I moved away abruptly, tears in my throat. Mrs Ramdhune tried again. 'So how do you find Paris? It is an elegant city, no?'

'I have only seen the airport so far,' I replied.

'That is shockeeng. We must change it immediately. The only way to make you at home here is to make you love everything French, as we do.'

'Do you like it more than Mauritius then?' I blurted out.

Her eyes widened and some of the good humour left her face. Her mouth opened and then shut again. She continued to pat me on the head, but looked away towards her husband.

'Cecil,' she said to him, 'why don't we take them for a spin in the car after dinner?' She pronounced it 'speen.'

'Why?' he replied. 'I want to watch the match tonight.'

She looked at him sternly. 'Shouldn't we at least show the poor girl our beautiful Paris by night so she will forget her troubles?' Then she turned to me, the good humour back in place. 'My poor orphan,' she cooed, patting me on the head.

I looked down at my feet, inwardly furious. The silly woman was talking as if my mother were dead too. Before I could correct her, my aunt intervened.

'We offered to take her on a sightseeing tour, but Leela wanted to cook today,' she said smoothly. 'She is a homely girl, you see.' My head jerked up angrily, and my mouth opened to refute her. Then my eyes met those of my aunt.

'Leela is a very good cook,' she told Mrs Ramdhune calmly.

I looked at the carpet. It was mauve.

The group moved into the living room, arranging itself generation-wise on the rock-hard sofas. 'Aah yes, the girls of India. Such wonderful cooks. But I am sure your niece cannot cook as well as you, my dear Mrs Patel,' Mr Ramdhune said politely. He sucked on his pipe and continued, 'My grandmother, Sita, who followed my grandfather all the way from Bihar and looked after him while he built our roads and ports in Mauritius, was a marvellous cook. But these young girls of today!' he looked at Lotti in a half-regretful, half-proud way. 'Unfortunately Lotti only likes clothes and art. This is what happens when your child is born in Paris.'

Mrs Ramdhune rushed immediately to her daughter's defence, 'But she comes first in her class, in a first-class school, where they speak only French.'

Mr Ramdhune's cheeks swelled. 'And she cannot speak a word of our language, Bhojpuri. She cannot even speak to her own grandmother.'

'She doesn't need to speak to her grandmother when she has the whole world to speak with,' Mrs Ramdhune shot back.

Mr Ramdhune looked like a pricked balloon, 'I am not sure the one is better than the other. At least her grandmother loves her and would never hurt her,' he muttered.

The room became quiet. I looked at Lotti sitting next to me, playing with the absurdly large metal bracelet on her arm, and my aunt and uncle trying to keep their faces sympathetic but secretly enjoying the fight tremendously.

Mr Ramdhune continued, 'It's that silly school of hers, putting rich people's ideas into her head.'

Mrs Ramdhune turned suddenly to the rest of us. 'My husband is worried by Lotti's newfound passion for French art,' she explained. Then her eyes fell on Lotti and they grew tender, 'But my little daughter is a good girl, I know. When she grows up, she will soon forget about these silly ideas.'

Both parents looked at their daughter anxiously. Lotti pretended she hadn't heard. Mr Ramdhune began to look annoyed. 'That woman minister of education is full of strange ideas, she wants the *banlieusandes* in the museums instead of at work.'

My uncle guffawed and clapped his hands, 'Very true, very true, Mr Ramdhune.'

Mr Ramdhune looked a little surprised, even a little irritated. He stared frostily at my uncle. Then suddenly he smiled condescendingly at him and continued, 'Now what I call a good minister is M Bestiole of *la poste*. Why, when he came to our post office. . . .'

His wife sighed. 'There he goes again, about his Monsieur le Ministre.' She began to rearrange the pleats of her sari.

Taking the gesture as her cue, Aunty Latha gushed, 'What a beautiful sari you are wearing, Mrs Ramdhune! Where did you get it?'

Mrs Ramdhune smiled, 'It is French chiffon you know, very expensive. But I got it in Lyons, at half the price you would pay for it in Paris. You must come with me next time, Lathaji.'

My aunt's face was a mixture of envy and desire. 'I would love to,' she replied, 'but I have my home to run, and there is the store. You know how Krishenbhai is useless with the accounts.'

'Such a pity,' Mrs Ramdhune replied. 'They have such wonderful choice there.'

'Paris has just become too expensive,' my aunt agreed, sighing.

'Yes, that is why we moved to Bobigny. We get everything for half the price there,' Mrs Ramdhune added.

I suppressed a smile. I could see why my aunt and Mrs Ramdhune got along so well. 'They are best friends you know, because both love money so much,' Lotti whispered to me softly. The smile I was trying so hard to hold inside, came to the surface.

'Come, let's go somewhere where we can talk,' Lotti said, smiling back. She took my arm and led me onto the minuscule balcony.

'Ah, I feel better. It was so stuffy inside.' She thrust her head into the wind. It was cold on the balcony. I shivered. 'But you're cold,' she said quickly. 'I forgot you aren't used to our weather yet. Shall we go inside?'

'No, no, please,' I said quickly. 'I like it here, it is the first time I have been outside since I arrived.'

'What?' her eyebrows climbed halfway up her forehead.

I laughed ruefully, 'My aunt says it is too dangerous to go outside— even on the balcony.'

Her expression became even more incredulous. 'Aunty Latha must watch too much TV,' she shook her head. 'There are no problems here. The really bad *banlieues* are farther south and to the west. We are almost in Paris here.'

I felt a rush of relief at her words, followed by a tremor of excitement. So Paris was not so far away after all. Slowly I turned to face the icy wind. It made my skin tingle, blowing away the smell of food that lingered on it. 'Ahh. Now I feel that I am in France.'

Lotti brought her warm face close to mine and gripped my hand tightly. 'Of course you are.'

eight

I spent my first month in Paris waiting for my mother to call me. I waited with a single-mindedness that even the claustrophobia of the flat couldn't dent. Sometimes the tension of constantly straining my ears to hear the ring of the telephone gave me headaches. I found it difficult to sleep. When they woke me for breakfast the next day, I would be bleary-eyed and lethargic. The stale sad smell of the flat clung to me, making my isolation complete.

Then one evening, as we sat eating dinner, the phone rang. My head came up with a jerk.

My aunt looked at me and frowned. 'It's probably the Ramdhunes. Let your uncle answer it.'

My uncle got up obediently and walked unhurriedly to the phone. He picked it up on the sixth ring.

'Hello?'

'Yes. This is he,' he looked unsure, as though the speaker were someone he didn't know.

Suddenly my uncle's voice changed. 'Yes, yes,' he said excitedly.

I didn't wait to be called. I knew it was she. I ran to the hall and waited impatiently while my uncle greeted her and asked her the usual questions. He was excited too. The hand holding the telephone was trembling. Finally, he handed the receiver to me.

'Leela?' Her voice sounded so near.

My throat went dry. I tried to say something, but no sound emerged.

'Say something,' Krishenbhai poked me between the shoulder blades. 'She isn't paying all this money to listen to your silence.'

I stared at the talking instrument in my hand. There was so much I wanted to tell her.

'Leela, are you there?' my mother's voice was tinged with anxiety. I cursed myself. The moment was turning sour with the inevitability of milk left too long in the sun.

'Maa, I'm here,' I managed to say finally.

'Yes, I know you're there,' she answered, sounding irritated. 'Do you like Paris?'

'Yes, Maa. Everything is . . . is fine.' That's what she wanted to hear. And my uncle and aunt were both listening avidly. 'How . . . how are you?'

'I'm all right. The house is very small though. And it is cold and raining all the time. We haven't seen the sun for a month.' She laughed a little shakily, 'Now I know why the English are the way they are. They can't get the damp out of their bones.'

I laughed too, but in my mind a question had formed. When are you going to get me out, Maa?

'And what are your plans, Leela? Will you be going to college? You mustn't stop your studies, or your mind will become rusty.'

'Here?' I was startled. 'But how? Everything is in French.'

'There must be classes in English, everyone can't speak French. Ask Krishenbhai to find out for you. I'm surprised he hasn't done so already. Let me talk to him.'

'But Maa, why bother? I can go to university in England when I come to you. I'll only have missed this year, and I can read the books at home with you.' I marvelled at my own cunning. What a wonderful opening I had given my mother for telling me when she was bringing me home. I took a deep breath.

There was a long silence at the other end of the line. When she spoke, her voice sounded different, faraway, 'Leeela,' she said, drawing out the 'e' the way my father did when he was about to give me bad news, 'I . . . I can't have you come here this year. . . . Atul's house is too small. Sunil and Anil are so hard to control. There are no servants, I have to do everything for them by myself. Sheilabehn hasn't said anything, but I keep feeling that we are an imposition on her. I would like to move out—find a flat for myself, but London is so expensive. More than I had ever imagined . . .' She trailed off.

I could not speak. My disappointment was choking me. I gripped the telephone as if it was the last link to my family.

'Leela,' my mother's voice was beginning to break, 'your aunt and uncle love having you. Soon, as soon as I am able, I will come and see you.'

I didn't say anything.

'Leela? Are you there?'

I made a strangled sound. 'Let me speak to your uncle, Leela,' she commanded.

Mutely I handed the phone to my uncle and ran into my room.

I lay there, unable to sleep, replaying the conversation in my mind. Was she angry with me? Had Krishenbhai complained about me before I spoke to her? I stared up into the darkness, dry-eyed. I felt as I had at the cremation, as if I had arrived at the end of time, and everything within me was grinding to a halt.

Then I heard footsteps come down the hall and stop at the door. 'Leela?' my uncle whispered. I shut my eyes and pretended to be asleep. 'Leela.' He opened the door a crack. He stood there watching me for a while and then he shut the door softly. I kept my eyes tightly shut and must have fallen asleep eventually because I was woken up by loud voices in the dark. Aunty Latha and Krishenbhai were arguing with each other.

'Shhhh . . . don't talk so loudly, she'll hear you,' Krishenbhai said in a loud whisper.

'I don't care,' Aunty Latha replied in her normal high-pitched voice. 'Let her hear. I'm not saying anything that's not the truth. You don't know how lazy she is—sleeping late, wandering about the house, saying nothing, looking down her nose at us. I've had enough. I can't stand it anymore.'

'We can send her to college. She'll pick up French soon enough— we can send her for French classes first. Her mother asked me to.'

Aunty Latha cut him off with a small sound between a scream and a hiss. 'Send her to college? And where will we find the money for it?'

'Public university doesn't cost much,' Krishenbhai said hesitantly.

'Rubbish, everything costs money here, and we have a mortgage and our future to think of. Besides, haven't we done enough for her—giving her a home, food, and clothes? If she wants to study, let her mother pay.'

'Have you no heart? She's my brother's daughter. What do you want me to do with her?' Krishenbhai's voice drowned out my aunt's. They were both shouting now.

'Take her with you then, since she's *your* brother's child. I don't want her mooning about my house,' Aunty Latha shouted back.

'All right, I will,' I heard Krishenbhai say quietly. 'Tomorrow she comes to the shop with me.'

I heard the door of their bedroom slam, and then the silence reestablished itself.

Next morning Amma shook me awake. 'Get up. They want you,' she said, and left.

I dressed quickly and made my way down the hall to the living room. They were waiting for me, seated stiffly side by side on the sofa.

My uncle began to speak, 'We have decided, your aunt and I, that it is best for you to come and work in the store. You spend too much time inside, it is not healthy.' He said it kindly, but his eyes would not meet mine.

I nodded, pretending, too, that I had heard nothing the previous night. Suddenly a huge wave of relief swept over me. I wouldn't have to see Amma and listen to the soundtrack of Aunty Latha's Indian films through the day as I slaved in the kitchen. I wouldn't have to remain locked in the blood-red apartment with its nailed-down blinds; wouldn't have to cook and cook and cook till my nails turned yellow and my hair, even my sweat, smelt of spices.

Then I felt a stab of anxiety. 'But what if Maa calls when I am away?'

'It is most unlikely,' he assured me. 'She works all day in her brother's shop, doesn't she?'

'Yes,' I nodded slowly.

'And in the evening you'll be back before she calls.' I looked uncomprehending. 'Don't forget, London is one hour behind us,' he explained.

'But . . . but what if she's coming to get me and calls to tell us that?' I said desperately.

They exchanged glances, and my unease grew.

Then my aunt caught me around the shoulders and gave me a hug. 'If that happens, I'll call you at the shop and you can call her right back.'

'You mean I can call her in England?'

'Of course.' They nodded.

'Thank you, thank you,' my voice came out squeaky with relief.

They looked back at me, some of my relief reflected in their faces.

I never brought up the subject again. I could not afford not to believe them.

nine

L̶ife with Krishenbhai and Aunty Latha soon settled into a routine. From being just a series of meaningless impressions against an endless background of expectancy, the days became familiar and predictable. I worked with my uncle in the store through the week and spent the weekends at the Ramdhunes'. The unvarying pattern gave me a sense of security and permanence. At last the feeling of walking on eggshells that had become so much a part of me since Nairobi began slowly to fade. Even my eventual departure for England started to seem distant and oddly unreal. I still missed my mother and my brothers. In the cold, alien world I now inhabited, I clung tightly to my memories of them. They were my family—mine—in a way that my aunt and even Krishenbhai could never be. But the ache of longing slowly subsided into a numb acceptance of separation. My family, our house in Parklands, even my father, slowly retreated into my dreams.

MY DAYS BEGIN at six in the morning. As soon as I leave the building now my home, I breathe deeply. The dark emptiness of the morning is restful, it demands nothing of me. I feel a calm descend upon me. I walk towards the Métro station. At this hour people are moving in little knots in the same direction. The cafés and the *boulangeries* are bright with a warm golden light. The wonderful smell of freshly baked bread follows me as I walk past.

Usually by the time I arrive at the Métro, the eastern sky is a pale grey. The delicate light smoothes out the lines and softens the ugliness of the buildings. I take the steps down into the bowels of the earth and am assailed by the night smells again. The 6.45 train into Nation is always fairly full of people—the night shifters coming off work and the early morning telephone operators, policemen, plumbers, and construction workers going in.

Those off the night shift sit in strange positions, full of suppressed tension. Their bodies are a battleground of sleep weariness and work energy. The day workers are quite different. They look empty. The women's make-up is patchy, as if applied with sleep-numbed hands. They sit slumped on the benches like rag dolls.

From Nation, I climb up to the aerial line, one of the oldest Métro lines in the city, which will take me to La Chapelle. I love the fragility and strength of the metal web that holds the train up.

One day in the depths of winter, I see a woman feeding the pigeons beneath the beams, talking lovingly to them. She is bundled up in a huge black overcoat, her body a large irregular square. On her head is a tweed hat with a green felt ribbon. Grey scraggly hair sticks out from beneath it. I am touched by her love of the birds. She seems a lonely old eccentric without anyone to talk to. Then I see the bag beside her and realize that she is poor and a huntress. I want to shout out and warn the birds, but the train does it for me. It comes screeching to a halt over my head, scaring all the pigeons away. The woman looks up, her face hot with rage, and screams at the train. Her upturned face is terrifying. Her features have melted into each other as if someone has rubbed them away with a powerful corroding agent. Her mouth looks like an unprotected wound. She sees me staring at her, and moving with the speed of a young woman, sprays me with bread crumbs. I recoil and rush away, followed by curses I do not understand.

I reach the store by 7.15. All around the streets are slowly wakening. The Sri Lankan Tamils and Arabs talk softly to each other in their own languages as they sweep the fronts of their stores and lay out the boxes of vegetables. In front of the cafés, waiters lay out tables on the sidewalk, unfolding the chairs with practised ease. Sometimes one of them whistles at me or says something that I don't understand in French.

I sweep the place, carry out the crates of vegetables and lay them out nicely, and dust the window display. When all these tasks are done, I light a couple of incense sticks before the brightly coloured pictures of Vishnu, Lakshmi, and elephant-headed Ganesh. This is Aunty Latha's idea. She insists that I do it every day. I don't like the way the incense smells. It makes me feel suffocated. But by this time it is around 8.30, time for the morning work rush. And so I take up my position at the door.

I watch them go by. Men in suits and long coats, women with high heels and elegant handbag-briefcases. Nobody talks. They just walk quickly—heads bent, feet in tune—in transition, moving between the night world and the day world. For twenty, thirty minutes they stream past without stopping. Then crowds thin, and end in a trickle—usually the housewives or the unemployed.

I like to watch the office crowd go by. Standing in the doorway, I suck in the air of their worlds—the dry metallic smell of the air conditioning, the salty smell of dried perspiration, coffee, cigarettes, and then something I do not recognize. It brushes ever so lightly against the nostrils, so fine and delicate that it is hard to pin down. The people don't notice my quivering nostrils, and if they do, they don't care.

I long to be a part of them, to wrap myself in their arrogance, my feet keeping time with theirs. To me they seem like gods. And I long to be invulnerable, as they are.

At the tail end of this crowd, around nine o'clock, comes my uncle. His long black coat is draped without a wrinkle over his shoulders. His hat is tilted at just the right angle. He looks like a customer. Even his breath smells French—like bitter black coffee.

'Good morning, my pretty little one,' he kisses me on the face. His lips always feel wet. I turn away and try to wipe off the feel of his lips. But he sees me, and every day he waits for that gesture. Then some unnameable emotion sweeps through his face, making little muscles jump like silverfish in his cheeks. He turns and looks out at the street. We both do. When he turns around, his face is still. 'Have you done everything?' he questions brusquely, moving away from me. 'Lit the agarbattis, have you?' His eyes dance over to the statues on the wooden shelf nailed to the wall. 'You know Aunty Latha would . . .'

'Yes, everything is done,' I cut him off hurriedly.

My uncle seats himself behind the video counter and pulls out his newspaper. 'To work now, my dear, we have lots of things to do today.' It is the cue for me to retreat into the back room.

But I remain standing awkwardly before him, trying to stretch the time I spend outside it. 'What's in the paper, Uncle? Anything about home? Any more riots?' He pretends to scan the paper. Then slowly he looks up, 'No, little one. Nothing about Kenya. Nothing about Africa at all today.'

Together my uncle and I wait for the customers to trickle in.

Mme Gunashekharan, the widow of the man who sold my uncle the shop, comes in every morning like a queen. She still expects my uncle to give her all her groceries for free, as he did for six months after her husband died.

Now she pays, sniffing at the prices, saying that they are higher than when her husband was the owner. I think it gives her more pleasure now that she can insult us while paying than when she had to be nice to us because she wasn't paying.

I am always the one to deal with her when she comes. I try to entice her into the back room, on the pretext of showing her fresh spices from Sri Lanka so that her loud remarks about the prices won't scare off the other customers.

After her come the Bangladeshi men from the Indian restaurant, the Sitar. They speak to my uncle in Hindi. My uncle answers in French.

He does it to discourage them from becoming too familiar. He is afraid that if he talks to them in Hindi, they will ask for favours—and my uncle hates to say no to a direct request. They come every day but buy only small things from us—spices, papad, pickles. Meats, rice, and vegetables, they order directly from the wholesalers, the same ones who supply us.

As they shop, I see them peeping around the corner at me. The thought crosses my mind that they might be coming to the shop to see me, but I shrug it away. It is more likely that they come to inspect the video films and to rent one quietly for the night. Eight of them live in one room, a studio off Montmartre, one of them tells me. And their landlord makes them pay 2,800 francs for it, when there isn't even running hot water there, nor an attached bathroom.

The Tamil housewives come in around eleven, after they send their husbands to work and their kids to school. They wear nylon saris, their black hair is oiled and either braided in plaits that hang down their backs or pulled into tight little buns. They linger in the shop sniffing at the masalas and poking at the rice and the plantains that we import at great price from their country.

Sometimes the housewives' visits coincide with 'the lovers'—a strange couple who live not very far away. They make two or three trips to the store every day. The first one is around 11.30 in the morning to buy beer, cigarettes, and mineral water. In the afternoon they come to buy food, usually ready-made foodstuffs in tins, and condoms. The latter my uncle hands to the man with the bad teeth while staring pointedly at the woman's navel, which can always be seen between her jeans and the sari-blouses she wears as shirts. They are always linked, either by their arms, legs or lips. The housewives stare at them, not bothering to conceal their disgust. But the lovers don't care. They leave with their hands in each other's pockets.

I become accustomed to my new world. One predictable day follows another almost as though I was at school in Nairobi again. Only now, instead of getting an education, I go to work at Krishenbhai's store. I never feel at home on the streets of Paris as Lotti does. Like my aunt and uncle, I am a stranger to the life here, a street urchin looking into the candlelit glow of a family supper. My world remains the flat with its blood-red curtains and the shop.

ten

As I got to know Lotti better, my admiration for her grew. She was beautiful and intelligent. Mrs Ramdhune had not been boasting when she said that Lotti was at the top of her class. And she spoke French beautifully. What I found hard to believe was that she had chosen me for a friend. One day, I asked her what she saw in me. Lotti laughed. She liked to laugh. Then she looked me over appraisingly like a man. 'Well, for one, we complement each other,' she said. 'I'm short and round. You're fair-skinned, and tall and everything about you is fine and delicate like an Indian statue.'

'An Indian statue? Where did you see one of those?' My eyes widened in horror, 'You can't mean one of Aunty Latha's statues?'

She laughed, 'No, no. Those aren't real Indian statues. I mean the ones that are in the Guimet.'

'Geemay? What's that?'

'The Musée Guimet? It is the most wonderful museum in Paris.'

'But how is it that they have real Indian statues?'

'Because someone made a collection of them—along with other things from China, Thailand, Japan, all of Asia in fact,' Lotti answered. 'And all of them are housed in a beautiful chateau in the middle of a garden that is like heaven in spring. It truly is the most beautiful of all the museums. You must tell Aunty Latha and Krishenbhai to take you there.'

I thought of Krishenbhai and Aunty Latha and knew the impossibility of such an event. In all the weeks I had spent with them, I had not once heard them refer to a restaurant, let alone a museum. I tried desperately to sound indifferent as I asked, 'Why would they want statues from India anyway?'

'Because they are beautiful,' she said. Her eyes began to glow. 'In this city they admire beauty no matter where it's from.'

I sighed. 'I wish I could see it.'

'Of course you can. Anyone can go to a museum.' She pulled out a book and began flipping through the pages. 'Here, I'll show you where it is in the map.'

She pushed the opened page at me, 'Here, look, in the sixteenth *arrondissement.*'

I frowned at the little pink squares on the paper. Then I looked away.

'What's the matter?' she asked.

'It's nothing,' I mumbled, ashamed.

'No, tell me. What's wrong?' She swung me around to face her.

Reluctantly I told her, 'I don't know French. I'm scared to go anywhere.'

She looked stunned for a minute. Then she began to laugh. 'Of course, how silly of me. I can explain how you get there. I can even draw you a map if you want.'

'No, don't bother, Lotti. I'm . . . I'm too busy to go,' I mumbled.

'Why? Why don't you go on Sunday?' she insisted.

'Forget it,' I said irritably. 'I just won't.'

She stayed silent for a minute. There, I've lost my only friend, I thought miserably.

When at last I looked at her, she was watching me, her eyes laughing.

I smiled in relief.

'Don't worry,' she said. 'I know just what you need.'

LOTTI WENT ABOUT it with Machiavellian cunning. First she convinced her parents that I had to learn some French. 'It is all right for

Uncle and Aunty not to know much French, Papa. But what about Leela? Will she stay without a tongue all her life, working as a slave in that poky little shop of theirs?'

'I'm sure that's not their intention, Lotti,' replied Mr Ramdhune. 'Surely she will be married one day to a good man, just like your dear grandmother was married to my grandfather.'

Lotti gave up. Next she tried with her mother. 'Maman, can you not convince Aunty Latha to let Leela go to French classes at the Alliance? The poor girl has no tongue.'

'But the expense, my dear,' her mother replied reasonably. 'And who would look after the store and cook in the hours that she was gone?'

'Hmmm.' Lotti's mother's logic was unbeatable. 'I could teach her, Maman—on Sunday? And it would help her serve the clients better at the store, wouldn't it?'

This time it was Mrs Ramdhune's turn to be silenced by her daughter's logic.

'I see your point, my daughter,' she said. 'But I don't want you to get involved in something far too complicated for you. You have got your *baccalauréat* in sixteen months, you know. I don't want your work to suffer.'

'How will my work suffer, Maman?' Lotti said impatiently. 'Papa never lets me work on Sundays anyway. I will be revising what I have studied as I teach. For there is no better way to learn than to have to explain to someone else. And this is the best way to practise for the teachers' exam. You, want me to be a teacher, don't you?'

Mrs Ramdhune's face brightened. She dearly wanted Lotti to become a teacher and sit the exam for the teachers' training college next year. A teacher in France! That was even better than being a postmaster. Mrs Ramdhune shut her eyes to savour the image of her daughter teaching little French children.

Lotti smiled triumphantly.

'YOU KNOW, MY dear Mrs Latha, our Clothilde loves your Leela so much,' Mrs Ramdhune began.

My aunt nodded. 'Yes, I am glad to see that Leela is quite well behaved. I was afraid she might be a little savage, with no manners or culture.'

Mrs Ramdhune continued, 'It is such a relief to me that they get on so well. Lotti has never had any Indian friends before. But Leela's been such a good influence on her, teaching her our Indian values.' She turned to her husband, 'Hasn't she, Shiva?'

Mr Ramdhune murmured assent, and concentrated on cleaning his pipe. I kept my eyes fixed firmly on the carpet.

'You are too kind, Mrs Ramdhune,' my aunt said. I glanced quickly at my aunt's face. Some of the tension had gone from it, and she looked almost as if she would smile. I looked down again.

Mrs Ramdhune continued dulcetly, 'Well, our Lotti has come up with a wonderful idea. She can teach Leela some French. Instead of wasting their time on Sundays talking about silly things, boys and clothes and whatnot, Lotti can give Leela French lessons.'

My aunt's face stiffened immediately. 'Oh no, no. We wouldn't want to trouble you. Lotti's studies . . .'

'It would be no trouble.' Mrs Ramdhune reached over and patted my aunt's hand reassuringly. 'Lotti is going to be sitting the exam for teachers' training college next year. It is good practice for her.'

My aunt and uncle were still not reassured. 'But it would be taking advantage of your kindness—we couldn't pay,' my uncle said.

'We wouldn't want to impose,' interrupted my aunt.

'No, no. There is no question of imposing,' Mrs Ramdhune reassured her. 'It will be most profitable for our Lotti too. Besides, she wants to do it for our dear Leela.'

Mr Ramdhune joined the conversation suddenly. 'It is important for Leela to learn some French, you know. Times have changed. The government won't allow any more immigrants who cannot speak the language, they want to throw them out.'

'But we pay our taxes,' my uncle cut in angrily.

'Yes, yes. But these crazy French nationalists are getting more powerful every day. We have to change with the times, to adapt,' he explained.

'And it won't cost you a penny. Free.' Mrs Ramdhune was better prepared with her arguments.

'And it will be an asset in the store with the customers,' Lotti added.

My aunt gave in. 'You are right, of course,' she said, looking at Mrs Ramdhune with tears in her eyes. 'What good friends you are to us!'

'You are a very lucky girl,' my aunt told me that night, coming into the room as I changed into my nightie. 'I hope you are truly grateful to your uncle and me for what we have done for you.'

I didn't really care whether I learnt French or not. 'Of course, Aunty,' I replied humbly. Her face softened. She patted me on the shoulders. Her eyes flicked to my legs and her mouth tightened.

'Don't you have any nightdresses that are not so indecent?' she exclaimed.

'But I only wear it to sleep in, Aunty Latha,' I defended myself.

'So what? Bad habits begin in the night when the mind is caught unawares,' she said, glaring at me.

I hung my head.

'Make sure it is only French language that you learn, not French culture. Remember, I won't have a bad girl in this house.'

'Of course, Aunty. I will try to be a good student,' I replied.

AFTER THAT, WHENEVER the families would meet, Lotti would drag me away for a French lesson. At first I was unconvinced. After all, my mother would come for me any time and then what use would the lessons be to me? But faced with Lotti's enthusiasm, I could hardly refuse. Soon I began to enjoy the classes and looked forward to them all week. For Lotti was a wonderful teacher. And she didn't just teach me French out of a book, she taught me lots of other things as well. They ranged from the mundane—like how to get fish and meat at half price from her neighbourhood butcher in exchange for a little feel, a squeeze of the breast or the bottom—to the sublime—like the time she took me to the Musée Guimet to see the Asian sculptures of which she swore I was the spitting image.

'See their little high breasts which point outwards diagonally like yours,' she whispered in front of a statue of Yashodhara.

I stared hard at the beautiful statue. Lotti was right, my breasts were like hers. I felt a thrill of pleasure—Yashodhara, the plaque said, was made in the third century AD. 'What are breasts in French, Lotti?'

'*Sein*,' Lotti replied, loud enough for her voice to echo strangely in the room.

The guard's head snapped up. 'Shhh,' I said in alarm, my hands flying to my mouth.

'Don't be silly, if he could see them, he'd probably tell you the same thing,' she said. 'All men are like Alain the butcher, you know.'

As the weather improved, Lotti took me farther and farther into the city of Paris. The city was her oyster. It nourished her and instilled in her a love of flamboyance and beauty.

Lotti tried to share her Paris with me. She took me through the covered corridors of the place des Vosges, the twisted streets of the Marais, the gigantic cold splendour of La Défense, the slow barge-filled river with its many bridges, each one different, and quays with lovers and lonely men. We marched on the grand boulevards, listened to strange American music at the Virgin Megastore, got lost amongst the little streets of the fifteenth and sixteenth *arrondissements*, and stared at the gravestones in the cemetery of Père Lachaise. We ate Chinese food in Chinatown, and Vietnamese food a few streets down, crêpes smothered in nutty chocolate paste in Les Halles, and spicy merguez and couscous at Barbès. And we stared into the French restaurants and the cafés and watched the people eat. They pretended not to notice us, and we laughed at them, and made faces until the maître d'hôtel or a waiter shooed us away.

We sat on benches in the bus shelters in the sixteenth *arrondissement*, where the old women watched us suspiciously, as did their dogs. We rode the Métro, and played silly eye games with the men. Lotti sometimes got carried away, and the victim of her dark eyes would get up and come over to where we sat to invite her for a drink. She always agreed, and fixed a date for another day. We would laugh all the way home after that. But I could never be as bold as she was. I couldn't blind myself to the feeling that I didn't belong there. The streets were too beautiful to make room for what I carried within me. Even on my first trip into the city, when Krishenbhai decided to make a small detour on the way to the Ramdhunes' in order to show me Paris, it wasn't the buildings that had filled me with wonder, it was the people on the streets. They walked with a self-conscious grace that seemed to say 'Aren't we lucky to live in Paris?' Each face, no matter how different, held the same shared confidence in the future. I did not belong with them, could not belong, because my future was waiting for me in another country, one I hadn't as yet set foot in.

What I loved best was squeezing into a crowded carriage in the Métro just before the doors closed. I loved being pressed against those strange French people, feeling the curves of their arms and backs, and the hard edges of their briefcases digging into my body, and with the salt-and-bacon smell of their sweat in my nostrils. I felt a part of them then, like I had felt a part of the crowds in Nairobi. I loved the powerful smell of the Métro, with its compressed odour of people from everywhere.

But as the days lengthened and spring became summer, the Métro ceased to be a pleasure. The strong scent of clothes, sweat, and flesh that characterized it crossed the threshold of pleasure, and became suffocating. So Lotti and I abandoned our underground games for the Luxembourg Gardens.

These gardens fascinated me. I had never seen a formal French garden before, and I marvelled at the symmetry of the trees with their stiff lines and boxy shapes—like a child's drawing of trees I thought—and the straight avenues. The pond and fountain at the centre came as a delightful contrast to the stiff lines. Even the naked curves of the statues seemed to echo the sudden relaxation of tension that the sight of the water brought after the formality of the avenues.

'Lotti,' I asked one day as we sat by the pond in the garden, 'what do you want to become?'

'*Quoi?*' Lotti asked sleepily, opening one eye and looking at me. She was lying on her stomach, her sleepy face cradled in an open book.

'What do you want to become when you grow up? I mean, in the future?' I corrected hastily, seeing Lotti's face crumple into laughter.

'Oh, I don't know,' she replied when she had stopped laughing. She pushed herself up onto her elbows and stared at the water. 'Maybe I will become a teacher like Maman wants me to, and marry Jacques. That would make her happy too, I think—but not Papa. Or maybe . . . '

'Would you be happy with that?' I cut in. 'What about your art history? What will happen to that?'

'Oh, I don't know. That is a dream. I don't think it could ever be.'

'But why not?' I asked. 'You do so well in school, you could go to the university.'

'Yes. But that is not the point. It's hard, you have to work a lot, at least seven years after school. And then I'll be an old woman, who'll marry me?'

'But what about your ambition to work at the Musée Guimet? I know you love those old statues and things,' I said.

'Oh, okay. Of course I'll study art history. But it's a drag—before I get to Asian arts, I have to study the whole history of Western art. I'll have to remember the names of all these artists whom I don't even like. And for what? For a few golden statues made three thousand years ago? Must I give my life for them, even if one of them looks like you?' she joked. But her face remained serious.

We stared at each other in silence. Lotti, who seemed so free, so confident, suddenly seemed very small . . . almost dull. I could picture her, not as she was now, but when she was her mother's age, plump and predictable. I felt sad.

'And what about you?' Lotti asked, turning the tables on me. 'What do you want to become?'

I sat up sharply. 'Me?'

'Yes, you. Don't look so surprised.' She laughed. 'You have a future too.'

'Hah,' I laughed bitterly, 'what future do I have, apart from the store? I'll be a spice girl—what is it in French, an *épicerette?*—all my life.'

'*Epicerette?*' she laughed. 'There's no such word, silly. But it sounds good. You have invented a new word.' Then she became serious again. 'But . . . leaving that aside, what would you like to become?'

'Well, I suppose . . .' I paused, thinking for a moment about my father and his plans for my future. He'd never have let me give up my education. I looked around at the people in the chairs clustered around the pond, all of them wearing very little and basking in the sun. 'I'd like to be invisible,' I said finally.

'What?' Lotti was so surprised that she sat up straight. 'What do you mean—invisible?'

'Just that, invisible. So that I can pass amongst these people as one of them and not have to feel ashamed that my clothes are all wrong and that I stick out.'

'That's not being invisible, that's called becoming like them,' Lotti exclaimed. Her lip curled scornfully, 'And you'll never be that because they'll never accept you—so don't hope for the impossible.'

'I know, I know,' I said defensively. 'But I'd still like to be able to melt in with them, be so much like them that they wouldn't even be aware I was there.'

'Why?' asked Lotti. 'Why would you want such a thing? Not to be noticed is the worst fate possible.'

'You're wrong, Lotti. To be different is the worst fate of all,' I said, thinking of my father.

Lotti realized what I was referring to and she squeezed my arm. 'Don't worry,' she said pragmatically. 'Pain doesn't stay fresh forever. After a while you won't notice it any more.'

I didn't meet her eyes. Instead I stared blindly across the pond at a pair of lovers kissing on the other side.

My thoughts flew to my mother's most recent letter. She sounded much more cheerful. She had found two rooms for herself and the boys, above a grocery store owned by a certain Mr Shah. He was a widower who lived in the adjoining village. She was going to manage the grocery store. And yet, despite the good news, something in the letter bothered me.

I thought back to her earlier letters. The first letter had arrived shortly after I spoke to her. It had been short and full of affection, but held no plans for the future, or for my joining her in England. Although she never said anything explicitly, I could tell that she had problems with her brother's wife. The second letter, a month later, was even more subdued. She had been ill, she said, because she got wet in the rain while hunting for a job. Why was she looking for a job, I wondered. She talked about the weather and how the cold never quite went away. 'Everything is grey here,' she wrote and I knew she was talking about her heart. I felt it too. As if the grey outside had seeped into our hearts and was slowly killing all feeling. I wrote to her, telling her about my job with my uncle in the shop. That way I could spare her the cost of my airplane ticket to England when the time came, I hinted gently. Her next letter scolded me for not studying but didn't insist that I go to school in France. I took that as a tacit acknowledgment that I could continue my education when I joined her in England.

And so the letters went back and forth across the English Channel. Sad letters, many of them, but brave ones, as both of us tried to cheer each other up by painting interesting pictures of our new lives. Then came yesterday's letter, and it had seemed too good to be true. How could things change so quickly? And if they had, why hadn't she said anything about my going to England in the letter? That, I realized suddenly, was what was missing.

'Why so silent, Leela?' I heard Lotti ask.

'Oh, nothing,' I replied. 'I was just wondering what England is like.'

'Boring,' Lotti answered, 'and rainy. And their food is terrible.'

eleven

After Lotti's holidays began, she and I went into Paris more frequently. One Sunday in late August, when the world was bathed in sunshine, we went to the Parc Monceau, to see—as she said with a mischievous twinkle in her eye—the brass band, the bourgeois ladies with their dogs, the children with their bored *au pairs* and the dirty old men who ogled the young girls and boys from behind their newspapers. When we were settled under a tree, after a spell of battling with my halting French, Lotti suddenly lay down on the grass and turning her face towards me, asked, 'Tell me what do you do in your uncle's shop.'

'What do you mean, "what do I do"? I just sell things and speak French to myself.'

'No, silly! I know that. I mean doesn't anything happen that is worth remembering? Is there never any excitement?'

I think back to the long afternoons and wonder whether I dare to tell Lotti about Krishenbhai; whether I can trust her to keep my uncle's secrets. Suddenly, it doesn't seem to matter.

'In the afternoons,' I begin, 'the store is quiet. But my uncle smells of perfume. His hair is freshly oiled. After a lunch of spicy vegetables, rice, puris, and a sweet from our refrigerated shelves, he makes a point of brushing his teeth. He is terribly restless, the newspaper long since abandoned. He stares out of the crowded display window at the street.

'She comes in very quietly, looking over her shoulder as she pushes the door open.'

'Who's she?' Lotti asks impatiently.

'Wait,' I command her. 'I'm about to tell you.

'Her ample middle-aged body is wrapped in a grey coat. She wears a little round brown hat on her brown head, and grey gloves on her tiny hands. When she looks at you with her large brown eyes, she opens them wide and pulls her face up just three inches short of your face. But she smiles as she does it, and that stops you from being scared or thinking she's mad. She goes straight to the prepared foods counter. There she lingers, undecided, her back to my uncle. He opens the folding part of the video counter with much noise, walks up to her, and clears his throat. She turns, a smile of surprise pinned to her lips. But she is a bad actress, for the smile disappears the moment she sees him and is replaced by another altogether different expression.

'A few minutes later my uncle and Mme Meunier, as I later found out her name was, come into the back room where I sit. "*Voilà c'est là qu'on garde l'essence de l'Inde,*" my uncle says, pointing to the sacks of rice, dal, and garam masala.'

Lotti giggles but doesn't say anything.

' "What can I show you? my uncle says in English, winking at me. Then he continues in French, rattling off the names of the spices with practised ease, "Some basmati rice, the best rice in the world, some cardamom, some cinnamon, some pearls, some aphrodisiac?"

'And she replies, "Some spices, yes. I love spice—cumin and garam masala—but don't you have something special, with a flavour all of its own, something unusual?"

' "I think I may have something for you in my office," my uncle says mysteriously, and pushes aside the heavy curtains to usher her inside.

'During the entire charade, I keep my face buried in the accounts.'

'You know how to do accounts?' Lotti asks.

'Yes, it's easy,' I reply.

'I can't imagine Aunty Latha allowing you to do that.'

'Oh, she doesn't. A week after I began working at the store, my aunt shouted horribly at my uncle for messing up the accounts register. He brings the book home for her to check every evening. He looks more like a schoolboy than her husband when he stands before her as she checks it. Through the entire dressing-down that she gave him that evening, he looked more miserable and guilty than I thought possible.

I felt sorry for him, so the next day I said, "Let me do it, Uncle. I took book-keeping in high school and did all Papa's accounts for him." His face lit up.

'From then on I do the accounts—and Aunty Latha has never again complained. I think she suspected something. For the first few weeks, she'd check each line in the book, her beady eyes swivelling to the left where she could see me cooking in the kitchen. After a few months, she checked sporadically. Then she stopped checking altogether.'

'Wonderful,' Lotti says.

'But there is more,' I tell her mysteriously.

'More what?' Lotti asks.

'More women, of course,' I reply, laughing.

Lotti rolls her eyes. 'I never dreamed he was so interesting. I thought he was boring like my father.'

'Although I like Mme Meunier the best, she, poor thing, isn't the only one who frequents my uncle's back office. There are other women who come to see him. He takes them all into the back room. And there—amongst the sacks of garam masala and coconut and mustard oil—they stay. I can hear the sound of the different kinds of grains rubbing against each other. They make a loud whispering sound, like castanets. When the women emerge, their hair sits perfectly on their shoulders and their skirts fit snugly without a wrinkle over their hips. But they smell of garam masala and crushed red chilies. And another scent as well, one that lies under the common odours of the store, a scent that clashes with the others because it is different—faintly warm, salty, and unwashed.

'My uncle escorts them out of the store courteously. Afterwards he stands on the pavement and lights a cigarette. The Arab grocer's helper, a Mauritian boy, Sankar, hails him in Hindi, "What, you caught an-other fish today. Tasty fish?" he asks. My uncle pretends he has not heard, but I can tell from the way his back straightens that he is pleased. "When one works and one dies in a foreign land—one must adapt to the local scenery," he spits, "They are not as juicy as our Hindu women." '

'His Hindu women indeed,' Lotti hoots with laughter. 'If your Sankar ever saw Aunty Latha screaming at Krishenbhai, he'd soon see just how juicy their marriage was.'

'I should be shocked, I know. But I only feel relieved when they come.'

'Why?' Lotti asks curiously.

'Because then he doesn't pay so much attention to me. And I get to sit in the front of the store while he is with them and look out at the street.'

'You exaggerate. It can't be so bad.'

'But you haven't seen the back room, Lotti. It is dark and the smells suffocate you. There are no windows, nothing to see. It is like a prison.'

'But what about the other people? You must get some interesting people in the evening?' Lotti insists, looking uncomfortable.

I shake my head. 'In the evening we get the working people on their way home. Men and women trying to decide what to buy for dinner, looking for a little something different to spice up their evening, or just to buy a bottle of water or cigarettes. At quarter to seven I leave my uncle to close the shop and walk to the Métro.' I laugh bitterly. 'My uncle makes me go ahead so Aunty Latha will not be made to wait for her dinner.'

'You poor thing,' Lotti exclaims, 'they make you cook for them as well?'

Her remark makes me feel uncomfortable, as if I have crossed the line between disloyalty and treason. 'Sometimes the crazy professor comes just as I'm leaving,' I say quickly, knowing it will distract Lotti.

'A professor?' Lotti perks up. 'How is he? Is he young, old, handsome?'

I laugh. 'Lotti, you have a one-track mind. Forget it. He is old, and his hair is grey and flies around his head and curls over his ears like a girl's. He has deep lines around his mouth and under his eyes.'

Lotti looks disappointed, 'But professors are sexy, you know. It is their only form of exercise.'

I try to look shocked, but fail. 'Well, he has nice eyes, blue ones, very bright,' I admit shyly.

'You see. There is hope for you still. Talk to him. Flirt with him.'

'How? He speaks Sanskrit or something. Even Krishenbhai can't understand his Hindi.'

'Wow,' Lotti's eyes grow big. 'You mean he is an Indian professor?'

'No. He is French,' I tease her, 'but he teaches India.'

She tickles me in revenge. When at last I recover my breath, I continue.

'I take the Métro home. I have a special friend who I meet each evening.'

Lotti sits up, as I knew she would, 'You have a *copain* and you do not tell me? You are a rat.'

'No. He is,' I say poker-faced.

'*Quoi?*' she squeaks.

'My friend is a rat,' I say happily. 'He is quite beautiful too. So elegant.'

'Your friend is a rat,' she repeats incredulously. 'You mean like those that run around on the tracks. Ugh.'

'Yes. A real rat. And he doesn't run around the tracks. It is his home,' I correct her.

She shakes her head slowly. '*Incroyable!*' She looks inquisitively at me, 'Why do you call it your friend?'

I become thoughtful. 'When I saw him that first day, I was all alone on the crowded platform and I couldn't speak a word. I felt alien. It was getting dark and only the Sacré Coeur shone like a light in the sky. Then I saw him. He was perfectly happy to be alone. He didn't care for the people on the platform. He didn't need them. And looking at him, I thought, how I wish I could be like him.' I shrug, 'I don't understand it myself. But every day, he seems to know when I'm coming, and he is there. I have only to look for him.'

Lotti still looks puzzled, and I feel a great gulf open between us.

'Oh, *arrête de faire l'intéressanté*,' she says sharply, giving up.

'What?' I ask, stung. 'Can you speak English please?'

'It means don't be pretentious.'

I don't really understand what she means, but I decide not to ask. I hurry on with my story.

'The night is still the worst part of my day. I reach the house at eight. My footsteps get heavier and heavier as the building nears. It requires all my strength to open the scarred doors of the elevator. My aunt has very sharp ears. No sooner do I step into the corridor than I hear her tinny voice call out to me, "I'm hungry. Hurry up and cook our dinner, beti." '

'I can't blame her. Just thinking of your food makes me hungry.'

'But I hate cooking, Lotti,' I say harshly. 'The smells haunt me, they talk to me—telling me about their loves, their hates, their need of company and warmth, their fear of dying. I cannot rid my brain of their feelings.'

Lotti stares at me, awed and a little fearful. But I can't stop myself. I have to make her understand. 'Each time I emerge from the clouds of cooking smells, I hate myself. I cannot protect myself from them. They have permeated everything—even my pee. At night, I wake up sweating in the overheated apartment and my sweat is tainted with the same sad smell.'

Something about the way Lotti listens tells me she believes me now. I relax and continue more calmly. 'Each night I swear I will tell her that I won't do it anymore. But you see, Lotti, I am a coward.'

'No, you are not. You're very brave,' Lotti says warmly. 'Anyone in your position would have run away by now.'

'But that is where you are wrong, Lotti. It takes courage to run away. I am too scared.'

As autumn shaded into a wet November, Lotti and I were once again confined to the house. After our glorious summer, staying inside and in such close proximity to our minders was even more difficult than it had been before.

twelve

Ayear went by. I grew almost reconciled to my new life. Aunty Latha ceased to frighten me, and Krishenbhai, whose secrets I shared, felt more and more like a friend. Lotti was like the sister I had never had. The sullen smell of the apartment I hardly noticed anymore. But I never stopped hungering for my own family. I dreamed of the day when we would all be together again, a family, complete. And my life, like a movie that had stopped for a change of reels, would begin again.

'Oh, by the way, there's a letter for you,' Aunty Latha told me casually at dinner one day.

'A letter?' I stopped eating.

'From England,' Aunty Latha said. 'Your mother, I think.'

The spoon fell from my hand. It was only ten days since I had received my mother's last letter.

'Can . . . can I have it?' I asked eagerly.

'Not now,' she replied, her mouth full. 'After dinner.'

'Please Aunty Latha, it may be important,' I pleaded.

'Go and get her letter, Latha,' Krishenbhai interceded on my behalf. 'You can see that she will not be able to eat any dinner otherwise.'

Grumbling under her breath, Aunty Latha rose and went to fetch it.

'I hope it's not bad news,' she said as she handed me the letter.

'Don't say that!' my uncle told her irritably. 'Why must you always imagine the worst?'

I didn't say a word. With trembling hands I tore open the letter and began to read, turning sideways in my chair so that all my aunt could see was my profile.

Dear Leela,

How are you? I hear from your aunt and uncle that you have settled down nicely. They are full of praise for you— how well-behaved and obedient you are, how helpful. I feel so proud when I hear them say such wonderful things about you. It eases the worry that lies heavy upon my heart to know that at least you are happy and well taken care of.

'When did she call?' I asked them accusingly. 'Why didn't you tell me?'

'She said she'd call back,' Aunty Latha replied quickly, 'we didn't want to spoil the surprise.'

'What surprise?' My heart began to beat faster.

'Read your letter,' Krishenbhai put in hastily. 'She said she had already written to you.'

Your brothers are still in the local school here, but I am not happy with it. It is filled with brutes and bullies. I am looking around for a private school where the boys will be more gentle. But private schools here are so expensive, and after your poor father's death, I don't know how I will manage. But let me not burden you with these worries. You are far from them, thank God. In another few years you will be married with a house and husband of your own.

The shop in Nairobi was sold. We did not get much for it. But from the money we received I have bought a little shop in a village south of London, called South Oxney. Your uncle Atul says that it is a very good property as London is growing all the time. Mr Patel helped me buy the shop. We are going to get married in a month.

I stopped reading the letter. How could she get married? What about us? Where would we go? I looked up. They were staring at me, both of them, their expressions apprehensive. Krishenbhai's face was even slightly guilty.

'What's the matter?' he asked.

'Don't pretend. You know what it is,' I snapped. 'She told you when she called, didn't she?'

Krishenbhai looked away. Even my aunt said nothing.

I got up from the table, pushing my chair back violently. 'You could have warned me,' I cried.

I ran into the bathroom and locked the door. I sat on the toilet and continued to read.

> We will be married very quietly, in a civil ceremony before an English judge. Then I shall be able to send the boys to private school, and one day you can even come and visit us for a little while. Maybe we can even take a holiday in France. Shahji says it is a very beautiful country. Then perhaps we will visit you and your uncle and aunt in Paris. Not for too long, of course, for I hear the house is small. But maybe for a weekend.
>
> I'm so happy for you, beti, and for us all, because God has been kind and we are all well-settled.
>
> Your loving Maa

I turned the letter over, thinking that perhaps there was more on the other side. But the page was blank. I re-read the letter again, hoping that perhaps I had missed some vital sentence. Slowly I crumpled the letter in my fist and, forced myself to look squarely at the truth: My mother had abandoned me. I felt a burning begin in my throat and spread slowly to my chest. My stomach heaved, and I lurched forward to the sink.

I stared at myself in the bathroom mirror. The face that stared back was so much like hers. But she hadn't seen that. She had never really meant to take me to England. My uncle and aunt must have known this. Krishenbhai and Latha, my mouth twisted in bitterness. I was their child. Everyone knew it except me. No one had bothered to tell me. I was only supposed to accept what came to me as fate.

In the days that followed, I needed Lotti desperately. But Lotti, too, it seemed, had been taken away from me. She was in Mauritius for a holiday. I had never felt so alone. I stopped going to the store and lay in bed all day, or watched movies with my aunt. I took refuge in cooking enormous meals, most of which I never tasted.

When Lotti came back, full of stories about her cousins and aunts and her various prospective husbands, I laughed loudly. My mouth moved and heavy bursts of sound came out of my throat. But I laughed out of a sense of duty. Lotti and her life seemed distant, and now quite unrelated to me. Lotti looked at me strangely.

Her father said, 'They love her so much there, they want her to marry and settle down there amongst them. We had a terrible time bringing her back.'

I laughed even louder this time.

'It is good to hear her laugh, isn't it, Latha?' my uncle said nervously. He turned to the Ramdhunes and explained, 'She has been very quiet lately.'

Lotti stared hard at me. I continued to avoid her eyes.

'Why, what happened?' Mrs Ramdhune asked Aunty Latha.

'Her mother got remarried,' Aunty Latha whispered.

'Oh,' Mrs Ramdhune whispered back, 'the poor child. At least she has you to look after her.'

Later Lotti pulled me out onto the balcony. She didn't say anything, but her eyes filled with tears as she held my face in her hands.

After that, things went back to being normal, or seemed to. I returned to work at the store, but it was no longer the same. Lacking a foreseeable end to my days there, time in the store began to stretch indefinitely, one day blending seamlessly into another. So I began to steal little bits of money from the till, fiddling the accounts each day by five francs here and there. I don't really know how it began. Maybe the first time, it had been a genuine mistake. But then, it became a habit, a small way to break the monotony of each day. A small measure of the day's worth in a life that had begun to drift again.

Thirteen

One afternoon, around 5.30 p.m., the telephone rang. I had just finished ringing up a purchase of cigarettes for a customer. The money was curled in my fist, waiting to be secreted away with the rest of the money I had stolen.

My uncle was occupied in the back room. He had a new woman with him. She was young and very white with red hair. And she chewed gum. My uncle looked so proud of her. He had taken her to the café down the road for a coffee and sat with her in the open on the sidewalk. She wore a miniskirt even though she was fat. Her thighs wobbled as she walked and brushed against each other, and her stockings made a swishing sound.

The telephone continued to ring. I stared at it in fright, certain that it was Aunty Latha. I let it ring about twenty times. Then it stopped. Two minutes later it began to ring again. I lifted the receiver and said yes very hesitantly. It was the professor. I recognized his scratchy voice and his special brand of Sanskrit-Hindi. He wanted us to make a delivery immediately. There were spices he needed. 'One moment, please,' I told him and ran to the back room. From behind the curtain I could hear the whispering of the grains and a woman moaning. I shouted in Gujarati, 'The old professor wants some things delivered right now.'

My uncle didn't reply, but the silence behind the curtain was palpable. I could sense his dilemma—should he abandon his young mistress and take the groceries himself, or let me take them to the professor and risk Aunty Latha's wrath? The bags of rice and dal rustled, the seeds moving against each other. Finally, he took the easy way out, as

I knew he would. 'You take it to him, my dear,' he called to me in Gujarati, 'but be sure to come back straight after. I don't want you in the streets after dark.'

Outside the sky was a brilliant blue and the street was bathed in the golden evening light. Joyfully I packed a bag with things that the professor wanted. I let myself out of the store and sucked in huge lungfuls of the light crisp air.

The professor lived towards the edge of the eighteenth *arrondissement*, halfway up the hill of Montmartre. It was a very elegant neighbourhood, filled with wonderful boutiques of beautifully arranged food and wine and cheese.

At No. 19 rue d'Abbesses, the professor's building, two stone gargoyles regarded me with bared teeth. I punched the numbers of the code, and the huge ten-foot wooden door clicked open. I found myself in a large courtyard where spring had already come in crimson and yellow and purple in the flowerpots that lined it. The lobby was small but filled with sunlight. In the middle was a long curved staircase. At the top of the stairwell there was a big white dome made of milky glass. It had a design of grapes and little round cherubic faces etched around its rim. On each floor huge diamond-paned windows, like those in a church, let in even more light. I thought of the dark stairways in Uncle's building. I wondered what kind of people would go to such trouble to decorate a staircase that was outside their own homes, that belonged to no one. On each silent landing, I stopped and stared hard at the closed doors all around me. What kind of people lived behind them? What did their homes and they themselves look like?

On the fourth floor, where the professor lived, I guessed which door was his immediately. It was wide open. Strange music emerged from the apartment. Above the door was a little red Ganesh in clay. Tentatively I rang the bell. 'Come in,' his voice roared through the music. 'The kitchen is at the end. You can put the things down on the counter.' I took a deep breath, my throat felt dry. All Aunty Latha's warnings about strange French men came to the fore. I stepped across the threshold cautiously.

I found myself in a long low-ceilinged corridor lined with books. The floor was made of wood and shone with rich streaks of brown and gold and red. White bookshelves curved along the wall, heavy with books. I stared at them hungrily. Even in Nairobi, I had never seen so many books outside a library. Suddenly I realized how much I missed books. My uncle only read newspapers. Sitting in the store day after day, and night after night in bed, I read and re-read the very few books I had, the stories giving meaning to my days. And now here I was looking at more books than I could read in a lifetime. I felt giddy with delight.

The corridor curved sharply to the right and then ended abruptly. Three white doors opened out to the left and to the right of me. One was closed and behind it, I could hear the music and click-click of someone typing. The other two doors were open. White walls and long windows, floors covered with carpets in warm sweet colours–reds, yellows, maroons, and ochre. The light jumped from one surface to the other, emptying into the corridor. The colours added to my sense of having wandered into another world altogether. I had never seen such gentle clear colours. Everything in my uncle's house, and even in Lotti's house for that matter, was dark and muddy-coloured or else so bright that it hurt the eye. I shuddered with pleasure and wished that I could become a book or a sunbeam and remain in the professor's house forever.

The floors of the kitchen were made of large green and blue tiles set in a geometric pattern. The walls were also painted pale blue and green—but the colours were cooler and more quiet. In one bay window, there was a window seat and in the other, a small wooden table with two chairs, from which you could look out onto the street. Evening noises from the street floated through the open windows, and on the stove a pot bubbled.

I placed my bag on the table. Then I gasped. For around the room, pinned or stuck onto the cupboards and on every other available wooden surface, were postcards from all over the world. Horsemen galloping across a pastel-coloured desert, white sailboats against a silver sea, grenade-shaped fruit and women with mysterious eyes in red saris, and gingerbread houses with onion-shaped domes. I stared at them hypnotized.

'So you like my postcards, hein?' the professor said, coming up behind me. I looked at him nervously. In his own house he looked larger and more substantial than he did in the shop.

'Do you like to travel?' he asked easily, smiling at me.

'I have never really travelled,' I replied stiffly, 'except in Kenya.'

'Kenya?'

'I was born there.'

Curiosity made his eyes shine. 'Really? I have always wanted to go there. I hear it's a beautiful country. Lots of animals.'

'It is the best country in the world,' I replied proudly, but even as I said it, I knew that I was acting. It wasn't the best country in the world. Just the only one I knew.

'Then you are not Indian? But your beauty is all Indian.'

'I'm half-Gujarati,' I replied quickly. 'My mother came from there.'

'You have never lived in India? But your family is Indian?'

I couldn't think of a reply, it was too complicated to explain.

He laughed. 'Doesn't matter. Let's not worry about who you are. Do you like to cook?'

'Y-yes,' I replied hesitantly.

'Then let us see what you think of my cooking.' Taking me by the elbow, he led me over to the stove and lifted the lid off a large brass pot. My head jerked back in surprise. Inside the pot a bitter war was being fought between the spices and the chicken because no attempt had been made to marry them. I stepped closer cautiously. An over-abundance of coriander and ginger dominated the ranks. The spices had not been ground together beforehand. The resulting mess made my stomach turn. 'Go on, taste it.' The professor dipped a spoon inside and held it expectantly to my lips.

I couldn't bring myself to taste it. The smells had already told me the entire story. I turned back to him, saddened. 'This is terrible. You have . . .' I stopped, afraid he would think me rude.

'I have what? Spoiled it?' he asked, looking worried. He seemed less frightening now.

'I think you need a little garlic and some more turmeric . . . and salt,' I told him gently.

'But I already added those.'

'C-can I do it for you?' I said suddenly, breathless at my own daring.

His eyes widened. Then he laughed. 'So you really like to cook, hein? Then you must be a good cook.' He stared at me and suddenly his expression grew cunning. I licked my lips nervously. 'Please,' he said pointing to the cupboards, 'be my guest.' Quickly I moved away and began to concentrate on the task at hand. I took a little ceramic bowl, peeled some garlic into it, and threw in a little turmeric and some chili. These I crushed together, gritting my teeth as the smell of their melding came to me.

Tears filled my eyes and I blinked them away. I looked at the professor again. He was watching me intently. The room filled slowly with shadows as night entered through the opened windows. As it grew dark in the kitchen, I became more and more conscious of him standing there watching me silently, and somehow I felt proud. Then I remembered what Aunty Latha always said about French people. I turned my attention to the food on the stove, unable to meet his eyes.

I put spices into the pot, stirred quickly, and put the lid on. 'Can you give me some yoghurt?' I asked without looking at him. 'And some sugar.' He handed both to me silently. I mixed in the yoghurt. Slowly the bitter acrimony in the pot subsided. I turned the fire down low.

'Leave it for another ten minutes and then switch the fire off,' I said.

He moved to the stove. 'Shall I taste it?'

I nodded. He took a spoon and dipped it into the pot. As he tasted, he stared at me intently. Then his face suddenly relaxed as pleasure filled it.

He smiled at me and took my hand in his. Instinctively my hand curled itself into a ball. Gently he prised open my fingers, kissing each one separately. I snatched my hand away and closed it into a fist once more. He laughed. 'Thank you, *ma princesse Indienne*' he said. I felt terribly excited. No one had ever called me princess before. I smiled at him shyly.

Then, quietly, he said, 'It is a pity you are so young.' He moved away from me, to the little white table by the window where my coat lay. Then he turned back to me. 'We wouldn't want to offend your uncle, would we?' he laughed and held my coat up for me to slip into. I put out my hand to take it from him. But he wouldn't let me. 'No, no,' he shook his head, 'in France we do it like this.' He held up the coat again for me to slip my arms into. My face burned.

Very formally, as if I were an honoured guest, he accompanied me back down the corridor. At the entrance I turned to look one last time at the professor's apartment, but instead found myself staring into his face. In a flash, it swooped down upon mine, his mouth sucking at my lips. I felt sick and tried to push him away. 'Please. I . . . I h-have to g-go. I'm l-late,' I stammered. His body felt soft and heavy, not unlike a cushion. Then he released me. He pressed some notes into my hands, 'For the cuisine. *Au revoir*.' My hand closed into a fist. I stuffed it into my pocket. '*Merci, et au . . . au revoir*.'

I crossed the old inner courtyard slowly. All around me white buildings loomed, and above them was the sky. It was very quiet in the courtyard. I stood there feeling that at last, at least for a little while, I had become a part of the beauty of Paris. I felt something settle inside me, giving me weight and a steadiness that had not been there before.

WHEN I REACHED the store, it was dark and the shutters were already three-fourths of the way down. I squeezed under them. Inside my uncle was pacing up and down in the semi-darkness. 'Where were you?' he yelled as I came in. He grabbed me by the shoulders, 'What took you so long? Your aunt called twice. I thought you had gone home directly ages ago.'

'Uncle, I was just . . .' I began guiltily.

'Just answer my questions.' He shook me like a bag of rice, 'What were you doing with that man?'

'N-nothing, Uncle,' I stammered.

His eyes narrowed. 'Nothing?' he sneered. 'You were doing nothing for two hours?'

'Please, just listen. I'll explain.'

He turned his face away. 'I don't want to hear your lies.'

'Uncle, please . . .' I began to sob. 'I have done nothing wrong.'

'Nothing wrong? You ungrateful bitch.' He shook me again, digging his fingers into my shoulder blades. 'You have betrayed us.'

'That's not true,' I shouted. 'He asked me to look at his chicken curry and it was awful. So I made it for him.'

He laughed at that, his mouth dripping disbelief.

I stared at him wildly, feeling my face burn and go numb. 'I promise it's the truth.'

'Of course you just cooked his chicken, you liar!' His mouth twisted into a sneer and he hit me across the face. I fell backwards into the cooked food counter and lay still, eyes closed. Maybe this was a dream, I thought.

'Leela.' My uncle's voice sounded anxious.

Cautiously I opened my eyes. 'You shouldn't have gone away like that,' he said.

'But Uncle, you told me to go. I did nothing except cook, I swear upon my mother.'

His face changed. 'Don't bring your mother into this. She would have died of shame had she been here today.'

I stared at Krishenbhai, suddenly seeing all the things that made his face so different from that of my father. I felt terribly alone.

Krishenbhai began speaking again, his voice sounding distant. 'You see, I know all about you.' He opened his right hand and threw something at me. Instinctively, I held up my hands to protect my face. Something cold and hard hit me, then paper money fell more gently around me. It was the money I had kept out of the register to put away with my secret stash. I began to feel sick, but somehow pushed the feeling back down my throat.

Quickly I gathered all the notes together and stood up. 'Uncle, I'm sorry. I meant to put it inside the register. I must have forgotten,' I said, holding the money out to him.

He would not touch it. 'Don't say anything. I don't want to hear more lies.'

'Please, I . . . Uncle, you're not being fair,' I pleaded.

He cut me off again, 'Don't talk to me about fair. You are the one who has not been fair. And after all we have done for you—saving you from that godforsaken continent, giving you a home, trusting you . . .'

Anger forced out the fear that had clouded my brain. I became suddenly calm. 'I haven't betrayed your trust. Call the professor and ask him to save a little of his dinner for you.'

My uncle looked at me uncertainly, his face softening slightly. 'Well, maybe I will or maybe I won't,' he said. Then, glancing at his watch, he continued, 'You had better go. Your aunt is waiting anxiously.'

I stood up relieved. 'Thank you, Uncle,' I said. He said nothing, still looking troubled. I turned and walked to the door.

'Leela.' Something in his voice stopped me. 'There is something you should know before you go to her.

'When your aunt called,' he said without emotion, 'she was so worried that I thought she would have an attack. So I got angry and . . . I told her that . . .' He stopped, fear and regret on his face.

'What?' I felt nervous. 'What did you tell her?'

'That you went out on your own. That it was your decision,' he said finally.

I froze. 'You *what*? You coward, you told her it was my decision?' I spat furiously. 'How could you do that?'

His eyes slid away from mine. He shrugged his shoulders helplessly and turned away, 'I couldn't help it.'

I asked helplessly, 'What will I say to her?'

He looked at me sadly. 'You'll think of something. Go now,' he said, patting me on the back. 'I'll lock up and come later.'

'I . . . I can wait,' I offered hesitantly. 'We c-can go together.'

He refused to meet my eyes. 'No. There is no need. I may take some time. You go, there is the dinner to be cooked. Aunty Latha must be waiting.'

I could not argue with that and left.

I ran to the Métro. In the train and on the long walk home, I tried to plan what I would tell her. Almost before I knew it, I was walking past the tall beehivelike buildings in which we lived.

The flat was silent and dark. I paused uncertainly in the hallway.

The door to my aunt's bedroom was partly open and behind it was darkness. I took a step towards it. The silence seemed to breathe and shift suddenly. I could feel her waiting for me.

I began to tiptoe down the hall. As I passed her room, she called out to me. 'Leela.'

'Aunty Latha?' I answered hesitantly. 'Are you awake?'

'Yes, I am. Come inside,' she answered.

I opened the door wider and stood at the doorway. There was enough light for me to make out the contours of the furniture and my aunt's huge bulk on the bed.

She raised herself slightly as I entered.

'Come right inside, child. Don't just stand there.'

I stepped into the middle of the room. She sounded calm. It was too dark to read the expression on her face. I began hesitantly, 'Aunty, I . . .'

'You're late,' she cut in quietly, 'and I've been lying here half fainting with hunger, waiting for you to arrive.'

'Yes, I'm sorry, but . . .'

She interrupted me again, 'While you were running off with some dirty Frenchman.'

'Please let me explain,' I tried to stay calm.

'No,' she shouted. 'I don't want to hear any of your lies. I know where you have been and what you have been doing.'

'You cannot know anything, Aunty. Only I can tell you what happened. Won't you just listen?' I burst out.

My aunt stopped, amazed. It was the first time I had ever raised my voice in front of her.

I continued quickly before the surprise wore off. 'I went to deliver the groceries because Uncle was . . .' I paused, unable to tell her, 'was busy.'

'Don't lie,' she said. 'You just walked out of the store without a word while your uncle was helping someone in the back.'

'That's not true,' I shouted.

She shouted back, 'Yes it is. You went off because you couldn't wait to take your clothes off and lie with a filthy foreigner.'

'I am not lying,' I pleaded. 'Have I ever done such a thing before? And if I had been guilty, would I have come back?'

'Perhaps not,' she said more quietly. 'But you have stolen from me.'

For a second everything went red. Then through the red haze, I saw Krishenbhai's face. I saw his weak mouth and his greedy sucking eyes. My voice emerged, little more than a hiss. 'You dare to call me filthy, to accuse me of sleeping with other men when your husband . . . ' as I said the words, I began to tremble, 'your own pure husband has slept with not one but three Frenchwomen in the last year.'

'Liar,' my aunt screeched, 'filthy whore, thief!'

I stood absolutely still, letting the words wash over me.

At last I spoke softly, coldly, like a scientist, 'Yes, yes. Maybe I am all that and more. But why don't you come to the store in the afternoon sometime, and look into the back room. Why don't you see for yourself who is in the habit of lying?'

My aunt pushed herself up on the pillows, her mouth opening and closing like a fish out of water.

'Or perhaps you already know . . .' I taunted.

Aunty Latha half-lifted herself off the bed in her fury. 'Get out,' she shouted, 'just get out.'

I stared at her, suddenly frightened, the ice around my heart breaking. I turned and left the room, closing the door quietly behind me.

PART *two*

o n e

~I stood uncertainly in the corridor. Behind me I could hear
Aunty Latha moaning and the bedsprings singing under the weight of
her convulsive sobbing. The sound cut through me and bounced back
and forth in the narrow corridor. I backed away from it. The hall was
calm, undisturbed. My eyes swept over the room, letting its uncluttered
order imprint itself onto my senses. The room was shrouded in darkness, only a thin stream of light slipped under the front door.

I don't know for how long I stood still in the dark. Suddenly I
became aware of the presence of someone standing at the door. I
looked up, the blood draining out of my cheeks. Aunty Latha looked
terrible. Her cheeks and eyelids were swollen and her eyes had become
little more than slits.

I felt an immense sense of remorse. 'Aunty, I'm . . . s-sorry.'

'For what?' she laughed bitterly. 'You think "sorry" can make a broken thing whole? It's a very nice word, no? You kill someone and then
you say you're sorry.'

'Aunty, please, I didn't mean what I said.'

'You didn't mean it? You were lying then?'

'No, but . . . I'm sorry, I was angry . . . I . . .'

'Not that word again,' she shouted. 'I hate it, I tell you. And I hate
you.'

'No, please.' I began to sob.

'You have destroyed me. You and your selfish little anger.' Aunty
Latha's voice cracked and her pain was terrible to see. Her face looked
as if it was breaking as she spat out the words. 'You have made my
life, our lives, our home hell. Get out—leave.'

There was nothing else I could do. I walked slowly to the tube-lit corridor, closing the door quietly behind me.

Outside the building, the street was empty, except for the garbage that had accumulated everywhere in the street corners and doorways.

The wind made an unearthly hissing sound like steam from a pressure cooker as it swept through the alleys. Nothing moved except for the things that were propelled by it. I turned the corner of the building and was grabbed by the wind. I let it carry me down the street like a piece of newspaper, blowing me along, homeless and strangely free. I felt light, almost weightless. Silent buildings towered above me, their faces mottled. I laughed at them standing there so solidly, unable to keep up with me, until I felt tears on my cheeks. Then I was past them and on the open road. The wind pushed me farther down the street.

Suddenly my ears caught a new sound coming out of the darkness—footsteps, half-running, half-slithering across the paving stones. I began to walk faster. The steps behind me seemed to quicken as well. My feet hastened their pace to a jog. The area of darkness between one streetlight and the next lengthened. I could no longer make out the sound of the footsteps against the thumping of my own heart. I turned a corner and suddenly the wind deserted me, pushing itself in my face as I ran. My lungs began to hurt and I was gasping for breath. I felt so scared I could hardly remember how to breathe. My energy began to ebb and my footsteps slowed. I tried to scream. But no sound emerged. The streets were completely empty, shrouded in silence.

I kept running until the mouth of the tunnel beneath the highway appeared. The tunnel exploded with sound. I felt phantom fingers grabbing at me from all sides. I ran on heedless until the lights of the village were in front of me. Then I slowed to a walk. The village looked deserted. In the stillness, my footsteps echoed loudly. A motorcycle engine came alive in an alley behind me. I jumped to the side, into the shadow of a doorway and stumbled upon something soft and protesting covered in rags.

Eventually, I arrived at the Métro and descended underground thankfully. The station was almost empty. I stood at the edge of the platform. On the opposite side, a group of men stood smoking and talking. They looked at me with the cold eyes of predators. I stared down at the rail bed.

At last the train arrived.

I rode the Métro for what felt like hours. The noise of the train spared me from thinking. The other passengers kept a safe distance from me.

Finally my stomach began to chew upon itself, the muscles clamping and unclamping endlessly to satisfy the hunger that lay within. I roamed the near-empty carriages looking for food. Eventually I found some, a half-eaten packet of caramelized peanuts. I gobbled them down, barely pausing to chew. The pain in my stomach increased. At one o'clock I got out of the carriage at the terminus. Policemen with dogs were everywhere, throwing the homeless out of the carriages. They gave me a glassy stare. I avoided their eyes and followed the crowd up the stairs and to the exit.

Outside an alien world welcomed me. There was an urgency to those who walked the streets, little more than shadows until they were impaled by the headlights of a fast moving car; men who moved with a loping pantherlike step, at once confident and threatening. Their eyes cut through me, cold as the winter wind, icily familiar, sizing me up. Like the great hunters of the African grasslands, intimately knowledgeable about their prey.

Instinctively I moved in the opposite direction, lingering in the shadows until I was alone on the street. Dead leaves littered the pavement and lay in dark heaps under the bare trees. They clutched wetly at my ankles as I moved past. Don't leave us here to die in the cold, they seemed to be saying. I brushed them off fiercely with hands that were numb and icy.

I squeezed my hands into the pockets of my skirt, and felt paper crackle beneath my fingers. I pulled the paper out without curiosity, and there clutched in my fingers was money. Suddenly I felt better. I could sleep the night in a hotel, and the next day, or even the day after, when Krishenbhai and Aunty Latha were really worried about me, I would return.

At last I found a hotel in a little street off avenue de la Republic. There was a buzzer beside the door. I pressed it.

The concierge stepped out from behind the desk. He looked me up and down. Before he could say anything I asked for a single room in a loud voice.

He kept staring at me. 'We are full,' he said.

'But you have a sign outside which says you have a vacancy.'

He opened his mouth to say something rude but I cut in quickly, 'I only need a place for tonight.'

'Tonight. That's what they all say.' He had the strangest set of teeth I had ever seen. They all slanted inwards at an angle of sixty degrees. I stared, wondering how he managed to eat. He shut his mouth.

'I only have a double,' he muttered sulkily, 'and it will cost four hundred francs.'

'What!' I exclaimed. 'Outside it says doubles cost only three hundred francs.'

'Well, that's all I have. You should be grateful I didn't throw you out.'

I said curtly, 'Show me the room.'

Grumpily he pushed a register towards me. 'Sign here. And I need your passport or *carte d'identite.*'

I froze. I had no papers with me. My uncle had taken my passport from me the day I arrived. I took a deep breath and pulled out my last hundred francs. 'My passport is at home. I didn't think to bring it. I wasn't planning to stay out tonight but I missed the last Métro,' I said with as much dignity as I could. 'Will this be enough of a security?' And I pushed the hundred-franc bill into his hands.

two

The next morning Paris looked different. The shops were open, their windows ablaze with light. The sound of the traffic, horns blaring, and car engines running was at once deafening and reassuring. The streets and cafés were filled with people. Nobody looked at me strangely, or noticed me at all.

I went to a telephone booth and called Lotti at school.

'Where are you?' she asked. 'I was so worried when your aunt called last night asking if you were with me . . .'

'In a hotel.'

'You planned it then, to run away? How brave!' she exclaimed.

'No, it just happened. My uncle . . . Well forget it, it's too long a story.'

'Where are you calling from, the hotel?'

'No. I'm not sure where I am, somewhere near Nation I think. In a *tabac*.'

'I'll come and get you. We can go back and face them together.'

'Lotti,' I said slowly, 'I don't think they want me back. My aunt . . .'

'Why? What happened?' Lotti asked impatiently.

'I told her about Krishenbhai's afternoon encounters.'

Unexpectedly, she laughed. 'That explains it.'

'Explains what?'

'I heard your aunt say to my mother last night on the phone that they had been nurturing a snake in their bosom. They said you had no morals and were a thief.'

'What? I'm not a thief. They're the ones who make me work without even paying me,' I replied angrily.

'I know, I know,' Lotti said, trying to soothe me. 'They were probably just speaking out of anger. But then,' she added, almost in spite of herself, 'Aunty Latha sounded very calm, she didn't even sound out of breath.'

We were both silent.

'Look, Leela,' Lotti said finally, 'I have to go back or my teachers will wonder what's wrong. What is the name of your *tabac?*'

'Le Scorpion.'

'Which street is that on?'

'It's beside the Métro exit, at the corner of rue du Rendezvous and boulevard de Picpus.'

'I'll retrieve you from there in one hour.'

'Okay.' I was so relieved I forget to tell her that retrieve and *retrouve* were not the same thing.

WHEN LOTTI ARRIVED, I clung to her. We ordered coffee and croissants. Lotti paid. 'Keep your money. You're going to need every penny,' she said. 'I don't think Aunty Latha wants you back in a hurry. She called me at school, right after you hung up.'

'What!' I was stunned.

'Yup. She told me to tell you not to come back.'

I shuddered and shut my eyes, reliving the events of the previous night. When I opened my eyes, my mind was made up. I looked at Lotti, who was staring at me anxiously. 'Lotti, I'm never going to go back. I'd rather be a whore.'

Lotti began to laugh, *'Quel melodrame. Tu n'est qu'un bébé!'*

Her face became serious again. 'Tell me everything,' she ordered.

I told her everything, starting with the professor's phone call and ending with my night at the hotel. She remained silent after I finished.

'I brought you something of yours,' she said at last, handing me a plastic bag. The flame-coloured silk inside flared as it caught the light. It was my mother's wedding sari.

'How did you find this, Lotti?' I asked.

'It was lying at home. Remember you brought it over last weekend, to show me how to wear it.'

'I'm so glad. Thank you. This is the only thing I did not want to ever leave behind.' I clutched the bag to me and hugged Lotti along with it.

Her face became serious again. 'What about your mother?' she said hesitantly. 'Shouldn't you tell her?'

'My mother has a new life.' I said bitterly. 'And anyway I don't know her telephone number.'

'You must write to her,' Lotti said finally.

My heart sank. 'But it might take her weeks to come.'

'I know. But I think I know someone who could help.'

'Who?' I asked eagerly.

'Do you remember the girl I told you about, whom I met in an Indian *épicierie?*'

'You mean the one who's a model?' I looked at her blankly. 'What would a model do with me?'

'Silly, Maeve's been living on her own since she was fifteen. She could let you stay with her.'

Before I could demur, she made her way to the telephones, her hips swinging saucily at the men over by the bar.

Five minutes later, she came back, her face alight. 'It's all arranged,' she said happily. 'Maeve said I was to bring you to her apartment right away.'

'B-but Lotti, what will I say? She . . . I've never lived with a French person before. And I'll have to speak in French all the time too. I . . . I don't know if I can.'

'Of course you can,' Lotti said encouragingly, 'you've spoken French any number of times.' Suddenly she grew angry, 'You wanted to escape, remember? Welcome to France.'

'I never wanted to come to France in the first place,' I replied hotly. 'It was my mother's idea.'

We went down into the Métro and caught a train to place d'Italie. This part of Paris was new to me. It was a strange mixture of old and new buildings and wide avenues. In one corner there was a Mc-Donald's, the plastic furniture and garish artificial colours making the place look cartoonish and unreal. On the other corner was an old brasserie with huge banks of ice on the outside with shellfish laid out on top. We crossed the street towards the McDonald's. An old woman, with white hair and thick legs, stood holding a placard, begging. I shivered, imagining myself in her place.

We walked to the quiet side street where Maeve lived. Her apartment was in a narrow five-storey house squashed between two fat grey buildings. They were not very different from the building that my aunt lived in. The only difference was that here there were well-kept cars lining the streets, the walls were free of graffiti, and the pavement was solid unbroken concrete.

Lotti punched in the code and we entered a small dark foyer. The roof was very low and the foyer was long, like a corridor. We climbed five floors of circular stairs and found ourselves on a landing with three doors leading off it. The one on the left opened and a tall figure dressed in black stood framed in the rectangle of light.

Maeve was really tall. Her body, silhouetted by the grey light, was long and curved: long legs, round hips, a long narrow waist, full breasts. I hung back, feeling like an intruder.

'*Salut, ma petite Lotti. Ça fait longtemps. Qu'est que tu deviens?*' Maeve ceremonially kissed the air above Lotti's cheek, and then, to my surprise, gave her a quick hug. Her eyes flicked over me briefly. She didn't seem to like what she saw, for she ignored me, fixing her attention on Lotti again.

'It's nice to see you, Lotti. Why don't you come more often? I need someone to show me how to use those spices we bought together, remember?' she said in a low throaty voice.

Lotti smiled and shrugged elegantly, still staring up at Maeve like one bewitched. 'I've just the person for you then, Maeve,' she laughed, and pulled me forward. 'Meet Leela. She's an amazing cook and a wizard with spices.'

'Really?' Maeve looked at me a little more closely and smiled briefly. She opened the door wider and bade us come in. Without waiting to see if we followed her, she turned and walked inside. We trailed after her into the apartment, Lotti in the lead, with me making up the rear.

At first the light blinded me. Then as my eyes grew used to the brightness, I realized that the room was actually quite small but the lack of furniture, the huge windows and white walls made it look big. It smelt new and impersonal, like it had just been moved into. There was nothing soft about the room, everything was tall and angular: high steel stools, slim table, and a narrow black couch. On the walls were three paintings in shades of black, grey, and white—strange moonscapes. The paint was applied thickly on the canvas, giving the paintings a rough layered feeling. I stared at them intensely.

'So what do you think of them?' Maeve asked, coming up silently behind me. Amidst the sparse modern decor, she looked strangely exotic. She had deep honey-blonde hair and creamy skin. Her eyes and her eyebrows were dark. But all this I noticed afterwards. To begin with, I was blinded by her lips. Their surface was shining and bumpy like the skin of a strawberry. The ridges and clefts that dotted them only emphasized their extraordinary roundness. A tiny brown beauty spot on a corner threw into relief the extravagance of that mouth. Maeve's lips incarnated a sensuality of the flesh that one fantasized about, but could never clearly picture. Until one saw her lips.

'They remind me of the walls of the old town in Mombassa with their many layers of peeling posters stuck haphazardly on top of each other, the colour washed away by the rain,' I replied.

'Really? No one has ever said that before.' She smiled, and for the first time the smile reached her eyes. They were strange eyes—like muddy pools of water reflecting dark grey rainclouds. They looked flat and depthless. Wintry eyes, I thought. They were made even more mysterious by the way that the heavy curved eyelids drooped downwards slightly at the edges. 'But I think you're right. That's a good description of it,' she said.

I smiled back at her, relieved, and fascinated. She didn't seem to mind that I was staring at her so frankly. Her smile reappeared. 'Come, let's sit down and talk,' she ordered.

Obediently Lotti and I moved towards the narrow black sofa that was placed against the wall opposite the paintings.

'So did you find the house easily?' Maeve asked politely.

'Oh yes,' Lotti replied. 'Your directions were perfect.' I looked at her in surprise, she didn't usually praise so extravagantly, and for so little. It sounded almost overdone. But Lotti, too, was transformed by Maeve's beauty. In front of her, she seemed different, smaller, dumpier, darker—a muddy dwarf beside a tall fairy queen. 'I brought Leela to you,' I heard her say, 'because you ran away from your parents in Strasbourg and came to Paris when you were sixteen.'

'Not quite.' Maeve said dryly, 'I did not run away from my parents. I left them—to be free.'

I turned back to her, wanting to say something in Lotti's defence. But I couldn't think of what to say. Maeve's world was a totally alien one. I looked down at my feet, sharing Lotti's embarrassment.

Maeve looked at the two of us, and suddenly she asked in English, 'Would you like some coffee?' Her accent was faint, mixed with something American. I began to refuse out of politeness, but Lotti gave me a warning look and nudged me. As Maeve turned and walked over to the tiny kitchen area, Lotti hissed, 'You must accept coffee the first time, or you'll never get to know the French. And don't ask for milk, she may not have it and won't like to be embarrassed.'

'How . . .' I was about to reply indignantly, angry at Lotti for making me feel so ignorant, when she put her finger to her lips. Maeve was coming back, carrying a tray with three tiny cups and a blue ceramic pot of sugar cubes on it. I stood up to help her, but she ignored me, putting it down with a fluid grace on the little glass table before us. Then she went back for the coffee. She's like a green mamba, I thought, beautiful, strong, subject to nobody's rules but her own.

'Don't worry. She's very nice once you get to know her,' Lotti said. I looked sceptically at her.

'Actually, she's a little different in her own house,' she amended. 'I had only met her on the outside.'

'Then how did you have the guts to ask her to let me stay?' I muttered, aghast.

'Well, who else could I ask?' she replied, indignant.

'But what if she had said no?'

'But she didn't, did she?' Lotti said coolly.

Maeve relaxed after the coffee. 'Why did you run away?' she asked me. 'Isn't that rather unusual for an Indian girl?'

'I wanted more from life than my uncle's grocery store,' I lied.

She took a sip of her coffee. 'My parents live in Strasbourg. A terrible place, small, provincial. Everybody knows everybody there. I wanted something more. So I came to Paris.'

'It is a great city,' I said, woodenly echoing what my uncle had said to me when I arrived. Suddenly I missed those days. I had been unhappy then but it wasn't the same as I felt today. It was all my fault, a merciless voice inside me pointed out. I forced myself to concentrate on Maeve. 'Provided you know the right people,' she was saying. 'Otherwise it can be hell. You become invisible and fall through the cracks in the pavement.'

'Who are these people?' I asked nervously.

'Oh, journalists, artists, models, designers, *hommes d'affaires*. The people you see at all the parties, and in the magazines.'

'I see,' I felt overwhelmed.

'I know many of them,' Maeve said with pride.

I looked at her beautiful face. 'They must enjoy knowing you,' I said spontaneously.

Her face tightened. She looked at me suspiciously, 'What do you mean?'

'That . . . that you're so beautiful, I'm not surprised that you know everybody,' I replied shyly.

Her face relaxed and she laughed. 'I like having you around already. You're welcome to stay here as long as you want.'

She lit a cigarette—gold coloured like her hair. 'Do you smoke?' she asked me. The cigarette drew attention to her beautiful hands. She had long elegant fingers.

'No,' I replied.

She shrugged, thin smoke curling out of slightly flared nostrils.

'I'd like to learn,' I said following the smoke with my eyes.

She smiled, her dark grey-brown eyes becoming slits. 'Don't. It's a bad habit—unless you can do it more elegantly than every other person who smokes. That includes me.' She brought the cigarette back up to her mouth. Her red lips pursed into a bud as she inhaled deeply, then opened again as she exhaled.

I watched her and wished I had lips like hers. 'I'll never smoke then,' I said.

Our eyes met and Maeve smiled.

Three

I stayed with Maeve for three months. I did very little except sit on her tiny balcony, staring at the neighbouring windows and at the street below. Sudden freedom made me apathetic. Now that I found myself living in it, the city no longer seemed seductive. The streets were filled with hostile faces. I made Maeve's apartment my prison, and stared at Paris from the safety of her balcony.

Soon I knew the routines of the people in the neighbourhood by heart. I watched the cars pull in, park, and pull out, and the people in them. Their bodies would collapse into legless dots when they got in and then unfold into the human form as they got out. I watched the young mothers emerge from their buildings at around eleven with their babies in prams and head for the park. In the afternoon I watched the little girls from the Ecole Maternelle troop out of the building and into the arms of their parents. I watched the world just as the old couple in the building next door did. But I watched them too. He wore a red dressing gown and she wore a flowery one. They never spoke to each other or shared the balcony. He came out in the morning to read the paper. She came out at eleven and at two to watch the little children and the babies. When the utter predictability of the scene made me sleepy, I went into the room and slept.

Once a week, Lotti would telephone or come over. She brought me money sometimes, and news of Aunty Latha and Krishenbhai. A week after I disappeared, they came to Lotti and tried to bully her into telling them where I was. They threatened to take her to the police. That's when Lotti's parents stepped in and threw them out of the house. After that, the two families stopped seeing each other. I felt sad for Aunty

Latha when I heard that. I had robbed her of her social life and her faith in her husband. But I felt worse when Lotti told me how her father had reacted when Lotti confessed that she had hidden me. He forbade her ever to see me again. I felt terrible. I hadn't done anything wrong. Why were the Ramdhunes bent on punishing me? Lotti had no answer. We didn't talk of her parents after that. Her visits grew further apart. When she came, she was full of bright and cheerful stories about her neighbourhood and her classmates. But her stories annoyed me now. They reminded me of a world in which I no longer had a part. Only with Maeve did I feel alive. Paris was her city, its life seemed to flow around her, full of excitement and promise. When I was with her, I felt that I was a part of all that.

I wrote to my mother and begged her to bring me to England. I promised her I would work hard and pay her back for every penny she spent on me. But her only advice was to return to my uncle and aunt's house, apologize for what I had done, and beg them to take me back. 'You have disgraced me,' she wrote. 'How can you be so ungrateful? Your aunt and uncle gave you everything. Go and beg their forgiveness. Krishenbhai has already forgiven you. You have hurt Aunty Latha terribly, trying to destroy her most precious thing, her home. But you are still family, she will take you back.' The letter ended without any mention of England. I never wrote to my mother again.

After a month I started looking for a job. I did odd jobs, ironing, washing clothes, cleaning houses. But the jobs were few and the applicants many. I hated standing in line with three or four sad-looking middle-aged women, asking for a job I didn't want to do. I wondered what their lives were like. We never spoke with each other—even when we met more than once, asking for the same job. Finally, I managed to get hired for one week at a bakery. Every morning I had to be there by five. My job was to pull out the bread and the croissants from the oven and set them on a long steel tray to cool. Then I had to arrange them on the shelves. The smell of the bread delighted me and the young bakers flirted with me with their eyes. And I could take some bread home free. At the end of the week, they asked me for my papers. 'What papers?' I asked, my heart sinking.

'Your *carte d'identité* of course. We need it for the taxes,' the woman snapped.

I . . . forgot it at home,' I said guiltily.

She looked at me suspiciously. 'Then we'll pay you tomorrow when you remember to bring it,' she replied. I didn't go back. I couldn't think of what to do. I longed for Lotti.

One day she called. 'I'm off to Toulouse,' she said abruptly.

'Oh, I see. What for?'

'For a holiday.'

I felt relieved. 'How . . . how long will you be away?'

'Three months.'

'What? Why?'

'Because . . . well . . . I've met someone, and I want to be with him.'

'He's from Toulouse then?' I said stupidly.

'No. He's from Paris. But his grandfather has a farm near there which he willed to him. We're going to go there together.'

What about me? How would I manage? 'And . . . and your parents?' I asked. 'What do they say?'

'They don't know. They think I'm going to a special tutorial programme to prepare for the teachers' exam.'

'Oh.' I wanted to ask her not to go. I opened my mouth to tell her about the bakery. But suddenly, I felt that she wouldn't care. Like my mother, what could my problems signify to her now?

I stopped looking for jobs after that. Maeve didn't mind. She didn't seem to work very much either. On most days, she rarely emerged from her room till lunch. She would stumble out, her hair all tousled, traces of make-up still on her face, the smell of stale smoke and morning breath clinging to her. Without looking at me, or even saying good morning, she'd reach for the coffee that I held ready for her. She'd gulp it down and rush back to her room to get dressed. She always lunched out, either with one of a succession of men who came to pick her up and whom she kept waiting for at least half an hour, or else with a group of friends in some trendy *terrasse de café*. After she left, I would clean up the house and make her bed.

Maeve usually came home around four, almost always with a shopping bag. We'd drink coffee together in little miniature cups and talk. Or rather she would talk, and I would listen. I was a good listener and Maeve's life seemed enchanted. I listened open-mouthed to her tales of the people she met and the parties she attended. I wondered when she earned her money. To me, Paris seemed to have become a giant gutter, sucking away every last drop of money I had. When I asked her shyly about her work, she would become evasive. 'Models get paid a lot, you know. It's a pity you're not taller.'

'Or beautiful like you,' I added. And her face glowed.

After our little afternoon coffee ritual, she would go back inside her room until it was time to get ready for the evening. I'd go out onto the balcony again, or watch television. At night she went out with other men, returning at two or three in the morning or sometimes after the sun was pouring into the flat. Then she would walk straight past me into the bathroom without even saying hello. At those times I felt she resented my presence in the flat. But when she emerged from the bathroom, her hair wet and her skin scrubbed clean of make-up, she would smile sweetly at me over the cup of coffee I silently handed her and tell me about her exciting new lover.

One day I woke up in the morning to the smell of coffee and the sound of two voices. One was male and unfamiliar with a slightly flat nasal accent. Opening my eyes, I saw Maeve preparing coffee for a stranger wearing boxer shorts. He was perched upon a high stool before the folding table that was fitted to one wall, next to the mini-kitchen. He was much older than she—at least twenty years older. His stomach spread quite unselfconsciously before him and his hair was thin and greying. As I watched them through half-closed eyes, Maeve came back to the table and put the steaming coffee pot down in front of him. He pulled her between his legs, reached inside her dressing gown, and started fondling her breast. I shut my eyes tight and pretended to sleep. In a little while, they went into the bedroom. I crept out of bed, put on my clothes, and quietly left the house.

When I returned that afternoon, the flat was empty. I washed the dirty cups and stacked them by the sink. Then I went to the balcony and stared down at the street below. It was almost dark when I saw

Maeve step out of a bright red sports car. The man was driving. In the back of the car, there were a few shopping bags. Maeve leaned across and kissed him quickly. Then she picked up her bags and walked inside the building without looking back. He watched her enter and drove sedately away.

I learnt that his name was Jean-Jacques and that he was a diamond merchant from Antwerp. Each time he came, he brought Maeve fresh flowers and little jewel boxes wrapped in Indian silk purses. I was surprised that someone as beautiful as Maeve would befriend a paunchy old man. But I was too shy to say anything to her and we never spoke about it.

I lost track of time. Maeve went back to her usual routine of lunches and afternoon shopping expeditions and I to housekeeping and sitting on the balcony. Jean-Jacques reappeared for a few days every month. He became part of the routine too. Then one morning some months later, I awoke to the sound of spoons rattling angrily in coffee bowls.

'How much longer are you going to keep her here?' I heard Jean-Jacques saying. My heart stopped. I listened very carefully.

'Why?' Maeve retorted. 'What business is it of yours?'

'What business is it of mine?' Jean-Jacques's voice rose and he thumped the table loudly. 'This is my house. And I decide who I keep here.'

'Indeed?' she replied coldly. 'I suppose my wishes have nothing to do with the matter.'

'Of course they do, darling,' he said, his voice becoming almost pleading, 'but I want you to myself. I'm tired of seeing her lazy body in that bed at noon. She is so dull and mousy. How can you stand her?'

'I've already told you, she cooks well.'

'But what if I want to make love to you here, on this table,' he whined.

'It wouldn't hold your weight,' she replied.

I held my breath, waiting for an explosion. But it never came. Suddenly I heard loud sobs—a man's sobs. 'You are so cruel, Maeve, terribly cruel. I wait for the day you will be old too.'

Maeve said nothing. I heard her get up and walk into her room. A few minutes later he followed. I got up very quietly and left.

The next night, after Jean-Jacques had left, Maeve brought up the question of my future for the first time.

'You don't have papers, so you cannot work legally.'

I nodded humbly. 'Then what can I do?' I asked, feeling very small. I wished Lotti were there to help, but she hadn't come back from Toulouse yet. I stared at Maeve hopefully.

'You can be an *au pair*. It's not very glamorous, but it's all I can arrange right now.'

'What's an *au pair*?' I asked, puzzled.

'You stay with a French family and look after their children.'

'Stay with a family? Won't they want references and things too, if I am to take care of their children?'

'I have a family in mind. They are very well-connected. The wife is from one of France's oldest families—at least, on her mother's side. Her father was a jeweller. Her husband, he is of the bourgeoisie, but a very nice man. He's a computer wizard. I modelled for him for a while. He owes me a favour or two.'

'But will they take me?'

'They will take you because I will tell them to. I will be your passport. Then it is up to you.'

'Up to me to do what?' I asked.

'To find another passport,' she replied.

four

I moved into the home of Monsieur and Madame Baleine, at 20 rue Victor Masse, to look after their two children Thérèse and Marie. 'The house of whales,' I named it in my mind, delighting in my new-found ability to play with French names and their meanings. They accepted without question the story of my life that I gave them. But they called me 'Lily'. 'It is easier for the children,' Mme Baleine explained, 'less foreign.'

Catherine Baleine was the chief buyer of home appliances for the Galeries Lafayette. She took her job very seriously and fancied herself a paragon of good taste. The house was filled with modern gadgets and beautiful objects—five long-stemmed crystal goblets that looked like frozen lilies, and bone china from Dresden, a family heirloom. The sofa was covered in Chinese brocade silk with chrysanthemums woven into it in the same thread. The table linen and bedsheets were pure heavy linen edged with embroidery done by nuns in China. The fluffy white towels had black satin roses on them. But they, like the crystal and fine china, only came out when they had guests.

Mme Baleine was in her late thirties, tall and slim. Her skin was taut and stretched tightly like a canvas across the high cheekbones and bony planes of her face, and tanned a gingerbread brown. She was terrifying in her elegance and height. She also had a terrible back problem—from always wearing impossibly high heels. This I deduced from the fact that she never once invited me to sit down in her presence. She would always sit on the grey silk sofa, and give me instructions—the children must be bathed by seven o'clock, Thérèse must go for ballet class at four o'clock.

M Baleine was shorter than his wife, with fashionably long hair and slightly yellow skin—the kind that tanned very easily in the sun. And when he smiled, which he did a lot, his brown eyes became little glowing slits and little laughter lines fanned out beside his eyes. His movements were quick like a sparrow's. He designed images for food commercials that were shown on television. He could tell you exactly which image had been created by a computer and which one hadn't. In his spare time, M Baleine, or Bruno, as he insisted I call him, fancied himself an artist of the twenty-first century—a computer artist. He was constantly asking me about Hindu gods and Indian music. He wanted to make an animated film about multiculturalism on computer, with Indo-African music in the background. His cousin, a composer of contemporary music, was to make the soundtrack. I remembered little of my grandmother's tales. We had never been very close. She preferred the twins and only spoke to me in 'don'ts'. But I told M Baleine what I could, drawing on my grandmother's and mother's stories. His curiosity was endless and as he listened to me he looked at me as if I were the most important person in his world.

The two children, Thérèse and Marie, also had dark hair and brown eyes like their father. At seven, Thérèse already knew how to use a computer, to embroider stories, and humiliate people. She made me nervous. Marie, at three, was a little parrot and faithfully repeated everything anyone told her. But they were affectionate children and soon began to give me the simple uncomplicated love that I had once received from Sunil and Anil. Little Marie was the first one to show it, insisting that I, and I alone, should bathe her. Then one day Thérèse surprised Madame—as she liked me to call her—and me by insisting that I be the one to read to her. I began haltingly, convinced that Thérèse was doing it to humiliate me, for as soon as I mispronounced or misread a word, she would correct me. But as I read further, the story took hold of me and I forgot my audience. I never noticed when Thérèse fell asleep, and only stopped when Mme Baleine caught my hand and gestured to me to switch off the light.

The Baleines lived in an old parquet-floored brick house, set in a sunny courtyard, with big bay windows and a tiny garden with roses climbing up the walls and curling around the first-floor windows. Inside, the house was divided into two zones, the family zone and the forbidden zone—to be entered only when ordered. The family zone consisted of the kitchen and the adjoining dining room-cum-study on the ground floor and the children's bedroom on the first floor. To these spaces I had complete and unrestricted access. The grand salon, the formal dining room, M Baleine's studio, the Baleine's bedroom and Mme Baleine's dressing room, and the guest bedroom constituted the forbidden zone. My room was on the second floor, a sloping space carved out of the attic with skylights, right above the master bedroom. It took me a few days in the beginning to get used to the restrictions. In our home in Nairobi, there had been no such restrictions, even for the servants. But soon I realized that there was a difference. At the Baleines, *everyone* followed rules. Most of them applied to the children and to myself. But the grown-up Baleines, I soon realized, had their own rules too. For example, they never went into each other's rooms without knocking first. They rarely went out together, unless it was to Mme Baleine's mother's house in the country over the weekend. And when Catherine said something had to be done, Bruno had to obey. Or when they both had parties to go to, then it was he who stayed behind till the children were in bed.

'Why do you think I got an *au pair* if not to put them to bed when we're not available?' he scowled at her. 'I assure you she is perfectly capable.'

'She may be,' Catherine returned calmly, 'but I still want one of us to be there when they go to sleep every night. We are their parents.'

'Don't load your guilt onto me, Catherine. The children know I am their father—whether I sit prettily by their bed when they fall asleep or not. Why don't you put them to bed this time? I'm sure they'd love to see you.'

'Because I have to go to dinner as part of my job. You forget who works around here.'

'Yes, yes. That's all you ever think about,' Bruno said bitterly. 'You're not a woman, you're an office slave.'

'If I'm an . . .' she gave a dry laugh, 'office slave, as you so quaintly put it, it's because you don't work enough.'

Bruno went silent. I heard him mounting the stairs, and ran back into the children's room.

My life soon fell into a routine. In the mornings I would get the girls dressed. Mme Baleine would have picked their clothes out for them the previous night. She was very particular about that. I would give them breakfast and prepare Mme Baleine's coffee. Then I would sit the children down to watch cartoons while I took Catherine her coffee. When I came downstairs, M Baleine would already be there, helping himself to coffee and reading the paper. He would take Thérèse to school while I played with Marie some more before taking her to the *crèche*.

When I returned, Mme Baleine would have left for work and M Baleine would be in his studio. She sometimes left me instructions or a shopping list on the kitchen table. Silence would descend upon the house for a few hours, while M Baleine worked away in his studio across the hall. In the afternoon I would fetch Marie from the *crèche*, feed her, and put her to sleep. Thérèse would return a little after four. I would make her tea, wake Marie up, and take them to the park, where we would play till six. Three times a week, I would take them to ballet class. Sometimes M Baleine would take a break from his work and play with the children for half an hour before turning them over to me. They were always a little sulky and disobedient after he left, and would treat me like a servant. At those times I wanted to hit them. But I soon learnt how to distract them—making up silly games to amuse them, or suddenly talking to them in English, to which they listened in awe. At seven-thirty we had dinner, and I put the children to bed. Then I would be free. On some days, after dinner, I would go to the movie theatre next door. Sometimes, especially in summer, I would just go for a walk, and watch the light fade and the windows glow. But I would avoid the grand boulevards, seized by an irrational fear that I would come across my uncle or the Ramdhunes, and they would learn of my descent to the status of a servant.

five

M Baleine rarely invited anyone to the house. His wife, on the other hand, had elegant dinners for ten or fourteen people at least once every fortnight. So I was surprised when one day he gave me a shopping list and told me that his cousin, the music composer, was coming to dinner with his new girlfriend and that they were all going to have dinner together *en famille*. That includes you,' he added kindly. And so I found myself later that night sitting around the dinner table with Marie to one side and Thérèse on the other. Throughout the dinner, the girlfriend, who was covered in futuristic jewelry, looked right through me, as if I weren't a person at all.

M Baleine had cooked duck with orange sauce. But the girlfriend was a vegetarian, and that put him in a bad mood from the start. The composer never spoke very much anyway, and tonight he appeared to be absorbed in some music that the rest could not hear. Mme Baleine, too, seemed distracted and unusually silent. She bent over Marie, fussing and scolding at the same time, as she tried to make her eat without making a mess.

Conversation was therefore strained throughout dinner. Except for the guest of honour, who talked throughout the meal, first about how she was always being hurt by others, especially men, because she loved them too much, and then about the benefits of vegetarianism. M Baleine's face grew slowly blacker. Even the composer became aware of the tension and tried to make up for it by heaping extravagant praise upon the duck. 'Quite professional,' he said, 'you could be a chef. Open a restaurant. With all the people Catherine knows, it would be a runaway success from the day it opens.'

M Baleine's face twisted, 'Shut up, Claude,' he said, 'and drink some more wine.' He reached across and refilled his own glass as well as his cousin's.

All at once the girlfriend, who had been talking to Catherine all evening, turned to M Baleine and said, 'So tell me, are you happy making pictures of smiling dogs and steaming dogfood?'

M Baleine looked at her through his wineglass without saying anything. Other conversations stopped. Everyone looked at him. He said in a tight careful voice, 'Well, it's better than buying the leftovers of someone else's tired imagination and festooning yourself with them thinking it will make you more interesting.'

The girlfriend went white. There was an awful silence. Everyone seemed paralysed. Except Marie, who suddenly chirped, 'Maman, why does Lily have brown nipples when yours are pink?'

Around the table, everyone shifted uncomfortably in their seats. Then Thérèse giggled. M Baleine seemed absorbed in his empty plate. Mme Baleine looked disapprovingly at me as if to say What were you doing allowing my children to see you in the bath? M le Compositeur quickly put his napkin in front of his mouth. His girlfriend gazed at the ugly academy-style portrait of Mme Baleine's grandfather. Poor Marie had by now realized that she had said something she wasn't supposed to have said and her face turned red as she struggled to hold back her tears. I began to laugh, shakily at first, and then with more conviction.

'You know, Marie,' I told her, 'I have dark nipples because they match my brown skin.' Marie's brow cleared and her tears receded.

Thérèse clapped her hands and said delightedly, *Mais c'est évident ça, Marie tu vois.*' There was an echo of masculine laughter around the table; even the women smiled. I looked up relieved, and was transfixed by M Baleine's eyes. They were shining as he watched me.

The next day he called me into his studio. I entered hesitantly. It was cool inside the room, and dark. Huge boxes and machines were stacked against the walls. The little space left in the centre was dominated by a large TV screen, several little monitors, and a big white desk upon which sat a computer. On the screen was a picture of a jar of mustard on which there was a woman's face. I stared at it. Music flooded the room, high chanting music that twisted around itself without form. The mustard and the face began to spin, until one could no longer make out the shapes. The music reached a wailing crescendo, and out of the whirling bottle burst fountains of sunflowers. Then came the beat of African drums over a softer melody. Now there was the beautiful woman's face filling the screen. Her ruby lips stretched in a smile, and then the face began to change. The eyes grew bigger and darker, dark brown, the blond hair went black, the lips swelled, and suddenly it was an African face on the screen. And then the face split apart into a spider's web, and in the centre lay a woman, naked. She had a tiny waist and full sensuous thighs, and she was the colour of the dark heart of the sunflower. I took a step forward, fascinated. Nestled in her pubic hair was a purple-green spider. The music stopped suddenly but the image remained, frozen and lifeless on the screen.

'This is my work. Do you like it?' His voice came softly out of the dark. Behind him the computer screen glowed blue and green.

'It's . . .' I felt nervous. I was awed by the strange image that remained fixed upon the screen. 'It's another world,' I said breathlessly, and then realized how stupid I must sound. I began to sweat, despite the air-conditioning. Little beads of perspiration dotted my spine, sending shivers up it as the droplets evaporated quickly in the cold dry air.

He chuckled. 'Another world. That's one way to describe it. It's a world that exists only in the head.'

'What is it for?' I asked curiously.

'It's a perfume advertisement I did not long ago for a magazine. I thought I'd have some fun with it, and so I added the music later, and fed in some more images.'

'What will you do with it now?'

'I'm not sure,' he replied. He turned and stared at the screen, pressing some buttons on the keyboard. The images came alive once more but without the music. 'I think perhaps I'm trying to make a statement. About smells. We're very smell-sensitive people, we French. After all, we invented perfume!' He continued to gaze intently at the screen. 'But advertising has turned everything around. We no longer react to something because of its smell, we only see it, visually. Eventually, human beings will lose the other senses because they won't be needed anymore. Perfume, mustard. They will all be the same, distinguished only by the shape and colour of the packaging.' He added violently, 'That's not very original. And to be an artist today, you have to be original, or you're worthless . . . words, words. I hate them.'

I stood silently beside him, wondering whether I should leave or not.

Suddenly he became conscious of me peering over his shoulder.

'Would you like to try it yourself?' he asked. He pulled the white oblong mouse lying next to the computer towards me and placed my hand on it. 'You see the little arrow on the screen there, the mouse controls that.'

'Oh really? How funny,' I giggled nervously.

He frowned. 'What's so funny?'

I stammered out an explanation, 'I like rats. My first friend in France was a rat. I saw him in the rail bed of the Métro. Though there are many rats down there, he was alone—like me.' I stopped suddenly, afraid I had betrayed too much.

But M Baleine was looking at me warmly, his eyes full of compassion. 'My poor dear, I had no idea things were so bad for you.' His hand reached for mine and he patted it awkwardly. Then he said softly, 'I feel terrible that I have never asked you how you are. Is everything all right? Are the children behaving themselves with you? Are you happy here?'

Why do you ask now, after all this time, I thought. 'Everything is fine, Monsieur. The children are very sweet. I'm quite happy, thank you,' I said quickly.

He licked his lips nervously. 'I'm happy that everything goes well for you,' he said formally. I looked up, expecting to be politely dismissed. But he continued to speak, his voice warming. 'You have a very strong character, I think, non? Paris must be so very different from your country. Yet you seem to be perfectly à l'aise here. I remember how self-possessed you were at the table when Marie said . . .' He paused, suddenly embarrassed.

'That I had dark nipples,' I finished for him.

He laughed, and his ears turned bright red. 'I didn't mean it to come out that way,' he said, 'but I'm glad you said it for me.' He stared hungrily at me. 'I dreamt about you last night.'

I felt thrilled, but also shy. Did he see me lying before him like the naked woman on the screen? I said nothing, only looked at my feet. He moved closer and I could feel the warmth of his body. He smelled nice, of cinnamon and salt and cigarette smoke. But I must have noticed it before, I realized, because the smell of him felt almost familiar.

His hand curled under my chin, tilting my face up to his. I shut my eyes hastily, wanting to postpone what was coming.

He laughed softly and his grip on my chin tightened. 'Your eyes hide many secrets, my little one. How much of life have you seen, I wonder.' His voice sounded muffled, far away. I opened my eyes. His eyes were alight. Very gently he kissed me. His long supple lips enveloped mine, gently prising my mouth open. I heard him sigh. I opened my mouth wider, feeling the texture of his lips. How strange that a man's lips should be so soft. I had expected the kissing to be hard and strong—that's how it looked in the movies. A part of me felt strange to finally be doing what I had seen other people do so often on the screen. It felt unreal, as if I were the watcher, removed from what was happening to me, absolved of responsibility.

Finally he pulled away and stared down at me. 'I've wanted to do that for a long time,' he whispered. He looked different—his eyes had lost their sharpness, the light in them muted. I felt a moment of dismay, maybe I had disappointed him. I reached my face up for more. His eyes lit up again. This is what it means to be beautiful, I thought exultantly, that I can make a man's eyes shine with love!

Then he was kissing me again and I pressed back against his lips with my own, tasting them as he tasted mine. His hands moved inside my shirt. I imitated him. His body shivered in response. He pulled my hips hard against him. In my lower stomach there was a sudden change of pressure, bones and muscle began to liquify and churn and spin.

We made love standing up, my legs curled around his waist like a belt. And though for a second I felt terrible pain, it was washed away by the knowledge that I was being loved, and I pulled him towards me tightly. Afterwards he apologized for hurting me, wiping my bloody thighs with computer paper.

We faced each other silently, not friends or lovers. Finally he said firmly, 'Go along now my dear. I should not have done that.' I wanted to ask why but I could not trust my French sufficiently. So I continued to stare at him dumbly, my eyes full of questions.

In the shelter of my room, my body began to burn. My lips felt heavy and my hips seemed to move differently, tilting back and forth as if the memory of the movement it had just learnt had been branded into it permanently. I felt disgust well up from inside. My body had betrayed me.

I ran into the bathroom and locked the door. As I waited for the shower to get hot, I could still smell him on me. The smell curled around me, thick as steam. I began to feel terribly guilty. I had done wrong, it was my fault. Suddenly I thought of Maeve and her long showers. I remembered Jean-Jacques slipping his hand into her robe. I stepped under the burning water and turned my face up into the full force of the stream. Soon my face began to throb with pain, and still I kept my face tilted upwards.

When I finally stepped out, my face was an orb of pain, blotting out all thought. I staggered into my room and lay on the bed turning my face to the wall. I looked at my room, wondering if this would be my last night in it. I tried to imagine what he would tell her. I pictured her face contorted with anger and betrayal, throwing me out, with the children watching from the stairs. I wondered where I would go. This time Lotti, I knew, would not help. I had not spoken with her since I arrived at the Baleines'. And Maeve? She had hinted she could assist me no further. The flat was not hers, it belonged to Jean-Jacques, who didn't like guests. I had failed, I thought miserably, I had thrown away my chance of getting a passport.

six

That summer Bruno and I became lovers. I stopped feeling alone. I stopped envying other families. I was content. Mme Baleine took the children to her mother's summer house on the coast of Brittany. I didn't have to go along as Catherine's mother already had a devoted housekeeper who accompanied her everywhere and wouldn't dream of letting anyone else take care of the children. I felt safe. The heat continued through July and into the middle of August. As Paris emptied and was repopulated by tourists and ghosts, the streets became our playground and I grew to love the city in a different way.

Then one day, I woke up feeling cold. I looked up at the skylight, which was open. The sky was still blue but the air was no longer hot and still. There was a cold wind blowing. I reached up to close the window. Bruno was looking up at me, rubbing his eyes exaggeratedly. 'My, my. I cannot believe how good the view is,' he teased me.

I fell upon him, pretending to smother him. The game came to an end with me lying beneath him, my arms trapped under his hand. We stared at each other silently.

'The wind changed,' I said gravely. 'It's cold again.'

He pretended to look surprised, 'Is it? Well, I'll have to warm you then.'

I didn't laugh, and as he began to make love to me, my mind slipped away. I thought of Marie and Thérèse. And what they would think if they saw us like this.

Suddenly he stopped. 'What's the matter? Don't you find me interesting anymore?' he said irritably.

I looked at him dully. 'I was thinking,' I said.

'About what?'

'The future,' I replied.

He flipped onto his back and groped for his cigarettes. He lit one hastily and took a long drag. 'Women!' he said. 'I knew we'd come to this topic eventually. You're all the same.'

'W-what do you mean?' He was making me feel stupid, and ordinary.

He laughed bitterly. 'Ultimately you're only interested in yourselves.'

He left the next day for Brittany. This time, the loneliness was almost unbearable. I walked the streets wrapped in it, and no one came close, no one spoke to me. In the end I felt that it had all been my fault. I had hurt him by not responding to his caresses, and in the process I had ruined everything. I longed to talk to someone about Bruno, but the words that came to mind were not beautiful. So I could not speak about it.

When they returned, things seemed to go back to the way they had been. The children were their usual selves but taller and more golden and full of stories about their grandmother. Mme Baleine was distant and gracious, slightly more relaxed than she had been and almost chocolate brown. Only Bruno seemed nervous and strained.

Then one day, when I entered the gate after dropping the children at school, he was waiting for me in the garden. He started towards me and grabbed me. I remained passive within his arms. 'I'm sorry,' he said.

I looked away. Sorry couldn't make a broken thing whole again, wasn't that what Aunty Latha had said? 'That's an easy thing to say,' I said quietly.

He looked surprised, then uncomfortable. 'You're right,' he admitted reluctantly, 'I can't take my words back. But I want to explain. I do care for you. You're so beautiful, and gentle, and . . . and young. I want you desperately.'

'But what about Mme Baleine?' I asked him coldly.

'Catherine?' he laughed. 'She can stay my wife in name.'

'And what if she gets suspicious?' I asked nervously.

'We'll be careful. Don't worry,' he said, stroking my hair. 'And anyway, she's very civilized.'

'Too civilized to be jealous?' I asked sceptically.

'Absolutely.'

After that we found each other whenever the house was empty. But it was not the same. There was no freedom in it anymore. We were forced to meet in the house, surrounded by visible reminders of Catherine and of our own public selves. So it would take us some time to leave behind those public personae and grow comfortable with each other as lovers again. Then just as we grew used to each other again, we would have to separate and put on our public faces once more so that the children would not suspect, and Catherine would not sense how the atmosphere of the house changed when she went away. So the separation never ended. As the weeks lengthened my two personae, lover and *au pair*, became masks. I no longer felt natural in the house, or when making love to him. Her presence was always there, looking over my shoulder all the time. The house began to feel oppressive and I spent more and more time walking the streets, and remembering the freedom of summer.

One night, after making love, he suddenly asked, 'Why a rat?'

'What?' I had no idea what he was talking about.

'Why did you make friends with a rat?'

'Oh, the rat.' I had almost forgotten about him. 'I . . . I don't know. Because he was there perhaps.'

'That's no answer,' he persisted. 'Try to do better than that. I will put the question to you in another way. Why did you choose a rat for your personal totem?'

'W-what is a totem?' I asked hesitantly.

He laughed. 'A totem is a spirit of an animal which, because it shares some personal affinity with your inner personality, becomes your symbol—the symbol of your soul,' he explained as if to a baby.

'So would it be strange if I chose a rat for my symbol?'

'Strange? Why should anything seem strange anymore? I think it's rather interesting. And quite original.'

'Really?' I was on guard. 'Why? Why do you think the rat is my symbol?'

'Not just your symbol but ours,' he said. 'Perhaps I'll make a piece of video art out of it, like Tom and Jerry. While the cat was out the rats played, and when the cat came back . . .'

'The rats were trapped,' I cut in quickly. 'So tell her about us then. Tell Catherine you love me. Then you will feel normal. We can be together when we want, without these separations and pretences that make me feel half-dead!'

He went still. Then he began to laugh, his laughter mocking, sarcastic. 'Absurd child, who cares about what is normal? We have deconstructed normality, smashed it into invisible pieces that cannot be rejoined. We have stripped away the prudery and revealed the hollow inside.' He stopped to blow a smoke ring. 'Nobody wants to be normal, normal is boring. We all want to be different. Isn't this different enough for you?'

'But I don't want to be different. I want to be normal,' I cried angrily. But he continued in the same terrible monotone, 'As for our *cher* Monsieur and Madame Normal, they are figments of the imagination.' He lay on his back on my mattress, looking up at the ceiling. He blew more smoke rings that rose into the darkness, perfectly round till the end. 'Normality is dead.'

I felt him slipping away. In my mind I saw him picking up his clothes off the floor and leaving.

Quickly I threw off the duvet and lit the candle by the bed. On full-moon nights we didn't need candles, but tonight the moon was a crescent that gave off no light. I climbed on top of him, my thighs straddling his hips, and gave him the answer he wanted, 'The rat was my symbol because like me, he couldn't speak French.'

'But now you speak perfectly,' he said laughing. Never in my life had I felt so muzzled. I smiled twistedly. 'Yes, now I speak perfectly,' I answered, rolling my r's like Aunty Latha.

At first I didn't notice that I had begun to smell. Then one day there it was.

It was a sunny morning in October, after three weeks of cold wind and rain. The free empty day stretched before me. Marie was going to spend the day with a friend and Thérèse had to be picked up only at five o'clock. I walked along the edge of the Cimetiére de Montmartre and up the hill to my favourite café, Le Sandwich. It was a strange café. The decor was an uneasy cocktail of American fast food super-imposed on turn-of-the-century German art-deco. Giant hamburger cut-outs hung from the curly red-and-gold stucco ceiling. Ornate gold mirrors and dark wood panelling that looked centuries old covered the walls.

Their *pâtisserie* was excellent, and the owner, Jean-Luc, loved India. He had been there several times. When he told me this, I felt obscurely pleased. What Jean-Luc loved best were the Indian calendars with the elephant-headed Ganesh and Hanuman, the monkey god, printed on them. The calendars hung along the wall behind the service counter, and the carved mirrors on the opposite wall reflected them 'à *l'envers*'— which is how Jean Luc liked to see them. 'Ah, *L'Inde*,' he would say, '*c'est épatant*.' That's how I learnt the word, as an adjective for India.

The café was nearly empty when I entered. There was no one there except for the young half-French, half-Vietnamese assistant behind the counter. Jean-Luc himself never came in before eleven. The assistant had sexy eyes that followed you from under the shadow of his baseball cap. I tried to flirt with him. 'Give me that almond croissant there,' I said. And as he bent down to retrieve it from inside the glass counter,

I bent down too, pressing my body against the glass. His hand paused slightly as it reached for the croissant, then moved smoothly forward again. He handed me the pastry, his face blank. As I reached to take it from him, I let my fingers delicately brush his hands. But he refused to meet my eyes. I hesitated, waiting. That's when it hit me—a dark feral smell, too strong to be civilized, too powerful to be hidden. A smell so shameless, it belonged to the night or to those private moments of solitude that cannot be shared. I was surprised to find it here, in public, for everyone to smell. It clung to me, climbing relentlessly up my nostrils. I had never smelt anything quite like it before. I stared at the assistant, wondering if he smelt it too. His face remained closed. Then I looked around for the source of the smell, wanting to distance myself from it as far as possible. At the same time I was curious to see the man who had the boldness to allow such a private smell to go public. He must have no shame, I thought amazed.

But there was no one behind me. I was alone in front of the counter. The assistant had moved away to the back of the store to pick up the telephone. I could hear the low rumble of his voice as he talked into the receiver, a soft look on his face. The smell had to be coming from me. It was all around me. Perhaps I had stepped in some dogshit, I thought desperately. I walked away quickly from the counter towards a little table at the far end of the café. I placed my croissant on the table and bent down as if to tie my shoelaces, and almost fell over as it attacked me afresh.

I sat down quickly and draped my sweater over my groin. I had found the source of the smell.

My mind went blank. There was no doubt that it came from me. Then another terrible thought struck me. The assistant must have smelt it too. That's why he turned away, repulsed. I felt suddenly very cold. Everyone would smell it soon, Madame Baleine, M le Compositeur, the children and Bruno . . . *Pu, pu, puer*. The words echoed in my head. Soon they would all know it came from me. And I would be sent away.

I left my croissant and ran out of the shop. A cold wind had sprung up. It cut through my clothes, my open coat and sweater. I let it, hoping the wind would whip away the odour. But I could discern traces of it on the wind as it rushed past me.

I ran straight down the road, across the park, and down a broad street. I found a supermarket and entered it. I pushed my way past the other shoppers, to the *rayon beauté*. Here, on rack after pristine white rack, were stacked miles and miles of products to combat bad smells: shampoos, deodorants, antiperspirants, body sprays, talcum powders, soaps, *crémes, exfoliants, gommages, and collages*. They were for the outside. For the inside there were the toothpastes, mouthwashes, vaginal douches, stomach washes, enemas, and nasal washes. A special product dedicated to every kind of hole and dent in the body.

My heart slowed down to an almost normal tempo as I feasted my eyes on the multitude of sweet-smelling products. I would buy them all, I decided, one for each part of me. I would clean the inside and the outside, and then fill each and every crevice of my body with perfume. I began to pull them off the shelves one by one: lavender soap, White Linen bath gel, sandalwood bath oil, alpine bubble bath, *gommages* and *rinçages*, shampoos and exfoliants, three *dentifrices*, and douches for each and every orifice. And then I moved on to the creams—hand cream, body cream, face cream, lip cream, under-eye cream. I bought them all. At last I moved towards the shelves of perfumes. My cart was half-full and difficult to maneuver by now. I pushed hard. It went sideways and collided with another almost empty cart that lay unattended, blocking the aisle. *'Mince, mais qu'est-ce que vous faites?'* someone said in exasperated accents.

My heart leapt into my mouth. I recognized the scratchy sandpaper voice even before the woman to whom it belonged turned around. It was indeed Maeve. I had not seen her since I came to the Baleines nine months ago. She hadn't given me her number and I hadn't asked. Maeve's red-gold hair was longer, I noticed. But otherwise she looked the same, perhaps even more beautiful than I remembered, her green eyes and full red lips working their magic as always.

'Maeve, you look beautiful,' I began, gulping. It was customary to begin with an invocation to her beauty.

She smiled at me, her ill humour forgotten. 'So, it is my little *or-pheline indienne. Comment vas-tu?*'

'Me? Oh fine, just f-fine,' I stammered.

Her eyes darted casually towards my shopping cart, and her expression sharpened. 'My, my,' she purred, 'are all these beauty products for you?'

'I . . . no . . . well . . . not all.' I began to sweat, biting my lips out of nervousness.

'Uh-huh.' Maeve did not believe me.

'How have you been?' I said, trying to switch the topic of conversation back to her.

'*Ca va?*' she said, yawning, '*Ça va bien en fait.*' I left Jean-Jacques.'

'Good riddance, you were much too good for him.' I wondered how she had done it. He must have made a terrible fuss. 'How's the apartment?' I asked slyly, wondering if Jean-Jacques had thrown her out of it.

'I have no idea,' she replied, sounding bored. 'I've moved. I live not far from here now.'

'Oh.' I felt at a loss.

'I'm off to Jamaica next week. I came to pick up some suntan lotion. And maybe some perfume, something spicy but not heavy, you see. Perhaps you can help me choose,' her eyes flickered over my shopping cart, 'since you seem to have become quite an *amateur d'odeur!*'

I shivered at her words. Did she know? Could she smell it?

'Oh, I don't know,' I replied hesitantly, 'these things are so . . .'

'But you're from India, the land of smells, you must know about *odeur.*'

I felt as though she had slapped me. 'I come from Africa, not India,' I snapped. I saw ice form on her features. Hastily I tried to make amends. 'I'm sorry, it's just that I'm jealous. I never get to go anywhere, and I'd love to go to Jamaica. How lucky you are, Maeve. You'll come back looking even more beautiful with a tan.'

Flattery always worked with Maeve. Her face lost some of its frost. 'Jamaica is just wonderful—beautiful hotels, beaches, good music, fresh fruit cocktails, the men are terrific dancers. Such a lovely culture. Everybody just loves to have fun.'

'That's wonderful, Maeve.' I forced myself to sound enthusiastic. She was so lucky. I would give anything to be able to go on a holiday with Bruno. Thinking about him brought me back to the present with a jerk. I'd get the perfume somewhere else, I decided. I gripped the handles of my cart and got ready to move on.

'Leela, don't go yet.' Maeve stopped me. 'I've only one more thing to get and then we can leave together.' She reached up to another shelf and pulled out a bottle shaped like a teardrop. 'I think I'll choose my perfume myself after all. Who knows, you might just choose something ghastly for me, right?' Her mouth smiled as she said it, but her eyes were cold. She had not quite forgotten my words. 'And you,' she added, 'I see you haven't got any perfume yet. Your cart looks incomplete without it. What will you choose?'

I scanned the shelves nervously. Under Maeve's eyes, even choosing perfume became an ordeal. I always felt she was testing me, waiting for me to betray myself in some unimaginable way. My eye was caught by a red box with 'Samsara' emblazoned across it. 'Samsara,' I said, 'material world, world of illusion, of the body. How perfect.'

'Ah yes, *de chez Guerlain*,' Maeve said. 'It is not my style, too heavy and oriental. The smell envelops you like a blanket. But I can see how it would become you.'

I looked at her sharply. But her face was bland. I grabbed a large bottle of the perfume. 'Thank you,' I smiled at her. 'It's just what I need.'

After paying, we walked out of the store together.

'So, do you have a *copain?*' Maeve asked.

'No,' I replied shortly. 'I don't have the time for a boyfriend.'

She pretended to believe me. 'Thought so. I told your friend Lotti that's probably why you hadn't called her.'

I flushed guiltily and then tried to act surprised. 'Did Lotti call you then? I didn't know she was back.'

'Oh yes, and she's quite upset. I told her you couldn't receive phone calls either.' She smiled knowingly and quite suddenly unbent. 'What do you think of Bruno? Do you like him?'

'Who . . . what do you mean?' I stumbled.

'M Baleine. He has a penchant for exotic women. That's why I suggested he take you.'

I stopped in my tracks. 'You what? You suggested . . . ?'

'But of course. Why else do you think anyone would let you look after their children without references, or even a passport?'

'But I thought it was because of your recommendation,' I muttered.

'That played a part in the beginning. But I don't know Mme Baleine at all. So he must have liked what he saw and so he vouched for you.'

'Why would he trust me?' I asked.

'Because I was sure he'd be interested in you when he saw you. He doesn't like blondes, he told me,' she said gleefully.

'You can't be right, you don't know him. Why, he loves his children and . . .' I stopped short at the expression on Maeve's face. You naïve girl, it seemed to say. Suddenly another suspicion arose.

'How do you know him?' I asked abruptly.

She laughed. 'Don't worry. It's not what you think. He was a friend of an old lover. I only suggested that he meet you. I knew they were looking for a new *au pair*.'

So how come you two kept in touch, I wanted to ask. She was watching me, her eyes challenging. I forced my shoulders to relax enough so that I could shrug in that typically French way. 'You are full of surprises, Maeve. I take my hat off to you,' I said. To my own surprise, my voice came out soft and controlled, the accent and grammar in place.

Maeve relaxed. 'Come and have a coffee some time. I live right up the street, second building to the left. I'm on the third floor.'

We kissed and walked away in opposite directions.

eight

The house was empty when I returned with my shopping. I locked myself in the bathroom and turned on the taps to fill the bath. With trembling hands, I opened the many packages of aromatic bath salts, shower gels, and bath oils that I had bought. I washed my hair and scrubbed my skin with as many as ten different products. I cleaned my teeth and flossed them. With clumsy shaking hands I used the feminine douche. It felt strange to put my own hands inside a part of me that until very recently I had known nothing about. I touched the curved surfaces in wonder, feeling the tightly curled muscles inside.

The rubber tube I inserted felt like an invasion, and my muscles clenched in protest. Then I squeezed the round rubber base and felt a whoosh of water hit the tightened muscles inside. I half-lifted myself out of the water and then sank back with a sigh as the water, obeying the laws of gravity, began to trickle out. Slowly the fear seeped out of me. My mind began to go over my conversation with Maeve. She had to be lying. Bruno—it still felt strange not to think of him as M Baleine—wasn't like that. For a month after I arrived he hadn't shown the slightest interest in me. Maeve was just making it up. Maeve! She was little better than a whore.

I hauled myself out of the tub and began to dry my body quickly, beginning with my feet. As I straightened up, I caught sight of a stranger in the mirror. I let the towel drop and stared hard at the body reflected there. My nipples were larger, pointed like buttons. My high breasts were heavier. And my hips, too, seemed fuller. In contrast, my narrow waist looked even smaller and my thighs softly curving. I stared at my body as if I was seeing it for the first time—and felt a slight twinge of desire. This, then, was the body Bruno loved. I let my hands touch its curves the way he would and suddenly I could not wait to see him.

Diligently, thoroughly, I applied each and every lotion and cream to my skin. Finally, to make quite sure, I smeared some Samsara onto my pubic hair and in my armpits. Then, cautiously, I sniffed at my body. My flesh smelt predominantly of the green bubble bath I had used—a lemony, woody scent that felt very French to me. The rest of the cocktail of odours was barely discernible. But that was okay. I wasn't worried about the strange alchemy of scent and skin that made some smells stronger on some people than others. As long as whatever it was that I smelt of was easily identifiable and came out of a bottle I didn't care. It was the nameless smell I feared.

As I left the bathroom, the grandfather clock in the hall struck one. With a start, I realized that Bruno would be waiting for me. Hurriedly I threw on a sweater and a pair of jeans, and rushed out of the door.

After some persuasion, Bruno had finally agreed that we could meet outside. So, when the children's schedules permitted, he and I would go to a studio that belonged to one of his colleagues, off rue St-André des Arts, and spend the afternoons there. It was an unfriendly room, shrouded in shadow even in mid-afternoon, furnished impersonally with a big sofa bed at one end and a built-in entertainment system against the opposite wall. A damp sewer smell of stale sex always clung to the place. As we made love, I would stare blankly out of the window watching the shadows creep across the white wall of the building across the street. The room seemed to have the same effect on Bruno. After we finished, he would get up quickly, and we would leave soon after.

By the time I arrived at the Greek restaurant on the corner of the rue St-André des Arts, he was already there, waiting and munching on a sandwich. He kissed me lingeringly on the lips. 'Mmm, you smell very washed. I wish I had been there to watch,' he whispered.

I felt warm with happiness and glanced up at him shyly. He was watching me hungrily. 'You are so beautiful. I can't believe you are mine.'

'Where shall we eat today?' I asked gaily, reluctant to leave the sun and enter the dark impersonal room in the alley nearby. 'I'm hungry.'

His expression became wolfish all of a sudden, 'I can't wait to eat you, my dear.'

'But I haven't eaten yet.' I laughed, and deep inside I felt the churning sensation begin. Suddenly every little detail of the moment became more vivid—the heat of the sun, the thinness of the air that heralded the oncoming winter, and the smell of the Greek sandwich, so much like the Arab *shyawarma* that my brothers and I would eat in secret in the old port of Mombassa.

Together we walked the last few hundred yards down the nameless sidestreet to the studio. As we walked up the stairs to the room, my limbs became heavier and heavier. I felt as if I could barely put one foot before the other. Finally we were in front of the door. Bruno fumbled with the key in the lock. I took a deep breath.

And to my surprise, the smell of the room, old and intimate like used sheets, welcomed me. I stood stock still in the middle of the room, the smell all around me, surrounding me in warmth. It reminded me of my parents' bedroom, in the early morning, when we all crept into the big bed and lay there pretending to be asleep. Step by step, the smell took me over. First, it entered my clothes, my coat, then my shirt, and then it unclothed me completely. Bruno watched in amazement as I struggled to get my clothes off, not knowing what had set me afire. Then I turned to him and undressed him tenderly, patiently, drinking in his sharp strong male aroma, as it swam up to meet me through the layers of office and street odours. I removed the last of his clothing, and ran my tongue slowly over his ears, tasting the slightly dusty street flavour of them. My tongue continued down his neck, lapping in circles at his smooth skin, drinking in the sweat of him, still in the zone of public smells. Then I felt compelled to go deeper. My tongue swept across his chest, flicked lightly over his nipples, and smoothly rolled into his armpit. Bruno froze, my tongue stilled. He let out the air trapped in his lungs in one great sigh. My tongue began to move, eating up the deeply private flavour, frantically trying to cram as much of the taste of him into my mouth as possible. He went still, surprised by my impatience. '*Qu'est-ce que tu as, chérie?*' he whispered, pulling my head up so that he could see my face. 'I thought you didn't like it here.'

I felt surprised that he knew. 'I didn't, but I've changed my mind.'

He laughed, 'You are full of surprises.'

'Do you like it?' I asked, looking up at him. 'Do you like my surprises?' I slipped onto my knees. But he pulled me up until I was on my feet, facing him. 'God, you seem possessed today,' he said, shaking his head in amazement. He picked me up and carried me to the bed. Carefully he laid me across it. He stared down at me for a second, his expression unfathomable.

'Now it is my turn,' he said, and laughed happily as he began to taste me as I had been doing to him. As his tongue reached inside me, I inhaled deeply and tried to remain still. Every movement of his felt like a bow drawn across my aching nerve-endings. Then I couldn't control myself anymore. I began to writhe and scratch in a frenzy of excitement, my body burning with unsatisfied desire.

We made love with a fury, a madness, that did not come from me or him, but seemed to come from somewhere else. Someone else seemed to have inhabited my skin that afternoon, someone who revelled in the touch and the smell of men, who fearlessly dipped herself into the most inaccessible pools of sensations.

We finally slept, in an inverted U, my face nestling in his groin, and his in mine. When I awoke, he was sitting cross-legged on the bed, my head still cradled in his lap. I stretched lazily, feeling the gentle soreness of my muscles. At last I felt I knew him: the sharp metallic taste of his armpit, the bacon-like fragrance of his groin, and the milky smell of his scalp. I smiled up at him and teasingly licked the little hollow right above his groin.

He smiled tenderly down at me. 'My lovely, most incredible child. What did I do to deserve one as perfect as you? It was my lucky day when you came to my house.'

I felt suffused with warmth. Then Maeve's words came back to me like a sliver of ice. I pulled away from him. 'How did you know that . . . that I would be, *comment dire*, available to you?' I asked, turning to face him.

He looked bemused, sensing a pit opening up before him but still believing he might side-step it somehow. He replied placatingly, 'Your friend Maeve. She knows you well. She seemed to think we would get along well. And she said you'd be good with the children.' Then looking at my face, he quickly added, 'But I never ever dreamed . . . How could I have imagined you'd be so beautiful. And so gentle, so sweet.' He caressed my cheek. I turned my face away. 'And so passionate too.' He reached out to pull me back into his embrace, but I slipped out from under his arms and slid off the bed.

The room had gone back to its former ugliness. The damp on the left-hand corner was growing, I noticed. I turned and faced him again. His face looked lined and old in the light. I stared at the man in front of me and wondered what I had found so attractive in him. 'So what did you give her for finding you a nice docile mistress?' I asked, my voice rising with each word.

'Who?' he looked amused, and that made me angrier.

'Maeve, who else?'

'Maeve?' he began to laugh. 'Where do you get such ideas?'

His words only widened the gap that had appeared between us. Suddenly I became possessed with a wild rage. Against him, and everything that had robbed me of every vestige of security and cast me into this well of fear.

I ran into the toilet, slamming the door behind me.

'You're crazy,' he called after me. 'No one made you my mistress.'

He didn't follow me as I had half-hoped he would. I sat down on the pot, trembling, and waited. Five minutes later, there was a light tap on the bathroom door.

'*Ma petite, sois raisonnable,*' he said through the door. '*Je t'aime. Tu es mon seul amour, maîtresse de mon coeur. Sors de là, s'il te plaît.*'

I looked around me. The bathroom was small, and rather dirty. The shower curtains, patterned with rivulets of dirt, were strangely beautiful, I thought idly. Through the door, I could hear Bruno. '*Viens, sors de là ma princesse. Mon adorable,*' he called. '*Ne te fâche pas.*'

I put my hands over my ears. I did not want to listen. His voice made me sick. He was a liar. And he had infected me with a terrible smell. I reached across and locked the door.

He heard the lock click and began to bang upon the door. 'You can't do this, you bitch,' he shouted. 'You can't do this to me.' I stayed where I was, looking at the door fearfully.

I remained on the toilet seat, naked, unable to move for I don't know how long. When I finally managed to get up, it was dark outside and I was almost frozen.

AFTER THAT THE smell haunted me, surfacing when I least expected. Sometimes, when we were dining *en famille,* at the table I would smell it, hidden amongst the *coq au vin* and *quiche,* nestling in the leaves of a spicy Alsacienne *choucroute.* Sometimes as I rose to go to the bathroom, it would creep out of the sheets with me. Or when I went to the supermarket, it would whistle past me in the aisles filled with people. Sometimes, even in the Métro it would be there right behind me, as I stood face to face with a beautiful stranger. I avoided Bruno, speaking to him only when I had to, locking my room at night, and refusing to meet his pleading eyes.

After a while, Bruno's eyes no longer followed me when I left the room. He stopped coming into the children's room when I put them to bed, and spent much of the day away from the house or locked in his studio. I missed his attention. And there were no more presents tucked away where I least expected them. One day I caught him talking intensely to Catherine, their heads close together. They stopped abruptly when I entered and stared at me. I felt sure they were discussing how to dismiss me. I imagined the scene.

They would face me together, sitting side by side on the Louis XV sofa in the huge salon downstairs that was used only to entertain.

Mme Baleine would sit very straight. 'Bruno and I, well, we've reached a decision,' she would begin gravely. 'We . . .' she would pause and look at M Baleine. He would not meet her eyes, or mine. He would look instead at his shoes. 'Well, we feel . . .' Mme Baleine would say. Then she would stop and put her hand on M Baleine's knee.

'Bruno,' Catherine would say, 'you tell her.'

M Baleine would look up quickly and fix his eyes on the ugly Renaissance painting a little to the left of my head on the opposite wall. He would clear his throat and begin, 'The children, they are not happy with . . . they don't like . . .'

'Don't like what?' I would ask, willing him to look me in the face.

'You . . . your room . . . the . . . smell is . . .'

'Different,' Catherine would finish for him.

M Baleine: 'Yes, different.' His head would come up, his eyes sweep over me at last. But they would not rest on my face or body, they would look over my head into the distance. 'The children have been complaining about your smell.'

Me: 'My smell, how do I smell?'

M Baleine: 'There's nothing wrong with the way you smell, it's . . .'

Mme Baleine: 'Different, and you see children don't like difference. They want to be the same as their little friends. Difference makes them uncomfortable.'

M Baleine: 'It may even disturb their personality growth.'

Me: 'But they like me . . . Marie adores sleeping with me in my bed.'

Mme Baleine: 'Yes—but then she must go to school, and her friends say she smells different. So you see it really cannot go on.'

M Baleine: 'There's nothing wrong with you, you know. You're wonderful, just wonderful with the children, so kind, so generous. We will really miss you.'

Mme Baleine: 'Yes, we will certainly miss you. Thank you. We're very sorry about this, but you understand, surely? Children are children.'

M Baleine: 'And our children are very precious to us.'

Mme Baleine: 'We know this is very sudden, so M Baleine and I have decided to give you a present, for the good care you have taken of our children. We will give you a ticket to New Delhi, one way.'

Everything was so civilized.

nine

I had to know whether what I suspected was indeed true.

I called Lotti.

'Hello, Lotti?' I said hesitantly.

There was a long pause.

'Hi, *étranger*,' Lotti said finally, mixing her French and English as always.

I breathed a sigh of relief. 'Lotti, I need to speak to you.'

'You are speaking to me.'

'No, I want to see you and talk properly.'

'Well, I'm not sure I have the time. I'll have to check my calendar,' she said dryly.

I gulped. 'I'm sorry, Lotti. It's just that I thought you were going to stay in Toulouse for at least a year,' I lied.

She pretended to believe it. 'My dear, I am a big girl now, I am at university.'

'Wonderful. I didn't know. What? Art history?' I could not complete my sentences for the guilt.

Hurriedly I fixed a rendezvous for Saturday, my day off.

We met at noon at a café we both knew. I dressed carefully for our meeting in my long red coat—one of Catherine's cast-offs, a short red wool skirt from Agnès B. that Bruno had given me and a tight black sweater. The clothes were all new, and smelt new. I put a little Samsara onto my clothes and around my groin.

Lotti was dressed all in black as usual. But that's where the resemblance to the old Lotti ended. This new version was painfully thin. Only her lips remained full. But even those were painted a different colour, a dark purple, almost black, and her face was whitened with powder three or four shades lighter than her skin. It made her look like a dead person. And she had cut off her beautiful hair. It was as short as a boy's now and dyed purple. She also had a nose ring in addition to her many earrings. We greeted each other the French way. I watched her face carefully as she moved away, anxiously looking for signs of surprise or repulsion. But there was nothing. Her face didn't even twitch.

'You look different,' Lotti said straightaway.

I gulped. I wanted to ask her in what way was I different. But I didn't have the courage quite yet. 'Actually you look really different, too,' I replied instead, 'so . . . so grown up.'

She leaned towards me. 'And you've begun wearing perfume.'

I waited for her to say more, my throat dry. 'Samsara, isn't it? My favourite, too—even though it's a bit heavy. But too expensive for me.'

She continued her survey of me—her eyes hard. 'And your clothes, too,' she said, her eyes narrowing thoughtfully, 'Agnès B, *j'imagine. Tu as bien tombé*—they obviously adore you.'

'Don't be silly, Lotti.' I looked away, unable to meet her hard contemptuous stare. 'These clothes are Mme Baleine's cast-offs.' Lotti gave me a look that said she didn't believe me, but she didn't argue. We stared at each other uneasily.

'You look really different, too. Your hair, and your make-up,' I said.

'We all grow up, you know,' she replied dryly. 'And not all of us have your good fortune.'

'Good fortune?' I spluttered. 'You don't understand what good fortune is . . . You still have a family.' I stopped short, confused by the strength of my anger. Lotti looked uncomfortable, too. We both looked away.

I looked around the café. It was fairly full of the usual midday crowd of tourists and Saturday shoppers. In the middle of the motley gathering, a teenage couple stood out in sharp relief, heads bent close to each other, arms and legs intertwining. The girl was short and thin and Chinese. The boy was French: tall, long-haired, bespectacled. I turned to Lotti to point out the lovelocked pair, but she was already staring in their direction, a look half of pain, half of amusement on her face. She turned quickly, sensing my eyes upon her.

'You're in love, aren't you?' I demanded, recognizing the look on her face.

Her expression softened. 'Yes, I'm in love,' she confessed.

'With who? Not with Michel?' I asked eagerly, guilt and resentment forgotten.

'No, not him,' she said, making a face. 'He is too white, too uptight. He can never understand us people of the south. No, I'm in love with an Arab. He's at the faculty at Saint Denis, studying sculpture. He's wonderful.'

'Oh,' I said, taking it in slowly. I felt strange to imagine Lotti in love with an Arab. There were Arabs in Mombassa, but we never knew any. They were even more unknown than the Africans. 'So . . . so where did you meet him?' I asked.

Lotti leaned toward me, 'You won't believe it, but I met him at the farmers' market in Bobigny.'

'What!'

'You know, the Sunday market. He is the butcher's assistant. When he isn't taking classes, he works there for money,' she replied a little defiantly.

'You're crazy. What will your father say?' I almost shouted at her. 'How are you going to tell him that you are going out with an Arab sculptor who is a part-time butcher?'

'I don't know and I don't care. He's a wonderful artist,' her voice deepened. 'Maybe I'll have to run away next.'

'Don't be *folle*,' I told her, slipping back into our own special language.

The waiter arrived to take our order. I ordered a kir and a steak tartare to follow. If Lotti smelt something odd, she might think it came from the steak, not from me. Lotti raised her eyebrows and then followed suit. After the waiter left, Lotti teased me, 'So you really have changed, haven't you? What happened to the girl who never touched alcohol, not to mention raw meat?'

I smiled tightly. If only she knew. I wished I could tell her. 'Nothing is the way it seems.'

'And from a girl who is oh so *sensible aux odeurs. Quelle dégradation* she continued to tease me.

'That's enough, Lotti,' I said sharply. 'Your . . . your jokes are in bad taste.'

She looked as if she had been stung. 'Since when do you know about taste?'

'I'm sorry,' I said quickly.

The waiter arrived with our food. After he had served us and left, she said roughly, 'So let's get down to business then. Why did you want to see me?'

'I . . .' I stopped. I felt tempted to say nothing—to let the meal go by in trying to mend bridges, to win back her friendship, to laugh.

She waited for me to continue. Then when I remained silent, she raised the fork to her mouth and calmly began eating her steak tartare.

'It's fun being an *au pair*,' I said brightly. 'I really like the family I stay with. They are *très chic*. Mme Baleine is a buyer for Galeries Suf-fragettes. I've learnt all kinds of things living with them.'

'You mean Lafayettes,' Lotti giggled, her eyebrows shooting up her forehead as they used to.

I stared at her, 'What do you mean?'

'You said "suffragettes".' She chuckled.

'Lafayettes. Of course. How silly,' I laughed with her.

Then her face became alien again. 'But you didn't invite me here to tell me that,' she said bluntly. 'Let me guess, the master of the house is *fou de toi*. He ravished you and now you're pregnant. So you need my help.'

I replied a little shakily. 'Don't be silly. It's nothing of the sort.'

She didn't believe me. 'I knew it. Once he saw those breasts, how could he resist?' she teased.

'No. It's nothing like that. It's just . . .' I paused and bit my lips nervously. 'It's just this smell, a horrible smell. Can't you smell it?'

'What?' Lotti began to laugh again. 'You really are crazy. I don't smell anything except perfume,'—she sniffed theatrically—'something heavy with a base of sandalwood and musk.'

I stared into her face. 'You don't smell it then?'

'Smell what?'

'It. The smell—like an animal, but stronger, more spicy.'

'Like food, you mean?'

'The smell has nothing to do with food. It's much worse.'

She stared at me. 'A smell that is spicy like food, but is not food. Is this a riddle? If it is, I give up. I don't know what you're talking about.'

'Lotti,'—I grabbed her shoulders—'I'm talking about me.'

'You smell? Of what?' she asked, looking at me as if I were mad.

'I'm not sure,' I replied. 'All I know is that my smell has changed. I smell bad now—I know it. I'm afraid Mme Baleine, other people, will smell it sooner or later. And they will throw me out. I'm scared all the time, Lotti—on the streets, in the park. Sometimes I see people staring at me strangely and I know that they have smelt it. And if they know it comes from me, they'll probably lynch me, or throw me out of their country.'

It was out. My grip on her shoulders slackened and I slumped back in my seat.

Lotti was silent. Under the table, I clenched my fists in quiet desperation and waited for her to say something. 'How long have you felt like this?' she asked finally, as if she were at a loss for words.

'Oh, I don't know,' I muttered irritably. 'A month, two months? I can't remember how it began.'

'If you can't remember how it began, then how do you know it's real?' she asked reasonably.

I felt the perspiration begin in my armpits. 'I don't know. I can't say where it comes from,' I said desperately. 'All I can tell you is that when it comes, it is very real, and very strong, and . . . and unmistakable . . . rich and heavy like manure decomposing in an open field in the rain or decaying vegetable matter in a sewer in flood. But it doesn't smell exactly like any of these things—just bad like them.'

Lotti looked out of the window, a frown between her eyes. I wanted to shake her, to make her do something, to rescue me. I pushed my chair close to hers and leaned over so that our faces were only inches apart. She moved her chair back in surprise. I pushed myself closer.

'Do you see what I mean? Do you smell it? Answer me, Lotti.'

'No, I don't. There is nothing there.'

'Then you don't smell anything at all strange?' I asked excitedly.

'No,' she answered firmly, 'I don't.' Then she reached across the table to take my hand, 'I think you need to come home.'

I thought she had gone mad. 'I can't come back now,' I burst out without thinking, pulling my hand out of her grasp.

She didn't move, but her face showed that she knew what had happened. 'So he did become your lover,' she said quietly.

I nodded, unable to meet her eyes.

'Why didn't you tell me?'

'I couldn't. I was too ashamed, I guess.'

'And you?' she asked. 'Are you in love with him?'

I shook my head, seeing him as he had looked in the studio of rue St-André.

'You're sure?'

I hesitated a little, then replied, 'Yes.' Whatever I felt for him had disappeared with the coming of the smell.

'Then you must come back,' she said firmly.

'How can I?' I whispered.

'If you come home, you would soon forget about your smell,' she reasoned. 'You don't look happy, Leela.'

I looked at her thoughtfully. She was right. If I went back to their world—the world of my aunt and uncle and the Ramdhunes, my smell could be hidden behind the spices and the heavy fragrant oils of their food.

'We still go to your aunt and uncle for the Hindu festivals. Aunty Latha does the cooking now. The house feels strange without you. I think they miss you. We all miss you.' It was her way of saying that she wanted me back as her friend. I felt relieved and for a second I allowed myself to remember the Sundays at Lotti's and the wonders of my aunt's kitchen.

'How . . . how are they now?' I asked, my breath catching guiltily in my throat.

A shadow passed over her face. 'They seem all right now. For many months after you left, Aunty Latha was ill. Krishenbhai stopped going to work to look after her.'

'So they never looked for me.'

'She was very ill,' Lotti said. 'But slowly she got better, and now they visit on Sundays again.'

I stared at Lotti, hope and fear warring within. But if I returned, I thought, I would be trapped, unable to get out of their smelly cocoon. And what if Lotti were wrong? What if the smell was actually a part of me, but Lotti—with her nose dulled by spicy food—could not smell it? Then, if I went back, the smell might stay with me for the rest of my life. At least in the Baleines' world I could make money, I could buy the perfumes, the new clothes—find ways to fight it, submerge it, even if I couldn't completely root it out.

'I can't come back,' I told her sadly.

She looked at me with infinite regret. 'I think you're making a mistake.' But she reached across the table and held my hand. My eyes filled with tears. I tried to blink them away. I removed my hand from her grasp, 'Come, finish your steak tartare,' I said, 'or you will be late.'

We finished the meal quickly. Then both of us rose to leave. I knew by the sudden brightening of her face that she was going to see her lover. I envied her. Her love was so simple, so light. It was not dirtied by uncertainty like mine was. Lotti and I said goodbye at the door. I did not ask to meet again. Nor did she.

I watched Lotti walk away.

I saw a pair of girls put their arms around each other and stare at their reflections in the glass windows of a café. But I could only feel the terrible coldness of loss, as it wrapped itself around me. I remembered how Lotti and I would stand and admire our reflections in just that way. I was on my own now, I could walk anywhere in the city and no one could stop me. I thought suddenly of a song I heard on the streets in Nairobi, an American song, about a man who did nothing but walk. When other people stopped and talked, he just walked by.

So I walked on, surrounded on either side by shoppers. On the street, with my new clothes, I no longer felt looked at. I was dressed as well as the next person, and this feeling added to my sense of freedom. Even their stares no longer stopped me. My walk slowed. I stared at the boutique windows with their new winter collections and imagined how the clothes would look on me. The colours seemed terribly drab, greys, dark blues, and lots of black. All around me, people were engaged in the same things, watching, stopping, staring at their reflections and at the clothes in the windows. Like I was. Oh, Lotti, isn't this exciting, being part of a crowd like this? I pretended she was beside me. Then I shook my head. She would not want to be part of a crowd. She liked to stand out, to be different. But she looked strange now. And she wasn't beautiful anymore.

I caught sight of myself in a shop window. I was beautiful. Perhaps Lotti was right, there was no smell. Perhaps I had imagined it. Perhaps it was the meat in my diet, and the cheese. Or maybe the strain of living in the house with Mme Baleine was beginning to wear me down. I turned down a side street towards St-Michel. Hanging from a window on the first floor of a building was a little sign '*A Louer.*' I thought of Bruno. He was in the country, with his family. I imagined him surrounded by tall trees and old grey walls, in an old chateau, filled with beautiful things.

The telephone was ringing as I entered the house. I ran to pick it up, thinking it was the grandmother calling to tell me that the Baleines were on their way back to the city.

I grabbed the phone. 'Allo?' I said breathlessly.

'Leela. *Comment va tu?*' a familiar voice drawled.

'Maeve!'

'You sound surprised.'

I was very surprised. 'How . . . how was your vacation in Jamaica?' I asked breathlessly.

'Oh great. Pablo and I are living together now, he's even talking about taking me to Argentina to meet his family. We're having a little party next Saturday. I want you to be there.'

Maeve had never introduced me to her friends before. My head began to spin. 'Can I bring anything?' I asked.

'Just yourself. Pablo is taking care of everything.'

I felt guilty thinking of how I had cursed her over the last few months. 'Thank you, Maeve.'

ten

It was close to midnight when I finally arrived at Maeve's party. I was late because I could not decide what to wear. I knew I had to wear something that would make me look a part of the crowd. Finally I settled for the same clothes I had worn for my meeting with Lotti. At least some of the men would only notice my legs in the minuscule red skirt, I thought wryly. I carefully smeared perfume all over myself. The smell would not be allowed to betray me tonight. Then I slipped into my red coat and was ready to face them.

The taxi dropped me outside her building. I looked up at the third floor, to make sure that the party was not already over. But the apartment was ablaze with lights and through the windows I could see a mass of black shapes milling around inside. I breathed a sigh of relief and quickly punched in the code she had given me. The interior of the building was very modern and newly renovated. Many of the mailboxes on the wall hadn't even got names yet. The brand-new steel elevator had automatic sliding doors. But they made me nervous—so I walked up the old-fashioned twisting wooden stairs instead.

Maeve's landing was filled with people standing in groups, talking, smoking, and laughing loudly. I edged my way past the first group, shyly smiling up at them, as I murmured 'Excuse me.'

I walked across to another group and stood quietly on the fringes. The conversation was all about Hetty and Andrea, and an art exhibition by Jacques. I tried to appear interested and knowledgeable, all the while miserably aware of my ignorance. I didn't belong here. A tall redhead in a beautiful gold dress threw out an arm with a long cigarette attached to the end of it. It hit me in the chest and I smelt rather than felt the burn in my silk sweater. She turned around, an apology on her lips. Then she realized that she had hit an outsider and muttered something that sounded like 'You shouldn't stand so close.' I wanted to make a devastating reply but couldn't find the words. Her entire group seemed to be laughing at me. I turned sharply and walked away to the door of the apartment. The press of people around it made a black shield around the entrance. I was tempted to run back downstairs. But the arrogance of those long straight backs made me determined to stay, to breach their defences, and make them notice me—somehow.

Taking a deep breath, I began to shout 'Maeve' and 'excuse me' at the top of my lungs. The black wall parted like magic and I found myself in a short hallway with several doors. At the end of it was a large room, empty of furniture except for a bar against the far wall. People were crammed into every corner, flowing backwards into the hallway. Men and women stood back to back, knees touching, elbows entwined, heads moving back and forth as they talked. Music thrust its way through the burr of conversation, plugging holes in it with its steady throb. Tongues and hips moved ceaselessly in concert. The place stank of smoke, sweat, and the rubbery smell of synthetics. I began to relax. No one would notice my smell here.

A door opened to my right and I saw Maeve wrapped in the arms of a thin dark man with a ponytail. 'Maeve,' I called desperately, and the two of them turned around in surprise.

Maeve was the first to move. 'You made it,' she said in English. She broke away from the man's embrace and came towards me.

'I'm glad you are here. Come, let me introduce you,' she said. She turned to the man. 'Pablo, come and meet my Indian friend. She stayed with me in my old flat, and is a wonderful cook.'

He came up and formally kissed me on the cheeks. 'Nice to meet you,' he said in English. He had strange eyes, long and slanting slightly at the corners.

'Relax. *Tu as l'air d'un naufragé toi,*' Maeve whispered in my ear. She took my hand and pulled me towards the group nearest us. '*Viens, je te présenterai aux gens.*' I hung back, nervous.

Maeve tapped a beanpole of a man on the shoulder. He turned

around, his face brightening visibly when he saw who it was. I stared at him, feeling a little disappointed. He had a kind face, wavy brown hair worn slightly long, and watery blue eyes behind round glasses. He looked like a highly pedigreed boxer. Except for his height, there was nothing that made him stand out. But he did have beautiful hands—very white with long sensitive fingers.

Maeve pulled me forward. 'Olivier. *Je te présente* Leela. She is an old and dear friend of mine from India.'

He looked shyly at me, his eyes never leaving my face. '*Enchanté*,' he said, smiling. 'A friend of Maeve is what we all aspire to be.'

I felt like a fraud. All I knew was that Maeve had an 'interest' in me, as she herself put it. Whether that translated to friendship, I wasn't sure.

'Oh, come on, Olivier, stop flattering Maeve—she gets enough already from everyone else,' said a short thin girl with dark brown hair.

'This is Annelise, watch out for her tongue—it is forked like a viper's,' Maeve said, her red mouth curving into a smile. Everyone laughed. Annelise looked unperturbed. She had a short thick neck like a man's that did not match the rest of her body. She was dressed in a low-cut scarlet dress with black feathers speckled with bright yellow dots in her ears.

'*T'inquiete pas chérie*,' whispered an older man dressed in a dark suit into my left ear, 'Olivier will make verbal love to you too—when he knows you a little bit better. *C'est tous ce qu'il sait faire.*' I turned to look at him. He smiled and bowed. '*Je me présente*, Guillermo della Croce. Tell me, how have I missed you all these years?'

'Don't believe a word he says,' Olivier said, laughing. 'He's a liar—all Italians are. Especially in love.' I watched them in silence, not knowing what to think. Were these people really all friends?

The conversation moved back and forth between them, sometimes a third or a fourth voice chipping in. After each sentence everyone laughed. Five minutes later, or maybe it was half an hour, I had laughed so much that my mouth felt stretched and tense. I could feel twin lines forming, linking my mouth to my nose. Everyone in the group had them. I wondered if it was something peculiar to French speakers, whether it had something to do with the muscles that were used in speaking French. Bruno had the same lines around his mouth. I wondered where he was right now, what party he was at, who he was with, and whether his cousin the composer was there too. Claude knew all about me—and didn't seem to find it at all strange when one day I joined the two of them for lunch at a bistro on the Ile St-Louis.

The laughter cut into my thoughts. On cue, I joined in. The conversation was all about people who weren't at the party: Lucille who had stopped working with Bejeane and had started a business of her own about healing through haircutting.

'She says she can tell if a person is happy or sad by the state of his hair,' trilled a short man who had just joined the group.

'Oh no, that's ridiculous,' a tall girl with a protruding Adam's apple screamed. 'She left that faggot Bejeane because there weren't any men there.' They all laughed again. I laughed too, though my mouth hurt with laughing so much.

One story followed another about people who could have been the names of streets for all I knew. In a little while I could no longer tell whether they were talking about people, books, or exotic dishes on a menu. I could add no story of my own to the stream of anecdotes that fell in layers upon the conversation, over the laughter that bubbled endlessly beneath it. I remained silent. But nobody seemed to care.

Suddenly a familiar voice whispered into my ear, 'What are you dreaming of, princess?' I turned around, my eyes drinking in the sight of his face.

'M Baleine, you . . . how c-come you're here?' I stammered.

'Bruno,' he corrected gently. 'Why the formality? You used to know my name once.'

I started at him in disbelief. How could he be here, looking me over with such confidence?

'I used to know your first name,' I corrected him. Shrewdly he did not argue. Instead he handed me a glass of champagne and steered me towards the balcony. I tried to resist. But the group had closed in upon itself, arguing loudly about the merits of some painter called Largan. Reluctantly I followed him.

It was quieter outside and the air was cold. I took a sip of champagne and looked at Bruno suspiciously. He smiled back at me. 'I wanted to be with you, and only you,' he whispered, coming closer.

My anger shrank and was replaced by a growing warmth. It felt good to be wanted.

We kissed. I relaxed into his embrace. We kissed again. But now it was different. His touch was full of expectancy, but I felt suddenly empty, as if I had nothing to give. His lips moved upon mine unheeding. He let out a sigh.

'Come, let's dance,' I said and moved quickly into centre of the room before Bruno could pull me back.

We edged onto the dance floor, and the music, which from the edge of the room had sounded like noise, suddenly grabbed me. The rhythm I realized slowly was vaguely African, a galloping three-four rhythm laid on top of a steady pounding pulse. The music pulled me into itself quickly. My hips began to move of their own accord—dip, sway, dip, sway. My hands rose to embrace the sound and I stretched out my neck, shaking my head to the rhythm. Cigarette smoke hung in thick clouds above us. My body flowed and circled around itself like dough, smooth and fluid. In the middle of my body, around my navel, the rhythm beat itself into the big flat bones of my hips.

Bruno stopped dancing and moved away so that he could watch me from the side. I continued to dance where I was. Others stopped to watch me too. I could hear little whispers of 'Who's she?' floating towards me from the crowd. I kept on moving mindlessly. Then suddenly Maeve was dancing with me, and it was as if a spotlight had suddenly been turned on us. She raised her arms over her head, imitating me, allowing the spectator to absorb her beauty bit by bit—her face, her body, her legs. Her movements were slow, and designed to show off her lush body.

As usual, when I was with Maeve, I began to feel ill-proportioned and ugly. But I kept dancing, using the music to block her out of my mind. Another song began, also African but calmer. I slowed down the pace of my movements. Suddenly Maeve grabbed me around the waist, thrusting her pelvis into mine. The music fell away from me; I looked up into her face stunned. She grabbed me around the hips and tried to force them to move like her own. But I stood rooted to the ground.

After a few seconds she gave up and moved back a few steps till our bodies were no longer touching. She looked at me strangely. I caught a whiff of another whisper, '*Mieux que Maeve, qui est-ce?*' '*Une très bonne amie de Maeve,*' the other person replied. '*Une femme-amie de Maeve, tu blagues?*' I heard the first voice say. Then the ponytailed Pablo surged out of the crowd and began to photograph Maeve. She stopped dancing and started to pose, model-like. People began to clap and laugh at the same time. The crowd closed in around me, blocking them off from my sight. I slipped away towards the hall for a little quiet. Bruno was nowhere to be seen. But the hall was filled with smoke and latecomers. The group I had been introduced to earlier was still standing there, laughing on cue after every sentence. I did not want to have to speak to any of them. I stepped through a door on my left, expecting to find myself in a bathroom where I could be alone.

Instead I found myself in a black, white, and silver kitchen. The cupboards were of glossy black formica, the sink and its surroundings were shining aluminium. The only other thing in the room, the refrigerator, was painted black with silver edges. The walls still smelt faintly of the resin-based gum the decorators had used to stick on the black and white tiles. But the black-and-white order was violated by the mess that pervaded every inch of flat surface. Empty wine bottles perched precariously on top of the refrigerator. Some were already lying belly up, gently nudging the others to give in to gravity. Plastic glasses and plates of half-eaten food were piled into haphazard mountains. The room smelt strongly of camembert and red wine that was slowly turning to vinegar in the heat. On the silver-topped counter in the middle lay the remains of a large bird—a still life of dead pheasant and fruit. These were being carved up with infinite care and precision by a huge man. He looked up briefly as I came in but continued slicing.

I watched him prepare his sandwich. His movements were very economical for such a large man. His concentration was absolute. He laid out the triangular white slices of pheasant on the brown bread, added some dark green lettuce which he pulled out of a bowl of ice beside the sink, and finally threw on some little dark red Italian pomidori tomatoes. Then he paused. 'What else?' he said to himself, looking down at the sandwich.

'Radish,' I replied unthinkingly, even though the question had not been directed at me.

He glanced up again. This time he looked at me carefully, starting at my face, my hair, then moving down to my shoulders, my waist and then back up to my face. 'Good,' he said and smiled.

He rummaged amongst the leftovers of the pheasant and dug out a magenta radish. He put it on the board and chopped it rapidly into thin slivers. Carefully he placed them over the other slice of bread. He folded the two pieces of bread together and cut the sandwich in two.

'*Tu veux la moitié*,' he said, and handed me half without waiting for the answer. I let him slide the sandwich onto my palm, his fingers brushing along the length of it. The skin on the back of his hand felt smooth and warm.

I raised the sandwich to my face and drank in the smell of the pheasant, the garlic in the butter and the herbs. Then I became aware of the more subtle aromas of tomato, lettuce, and radish, and realized I was very hungry. I had not eaten since breakfast. I took a huge bite. It was delicious. I chewed slowly, lost in the pleasure of the food. The man watched me eat, seeing the hunger dawn in my eyes and suffuse my entire face. Only then did he pick up his own sandwich and bite into it, as if my hunger had ignited his own.

He took quick decisive bites. I ate more slowly, not really tasting the food, my thoughts completely absorbed in the person across the table.

We ate in silence, watching each other. He was older than I had realized at first. His eyes were set rather close together, emphasizing the feeling of power that emanated from him. He was still dressed in office clothes, a formal dark brown suit. But he had taken off his tie, and his brown-grey hair was messy.

We finished almost simultaneously. He wiped his mouth with the back of his hand. I licked the crumbs off my lips. He watched me in silence, a satisfied look in his eyes. They ran over my face, forehead, eyes, nose, and came to rest on my mouth.

In a single stride, he crossed the kitchen and was at my side.

He kissed me briefly and left.

I remained a few minutes longer in the kitchen. It felt empty without him. Then I walked out, determined to leave the party.

As I came out of the kitchen, I saw that the group I had been introduced to earlier were waiting by the door. The moment they recognized me, they pounced. Eager curious faces surrounded me. They waited for me to say something, but I remained silent, feeling suddenly shy, not sure of what was expected of me. 'I think I'll go now,' I said finally. 'It was nice to meet all of you.' They looked disappointed.

'Don't go yet,' said Annelise. 'The night is still young. Besides . . . you haven't told us anything yet.'

'About what?' I asked.

'What did he say to you?' Annelise asked, her eyes shining.

'Oh yes, do tell,' the one called Olivier imitated her.

'Do you know him? Have you met him before?' The small bald man stared at me, his eyes taking in my clothes and my shoes. Clearly he found me lacking.

'Actually I don't know him,' I said bewildered. 'Should I?'

They burst into laughter.

'Oh, she's precious,' the Italian man who had flirted with me earlier said. 'Who are you? Where have you been hiding?'

I didn't reply, feeling suddenly scared. What would they think if I said I was an *au pair*? They would probably laugh at me. I looked around at the group of faces, terrified. Then, unexpectedly, Olivier spoke up for me, 'Hey, leave her alone. Why should she know about the stars of our sordid nightlife?'

'The great M Bon Marché is hardly sordid,' the little man replied angrily. 'His stores are famous for being quite the most exclusive in the world—the Mecca of food fetishists. He is to the food supermarket what the Larousse is to *la gastronomie française*. I want to know everything, *chérie*—grunts, burps and farts.'

I looked at him coldly. 'There is nothing to tell. We did not exchange a word. He just gave me half a sandwich.' I didn't tell them he had kissed me. It had hardly been a kiss—more like a seal of approval.

'Oh, isn't she cute,' the Italian man hooted with laughter. 'She says he gave her a sandwich. Serves you right for being a curious old woman, Jean-Luc.'

'Wait till Maeve hears of this—I wonder how long she'll stay your friend after this,' Annelise said venomously. My mouth went dry. If the man really was as famous as every one made him out to be, then she would hate me. In which case, I didn't want to meet her again that evening. I looked towards the living room where people were still dancing and drinking, clustered like flies around the bar. I could not see her.

The story of the sandwich spread like wildfire, it seemed as if everyone was staring at me. I decided to find Bruno and leave.

I started to edge my way past the group who were now arguing loudly over the rival merits of two cooks or kinds of dishes—I wasn't sure which.

'Are you leaving already?' a voice asked, and a soft hand touched my shoulder.

I turned around. It was Olivier.

'I was thinking of it, yes,' I replied warily.

'Do you have a car or do you want me to call a taxi?'

I looked up into his bland face. A face like wallpaper, I thought scornfully. Maeve had not seemed particularly friendly with him. 'I haven't decided what I will do yet,' I said.

Strong arms grabbed me from behind and swung me around ungently.

'What were you doing with him?' Bruno demanded tightly.

'Who? What do you mean?'

His grip tightened. 'What were you doing in the kitchen with him? Must you try to humiliate me in front of my friends?'

'Let go, you're hurting me.'

'Bruno.' Olivier put a hand on Bruno's shoulder. He let go of me immediately.

'Oh, Olivier. How are you?' Bruno said none too warmly.

'I'm fine, thank you. And you?' he replied.

'All right I suppose, more of the same,' Bruno spoke distractedly, continuing to stare angrily at me.

After a few moments of awkward silence, Olivier said, 'Well, I'm leaving, so I'll go find Maeve, say goodbye. It was nice to see you again, Bruno.' Then, to my surprise, he addressed me. 'I enjoyed meeting you, Leela, perhaps we can meet again?' I looked at him in surprise. 'Of . . . of course. It was a pleasure,' I stammered, aware of Bruno looking at me. Olivier melted into the crowd.

When I finally dared to look up at Bruno, he was laughing. 'You seem to have made quite an impression on poor Olivier. How strange!'

'Why?'

'You are hardly his type—he's an intellectual.'

'Why? Am I not smart enough?' I asked sharply.

'No, *chérie*,' Bruno said easily. 'It is just that you are too far from his world. I know that I don't have to worry about him.'

'Maybe you are wrong. Perhaps our worlds are not so different,' I said softly, thinking of how eager everyone had been to know who I was after I came out of the kitchen.

At once his eyes narrowed, and some of the anger came back into his face. 'How do you know Philippe Lavalle?'

'Through food,' I replied, mocking him. 'He has a great appetite.'

Bruno's face darkened even further. 'Appetite? The man is always hungry. He gobbles everything without tasting—food, wine, women.' He ran a worried hand through his hair. 'I regret I ever asked Maeve to invite you here. But you'd better not think anything of it, or Catherine will kill you.' He began to laugh wildly. 'How ironic, I wish I could tell her. I'd love to see her face. She hates to be beaten, and by her own children's *au pair*.'

Suddenly I felt very tired. 'Let's forget him,' I said, turning to Bruno, 'I'll probably never meet him again.'

'That's true,' he agreed, his face lightening. 'You never will.'

eleven

After Maeve's party, Bruno would take me out with him to parties, and show me off to his friends. At first they showed some interest in me, mainly because of the story of the sandwich man. But after a while the story grew stale. Other stories replaced it, and they forgot me. I stayed on the fringes, known only as Bruno's friend. Only Olivier and Annelise even remembered who I was.

One day, Olivier came up to me and invited me to a concert.

'What kind of concert?' I asked him uncertainly.

'It is a young Spanish guitarist,' he replied. I was mystified, but hesitantly accepted.

I dressed for the concert as I had seen people dress for church. I made sure I used lots of perfume though, just in case the smell decided to emerge again. I lived in constant fear of it, but for the last few months it had been surprisingly good, hardly ever showing itself. When I met Olivier at the entrance of the Métro at St-Michel, he was dressed formally too. He took me through many little streets, past Tunisian sweet shops that would have looked the same in Barbès, or in Mombassa. Then we rounded a corner and found ourselves beside a small square church. It looked so plain I was disappointed. Inside, the ceiling was low and there were no decorations except for a large rose-shaped stained-glass window at the back. We sat down on one of the hard wooden benches close to the front. The church slowly filled with people. I kept turning around to see if I could recognize any of the people that hung around Maeve. But the people here seemed to belong to a different world. They looked ordinary, like the people in the Métro, and on the streets. And yet, there was something in their faces, in the quiet way they spoke to each other, that was different. That was a little like Olivier.

'So is this religious music we're going to listen to then?' I asked him.

'No. Not really,' he replied slowly. 'It's quite secular.'

'Oh. Is secular like rock then?'

He looked confused. 'I'm not sure I understand.'

'You know popular music, rock, like Led Zeppelin, Jethro Tull, and others,' I said, happy to be able to show off my knowledge.

He looked away for a second and coughed. 'I suppose it was popular music in its time.'

'When was that?'

'Fifteenth, seventeenth, eighteenth centuries.'

I was aghast. 'But . . . but why would people listen to music that old?' He looked embarrassed.

Just then, there was a hush, and a young man walked in holding a guitar. He was extremely thin, and his black trousers only served to emphasize it. His longish brown hair touched his collar, but receded in the front, exposing a huge expanse of forehead. But his eyes, which were dark and intense, saved him from being ugly. He looked around the church briefly and sat down, placing the guitar on his lap. He looked down at the floor, not looking at anyone. The silence was absolute. Then he began.

The music was full of different sounds, some rather sweet and smooth, others heavy and rough. They flowed together under his hands, sometimes fast, at other times slow. He bent over his instrument, paying no attention to the audience. He seemed to be wrapped in silence as he played. His music sounded strange, too full of melody to be ugly. But other sounds—dark unconnected sounds—interrupted the song and made it difficult to listen to. Somehow I could not get inside the music. I felt as if the sounds surrounded me but I found nothing I could hold on to. I watched the others around me. They sat still and straight, their faces serious. I looked at Olivier. His face was flushed, his eyes shone, and his body swayed gently with the music. My thoughts began to wander, and it was only the silence that brought me back to the present. I raised my hands to clap, glancing at Olivier. But he remained still. I quickly hid my hands in my lap. I looked at the man on my other side. He was slumped in his seat, looking at the paper in his hand. A few whispers arose from the audience, and a little shuffling and sighing. Then the room went quiet again. A woman came out and stood beside the guitarist. She began to sing. Her voice was sweet, high-pitched but full of strength. Though the language was not French, something in the way she sang, caressing the vowels, told me it was about love. I wondered where the song was going, whether it would have a happy ending. Then the guitar came in and from the first few notes, I knew that it was about the death of love. I looked around the church and wondered whether the others sensed it. Their faces were grave, as if they felt the sadness too. An excitement filled me.

The singer joined in suddenly and the music sweetened slightly, some of the tension going out of it. Then it came to an end and everyone began to clap. I felt confused, why were they applauding after this one and not after the first? Was it because they liked this one better? I glanced at Olivier. He was clapping wildly, his hair in disarray. He looked at me and smiled. I began to clap madly too.

The guitarist got up. His face was red. He bowed briefly and walked off the stage. People relaxed and began to stand and stretch.

Olivier turned to me and smiled. 'Did you like it?' he asked.

I smiled back. 'Very much,' I lied. 'Especially the second one.'

He nodded. 'I'm glad. It must be very different from the music you're used to.'

'Yes, very,' I said politely.

'Sometimes we have Indian music concerts in Paris too.'

'Here? Indian musicians?' I asked incredulously, images of dancing film stars coming to mind.

'I've been to some of them,' he said. 'They are very intense.'

I felt bemused. In Nairobi we had only listened to my grandmother's religious music. I had never liked it because it sounded strange and boring. 'Why? Why would you go to listen to Indian music?'

'Because your music makes one go inside oneself.'

'You really like it?' I whispered, still finding it hard to understand. 'But it's so different.'

He laughed. 'That's why I like it.'

The lights suddenly dimmed and the hall went quiet. I turned and looked at the stage. The musician came back. But this time a man accompanied him with a huge guitar, almost as tall as himself. There was a flute and a violin, as well as what looked like African drums.

'What is that thing—the big one?' I whispered to Olivier.

'It is a double bass.'

'Oh,' I mumbled, 'I . . . I forgot.'

He looked embarrassed and stared ahead once more.

In the second half of the concert, the guitarist switched to music he had composed himself. He made strange sounds, some that clashed like concrete being mixed, while others were almost too sweet, like fruit that was rotting slowly under a hot sun, sometimes bitter, at others pungent and strong. This time I was no longer outside the music. I sat up straight, excited. I had never imagined that music could talk: that it could express the fear, loneliness, and excitement that I felt. I sat silent long after it had ended.

Finally Olivier tapped me on the shoulder. 'We should go now.'

I looked around. The church was empty. But I could feel the music linger, unwilling to be forgotten. I waited a few more seconds and then rose.

Olivier took me through more tiny winding streets until we found ourselves in a cul-de-sac lined with restaurants. He led me down some steps into a small restaurant whose walls were made of large stones. It was a cosy space, with lots of little tables crammed in between large potted plants.

Over dinner we talked of various things. It was less difficult than I had imagined. 'How do you know Maeve?' I asked.

'I met Maeve at my cousin's New Year's Eve party, just before I finished my *baccalauréat*. She was very beautiful and I was eight years younger, so of course I had to know her,' he said with a strange smile.

'She is very beautiful. And smart,' I gushed.

He raised an eyebrow quizzically. 'Really? I suppose she is smart—in her own way. She may even be intelligent, but I don't think she tries very hard.'

I remained silent.

'But I defer to your judgement,' he continued, smiling at me. 'You must know her better than I. How did you meet?'

'Through friends of the family,' I said vaguely.

He nodded, satisfied. 'My mother's family comes from Strasbourg too,' he confided. 'Though our families don't know each other, I still feel some responsibility for her.'

I laughed suddenly. 'You almost sound Gujarati.'

'What is that?'

'It is where my family is from originally—Gujarat, in India.' I thought of my uncle suddenly, and wondered what he and Aunty Latha were doing now. That surprised me, I had not thought of them for a long time. 'But I have never been there!'

'Really? How sad.'

'Why?' I challenged him. 'Maeve hates Strasbourg, she never wants to go back.'

'But then Maeve hates easily, including herself sometimes.'

'But if you don't leave home you will never be successful—that's what Maeve says,' I said vehemently.

He didn't reply.

The food arrived and we ate in silence. I listened to the music playing in the restaurant. It was quite different from what we had heard that evening.

'What kind of music is this?' I asked suddenly.

Olivier looked puzzled. Then he realized what I meant. 'Oh, that's Greek—but not very good. I have better Greek music at home, if you'd care to listen to it sometime.'

'No. That's all right,' I said hastily, 'I just wondered, it sounds so different from what we heard.'

'Did you like the concert then?'

I turned to him, my eyes shining. 'It was just wonderful.'

Olivier's eyes lit up. 'I'm so glad,' he said, almost under his breath.

'I never thought music could talk,' I said excitedly, and then almost bit my tongue.

'Of course it does,' he replied, his face glowing. 'Why else would people listen?'

I felt confused. 'I don't know. I just . . . we never listened to much music at home.'

He looked surprised. 'Well, then, we'll have to make up for it now. Would you like to come and listen to some more music?'

I hesitated, but the thought of more music made me feel greedy. 'Yes, yes, of course.'

After dinner he took me to his apartment and played more music for me. After a while though, it all began to sound alike. I waited for him to try to kiss me. But he didn't. Instead he kept playing record after record, and giving me lots of camomile tea to drink. Eventually he handed me my coat and offered to accompany me home. I refused. But I let him put me into a taxi and slip some money into the driver's hand.

After that I met Olivier regularly. The evenings always followed the same pattern—concert, dinner, and then silently listening to more music at his house. He took me to a music store and introduced me to different composers, showing me various versions of the music we had heard together. He told me stories about composers and great conductors. When he talked about them, his face became almost attractive. And yet he never touched me, or gave me the slightest indication that he desired me. We never spoke very much about things that weren't related to music. I wondered why he spent so much time with me. 'Probably because he can't find anyone else,' I heard Maeve's voice whisper in my head. But I felt that Olivier was my friend because he, too, was an outsider to Maeve's world, like myself.

He wasn't really Maeve's friend, but her cousin's. He was the only son in a very rich and respectable old family from Strasbourg. But his parents had moved to Paris when he was twelve because his father, a lawyer, was nominated a judge at the Supreme Court. After his *baccalauréat,* he got into the best business school in France. But the classes bored him, so he would quietly sneak across the road to the faculty of

sociology and anthropology, where the classes were much more exciting. Eventually he graduated with two degrees—one from the business
school and the other in anthropology. But afterwards, when the best
firms in France were wooing him, he refused them all and vowed never
to go into a big entreprise. He had money, and so he decided to wait
and look for a job that he felt was worthwhile. That was eight years
ago. He still hadn't been able to make up his mind. This indecision
was evident in everything he did—in his diffident charm, in the way
that his hands shook slightly when he held a glass or lit someone's
cigarette for them, and in the hesitancy that was at the root of his
clumsiness.

ANNELISE AND I became friends in an altogether more dramatic
fashion. But Annelise was highly theatrical, just as Olivier was em-
phatically not.

In May Olivier invited me and a few others to the south of France
for the weekend. 'Jean-Marie, an old and dear friend, abandoned Paris
two years ago after a liver transplant. He now lives in a little village
near Cannes. We don't know how long his liver will last, but that
doesn't stop him from eating and drinking like a king. He would love
to meet you,' Olivier explained, making it sound as if I would be doing
him a favour by coming along. Bruno was going to the country to
Catherine's mother's home. I accepted happily.

The morning after we arrived, we decided to make a tour of the
village. We piled into the two cars and set off. I sat in the back and
admired the scenery, happy to be free of Paris. The road to the village
of Tourette sur Loup twisted around the folds of the hill. As we
rounded each curve, I caught glimpses of the fairy-tale village. It
seemed to have been carved out of a single rock and frozen in time.
The houses were all built out of the same deep gold stone, vivid against
the green of the hillside. They all had small high windows set deep
into the walls, with small balconies lined with pink and red flowers.

We rounded the final corner and found ourselves on the edge of
the central square. It was not quite a garden but a grove of dark droop-

ing trees, amidst elegant rose-and-gold cafés and restaurants, and shops with colourful awnings. On three sides of the square, the street had been taken over by the farmers' market. There was a small old church at one end of the square. And at the other end under the trees, there were tables where people sat drinking coffee and aperitifs. 'We'll meet there,' Jean-Marie said, pointing to a café behind us, 'at *midi et demie.*' It had a beautiful vine-covered patio on which little white wrought-iron tables were set. A group of red-faced men sat around one of them drinking milky glassfuls of pastis.

Our group split up. Annelise went towards the left to look at an art gallery. Signor della Croce, Pablo, and Maeve went meandering down the main road towards a bar they knew, and the rest of us headed in the direction of the farmers' market. We passed a group of old men playing boules. As I watched, one of the old men crouched, took two short running steps, and, with an unbelievably smooth motion of his arm, sent his steel ball rolling at great speed towards another similar one, twenty-five metres away. It seemed a long distance, but his ball hit the other with a resounding thwack and sent it careening away. I stared at them. It was strange to watch old men playing a game so seriously. 'It's a tradition around here,' Olivier whispered to me.

'They're so old,' I whispered back.

He laughed. 'So what? What else do they have to do?'

'But what about their children?'

'Their children have gone,' he replied. 'They are the only ones left.'

I became silent, suddenly remembering my grandmother. Was she all right in Mombassa? But she isn't alone, I reminded myself fiercely, she has my cousins and my uncle and aunt.

The farmers' market was a riot of colours. Well-dressed men and women walked between the stalls, looking at the wares. The women reminded me of Mme Baleine, expensively dressed, their skins perfectly golden. But unlike Catherine, here they all wore tennis shoes. The men were equally elegant. I suddenly felt very poor in my cut-off jeans and T-shirt.

We mingled with the crowd and wandered from one stall to another. I soon forgot myself in the scents and the sights of the place. The first few stalls sold the bright flowered cloth that seemed to be typical of the region. Then came the cheeses, mainly goats' cheese, and huge plastic pails and earthen pots of olives. The two powerful smells mingled divinely together. Some of the cheeses had a crust of herbs or peppercorns, which gave heaviness and maturity to the sharp aggressive aroma of the cheese.

'It's so different from Paris,' I remarked, looking at a small oil press that was on sale at a stall selling antique furniture.

'This is only a small market, mainly for tourists,' Jean-Marie replied. 'You should see the big one in Aix, or in Vence. Those are more authentic.'

Suddenly he dashed ahead and began to talk animatedly with a man wearing the bloodstained apron of a butcher. I hung back, admiring a stand of dried flowers and herbs. The scents were intriguing. The woman who ran the stall was plump and middle-aged, dressed in the familiar flowery prints. She had laugh lines at her eyes and there was a comfortable motherly feeling to her. I decided to ask her what the different herbs were for.

'Excuse me?' I said hesitantly.

She ignored me. I said it again, slightly louder.

Still she wouldn't respond. 'Christine, I think she wants to talk to you,' the cheese man next door said loudly, roaring with laughter.

Suddenly I felt as though all eyes were upon me. I looked around helplessly for the others, but they seemed to have disappeared. The woman was staring at me now, her face hard.

'What is it?'

'I . . . I just wanted to know . . .'

'I'm not selling knowledge here,' she interrupted me rudely. 'If you want something, point.'

'Well, how much is that?' I said, pointing to a bouquet of dried lavender and some yellow flowers with a strong peppery sweet smell, whose name I didn't know.

'Two hundred francs.'

I gasped. 'That's a lot of money.'

She sniffed, 'I don't ruin other honest businessmen by making my goods too cheap.'

I felt puzzled. What on earth was she talking about? I looked over my shoulder in case she had said it to someone else. But there was no one nearby. I started at her in confusion. Suddenly I realized what was bothering me. The flowers were marked a hundred francs. It said so quite clearly on a little white placard tied to it. 'But it says a hundred francs on it,' I said as firmly as I could, holding out a hundred-franc note.

She picked up the bunch of flowers and looked carefully at them, her eyebrows shooting up in mock surprise. 'So it does,' she said slowly, her voice heavy with sarcasm. 'I must have made a mistake. You see, this is the price for French people.'

I felt my ears burn and a humming sound begin. 'How . . . what?' My tongue felt heavy and sticky. Behind me I heard a titter followed by a deeper masculine laugh. I buried my face in the flowers to hide my burning cheeks. The smell of the flowers swamped me, suffocating me with their cloying sweetness. Then there came another scent, one I knew well. I turned and ran into the crowd, stumbling into people as I pushed forward. Suddenly the whole market seemed to be alive with angry imprecations. Hands reached out to grab me, but I ran on blindly, possessed of a superhuman strength. Only the smell followed me, dark as a shadow, ugly, hungry, and jealous.

At last I stumbled into the grove of cypress trees in the middle of the square. My heart was pounding, there was a roaring in my ears. My smell reached up to suffocate me.

'Leela? What happened? Are you all right?'

It was Olivier. He was perspiring and looked worried. I backed away from him, afraid he would smell it too.

'You ran away from the market as if there were evil spirits after you,' he said lightly. But his face was concerned.

'Nothing. I'm all right now. Thank you.' I tried to sound as calm as possible.

'You don't have to lie, Leela. I heard what happened.' Olivier caught hold of me gently and held me. I stood resting against him. His chest felt comfortable. I became conscious of the smell of fresh sweat with something slightly sharp, almost bitter, underneath it.

I moved away from him quickly and looked up into his face. It was full of concern, but I felt sure I had seen something else there just a second before.

'Shall we go sit down at the café?' he asked.

The others arrived shortly after we sat down. Olivier told them briefly what had happened. When he finished, I looked around the group. Their expressions ranged from uncomfortable to sympathetic to disgusted.

'Bloody Front Nationalists,' Pablo exploded. The men at the other table suddenly looked at us.

Jean-Marie shook his head sadly, 'I never thought it was this bad.'

'Fascists,' della Croce hissed.

Maeve, not to be outdone, leaned over and gave me a hug. 'My poor little sister,' she said,

Only Annelise kept quietly biting her lips, her face set in a heavy scowl. Suddenly she burst out, her voice strong with emotion, 'Those fucking bitches. I hope they rot. I hope they get leprosy and their flesh falls off bit by bit.' She slammed her fist on the table. The glasses jumped, and one fell to the floor and shattered. The men at the other table began to clap and boo.

The commotion brought both the landlord and his lady running.

'What's going on here?' the landlord blustered.

'What's wrong?' echoed his wife, hard-faced and blond.

'What's wrong?' Annelise jumped up and glared at her. 'I'll tell you what's wrong, you people are what's wrong.'

Men rose from other tables, fat and sloppy, faces red with wine and sunshine, and came ambling over. 'She's insulting us, can you believe it?'

'Parisian bitch.'

Annelise swirled around. The man who said it backed away before her furious eyes. I stared at her in awe, how was she able to get so angry? Was it really for me, I wondered.

'You lazy drunken good-for-nothings, when was the last time any of you had a job, huh? Instead you just sit here and hate the world,' Annelise shouted. She picked up another glass and threw it at them. 'Why don't you just drink yourselves to death?'

'What the hell?' one man took an angry step towards her, but Olivier stepped in between. The others got up as well.

The landlord finally recognized Jean-Marie. 'Monsieur Petit,' he said nervously, 'I think it would be better if you took your friends and left.'

Jean-Marie got up and reached for his wallet. But Olivier had already taken out a wad of notes and thrust it at the landlord. Jean-Marie shepherded Annelise outside and the rest of us followed. In the car, Annelise continued to berate the rest of them. 'You all are cowards, couldn't even stand up against a bunch of bumpkins,' she cursed. I felt embarrassed. I was the cause of the whole thing, and by now, they were all probably hating me for ruining their weekend. 'You're all completely selfish, you know that,' she went on. 'You are so determined not to let anything spoil your mood, you can't tell wrong from right anymore, just pleasant from unpleasant.'

'That's enough, Annelise, you're overreacting,' Olivier said calmly.

She stopped immediately, putting her hand to her cheek, as if he had slapped her.

I felt grateful to her, and furious with Olivier. The others looked uncomfortably out of the window. Silently I reached across and gripped her hand.

twelve

Maeve was married on a Saturday afternoon in late September, in the Eglise de Notre-Dame des Victoires.

I came to the church alone. Bruno and I were both invited—his card was addressed to him and Catherine. But she simply yawned when she saw the elaborate card and tossed it aside. 'I will not disappoint Maman and the children for the wedding of some parvenue. Lily can represent us.' She looked at me lazily. 'She's your friend after all.'

She turned over on her side, so that I could press the other side of her back. I felt like digging my nails into her, but controlled myself with some difficulty. 'Besides,' she continued, 'the children need the fresh air. Paris is becoming so crowded. Everyone inhales the germs of the stranger next door.'

'You are so wise, my dear,' said Bruno. He sauntered over to the bed, where I was massaging Catherine's back, and leaned over to give her a kiss on the back of her head. As he bent down, he winked at me. I pretended not to notice.

The previous night we had had a huge fight. Our relationship was becoming more and more strained—oscillating between jealousy and passion on Bruno's part, and hurt and indifference on mine. I was still smarting from what he had said. So I ignored him.

He knelt by the bed. I kept kneading Catherine's back. He began to caress her neck even as he continued to stare at me, his eyes pleading. I looked down at our four hands resting on her bony back. What a picture the three of us made, I thought bitterly.

'So you agree with me about Paris?' Catherine said, breaking the silence.

'Of course, my dear,' he answered absently, his eyes still fixed upon my face. I gave him a slight smile. His face lit up.

Catherine turned and pulled his head down over hers. I moved away but lingered by the door, unable to bring myself to leave the room. Then I heard her say, 'So shall we sell this house then and move into Maman's chateau? There is much more room there, and the children will have fresh air all the time.'

'But . . . but what about your work?' he extemporized. 'You know you cannot leave Paris.'

'I could sell this awfully large house and buy a small apartment, a *pied à terre* really. You could stay in the country and do your work in peace.'

'B-but my work? The office?' Bruno stammered.

'We'd have so much money you need never work again. You always complain about how work gets in the way of your real vocation as an artist. Maman's place is simply huge. There will be plenty of space for you to isolate yourself. Why don't you come with me this weekend and see?' Her voice changed, a thread of steel running through the soft controlled syllables. 'You haven't come down since May, Maman is beginning to wonder about you.'

That decided it. Maman was the real power in the family, the one with the money. Even the house in Paris belonged to her. So Bruno couldn't refuse. He cast me a despairing look. I looked away, knowing my time with him was coming to an end—unless he did something fast. This was Catherine's way of telling him so.

His eyes dulled and he looked down at his wife. 'All right, my love. I will do as you please,' he said and gave her another kiss. Then without looking at me again, he quickly left the room.

I followed him out. 'I want to talk,' I whispered urgently to him.

A few minutes later, he joined me in the courtyard. I was already smoking a cigarette when he arrived.

'You aren't serious about going with her this weekend, are you?'

He avoided my eyes and pretended to concentrate on lighting his cigarette.

'It's Maeve's wedding this weekend, remember?' I said, trying to make a smoke ring but failing and ending up blowing smoke into his face.

'Stop it,' he said irritably. 'If you can't smoke properly then don't.'

'To hell with the cigarette,' I said, grinding it under my heel. 'Tell Catherine you can't come, that you have work here in the city.'

'What work do I have over the weekend?' he said sulkily. 'Besides, that's what I told her last weekend and the weekend before that and the one before that . . .'

'Then tell her the truth,' I cut in. 'Aren't you sick of lying?'

He stopped short, his mouth falling open in surprise.

Looking at his expression, I realized that he would never leave her.

'I'm going to the wedding with or without you,' I announced quietly.

He looked relieved. 'Sure,' he replied easily. 'You're a free woman.'

I looked at him aghast. What did he mean by that? Did he not want me anymore? 'And if I never come back?' I asked lightly.

'That's your decision,' he shrugged. 'I've never tried to hold you. You stay with me by your own free will.'

'Free will?' I laughed scornfully. 'Nothing's free here, not even me.'

He laughed nastily. 'Then you're just cheap.'

THE MOMENT I saw the crowd of wedding guests outside the church I knew I had made a mistake in wearing a sari. I don't know what had made me do it. The sari began to feel like a disguise. I searched the crowd for a familiar face. Finally I saw Annelise standing on her own. I walked up to her. 'Where's Olivier?' I asked. 'How should I know?' she answered irritably, 'I'm not his keeper.'

I said nothing.

A few seconds later Olivier joined us. He smiled down at me gently. 'You look beautiful today,' he said, touching the soft silk of my sari. I smiled up at him gratefully.

'Shall I take you to see Maeve?' he asked gently.

I warmed towards him. He really was kind. 'Yes, please.'

He took me through a side door into the church, and along a corridor to a little courtyard filled with sculptures and rose bushes. We
crossed it and entered another corridor. He stopped and pointed to
the wooden door at the end. 'She is in there. I'll see you in the church.
Come sit with us.'

I timidly pushed the door open. Maeve was there in the midst of
what looked like a tiny greenroom. There were various people around,
but they all seemed to be involved in fixing the clothes of the brides-
maids. Maeve was alone, sitting before the mirror, putting the final
touches to her make-up.

I went up to her. 'Maeve, you look lovely,' I said by way of a greeting.

'So do you, my dear,' she smiled into the mirror. 'And Bruno? Is he
outside?'

'No,' I felt tempted to lie but didn't. 'He had to go into the country
at the last moment.'

She frowned slightly. Then she swung around to face me, catching
hold of my hands. 'Listen, Leela,' she whispered urgently. 'I want you
to be happy. But you can't wait for happiness, you have to go out and
grab it. You've waited long enough for Bruno. Find someone else now.'

For a moment I stared at her. Then tears came into my eyes. 'Oh,
Maeve,' I cried, 'what can I do?'

Suddenly a door banged and she seemed to recollect herself. She
turned back to the mirror to finish her make-up. 'There are going to
be lots of men here today,' she said casually.

Maeve was right. The church was filled with men. They all looked
similar—thin, hair shoulder-length in a ponytail, or cut very short,
with little round spectacles on long beaky noses. They all had big feet
encased in expensive patent leather shoes with inch-high heels. Would
one of them be ready to take Bruno's place, I wondered wildly. But
what did I have to give? I didn't even have a room of my own. Sitting
in the church with its huge arched ceiling and the music of marriage
all around, I felt miserable. The sari felt heavy and cumbersome, suf-

focating me. Suddenly I hated it for concealing so much. Who would look at me now? I shifted restlessly in my seat, wishing I had not worn it.

'Are you all right?' Olivier whispered.

I looked at him blankly. 'Yes, yes. I'm fine.' He sat beside me, and next to him was Annelise. She was filing her nails loudly, oblivious to everyone around her. We were in the second row, right behind the family pews. The nail file made a sound like sand rubbing on glass. But nobody paid the slightest heed to it. Olivier saw me staring and whispered into my ear, 'She does it at every wedding. Everyone's used to it.'

'Oh,' I mouthed back, smiling up at him. Would he help me if I told him the truth, I wondered. Or would his face melt into indecision as it so often did? It was difficult to say with him, his face gave away so little of what he really thought or felt.

I turned to look at Maeve, who had just come into the church on the arm of her father, a small nondescript man with wisps of grey hair. She walked up to the dais where the priest and Pedro waited. They knelt. Then the priest was blessing them, saying something in archaic French that I couldn't follow. A woman began to sing. It was a beautiful song, "Ave Maria." I decided to ask Olivier about it later. I surrendered myself to the music. The single voice wrapped itself around my heart. All at once, I felt terribly alone.

Olivier leaned down and whispered in my ear, 'Look who's just come in through the side door and is staring at you.'

'Don't tell me, I can guess,' I replied, refusing to turn my head. It had to be Bruno, I thought grimly. He must have found a way to slip the marital noose one last time and come running back to Paris to keep an eye on his mistress.

Olivier nudged me again. 'Look, it's Philippe Lavalle,' he hissed. Slowly I turned my head. And there he was, the sandwich man. He looked away as my eyes met his. A small current seemed to surge through the crowd, as heads turned to look at him. He remained standing in the doorway throughout the ceremony. 'What is he doing here?' I asked Olivier. But before he could reply, Annelise hissed, 'Don't you know, he's opening a Bon Marché in Buenos Aires. And Pablo's parents are his partners there.'

After the ceremony, we all trooped back into the sunshine to congratulate the newlywed couple and 'for the photos', Olivier whispered as he hustled me into line beside Annelise. At last we were all arranged in three neat rows on either side of the church entrance. Then the bride and bridegroom emerged. Everybody began clapping and throwing handfuls of rice at them. Finally the photographs began. Pablo insisted on wearing his Leicas, three of them, all squat and boxy looking, around his neck. He looked stupid, I thought. A *poseur!* They were all the same, I thought scornfully, my eyes slipping over the rows of almost identical faces. How could Maeve be happy with a man who looked as if he was pulled off a shelf of others just like him? I looked around for the sandwich man. But he had disappeared.

The wedded couple were flagged off with more rice showers and the guests began to disperse.

'Wonder where le Bon Marché disappeared to after the wedding. D'you think he'll come to the dinner?' Annelise asked as we stood on the steps in the sunshine.

'Well, he is doing the catering, you know,' I said. It was a silly remark, I realized. But it was too late, the words were out.

Annelise, unable to resist an opportunity to be sharp, pounced. 'My dear, try to use your brain sometimes—his company caters for every single party that takes place in this town.'

Olivier, the peacemaker, cut in hurriedly, 'He must have finished with her, that's why he came alone.'

'Finished with whom?' I asked.

'But, do you mean to tell me you didn't know? Catherine Baleine of course,' Annelise said, enjoying my surprise.

'I knew he was trying to tempt her into working with him—to set up his international food section,' I said weakly.

They hooted with laughter, 'Is that what she told him?'

'The hoodwinking husband gets hoodwinked—wait till I tell the others this,' Annelise said, wiping her eyes. '*Ils vont mourir de rire.*'

'You are both hateful,' I spat, and ran into the church. Inside, the fragrance of lilies still lingered. I grew calm, and began regretting my outburst. Someone tapped me on the shoulder. 'Mademoiselle,' a small grey man was at my elbow, 'I have something for you.' He handed me a little card. 'Have dinner with me tonight,' it said, and below that, 'Philippe Lavalle.'

'There is a car waiting for you outside if you will agree to follow me,' the man said. I clenched the card in my hand and followed him.

The car took me back into the city by the porte de la Muette and in no time I found myself standing on the pavement before a cold grey building on rue de la Pompe beside the Trocadéro. It was the kind of building that the area abounded in—with women, gargoyles and fruit carved out of the façade with the name of the architect on a little plaque in the middle. I stared through the black *fleur de lys* grill at a little foyer of marble and gilt with lots of mirrors. I pressed the buttons and shouted my name into the speakerphone. The red eye on the panel of numbers went on, and a voice said, *'Entrez et montez au troisième, s'il vous plaît.'*

There was a small wooden elevator at the end of the hall, but as usual I took the stairs. When I arrived, a servant took my coat and bade me sit down in a chair in the foyer. Monsieur Lavalle was not yet available but he would join me presently.

I was left alone to absorb the splendour of the hall with its gold-and-blue Aubusson carpets, yellow silk curtains, and a tapestry showing the gifts of the Magi to the baby Christ. The decor surprised me. I would have thought Philippe Lavalle to be a lover of everything modern, but the salon onto which the hall opened was crammed with antiques.

I had almost fallen asleep on my chair when he appeared. 'So you've come, have you?' he said without excusing himself for keeping me waiting.

He stood before me, full of impatient energy. I looked up at him towering over me and was made speechless by my body's instinctive response to him.

'Yes, I came some time ago,' I replied.

'I'm sorry to have kept you waiting,' he said perfunctorily, taking possession of my hands to pull me up. He put his hand under my chin and tilted my face up. I let him, feeling like a puppet in his hands.

He stared at me, as if he was seeing me for the first time. 'I had forgotten what you looked like, even though I have often thought about you—especially when I eat sandwiches.'

'I didn't know then what an honour I was receiving, or I would have thanked you more effusively,' I said demurely.

He laughed. 'I like your spirit, *ma belle*. You are wasted on the likes of Bruno Baleine.'

I felt my knees go weak. 'Of what concern is that to you?'

'Because I want you and I'm a busy man who doesn't like to waste his time,' he replied. We walked into the salon.

'This is a bit sudden,' I said lamely. 'You still have to seduce me, you know.'

'Oh really? You like playing those kinds of games?'

'I . . . I d-don't know. I just thought . . .'

'Well, I don't,' he cut me off. 'Just tell me what it is you want from me and I'll decide if the price is right.' He began to pace up and down the room.

I shut my eyes and tried to think. Then I heard his footsteps approaching.

'Since you can't decide what you want, what do you want to become?' he asked.

'Does it matter what I want to become when fate will be the one to decide in the end?'

'Aha! Fate,' he shouted with laughter.

'I don't see what is so funny,' I said coldly. 'How can you believe that you control your life when . . . when tomorrow you might be killed in a car accident or by . . .' I choked slightly, 'a bomb?'

He stood before me, leaning over me as I sat on the sofa. 'There lies the difference between your culture and mine,' he said, his voice low and triumphant. 'You believe in fate and end up enslaved. We believe in individual will, and so we are the masters of the world.'

'The Greeks believed in fate, too. And they were masters of the world in their time.'

'Who cares what happened thousands of years ago? Forget about fate. It doesn't exist.'

I remained silent for a moment. The man was a fool. To forget fate was to lose the past. How could anyone want to do that? But as I stared at the opulence all around and thought about everything that was Philippe Lavalle, I began to change my mind.

I raised my head and looked him in the eye. 'In that case, I want to be famous.'

'And how do you think you will achieve that?'

'I don't know,' I replied seriously. 'Perhaps you can teach me?'

He threw back his head and laughed. 'Teach you?'

'Yes,' I said simply. 'If anyone can, it's you.'

At last he came and sat down next to me on the sofa. I reached out and caught his hand. 'And if you were in my place, how would you go about becoming famous?'

His eyes began to glow. 'How does a woman go about becoming famous?' he growled, the words coming from deep inside his throat.

He lunged at me, pushing me into the cushions. One hand closed like a pincer over my breast. 'She joins herself to a famous man.' As his mouth closed over mine, I was swamped by the smell of him, sweet and meaty and buttery like *saucisson*.

PART *three*

one

~P hilippe's body smell was strong and unambiguous. It enveloped him like an armour, so that from the very first moment that he pulled me to him, I felt at ease. The sari came off with one impatient tug of his hand. The heavy silk coiled itself like a snake around my feet and I stood before him in my blouse and underwear, a twisted black cord that I used instead of a petticoat still around my waist. My underwear was a cheap cotton thing that my aunt had purchased. I quickly slipped it off, feeling ashamed. His eyes flickered slightly as I moved, and came back quickly to rest on my face. Fumbling a little under his scrutiny I began to undo the buttons of my blouse. At last he moved and pulled the blouse off my shoulders, his eyes feasting on my breasts. I put my hands on his shoulders. Tension held me rigid, coiled tight and waiting. His eyes came back to my face and he gave me a twisted smile. I did not smile back. My eyes remained locked into his. His hands fell to my hips and tightened painfully. Then without a word, he lifted me and carried me to the bedroom. As we passed the gilt-edged mirror in the hallway, I let my head fall back so that I was looking at an upside-down world. I smiled.

From the door, the room seemed endless. Other than a large four-poster bed made of some dark wood, it was utterly bare. A fluffy white carpet swooped up to meet a whole wall of windows, stretching from floor to ceiling. The curtains were pulled back. I could see a huge expanse of cloudy grey sky. He placed me on the floor before the windows.

Naked, Philippe's body looked even larger than it did clothed. The muscles in his chest and arms came to life as he swooped down on top of me. His mouth found mine and his tongue thrust its way inside. I kissed him back hungrily, feeling the air slowly leave my body. I tried to pull away and get some air. But he wouldn't let me. Strengthened by panic and the sense of impending suffocation, I clawed at his face, fighting him for air. He laughed and moved his face out of harm's way.

His weight lifted off my chest. The world came slowly back into focus. I drew a long breath, and felt myself relax as the oxygen was carried to the further recesses of my body. An immense languor filled me. I shut my eyes. I became aware of his hands stroking my waist, my hips and then my thighs, pushing them apart gently, tracing the crease of my groin. My knees fell open and I arched my back in readiness. The air felt cold. I grew hungry for the warmth of his body and strained upwards, offering my breasts, my neck, my mouth. But felt no answering weight descend upon me. My eyes flew open. I stared at Philippe anxiously. His face was twisted and red, his eyes far away. His flesh trembled and sweat clung to his skin. He seemed lost in a world of desire completely of his own making. My desire was replaced by a bitter sense of disillusionment. Philippe's face became that of a stranger. With both hands I reached up and tried to hit him as hard as I could. Suddenly he grunted and, with a single powerful motion, thrust himself deep inside me.

The pain ripped through me. My muscles went rigid with shock. He didn't seem to notice. He kept pounding away, oblivious to my pain. I stared helplessly at his chest, watching the muscles of his arms and neck clench and unclench. Then I began to feel the rhythm he was beating relentlessly into my body.

I had a sudden vision of my aunt, the flesh on her arms quivering as she ground the chilies and the garlic into paste. Only this time, it was my body that lay in that mortar. My body absorbed each thrust of his and the impact sent tremors of delight through me. Pain and pleasure spread through my flesh in ripples, merging at the edges so I was no longer conscious of which was which. I was caught in the relentless force that powered Philippe's movements, a force greater than both of us, a force that pushed him into me again and again, even as his body burned and melted. I was the cause of that power, I realized suddenly. Mine was the body that was forcing him into me again and again. My hips rose strongly to meet each of his movements. His body ground into me relentlessly, pounding my flesh till I felt I would melt. He thrust into me, faster and faster. The sense of being annihilated brought me to a shuddering climax seconds after him.

Afterwards we lay side by side with the white carpet reflecting milky light on the walls.

His hand found my face. His fingers traced its contours. I grabbed his hand and pressed his palm against my cheek. His fingers twitched and then became still. Still holding his hand, I turned slightly and stared across at his profile. It seemed happy. I ran a fingertip gently across the ridge of his forehead, along the bridge of his nose, down into the softness of his lips. I touched the little hollow in his neck and let my finger slide down diagonally to the flesh of his stomach.

'I . . . it . . .' I began.

He grabbed my hand before it could go any further and put his fingers to my mouth. 'Shhh,' he said. 'Don't speak.'

'But I want . . .'

'Shut up. You'll spoil it.' He turned away. I stared miserably at his enormous back, wondering what I had done wrong. I heard him fumbling amongst his clothes.

'I only wanted to thank you,' I muttered sulkily.

He didn't respond. I heard the click of a lighter being flicked open and saw the yellow-green flame.

Then he flipped onto his back again and puffed away at his cigarette, ignoring me.

Suddenly he said, 'Shall we eat?'

He was getting rid of me, I could see that. 'I shall think you very rude if you do not feed me after having whisked me away from the wedding feast,' I said bitterly.

He laughed dryly. 'Ah yes, indeed. You would otherwise feel cheated having given up so much in return for so little, no?'

'I can't sell myself too cheap, you understand,' I said sarcastically.

'But you just did,' he replied. 'You should have made sure of the meal first before you gave me what I wanted. My chef is the best in the world, he was trained by my mother.'

'My aunt is the best cook in the world,' I said, wanting to pierce his horrible arrogance.

'Oh really, so you have talent in your family?' he sneered.

'You're not the only one, you know.'

'Oh I don't have any such pretensions. I know I have no talent. But what about you? Coming from such a talented family, what can you do?'

'Take me to your kitchen and I'll show you,' I replied, stung to the bone.

'All right.' He sounded surprised. 'I'm hungry enough to eat anything. But don't give me something that will burn my mouth and then tell me that you Indians invented haute cuisine.'

I cooked all evening, fusing what I had learnt at the Baleines' with what my aunt had taught me. I used olives, roasted red peppers, and pine nuts in the chicken curry. As I worked, other ideas came to me. What if I organized the food differently, laying it out on each individual plate like the displays I saw in the windows of the *traiteurs*, matching the colours on the plate so that it looked beautiful to the eye? So I coloured some of the rice with saffron, leaving the rest plain. I cooked magenta turnip greens with spinach and tossed them with a creamy sauce of almonds and fresh goats' cheese, slightly sweetened with honey. The chicken had the dark earthy flavour of the olives and a lovely terracotta colour. I cooked the grated carrots lightly with lemon, olive oil, ginger, and mustard seeds. And finally, as the night came, I cut up raw papaya and oranges and white radish and garnished them with olive oil, lemon, honey, and coriander.

When I finally placed the plate with its fragrant contents before Philippe, he could not believe his eyes. 'This . . . this doesn't look like Indian food,' he said suspiciously. 'Where did you learn this?'

'I made it up.'

'You're lying. Nobody could make up something like this. Who are you? What cooking school did you go to?'

'I told you. I learnt to cook at my aunt's. Why don't you taste the food and see?'

When he finished, he was silent for a long time. 'This is unlike anything I have ever tasted before,' he said finally, very quietly. 'How did you do it?'

I felt unbearably proud. 'It is as if the smells themselves talk to me,' I confided. 'They tell me how they feel, and whisper to me what I must do to make them comfortable, to permit them to live out their lives in the way they have to, and how to help them die, so that they may give off the best perfume while doing so.'

'How extraordinary,' he said, somewhat sceptically. 'You talk as though it was they who taught you to cook.'

'No. Not in the beginning. My aunt did. And she learnt from her mother and grandmother.'

He groaned in mock-anguish. 'Oh, you Indians, so trapped in tradition. Why can't you be different?'

'But I am different,' I replied.

And it was true. I was different. Because tradition said mothers didn't remarry or sacrifice their daughters to an uncertain fate. Tradition had betrayed me. That's why I had been forced to change, to reinvent myself. That's how I had become different.

But Philippe didn't think so. 'You're not that different from the rest of your people. Compared to the differences that exist between any two occidentals, all of you seem very much the same.'

I said nothing. How could I measure how different I had become? Who could I measure myself against? All those who had known the way I was were no longer a part of my life. I suddenly felt very alone. Like the Brahmin dwarf in my grandmother's stories, I had changed worlds too many times, ruthlessly cutting the bonds of the old world to enter the new.

Philippe grew tired of my silence. 'So how are you different then? Tell me.'

'Because . . . because I don't want memories. I want to be free of the past.' The answer burst out of me violently.

He was intrigued, sensing a secret. 'Why is that?'

I felt trapped. Not knowing what kind of answer would satisfy him, I improvised. 'Memories, my mother always said, are seeds that sprout into huge trees overnight, blocking your view of the future.'

His face took on an intentness that worried me. 'I have never heard of that one before, but I like it.' He laughed. 'At last a piece of super-stition that makes sense! Now I know why I had to have you.'

I laughed with him, reassured.

IT WAS UNBEARABLY bright when I woke up the next morning. A clear sky, dusted with haze, had turned the vast picture window into a river of light. I groaned. The light danced before my eyes, giving shape to the pain that suffused my body. I felt exhausted and sore all over. But I was happy. I had survived Philippe's onslaughts. It seemed he could not get enough of me. Time and again, just as I was falling into the most beautiful of sleeps, he awoke me with his caresses, his hunger infecting me quickly. I looked at my body, half expecting to see that bits of it had disappeared. But it was all there, glowing hotly in the amber sunlight.

I looked at the pillow next to me. Philippe was not in the bed.

'Philippe,' I cried, feeling suddenly lost.

He came into the room, fully dressed, in a grey suit.

'I'm going to the Bon Marché,' he announced.

'Oh,' I said disinterestedly. I turned around to go back to sleep. He grabbed my shoulder and shook me. 'And I'm taking you with me. So get ready, you have five minutes.'

I sat up quickly and reached for my clothes. But I couldn't find them. With a groan, I remembered that all I had was my mother's sari. It was on the bed, entangled in the sheets. From our first hours, it had exercised a strange fascination on Philippe. And he had made me tie it and retie it repeatedly, and then folded the silken lengths around me in new and unimagined ways. But in the daylight flooding the room, the sari looked crumpled and tawdry.

'But . . . but I can't go out in this,' I said to him, pushing away the creased folds.

'I don't care. You're coming with me,' he said, looking pointedly at his watch.

My fingers were trembling as I tried to put it on. He watched me impatiently. He seemed distant now. I felt ashamed and that made me clumsier still.

'Hurry up,' he snapped.

'I can't. This is too crumpled and it's hard to tie it,' I replied irritably.

'Damn,' he swore, 'why don't you wear something else?'

'I don't have anything else,' I snapped back.

Finally, I was ready. The sari still looked crumpled and I had no make-up. I pulled his comb through my hair and tied it up. I looked dreadful.

In the car, he sat far away from me and gazed abstractedly out of the window. It was a beautiful autumn day. The sun was shining softly, turning the white of the buildings to cream. The sky was a deep clear blue. A cold wind whirled the leaves and dust around. As we drove around the Invalides, I caught him staring at me, frowning.

'I can't help being here you know,' I said, 'but if you tell the chauffeur to stop, I can get out now.'

He stopped frowning then and reached across to pull me to his side, his right hand absently cupping my breast. I felt my body respond in spite of itself. My hand reached up and covered his. He pulled me closer still and rested his chin upon my head. 'I don't know why I'm taking you to the Bon Marché. I've never taken anyone there before,' he said into my hair. 'But I'm going to give you a guided tour.'

two

P hilippe's father, a Sicilian by birth, came to France when he was twenty-two and by the time that he was thirty he had a small business making custom-made bathrooms for the villa owners of Provence. He also supplied cheaper readymade versions to the big supermarkets in France. But his biggest brainstorm, the one that made him his first million, was the signature bathtub—a bathtub with the signature of a famous film-star or writer engraved into it.

After that there was no turning back for Signor Lavare. He changed his name to Lavalle to sound more French, bought a villa in St Paul de Vence, in Provence, and took the first vacation of his life—a *tour gastronomique* of France and Switzerland.

In the little town of Annemasse, he stopped to sample *cailles au raisin* in a mysterious little restaurant, called Le Vigneron, on the mountaintop. No sooner did M Lavalle taste it than he fell in love—a strange love, more like an obsession, that made him hunger for a sight of the man who made the food as much as he hungered for the food itself. He stayed on in Annemasse, cancelling the rest of his trip, ignoring the frantic letters of his manager—unable to tear himself away from the little hut on the mountaintop. During the day he roamed the streets or sat in the cafés, trying to glean a little information about the chef. In the evening, at six sharp, he would walk up the hill to the restaurant in his best clothes and eat his dinner in solitude at the table of his choice—right next to the kitchen door. Summer became autumn. The crowds in the restaurant thinned, and the waiters all knew his order by heart. And still he had not seen the chef. Every day, along with his payment, he sent in his card and on it he wrote, 'Please may I speak to you for one minute.' His request was never granted. At eleven o'clock, the restaurant closed, and the waiters gently shooed him out. Finally November came, and with it, the first snow announced its arrival with heavy clouds and a sudden drop in temperature. 'You'll have to leave now,' the lady at the pension where he was staying told him spitefully. 'Winter is coming and the restaurant will be closed.'

That night as M Lavalle climbed up the hill to the restaurant, little snowflakes began to fall. They melted against his cheeks and slid down the rough surface like tears. The restaurant was empty and the waiters unusually loud, calling to each other about their plans for the winter. Even the food that was put before him that night tasted different, slightly oversalted and smelling oddly enough of lavender. 'All dreams come to an end, Lavarro,' he admonished himself firmly, and tried unsuccessfully to think of bathtubs. Then he motioned to the waiter to bring him his bill. But the waiter came back and told him that it was on the house. 'Please thank the chef for me, but it is not necessary. You see, I am a rich man.' And he put a thousand-franc note on the table. He got up sadly, picked up his coat and hat and left. Outside the snow had stopped falling, and you could see the stars.

In the distance, a high sweet voice called his name. He stopped, surprised to hear a woman on that desolate hilltop. He turned around to see a slight figure silhouetted against the snow and the stars. 'I . . . b-believe you wanted to meet me?' she said, with a pronounced stammer. 'I'm sorry, ma'am, I'm afraid you must be mistaken. I don't know who you are, and while I'm delighted to make your acquaintance, I cannot in truth say that I had desired it.' Saying this, M Lavalle politely touched the brim of his hat in salute, and turned to walk away. 'But, M Lavalle, you sent m-m-me your card every n-n-night this past s-summer. Mireille was still unable to admit that she was the chef of Le Vigneron. M Lavalle went cold. Slowly he turned around. 'You are the chef?' he asked softly, hardly daring to believe his luck. Mireille nodded. In a flash, he had her in his arms. 'I will never let you go now,' he told her triumphantly.

Unfortunately their love was shortlived. She died a year later in childbirth, leaving behind a lusty eleven-pound son, Philippe.

Philippe grew up spoiled and alone. Both physically and temperamentally he resembled neither his father nor his mother. While they had been moderate, quiet people, Philippe was flamboyant, rude, and prone to excess in everything he did.

In time, it became clear that no matter how different, he was the true child of his parents. From his father, he inherited a tradesman's imagination—knowing instinctively how to best package something to make it sell. From his mother, he inherited a love of food and a passion for exactness—not just in the end product that was laid down before him at meals, but food in every shape and stage of preparation. Everything from the smell of the melon for the melanzane to the exact thickness or thinness of the proscuitto had to be just right. And so, armed with these two talents, Philippe set out to create the most exclusive chain of food supermarkets the world had ever known.

To begin with, everyone thought he was mad. 'Nobody will come to a shop to buy what can be had on a Sunday morning fresh from the farm,' his father told him. But Philippe was maddening when he wanted something, and so with great reluctance M Lavalle gave his son an old warehouse in the fourteenth *arrondissement*. It was a run-down neighbourhood of warehouses, there were no shops or smart restaurants. But Philippe loved the place with its high ceilings and the light that flooded in from the long twenty-foot windows placed high up near the ceiling. It reminded him of a church. So he hired architects to put in a few rounded arches to create the feeling of a nave, and columns that soared upwards around which cunning displays could be arranged.

He hired experts from the Ecole des Arts Decoratifs to create the interiors. He made them paint medieval banquets and seventeenth-century still lifes of food, fish and fowl—*trompe-l'oeils* all, which merged into the actual food displays.

He called his supermarket the Bon Maraîcher, the name evocative of an old-fashioned peasant farmer. But people soon abbreviated it to the Bon Marché. The nickname was considered a good joke by all of Paris—because there was nothing inexpensive about the store other than its name. Everything inside was expensive, from the coffee in the café to the frankfurters in the *boucherie*. But everything was the best in quality, the most perfect in shape, size, and smell. 'Paris, I give you perfection' was his best remembered quote in *Elle,* which ran a ten-page photo feature on the store.

When the place was finally ready, the night before the opening Philippe threw a party in the warehouse. He invited great chefs to cook, beautiful women to decorate the evening, and politicians and journalists to provide ceaseless conversation. And he invited two TV channels, TF1 and M6, to come and film it, and somehow, no one quite knew how, clips of the party were shown on the news that very night, and all the next day. By the time the mayor of Paris actually cut the ribbon and declared the store open, it had become a national event.

When we arrived, I was awed by the size of it. It looked more like a palace than a supermarket, from the beautifully carved balconies on the second floor, to the fruit and vines, symbols of success and fertility, that were carved onto the bases of columns. The place was teeming with activity, with people going in and out of the sliding glass doors constantly.

But Philippe didn't take me through the main entrance of the store. He led me around the left side of the building to the service street, to a steel door that seemed only waist high. Three steps led down to it. The door looked about as welcoming as the entrance to a prison. He fumbled with his keys and pushed it open. I pulled back.

'Are you so ashamed of me that you can't take me through the main entrance?' I demanded.

He looked puzzled for a second. 'Don't be silly. I want you to see this from the bottom up. The way I planned it.'

We entered and found ourselves in a freight elevator. Philippe pressed a button.

'We're going down!' I exclaimed stupidly.

'I had them dig under the building and under the road, too, for storage space,' he explained.

The elevator stopped and we stepped out into a long and featureless corridor. This floor is where I store my wine,' he announced proudly. 'We're so far underground that even the vibration of the cars on the road can't reach us. Wines don't like movement, you see.'

I shuddered. It was absolutely quiet. Suddenly the street seemed an infinitely desirable place to be.

He stopped and waited, his face alight with anticipation. Did he want me to kiss him? Or was he waiting for me to ask him a question? I stared at him helplessly. 'Do you know why I store my wine down here?' he asked finally, frowning slightly.

'I can't imagine. Tell me, please.'

'Like me, it dislikes the sun,' he said.

'But wine is made from grapes,' I protested. 'They need the sun to grow.'

'Who wants grapes—they perish so quickly,' he replied irritably. 'Come, the wine cellar is this way. Here the grapes last forever.'

He put an arm around my waist and led me through another long corridor, this one lined with bricks. It veered suddenly to the left, and broadened. The air felt cold but surprisingly dry. We descended a flight of steps to a stout wooden door. 'My kingdom begins,' he said mockingly. Despite the dryness of the air, there were little beads of perspiration on his forehead. He was nervous, I realized in amazement. He wanted my approval. I felt a surge of happiness.

He quickly punched the digits on a console set into the wall beside the door, and it swung open soundlessly.

I peered inside curiously. The wine cellar was actually a series of long rectangular rooms, lined with racks upon racks of bottles. They reminded me of shelves in a library. As we entered each chamber, a dim light would go on. In each room the light was of a different colour. The racks, too, were not the same.

'The racks are made of different materials—cedar, oak, eucalyptus wood, apple, cherry wood, a special plastic that has no smell, or artificially hardened mud,' he explained when he saw me staring at them. 'Different woods affect the bottles differently. Some woods are warm and keep those wines which are sensitive to the cold cocooned in warmth. Other wines are very sensitive to smells—they cannot be placed with other wines. Nor can they be placed on racks of wood—for all wood has a smell, you know. So for these I had special shelves designed from a very special type of plastic.' He looked meditatively at the wine. 'Wine in the bottle can live a very, very long time—a somewhat circumscribed life perhaps, but one that gains in value with each passing year, unlike us humans.'

I remained silent. I had never heard anyone talk like this before.

He turned back to me and laughed. 'Provided of course that it is kept in a controlled environment.'

'A controlled environment?'

'Yes.' His voice grew elastic. 'The lights are special-temperature lights which give out almost no heat. Wines don't like light or changes in temperature. Yet there are some wines which like a little cool blue moonlight to bring out their flavour. So that's why we have the blue lights. Other wines like complete darkness, so I had special lights designed that are like the lights used in darkrooms. Good wines have to be protected from all extremes—like babies,' he said sentimentally.

I stared at Philippe, amazed at the change that had come over him. In the darkness of the wine rooms, he seemed to have lost that uncontrollable energy that both scared and excited me. Even his voice was transformed, becoming warm with love and knowledge, and his language had lost much of its vulgarity.

'And dust?' I asked flippantly, as we entered the fourth room where the bottles were covered in dust. 'Do some wine bottles like a nice blanket of dust to keep them warm while others don't?'

He laughed. 'That's to tell the ordinary wine from the really good stuff. Most of what is sold upstairs is dressed-up trash—good but predictable. But it looks right, is packaged right, and sits surrounded by expensive things and the right kind of people. So people feel beautiful buying it. You know what people taste with?' he asked abruptly.

I opened my mouth but he answered the question himself. 'The eyes,' he said, tapping his temple, his eyes shining. 'No, don't argue with me. Wait till you have seen the rest of the store and then tell me if you still disagree.'

We walked into the far end of the cellars. Immediately a pale blue light came on. This room was colder than the others. The wine racks looked old and neglected, and the walls were of unpainted brick, dark with age. I shivered in my sari, and wrapped the loose end firmly around me. He looked at me, amused. 'I see you don't like this room. I keep my favourite wines here, the high altitude wines, made from grapes from the high Himalayas.'

'From the Himalayas?' I said wonderingly. 'I didn't know they had wine there.'

'Indeed they do. It is their best kept secret, one that, thankfully, even most Indians don't know about.'

'Then how did you . . . ?' I asked, resentful of his remark.

'I spent two years there in the mountains,' he replied.

'Two years!' I looked at Philippe with respect. He had been to the country of my ancestors after all, and he must have liked it to remain there for two years. I felt suddenly proud of my heritage. A million questions jostled for space on my tongue. 'Wh-what did you think?' I asked at last, somewhat incoherently.

Philippe walked over to the shelf and pulled out a fat ungainly bottle. 'These are real northern wines, full of an icy fire, brewed by local tribesmen,' he said, turning the bottle slowly in his hands. It was made of dark blue glass. 'They have a crisp sharp taste, like the clean blue air of the mountains. To keep the plants alive under the ice, the locals cover them with layers of tea leaves and cowdung, and some-times human dung too.'

'Oh no!' I exclaimed.

'Indeed, yes. The women take the shit in tin pails and spread it carefully over the vines with their hands. If you had been born there, you would have had to do it too.'

'Why only the women?'

'Because the men leave the women to do the dirty part, they only brew the stuff, sitting like priests in their little huts.'

'But that's unfair,' I cried.

'You're wrong. I believe that the unique taste of this wine, and its special musky aroma, comes from the women, from their work of burying the vines in shit nine months of the year.' His face began to glow. 'They were the most sensuous women I have known.'

I found myself wanting to taste the wine in those bottles, so that I could possess the sensuality of those women and make Philippe my slave. I must have made a sound, for he turned from his contemplation of the wine to look more fully at me. His eyes came to rest on my mouth, half-open and dry with desire. I took a step towards him. He didn't move, his eyes fixed intently on my face. I licked my lips, forcing them into motion. 'I'd like to try some of your wine, please.'

His teeth flashed white as he laughed loudly. It sounded ugly in the stillness of that blue room. 'This wine is no different in quality from what you saw in the first cellar.'

'What!' I exclaimed, feeling terribly betrayed. 'But . . . but that can't be, you couldn't have made that up.'

'I most certainly did,' he replied. 'There aren't any grapes that grow at high altitudes in the snow. Grapes need the sun to give them sweetness.'

'But . . . but the manure . . . I mean . . .' I said weakly.

He laughed again. 'In the cold, even human shit freezes over like everything else.' He took a step towards me and pulled my chin up so that I was looking into his face, my body pressed against his. 'But my story excited you, didn't it?'

I turned my eyes away. 'It did, didn't it? Admit it.' He grabbed my hair and pulled, forcing my head up higher. My eyes flew up to his face.

Reluctantly I whispered, 'Yes.'

'I knew it!' he released me suddenly. 'I wanted to know what kind of woman you were. Now I know.'

'That's not true. You don't know what excited me,' I said hotly. 'You told me a story, you don't know what it was inside your story, or even outside it, that stirred me. How do you know that it wasn't because of the blue light on your face, or the smell of the wine and the wood, or the cold? How do you know I wasn't pretending just to please you?'

He took an angry step towards me. Then, quick as lightning, his mood changed, his face became benign. 'My, my. Now you're entering

186 • R A D H I K A   J H A

the realm of philosophy, my dear. Philosophy is what losers use to pretend that losing doesn't matter. I don't care about exactly what turned you on, all I care for is the effect. I know that I made you want to possess something that doesn't exist, can't exist really, something that you even found disgusting to begin with. I have a gift for creating desire in a person—and therefore I can have anyone I want, man or woman. That is why I can do anything I want. Don't you forget that.'

He was on the move again, dragging me along with him. 'We have to leave, we can't waste any more time here. There is all the rest of the store to see.'

As we walked back through the cellars, he talked compulsively. 'To be rich, you have to understand dreams, and you have to be able to turn dreams into stories, and stories into things. Business is based on this equation, good businessmen understand this. My father, for ex-ample, sold bathtubs. It was a sensual thing for him. He loved to bathe. He'd fantasize about his favourite movie star in there, Sophia Loren, Gina Lollabrigida with the enormous tits, Marilyn Monroe. So he de-signed bathtubs with paintings of these women lying naked inside them. On this idea he created little variations, and became enormously wealthy on his fantasy. He wasn't the only one, others have done it too.'

He stopped abruptly and opened a door on the left-hand side of the faceless grey corridor. I peered inside. After the sterile orderliness of the halls, the mess in the room stung the eyes. Cartons of fruit and vegetables spilled their contents on the floor. Shopping carts with oddly shaped wine bottles were stacked on one side. Wrapping paper of a particularly ugly shade of lavender was strewn all over.

'This is the reject room,' Philippe explained. 'Every consignment of food that comes in is first checked for faults.' He picked up a kiwi fruit lying close to my feet.

'What's wrong with it?' I asked.

'Nothing,' he replied, 'except that this little fellow is one whole mil-limetre larger than the average kiwi, and is unfortunately hairier than its brothers.'

'That's crazy,' I said aghast. 'What a shocking waste!'

'No, it's not crazy,' he said, looking annoyed. 'People don't taste food before they buy it. They know the food with their eyes, not with their mouths. They see it on TV, in magazines, and finally in the supermarket. Long before they can taste it, their minds have already accepted the verdict of their eyes.'

I looked at him dumbly, unwilling to believe him but unable to dismiss his words. He touched my eyes. 'That's why a woman must always look good enough to eat.' My eyes slid away from his. But what about when I became old, or if I had an accident? I shivered.

Then once again Philippe was hustling me back down the corridor. He whisked me into the elevator again and pressed a button. The elevator moved suddenly and I was thrown against him. He laughed delightedly and pressed my body to his. 'Do you like my storehouse?' he asked, looking at me intently.

'Of course, as long as you don't store me there,' I replied.

The elevator came to a stop. He released me and gave me a little push. I stepped outside quickly. We were in another narrow, tube-lit hallway, at the end of which were stainless-steel double doors. I stared at him fearfully, scared he would leave me behind in these featureless subterranean rooms. He took my elbow. 'Don't be scared, this is the last of my underground kingdom.'

I opened the doors and found myself in a glass-encased viewing gallery overlooking a huge room—so vast that I could not see the end of it. The room was very bright. The walls were white, and fluorescent light filled the place in such a way that the room was devoid of shadows. It was incredibly clean and orderly. The only sound there was a low gentle humming. Wrapped in plastic sheets, huge carcasses of beef and mutton hung from gleaming iron hooks in the ceiling.

'My God.' I had never seen so much meat.

'Enough to feed all of France for a day,' Philippe boasted. I began to feel sick, but could not tear my eyes away from the neat rows of headless animals.

He opened a door at the end of the gallery. I did not want to be left alone there and quickly followed him. We walked between rows and rows of gleaming steel racks hung with meat. At the back of the room,

three people—I could not tell whether they were men or women because they were completely encased in white like doctors in an oper-
ating room—were bending over a conveyor belt, huge steel measuring
rods in their hands. On the belt lay more carcasses. The three measured
them and nodded at one another and then pressed a button beside
them. An iron hook descended and they fastened the meat onto it.
Then another lever was pushed and the carcass rose into the air and
was deposited next to the others on the racks.

'Why is there no blood?' I asked Philippe impulsively,' and no
smell?'

'Because they are already freeze-dried by passing liquid nitrogen at
extremely high pressure over them.'

'And that takes away the smell of the meat?' I asked in wonder.

'Of course. And it stays perfectly fresh,' he replied proudly. 'Then
they are cut with laser knives, the kind that jewellers use. I had them
specially adapted for my purposes. It is the most brilliant of all my
ideas.'

We walked back. I took my time now, staring at each one of the
frozen headless bodies. Each animal was beautifully shaped, from the
curve of its shoulder to the smooth roundness of its belly and thighs.
I could almost feel the firm tight young flesh beneath my hands. I
shivered, this time because I was aroused. I leaned into Philippe, feeling the warmth of his body percolate through the silk. 'How did you
find such perfect animals?' I asked. 'They are all the same size, and the
same shape.'

He smiled at me. 'You notice everything, don't you? I'm glad I found
you.' He kissed my lips lingeringly. 'My man Alberto searches out the
best meats for me. I send him as far as Australia and Argentina for it.
We only accept the best-proportioned animals. Those that aren't the
right weight or lack the proper curvature of thigh, we reject.'

'But surely their meat is the same?' I asked.

He shrugged. 'Perhaps. But if they don't have the right look, they
are useless. We train our customers to recognize the "right" look. The
Bon Marché proportions are a seal of quality. People believe that.'

'Well, thank God, you don't sell the right human proportions too,'

I said tartly, and walked quickly ahead of him into the safety of the corridor.

I heard him laugh. 'You don't have to worry, your proportions are perfect.'

I felt chilled.

We went back to the elevator. My spirits rose as it gained height. When the doors opened, it was as if we were returning to life.

Huge glass windows, twenty feet tall, made a dazzling curtain of light against which the tropical forest of indoor plants seemed all the more lush. Parrots, cockatoos, and tiny jewel-like birds that I didn't recognize, fluttered around the miniature banana trees, their screeching conversations disrupting the steady chuckle of running water. A waterfall poured into a rock pond filled with scarlet and white lotuses. It was warm inside, and the air was heavy with a complex cocktail of the smells of exotic fruits and flowers. Hanging from the trees and from driftwood stands were baskets of colourful fruit. Tiny yellow bananas fanned out around a bottle-green pineapple, and huge orange mangoes from south India sat beside passionfruit from East Africa, mangosteens from Indonesia, and tiny mandarin oranges from China. There were bougainvillea bushes, a riot of crimson, magenta, and white, amidst which were little white wrought-iron tables bearing hors d'oeuvres or candied tropical fruit and marzipan.

It wasn't just the elegance of the decor but the sheer mountains of food that was overwhelming. From the sound of the water and the birds to the rich colours of the foods, the place radiated harmony.

Every detail was meticulously planned—next to the black cherries, for example, were quaint straw baskets laid out for the customers to use. I watched a darkly elegant woman begin to load a basket with fruit. She was very tall and her back, which was all I could see now, was broad, almost manly. Her red satin trousers hugged her muscular hips. I wished I could wear clothes like hers. In my sari with its lack of any definite shape, I felt frumpy. The woman moved over to the melons. Her long fingers prodded each one systematically. Finally, she chose a large green oval one. Suddenly she turned and saw me staring. She waved, '*Salut*, Philippe.'

I turned to look at him. 'Isn't she someone famous?' I asked naïvely. 'I feel as if I should know who she is.'

'Of course, the whole world knows her. She's Elizabeth Bouchon.'

I realized how little I knew of the world he was pulling me into. 'Do . . . does she come here often?' I asked hesitantly.

'Certainly, when she isn't making a film about some tribe in Zanzibar,' he replied, his eyes narrowing. Then his face cleared, 'I've often thought of using her in an ad. You know, with a sentence underneath the picture "when she isn't eating worms with the tribe of Shalli Wak, she's at the Bon Marché".'

I laughed dutifully, trying to memorize her name.

'What do you think?' Philippe asked, turning me to face him and looking deeply into my eyes. 'It's like a dream,' I whispered to him. 'I could never have imagined such a place, so exquisite, so perfectly calculated to delight.'

He smiled and squeezed my hand possessively. 'Nobody today could even have dreamed of such a thing. But I did. And only I could make it real.'

I looked at him with new eyes. He seemed so different from the overbearing man I knew. 'It's not just a dream, it's a fantasy come true,' I said.

'This is much more than a fantasy. For people who shop here, it is an obsession. They need to come here every day. They don't trust the food in other places, it doesn't satisfy the craving inside them, it isn't beautiful enough.'

We walked on and were surrounded by vegetables arranged like a fireworks display. Purple-blue brinjals surged out of the bright yellow and red of bell peppers. Green and yellow zucchini surrounded red tomatoes and magenta beetroots. Each vegetable was of the same shade, without blemishes, its skin moist and shining from overhead sprinklers that sprayed it with minuscule droplets of water. Behind the towering displays were more palm trees and bougainvillea bushes, and the birds called to one another. The sunlight poured in and reflected off the cunningly hidden mirrors.

Philippe continued, 'At first it was easy to make people buy—all you had to do was play on their imagination. But buying eats into the imagination. Attaching a fantasy to a thing creates desire only so long as it is not possessed. After that, it can no longer trouble the sleep.'

My head began to spin. I felt as though I were walking on a cloud.

'People can't dream for themselves anymore. They are so used to having their dreams converted for them into things they can buy that the things they want to buy have filled their minds, and replaced their imagination. And with less and less imagination at their disposal, they can no longer summon up the desire to possess new things. Buying doesn't satisfy them anymore, and they consume less all the time. It doesn't take away the boredom caused by the death of their imaginations. They feel empty without their dreams, they cannot imagine the future anymore, not even one filled with things to buy and to possess. They can only see time—they become obsessed with the hours, the minutes, the seconds of life passing by. They become preoccupied with death. It's all they have to think about. It is a hysteria that builds, because their future is so empty.'

He stopped and looked at me. I was still lost in what he was saying, the words pounding on my brain. He turned and waved to a short grey-haired man dressed in a strangely cut silver suit, his wet red mouth pursed in a kind of permanent pout. 'Simon, *mon cher ami*,' he said loudly, suddenly jovial, completely transformed from the person of a few moments before. Turning to me, he whispered, 'Stay here. I'll be back in a second,' and walked quickly forward. He and Simon talked intimately, their bodies close together. They look like they were old friends, I thought enviously. Finally they parted. Philippe came back towards me. 'A good man, Simon. He is the chef of La Pirogue.' My eyes widened. La Pirogue was the oldest and best known of the *nouvelle cuisine* restaurants.

'Simon was one of the first people to realize how the world had changed. He understood that people today will only buy two types of things, the bare necessities and the obsessions. So he invented nouvelle cuisine, a cuisine which set out to seduce all the senses and was so difficult to make that no one else could understand how to do it. It was very popular for a while but it never became an obsession. Can you guess why?'

I shook my head, knowing that was what he wanted. 'No, why?'

'What he didn't completely comprehend is that for something to become a lasting obsession, it has to challenge time. His food simply took too much time to prepare.'

'Time?' I asked, feeling lost.

'Yes, time, because it reminds us that we are dying.'

'And what could make a person forget time?' I asked. 'Sex?'

He shook his head. 'No, even sex is not good enough to sell things these days. It has been sadly overused by advertisers. They eat into images like locusts. But the answer to your question—he waved his hands like a magician—'the answer is all around you: food. Humans cannot do without food. And it can be had much more easily than sex, it can be consumed alone or with company. Food can be had in place of sex, or before it or after it or as an accompaniment to sex. If one gets bored with sex, one can live without it. If one gets bored with food, one still has to eat.'

'But food is a necessity. Therefore it is ordinary, boring even. How can that become an obsession?'

He seemed delighted by my incomprehension. 'Because one day I realized that if buying satisfies a craving of the imagination, then why shouldn't a craving of the body satisfy the craving of the imagination? And that is why I could create this great store.'

'I . . . I still don't understand.'

'Food,' he explained, uncharacteristically patient, 'because it has to be eaten again and again, day after day, conquers time, making it circular. And thanks to science, we believe that perfect food, like the elixir of life, conquers death. And I make people believe that perfect food is Bon Marché food.'

'But who . . . I mean, how did you learn all this?' I asked.

He looked at me for a second. 'It was simple. All the ingredients for the obsession were there already. My genius lay in putting them all together.' He flung out his arms, 'I have opened a new unending realm for the selling machine to conquer. But that is not all. I provide satisfaction too—endless amounts of it, and *soulagement* of the fear of dying. I have given people satisfaction that can be constantly remade and re-created every day. Suddenly they don't have to worry about what to want, to desire, and to dream about. All at once, life is no longer boring. What I sell isn't food, it is life. And I get richer and richer with every meal that is eaten.'

I stared at him, trying to digest what he had just told me. It seemed fantastic. But the evidence was all around me. Everywhere I looked there were beautiful and exquisitely dressed people, moving through the wares with the same concentrated serious expression. Suddenly I felt scared. How could I possibly satisfy a man as brilliant as Philippe?

I became aware that I was in the middle of a spice bazaar. I burst into slightly hysterical laughter at the familiar sight of chilies of all colours, sizes, and shapes hanging in huge clusters from the awnings of wooden carts. Cinnamon, cardamom; pepper in shades of red, yellow, and orange; turmeric, coriander, ginger, and garlic were all heaped onto multicoloured wheelbarrows. Between the barrows sat life-sized dolls in brightly coloured costumes from the countries where the spices came from, and stacks of earthenware pots and strangely shaped spoons and dishes in brass and copper. I thought of the dingy back room in my uncle's grocery store. I shut my eyes and inhaled deeply, wanting to absorb the different flavours of the beautiful spices. I could smell nothing but a faint dusty aroma. Then, hesitantly, the smell of the spices came to me. But they were meek and frightened, not the powerful self-confident scents that had demolished the smell of French bread so efficiently in my uncle's shop. Here the buttery smells from the nearby bakery section were far more overpowering. I shook my head, frowning.

'What's the matter?' Philippe asked, staring anxiously at my face. 'What's wrong?'

'They have no smell. Or very little smell,' I amended, not wanting to hurt his feelings.

His face cleared. 'So what?' he said, taking my arm. 'They look good, don't they? No one in all Europe has ever managed to sell spices to the French, except me.'

'But they have to have a smell. How do you cook if they don't smell? How can you tell if it's good?'

'You don't need to smell to taste. What difference does it make, as long as they taste correct?'

I began to laugh. He looked grumpy, exactly like a little boy who had been told that there was something he couldn't have. 'These have no smell. You cannot cook properly if you cannot smell the spices. You cannot taste either, for taste begins in the nose.'

'In that case, my dear, I should hate food because I cannot smell very well. I never have been able to, since I was a child, but I know my food. Forget your silly theories, they only show your ignorance.'

I had hurt him, I realized. Suddenly I saw him as he was in the flesh: a heavy, middle-aged man with his eyes planted too close together and his face running to fat. I felt a surge of pity. As I watched his face, the anger went out of it and was replaced by desire. 'You look lovely when you're angry,' he said softly.

I became aware of the hot sausage-sweet smell of him. It reached out to grab me. I began to back away, but the smell was faster, it encircled me. I turned and walked blindly through the aisles, by golden bags of coffee beans and crystal jars of honey in every shade from rusty red to straw gold. I ducked behind a wall of Parmesan cheese, and found myself in an enclosed semi-circular space surrounded by an aquarium filled with fish of the most dazzling colours, dipping and weaving incessantly between crimson corals. The effect was of a moving wall of colour. Hanging from the ceiling from hooks were the skeletons of two huge fish, encrusted with barnacles and seaweed. I paused to catch my breath.

Suddenly a beautiful man was at my elbow. In my old school in Nairobi, they would read us stories from the Bible at Monday assemblies. This man was exactly as I had imagined Jesus must have looked, with almond-shaped eyes the colour of wild honey. I stared at him, bereft of speech. He smiled understandingly, and touched my hair. 'Is everything okay? Can I help you?'

I raised my hand self-consciously to my hair. 'I'm all right now. Thanks.' I searched my mind for something more to say. 'The . . . these are v-v-very beautiful fish you have here.' I could feel myself blushing. He looked at me and gave me a slow intimate smile. 'They are, aren't they?' he said.

He walked me over to the counter and pointed to one end. He was standing so close I could smell the heavy salt odour of fish and blood on his apron. 'That's my favourite. It's a clawed shark, comes from the Baltic sea. Very rare, delicious meat. See the five claws on the edge of its fin?'

I leaned over the counter. He bent over me, bringing his body in direct contact with mine. We stood like that for a second. 'It makes a wonderful steak, madame,' he cooed into my ear. I heard footsteps approaching and quickly the man moved away. I straightened up and turned around. It was Philippe.

'Enjoying our special customer service?' he asked coming up to me and putting an arm around my waist.

'What . . . what do you mean?' I asked guiltily.

'Michel is very good at selling, especially to women. He is not afraid of human contact, you see. So they keep coming back.' He winked at the man.

A woman walked in. She was in her seventies, dressed expensively in a slightly old-fashioned tweed suit. She walked up to Michel without shame and draped an arm around his waist, purring up at him like a affectionate kitten. He replied in kind, putting his arm around her shoulders.

I drew back, suddenly ashamed. Philippe noticed it and laughed. 'Michel says that women are like fish. Once you hook them, they twist and turn and bleed, but don't run away.'

I looked again at Michel and felt sick.

'Come, enough of this. I will take you home,' Philippe said abruptly. We walked out through the main entrance. The car was parked on the curb. A cold and mischievous wind was blowing. It caught hold of me, lifting the end of my sari off my shoulder. I wrapped it closely, intensely aware of Philippe's eyes on me. I climbed into the car and lay back against the cushioned softness of the seat, my eyes closed.

The car moved on silently. I turned to Philippe suddenly.

'It only works if everyone desires the same things. But they don't, do they?'

He looked at me, puzzled. 'What are you talking about?'

'Your theory of selling. People don't all think of food as an obsession.'

'But I make them change their minds,' he snapped. 'I can make them want anything I want them to want. All one has to do is to be in the papers, in the magazines, and of course on TV.'

'But what about me?'

'What about you?'

'Can you make me into something everybody wants?'

He laughed. 'Easily, if I wanted to.' His eyes slipped to my breasts. 'But I prefer keeping you to myself, unchanged.'

I sat up angrily. 'Why? Why shouldn't I change?'

He avoided my eyes, looking out of the window for a while before answering.

'Can you not guess?' he said irritably. I shook my head. He brought his face close to mine, 'Because if you do, you'll lose yourself. Your culture is averse to change. They do it badly, and so would you.'

I shook my head. What he described felt all wrong to me. 'Are you sure I am so very different from you?' I asked.

'Of course, *ma belle*. That is what is so exciting.'

'Why?' I challenged him. 'Doesn't it scare you?'

'No, why should it scare me?'

'Because I might change you, make you different from everybody else too,' I cried passionately, hating his smug certainty.

His face cleared, he shouted with laughter. 'So what? I'm not scared of change. I know I am different, depraved actually. I drive women crazy—so I'm told. Don't you feel scared of me?'

'W-why are they scared?' I felt suddenly nervous.

'They say I hurt them.'

'And do you?' I asked in a whisper.

He shrugged, 'Only when they bore me.'

He took my chin gently in his hands. 'But you are different from the others, so soft and yet so impenetrable. I don't think you will bore me too quickly.' He touched my lips with his fingers. 'You are like a wonderful new game that I don't yet know the rules for.'

I looked out of the window. We were crossing the Pont Neuf to the right bank again. The trees were wearing their autumn colours, red and gold like my sari. They looked disguised, like women dressed for a party. 'And what if you never find out?' I asked, feeling the perspiration beading my skin.

He caught hold of me by my hair and pulled my face towards him till our faces were inches apart. 'Don't worry, I will,' he said confidently.

Three

In the space of a few weeks, I felt as though I had known Philippe forever, that I had always lived with him. I hardly thought of Maeve, or Bruno or Annelise. Even Olivier retreated to the shadows, except when I listened to music. But that was seldom, since Philippe did not like classical music. I rarely thought of Lotti, or my aunt or uncle. Or my mother. Occasionally I caught myself wondering if they would recognize me now.

There was one thing I missed from the Baleines' attic room—an old globe that stood on a wooden axis three-and-half feet off the ground. It was too big to be a toy, and the colours were rather faded. The axis was slightly broken, so that the earth stood straight up like a fairytale moon. The countries were marked out in different colours, with the capital cities encircled by little black squares. When it was plugged into an electric socket, the country on which your finger rested would light up. I thought of it more and more with each month spent with Philippe. Each time he and I boarded a plane for some distant land, I remembered it with longing, my fingers itching to trace on it the contours of that country.

I told Philippe about the globe early one morning when we were in Mexico City, both of us still awake from jet lag. I described how I spent hours at night after I had put the children to bed, spinning the globe on its axis, my eyes shut. I would put my finger on it when it stopped, trying to guess without opening my eyes which country my finger had landed on.

He laughed. 'Why do you think of that now?' he asked, running a finger across my collarbone and into the hollow at the base of my neck.

Because I was thinking of how the world has shrunk, how it was in fact not such a big place after all. I opened my mouth to say so. But his eyes were no longer on my face, they were following his hand as it pushed the sheet farther and farther down, baring my breasts and then my waist to the light.

I narrowed my eyes mysteriously. 'I can't tell you.'

His eyes came back up to my face and settled upon it expectantly. 'Why?'

'Because I'll have to show you.'

'It's a game then,' Philippe cried like a little boy.

'Yes, it's a game.'

I didn't tell him that when I played this particular game, I had a partner, Bruno.

One night when I had been playing with the globe in the dark he had entered so silently that I did not hear him. Placing his palms over my eyes, he had whispered, 'The country you are touching is like your left breast. Guess what it is.' When I couldn't guess, he had told me, 'It was Kenya, my sweet.'

'Oh,' I had said, still not understanding. 'How can Kenya be like my breast?'

'I'll show you.' With his finger, he had traced the shape of Kenya around my breast. The nipple had begun to rise. I had looked down at it, surprised. It had felt separate from me, distant. 'And my nipple is Mount Kenya, I suppose,' I had said wryly. He had laughed delightedly, and stuck his mouth to it.

I didn't like the game because it took away the magic of the world's sheer size—its huge unknown spaces, people, languages, animals, forests—and reduced them to ordinary things—a thigh, a breast, an ear. One couldn't escape into a body, the way one could into the world. But the globe and my body became equal, both waiting to be possessed. As I described the game to Philippe, his smile grew.

With Philippe, I came to know the world in a different way. My passport, a duplicate of the old one still with Krishenbhai that Philippe had obtained for me from the Kenyan embassy in Paris, began to fill with visas of all colours and designs, each one secured after a humiliating cross-examination by a supercilious official in Paris.

When we returned together from our trips, Philippe and I went through different gates. His was friendly and empty, mine was slow and crowded with dark faces. I longed for a French passport so that I, too, could walk though that gate beside him. But the only way I could get one was if Philippe married me. 'Be satisfied with your *carte de séjour*,' he snapped when I brought up the subject. 'In ten years you will become naturalized.' But I was impatient and scared. I could not imagine holding Philippe's interest for even half that long. With a French passport, no one could touch me because I would be one of them, I thought longingly. But I was powerless, and I could only dream dreams of the toy globe.

But wherever we travelled, the impressions in my mind blurred into one, dominated by the smell of Philippe. It went with us everywhere, filling the air we breathed inside and outside the house until I almost felt suffocated. Like a wall it surrounded me. Even when he wasn't present, his smell, loud and demanding attention just as he did, followed me—into the bathroom, and outside on the streets of strange cities we travelled to. It was like a bodyguard, giving me no privacy at all. I was sure it was what made people stare, making men do no more than look at me, and the women sniff audibly while their dogs barked.

Then, one day, without telling me, Philippe went away and did not take me with him. His smell slowly dissipated, growing ever fainter each day he stayed away. As the house emptied of it, the rooms became silent, the very air in them seemed cold and inert. I wandered from room to room in that large ornate apartment filled with the expensive antiques he loved to buy, looking for a little whiff of him somewhere— in his favourite chair, in his study, in his dressing room with the huge built-in cupboards, half of which were now mine. In the bathroom I searched among the dirty clothes that he had thrown away before he left. But the clothes disappeared soon after he left and were replaced by clean lifeless smells. I even searched his shoe cupboard for the smell of him.

When I could find it nowhere else, I returned to our bed and buried my face in his pillow. I inhaled deeply. There it was nestling in the pure cotton fibres. The smell was stronger and more concentrated, like an essence preserved in the oily base of a perfume. For a few seconds I could almost feel Philippe lying beside me, his heavy breath covering my own, his leg thrown carelessly across my body. Then, as the smell of him faded, my worry began. What if he never came back, I asked myself, staring at the ceiling. What if he stopped wanting me, and just sent me a note with the chauffeur telling me to leave? I was certain the chauffeur and the cook despised me. It was in their eyes, barely veiled, whenever they looked at me. They knew I was not going to last, and made no effort to talk to me. I stopped going out. Nothing interested me anymore. I wanted to meet no one. All I could think of was Philippe.

As the days dragged into weeks, the need got so bad that I was unable to get out of bed in the morning. I lay in the empty anonymous bed all day, alternately sweating and shivering, trying futilely to re-member what he felt like, what he looked like when he spoke to me at night. What did Philippe see in me, I asked myself again and again. What was the essence of my charm that made him choose me? How could I keep it alive if I didn't even know what it was? The questions chased each other around endlessly in my head till it was empty of all other thoughts. And I ceased to exist outside those few questions.

I turned my head into the pillow. Philippe's smell was long gone now. It had lasted about a fortnight, and then it had disappeared. It had been over three weeks now and there was not a trace of the smell left anywhere. I lay immobile in bed and stared out of the window. The light seemed to leap off the walls, and drip off the ceiling. I could almost see the little beads of light falling off the ceiling onto the bed, like little drops of sweat, covering my flesh, ice-cold and unforgiving.

Finally, when I could bear it no more, I went shopping. The smell of new clothes drove the fear away. It brought Philippe alive again. He made everyone else seem so small and so powerless. I replayed our conversations in my head. No one else understood the world as he did. That's why I couldn't meet anyone else. Even the thought of An-nelise and Olivier and the inane conversations of their friends bored me. So I preferred to go shopping alone, with Philippe's ghostly voice for company. In the beginning he had always accompanied me on our shopping trips, guiding my eye towards the kind of clothes he wanted me to wear, giving me advice on what to look for. He knew my body better than I did, I had realized with amazement and pride the first time he had intervened with the shop assistant. I revisited the shops he had taken me to, enjoying the recognition on the saleswomen's faces. And when I paid with the Carte Bleue Philippe had given me, I felt doubly proud, not just because I was the owner of such beautiful and expensive things, but also because the card showed that it was Philippe who owned me.

Philippe returned eventually, armed with presents and his overwhelming hunger. For days we hardly left the bedroom. The air in the house changed, became liquid and alive.

Later that week I told him about the smell.

We were sitting in a little restaurant just off avenue George V. It was one of Philippe's favourites, not because its chef, Jean-Marie, happened to have received three stars from the Michelin and was one of the Bon Marché's most prestigious clients, but because he claimed the *caille au raisin* they served there was almost as good as his mother's used to be.

'Did you miss me?' he asked as we sat down at a table in the corner of the glass-enclosed patio.

'Only a little to begin with, terribly later on,' I replied honestly.

He pretended to look sad. 'Why only a little in the beginning?' he asked in a little boy voice. '*Ma belle*, that is not good enough. I'll have to go away sooner next time.'

'No, no, no. It's not like that at all,' I said quickly, unable to bear the thought of separation so soon. 'Please, I beg you, don't leave me.'

He looked cruel. 'Why?'

I began to explain breathlessly. 'You see, after you leave, your smell keeps me company, almost as if you were still there. It comforts me. But it begins to fade after a few days. And I run through the house searching for a little whiff of you like an addict. I go to your cupboard and bury my nose in your clothes, or in your pillowcase, in our sheets.

When your smell finally disappears and there is nothing left to comfort me, I think I'll go crazy, I miss you so much.' I didn't tell him about that other smell that still haunted me. The smell that ate into his smell—redolent of oil, stale spice, cabbage, and urine—so that I was forced to clothe myself in heavy cloying perfumes to hide it.

I looked anxiously at his face. He was not looking at me. He was staring at the tablecloth.

'Philippe?' I whispered, my throat dry. He averted his face and looked out towards the restaurant. 'Why are you angry with me? Should I not have told you?' My voice came out thin and tense as an electric wire.

He looked down at his hands, avoiding my eyes. 'You have made me speechless—that . . . that is the most beautiful thing anyone ever said to me.'

'Why don't you look at me then?'

At last he looked up. His eyes were shining with unshed tears. He looked at me with such love that I felt locked in his embrace. 'I don't dare look at you because I want to take you home right away and make love to you.' He laughed shakily. 'But I am afraid Jean-Marie would be terribly offended.'

My body went limp with relief and I managed a shadowy smile.

As if Philippe's words had conjured him up, Jean-Marie arrived.

'M Lavalle, what an honour. I thought you had forgotten me,' he said in a high piping voice.

'I would never forget you, Jean-Marie. My best customer, the best advertisement for my food. I trust they have looked after you well at Bon Marché in my absence? I have been in Japan and have missed your food terribly.'

I listened with amusement to Philippe's speech; he said the same thing to each of his thirty customer restaurants. When he spoke to them, he made it seem as if he were saying the words for the first time. The chefs were a vain lot, and it seemed to endear Philippe to them. Jean-Marie was beaming.

'*Au Japon? Ils n'ont pas la cuisine là-bas. Mais, si vous m'aviez averti, j'aurais produit un repas digne de vous,*' he replied, displaying a proper deference to Philippe and a French chef's disdain for foreign cuisine. He ignored me completely.

'Anything you cook will be more than worthy of me,' Philippe replied graciously. 'What are you going to give us tonight?'

Jean-Marie's rather purple face lit up. He puffed out his chest until he looked like a penguin. 'For entreé, I suggest *la barbe de Barbebleu*, followed by M'sieur's favourite *cailles* accompanied by jade eggs in serpent's nest, made with my own hands,' he thrust his hands before us to emphasize the point, 'and finally for dessert, *une île noire dans un lac de sang*.' His hands came to rest neatly folded across his apron, supporting his small but stiffly protruding belly.

'You seem to have become very bloodthirsty in my absence, Jean-Marie!' Philippe laughed. 'What on earth is a black island in a lake of blood?'

'Aha,' Jean-Marie's eyebrows went up haughtily, 'these are secrets you will only know when you taste it. And even then you will not know it all.'

Philippe looked at him like an indulgent parent. 'And the wine?'

'I have a good St Emilion waiting for you. Followed by your favourite Nuits St Georges. And then, with dessert I have a delightful wine—redolent of apricot with an aftertaste of walnuts. It comes from my region, *au dessous de Bordeaux*. It is very rare. The proprietor only makes a hundred bottles—and he only sells to friends. I keep twenty bottles—for special guests.'

Jean-Marie's enthusiasm made my stomach respond. My appetite returned, magnified by the days of near-starvation during Philippe's absence.

I turned to Philippe excitedly. But his expression baffled me. It was detached, unmoved.

'Thank you,' he nodded royally at Jean-Marie, his movement containing both approval and dismissal.

Philippe turned to me as Jean-Marie departed. His face changed. It became softer, and his eyes filled with light. I sat back, letting the warmth of his regard fill me.

'So tell me, *ma chère*, what do I smell like?' he asked lightly.

I gulped. It was not the question I wanted to answer in public. 'Can I . . . do you want me to tell you right now?'

A shadow passed over his face, and his eyes became less warm. 'Of course,' he said irritably, 'why else would I ask you?'

'But . . . but in public?' The idea unnerved me.

We're quite private here,' he turned around impatiently. 'Look. The restaurant is almost empty.'

'All right.' I stared hard at him, drinking in his intelligent brown eyes, the grey in his hair, the lines of tiredness that mapped his face. My eyes fell to his throat, taking in the curious breadth and thickness of it and the way his head seemed small in comparison, like the head of a leopard. He smiled at me greedily, his eyes gently sucking at my mouth.

Without warning I could no longer remember what he smelt like. A swelling panic rose in my throat.

I forced my eyes shut, telling myself to be calm, to remember. When I finally opened my eyes, he was watching me as he would look at something he had just bought, a look both hungry and gloating— certain of possessing.

I began to speak, the words tumbling smoothly off my tongue, 'Mmm, let's see. You smell rich and heavy and sweet and buttery like . . . like . . .' I searched for the word, thinking of blood and milk and raisins, of sausages. 'L-l-like *boudin*,' I announced defiantly. I paused and peeped at him quickly. He didn't look angry at being likened to the famous sausage made from blood, apples, and raisins. 'And when we make love . . .'

He was enthralled, watching me intensely, his body immobile. 'And when we make love, your smell intensifies, the fruitiness that lies just under your skin gets accentuated. It has the consistency of wine. Its edges curl around me, lifting me up. All around me are smells like the tropical rains, sweaty and moist, like earth and salt, water and wine and fish all mixed together. There is a little of everything in your smell—things dying, things coming to life.' I stopped, carried away by my own description, a familiar pressure beginning in my groin. I pressed my thighs together tightly and wished we weren't in the restaurant. I looked at Philippe. He seemed equally excited, his face was puffy and flushed, his eyes burning.

He reached across and gripped my hand. 'Very beautiful, I want to take you away with me right now so you can tell me again properly.' Suddenly he looked almost timid. Then the words came out in a rush. 'I missed you very much on this trip,' he began, licking his lips tentatively. 'I didn't realize I would, but I see now that it was a test. And you won.'

Awe mixed with disbelief painted his face as he remembered.

'Nothing excited me, not even the most beautiful of their women interested me.' He paused and then continued, his voice rough. 'All the time it was you I thought of, your face, your expression when your face lies beneath mine, your eyes closed, faraway. It's funny,'—he shook his head slightly—'before I met you, I wasn't interested in *les femmes exotiques.*'

The words momentarily pulled me out of the fog of desire that surrounded me. I didn't feel very exotic anymore, dressed in my neat Parisian clothes, with my careful French smell.

'Do you know how I knew I must have you?' He raised my hand to his lips. 'Because of the way you ate your sandwich.'

I jerked back in surprise. 'What do you mean?'

He moved closer, his voice swelling with passion. 'Don't you remember? Your face when you eat . . . I can never forget it . . . It was so unbelievable a transformation. You looked scared when you came in, frightened and hungry. Then when I gave you the sandwich, your eyelids drooped over those big black eyes and I ceased to exist for you. You began to chew. Your face was serious, totally absorbed in the act of tasting. It was . . . primitive. Pure animal instinct.'

My throat became dry. I became aware of the space inside me calling out to me, clamping and unclamping its lips insistently. He leaned towards me and continued huskily, his voice filled with awe. 'I could feel how hungry you were. I wanted to be inside your head, in your throat, tasting the food the way you tasted it. After a few bites, your face became meditative. You were sated.' His voice became a whisper. 'All at once I knew I was in the presence of something new, something alien. Each time I looked at a woman, I saw your face with that look of animal pleasure. I had to have you then. I had to know why you looked that way.'

Just then, from the corner of my eyes, I saw the white flash of a camera. I looked back at Philippe; a veil seemed to fall over his eyes, but otherwise he was perfectly composed, his head tilted a little towards the room. Smiling for the camera or for me, I wasn't sure anymore. The moment lost its colour.

'Is it only coincidence that we always get photographed in restaurants, or do you telephone them in advance to let them know we are coming?' I asked sharply.

'Can I help it if we are so photogenic?' he replied, opening his eyes wide in order to demonstrate his innocence.

'We are?' I asked, acidly. 'I may be photogenic, but it is you he wants to photograph.'

'Then why are you so concerned? After all, am I not doing what you wanted—making you famous?'

'What kind of fame do I have?' I replied hotly. 'I am allowed to do nothing, except dress and undress at your command.'

Just then the wine arrived.

Jean-Marie himself came to do the honours. He opened the bottle with an old-fashioned blade, disdaining, as I had known he would, to use a more modern corkscrew. He opened it expertly and gently placed the wine on the table to breathe. He leaned his arms on the table and began a long and technical conversation with Philippe about the prospects of the Bordeaux wines that year. From wine they went on to discuss football and the Tour de France. My mind wandered.

Then Jean-Marie poured a tiny sip of wine into a crystal glass and handed it to Philippe so he could judge the wine himself. But Philippe handed it to me. 'Here, you taste it,' he ordered. Next to me, I felt Jean-Marie start.

As I took custody of the glass, I felt Philippe's desire reaching up to me. I lifted it to my nose, gently agitating the liquid. Then I held it beneath my nose and pulled the fumes straight up my nostrils.

The wine smelt at once sweet and spicy, like cinnamon and nutmeg, and sour and earthy. There was also a slight hint of chalk that hung back, almost out of sight. The smell filled my nostrils, delicate but well-formed as a gazelle. Then I took a sip. The wine slid across my tongue like oil, and slipped effortlessly down my throat. Underneath its silky coat, I could feel the muscle that held the various elements of it together. The smell gathered force after I had swallowed it, the warm juices that had been hiding beneath my tongue rushing into it, lifting it up and warming it so that the fumes rose through my throat, once again climbing the dark nasal tunnels to my brain. I said nothing and slowly took another mouthful.

Then I realized that both Philippe and Jean-Marie were waiting for me to say something.

I nodded curtly, trying to copy Philippe's royal way of making his wishes felt. 'It is okay,' I said, looking at Jean-Marie. He looked at me with respect. 'Very well, madame.' After he left, I took another sip of the wine.

Then Philippe spoke. 'I've lost you to the wine, hein?' he said.

'Yes, I'm afraid so,' I replied lightly. In the distance I could see a white-clad figure weaving his way through the tables towards us, carrying a huge tray in his arms. He seemed to be walking on air. I watched as he came closer, 'And you are about to lose me once more,' I told Philippe, still watching the waiter, 'to the food.'

It arrived and both of us fell silent. The beard of *barbebleu* was a warm creamy chèvre on a bed of blue-green arugula, with a blueberry *coulis*. The sharp salty cheese was transmuted into something warm and soft and sweet by the honey-sweetened blueberry sauce, but sharpened by a suggestion of mint. And then the slightly bitter arugula cut away the extra sweetness from the sauce, leaving a taste that was so perfectly balanced that it took my breath away. I surrendered myself to the cleverly constructed food.

Philippe said roughly, 'Tell me, what is it you feel? What do you think of when you are eating that food?'

I stopped, my fork in midair. 'W-what do you mean?'

Philippe began to speak again, but as if he were talking to himself.

'I envy you. You still lose yourself completely in what you taste. Even I cease to exist for you. Sometimes you wear that look when we make love. Your eyes become unseeing and your face glows, becomes even more beautiful.'

I put down my fork quietly, afraid to disturb him.

'How is it that you are more lovely when you aren't thinking of me?' he asked.

I was saved from having to reply by the arrival of the *cailles au raisin*, on an old-fashioned trolley. Silently the waiter cleared our plates. He placed two covered silver dishes before us. He looked very young. I wondered if he was a student, and what he was studying at the university. His eyes looked so clean and bright behind the round spectacles. Our eyes met, and immediately we both looked away. I stared down at the table, and noticed that his brown hands were trembling.

After the waiter left, I looked up at Philippe over the silver domes. He seemed far away, his head small and fragile next to the huge silver covers of the dishes. I picked up the wineglass and looked at him through it. His features twisted and broke into triangles and squares.

'Why do you look at me like that?' he asked. I looked up at him quickly, peering over the rim of the glass. The bits fell heavily back into place.

'Why do you look sad, all of a sudden? *'Tu m'en veux pas comme esclave?'* he asked teasingly. Underneath the smoothness of his words was an order: to stop being serious at once, to play.

'I am not sad, just wondering,' I said, still dwelling on the thought of him as my slave.

'Wondering what?' he asked possessively.

'If you ate my feelings as well.'

He laughed confidently. 'Ate your feelings? What stupidity!' His eyes grew serious. 'Don't think so much. It doesn't suit you.'

'Do you think that in possessing me, you can possess what I am feeling as well?' I insisted.

His face lost some of its confidence. 'It is nothing of the sort,' he snapped.

'Maybe you're right.' I agreed hastily, 'I was just being silly.' I touched his knee gently, 'I'm sorry. But I can't help thinking when I am alone too long.'

Jean-Marie arrived to unveil the quails himself. With a flourish he lifted off the silver covers. There they lay, two little headless birds of identical size, crisp and brown on the outside, surrounded by a bed of bright orange crispy vermicelli and two egg-shaped balls of spinach mousse. Suddenly I felt very full, as if I had ingested something hard and heavy.

Philippe attacked the food in his usual way. He was not a tidy eater and little specks of dark wine-coloured sauce soon speckled his shirt-front. Suddenly he looked up at me, catching me staring at him. Quickly I smiled. He began to speak, his mouth full. I watched the half-masticated food that lay forgotten in his mouth. Then, feeling immediately guilty, I looked up, trying to keep the whole of his face within my frame and pay attention to his words.

'You know, I have it. I've finally understood,' he was saying. 'The secret of my success is in realizing that in the modern world hunger exists solely in the brain.'

Unable to tear myself away from the sight of the food, I replied vaguely, 'Smell begins in the brain too.'

four

The key to knowing Philippe was to understand his relationship to food. He didn't taste it, he demolished it, and then he forgot all about it. Five minutes after he had consumed an entire four-course meal, he could no longer remember what it had tasted like. He couldn't tell what the main course had been, whether it had been hot or cold, whether the wine he had consumed was white or red, or even if he had eaten it with someone or alone. And so he was always hungry.

Philippe could not remember what he ate because he lived on a single plane of time—the immediate. What he wanted could only be enjoyed in the moment it was conceived. His desire struck like lightning and disappeared as quickly. Then something new had to be found to fill the void.

Philippe wanted to possess me, because I was the opposite of him. I lived in a time that was made up almost entirely of remembering. Perhaps remembering had always been a pleasure, a part of my personality, even a part of my genes. But with Philippe, it became a means of survival. For the Bon Marché was an exacting mistress. She had to be fed every day, and cleaned and protected from theft and competition. She had to be kept constantly in the glare of publicity. Fulfilling these demands took Philippe away from me a lot, once the media no longer found anything to say about our relationship. When he was away, it was as if I ceased to exist. The world grew empty and colourless. And remembering him became a way of staying alive. I meditated on our moments together, letting them expand in my mind until they filled the hours and the days to such an extent that I forgot the world outside.

Smell was the trigger into that world. Because smell, I believed passionately, began in the brain. Philippe never could understand where my pleasure came from, but he envied it. He took possession of my body instead, a strange kind of jealousy that made his passion brutal. But his hunger for me—like his other desires—was short-lived. And as soon as it was satisfied, it was forgotten. So I had to constantly invent new ways to capture his interest.

Out of this strange knowledge, I evolved a series of little games to lengthen his pleasure. But the smell game was his favourite. It consisted of my describing what different parts of him smelt like, at different times of the day, before, during and after our lovemaking. Sometimes we took a little cocaine before embarking on the game. Enflamed with lust, he would thrust himself at me. Afterwards we would lie together in a knot, tired and content. And we would talk. He would tell me about his work, his trips to different cities in the world, sharing his pleasure in his business with me. For it was the only thing that remained alive in his memory. I listened to him, occasionally offering a suggestion or commenting on what had passed. Soon our vocabulary of smells developed into a language of its own, pure and self-contained, needing no explanations. Eventually, the meaning of the game was lost in endless repetition, and became a ritual, sacred in itself.

Living uniquely in the immediate moment, Philippe had no use for the pleasure, or the pain, of love. For love, one had to have memory. Philippe's moments were lived without memory and without guilt—but it meant that his moments were like empty rooms, they had to be filled.

So he collected antiques in order to capture the past, and saw the future only in terms of the Bon Marché, a self-portrait in brick and mortar. His statement of immortality.

I made myself an expert on the exotic, from antiques to unusual foods. I joined a class on antiques and learnt to distinguish between the real ones and the fakes. Once I knew enough, I began to explore the old markets of France, in Lyons, Strasbourg, and Amiens. I travelled to Belgium and Switzerland and even Germany and Austria looking for the little things Philippe loved. I researched their histories painstakingly, and where I lost their tracks, I made them up. I would tell him stories about the things I bought him, and he would listen hungrily.

I searched for the *fournisseurs* of the best spices, and arranged for special heat-emitting lights to bring out their colour and aroma. But since smell also depended upon humidity, I created a perfumed fountain that spread the odour of rain on dry ground through the air. And, finally, to popularize the exotic spices, fruits, and vegetables, we hired some of the most famous chefs of *la nouvelle cuisine* to experiment and create a special Bon Marché cookbook. It became a global bestseller overnight, making the store even more popular.

But the more successful Philippe got, the more time he spent away trying to manage his growing empire.

To fill the time, I began to read voraciously. First the magazines, which used a more current French that was easier to understand than fiction, and then, as my French got better, novels, poetry, anything that took my fancy. As a result I grew more talkative when he returned, my mind brimming with ideas.

'But what happens, Philippe, when everyone's imagination is all used up?' I asked him one day as we lay together in bed. 'What then?'

'What do you mean?' he said. 'The imagination can't get used up. It is not petrol, you know.'

'Yes, but if people's imaginations are constantly being occupied by things for sale, they lose the power to imagine for themselves, *n'est-ce pas?*'

'*Et alors?*' He was listening, slightly impatient now.

'So then, in the end, they will have no imagination left and so no desire to buy?'

He didn't reply immediately. I looked at him closely. Finally, he admitted, 'Theoretically, yes, it is a possibility . . . but I don't think . . .'

I cut in excitedly, 'Then, when the imagination is eaten up, and all buying stops, what then? Will Europe be destroyed? What will come in its place?'

'Of course not,' he snapped. 'You Indians are quite illogical. As long as there are new babies being born, the imagination can't dry up.'

I smiled. I had already thought of that one.

'But will the babies of those without imagination be born with theirs intact?' I asked sweetly.

'Of course, every generation is different.'

'But they are still the children of their parents. They cannot be very different,' I insisted. 'If their parents are bored, if they can no longer imagine, how can their children?'

'Because it's biological,' he replied impatiently. 'They have to be born with imaginations. Like fingers, and toes.' He reached up to light his cigarette.

I kept silent, fearing I had begun to lose the argument. 'But deformed children get born all the time,' I said finally.

'If you had had an education, you would know that statistically they are worth nothing.'

'I wonder if children's imaginations get more easily filled than their parents', so that they are bored faster and faster,' I said hesitantly.

'Their imaginations are excited by different things, that's all,' he replied. 'They have less fear. And so their desires are bolder, more impatient. They have to be fulfilled that very instant.'

'But then eventually the things that excite their imagination will run out and therefore their imagination will too. It is a vicious cycle.'

He went still. I propped myself up on my elbows and looked down at him victoriously.

He looked up at my face. 'So, professor, what is the solution then?' he said sarcastically.

'Maybe,'—I pretended to think hard though the idea had been waiting to be aired for over a month—'that is why one moves on to other parts of the world, where the selling is not of the same level, where it hasn't reached the imagination yet.'

He laughed suddenly, looking superior once again. 'My little idiot, people everywhere sell in the same way. You move to another country to make more money, that's all.'

Philippe's sojourns in Paris became fewer and farther apart. I felt empty and irritable all the time. I stopped going on my antique-hunting trips. There seemed to be no point—for Philippe was hardly even there now. And the pieces would just lie around the house and gather dust, witnesses to my inability to hold him. But it wasn't my fault, I thought angrily, he had stolen my energy. I no longer had the will to go out on my own. I felt ugly and old. I was ashamed to meet the people I knew through him, scared of seeing the quiet triumph in their eyes. I did not have the courage to face Olivier or Annelise. The world outside the apartment was a reminder that Philippe was not with me. I dreaded seeing the inevitable advertisements of the Bon Marché, his face smiling confidently alongside. So, in frustration, I turned to cooking once more. Only this time I learnt to cook French food, from Alfredo, Philippe's father's cook and manager of the Bon Marché, Paris. I forced him to teach me all the dishes Philippe's mother had once made. And when I had mastered those, I made him teach me others which were even more subtle and complicated. French food was so different from Indian food. The challenge was not so much in the spicing and cooking of the food, but in the timing, and in the finding of the perfect ingredients. So I learnt to cook through memory, and with my eyes, bypassing the senses until I was sure that I had got the rest of it right. Then I began to experiment using my knowledge of spices to create new and different sauces.

I cooked huge elaborate meals and waited for Philippe to return. And when he did finally come back from his trips, his parties, his grand store openings, and his one-night stands, he devoured us both.

But such moments never lasted. For Philippe was never satisfied for long. He got bored with the game, with me, and with the apartment that had increasingly become my only world. He had to have more, something real, something from the world that was my enemy, the one outside. He needed a new challenge, another project, a new design for the store.

'I think it is time to redecorate the store,' he said one day as we ate breakfast together on one of his infrequent trips to Paris.

'But you only redecorated the international food part last year, and the housewares section in Brussels was remodelled six months ago.

New lights were put in the store at Rio three months ago. Just how far do you want to go?' I asked him, exasperated. 'Haven't you done enough?'

'Enough? There's no such thing as enough. When you say enough, you die. You must be constantly doing something or else the press forgets you. But actually, I was thinking of La Bon Marché in Paris. We are forgetting her. She is getting old. People will get tired of her.'

'That's not what the account books say!' I pointed out sharply.

'The account books are a year behind the times, my dear. I'm telling you. I can feel it here—in my stomach. People are beginning to get sick of the Bon Marché. It is becoming boring.'

'Boring to you or to them? You never spend any time in Paris, how can you be bored with her?'

'I do not need to be in her, to know what she needs. She is in my blood,' he replied, staring moodily at the salt shaker. 'I have neglected her for too long. It is time to bring her back into the public eye.'

And what about me, I thought angrily, when would I be brought back into the public eye? But I couldn't say that to him. He would enjoy my pain. It would just be another game to him. Except this game, I realized instinctively, I would have no control over. So I had to keep quiet. 'If you want the Bon Marché to be noticed,' I said dryly, 'try advertising.'

Philippe opened his mouth to ridicule me. Then he shut it. 'A new advertising campaign,' he said in tones of delight. 'We haven't done that since the store was opened. What a brilliant idea! And I'll have to spend the months of preparation in Paris now—with you,' he added condescendingly, making me realize that all my efforts at concealing my loneliness had been in vain. I quickly got up and left.

And so it was decided. The adman, M Binet, was called in. M Binet had been a friend of the family. Though his company was very successful, he managed to remain humorous and unhurried. Whenever he called, he took the time to talk to me. Philippe invited him to the house for dinner. I was excited about having a guest after such a long time. I wanted at least one of Philippe's friends to know that I still existed.

The doorbell rang at seven. The man standing outside was not old M Binet. He was much younger, less than thirty, and handsome. His face lit up when he saw me.

'*Oui, monsieur? Qu'est-ce que vous voulez?*' I paused, wondering whether the man had come to the wrong address. It was a pity, I thought, because the man looked nice.

The man smiled at me. He had nice teeth I noticed, white and straight. 'My name is Marc Despres, I am the chief designer for M Binet. He was called away unexpectedly, on a family matter.'

M Binet's wife, I thought, must have been complaining of neglect and M Binet had given in. I looked again at the stranger. He looked back at me, his expression admiring. Suddenly the evening brightened.

'*Tant pis,*' I shrugged, smiling, letting him notice my bare shoulders. 'Please come in.' I felt a shiver of awareness run through me. We stared at each other. 'I'm sorry M Binet couldn't come. I hope everything is all right with him.'

'Oh certainly, it is just bad luck that this meeting came up so suddenly, when he is wanted for a dinner party at home,' he said poker-faced.

I laughed, and my tension vanished. He laughed easily with me. 'M Binet's bad luck is my good fortune,' he said, when our laughter finally died down. 'I've heard so much about you. And seen your photographs.'

'But that was years ago,' I replied, amazed that he could still remember the days when our faces, Philippe's and mine, had been in all the society magazines.

'Maybe that is why they don't do you justice, madame,' he said softly.

'I'm not married, call me Leela.'

'Leela? What a lovely name.' He was clearly a flirt, I decided. I felt as though I had already drunk a glass of wine.

Suddenly Philippe appeared, looking surprised and then surly as I introduced the young man. It was clear he thought the man too young and became his most aggressive self. 'Why didn't Binet come himself, huh? It's the most important account he has, and he sends someone else. And why you? What do you know about the Le Bon Marché account?' He turned to me and said in English, 'How can I talk to this kid? Tell him to go away.'

I looked anxiously towards M Despres. I felt sure he knew English. But he didn't seem in the least upset. He addressed Philippe directly, 'I do actually know quite a bit about your account. I've been handling it for the last four years.' He turned slightly, so that he was addressing me as well, 'You have a wonderful sensitivity. Your attention to every little detail, the touch, the taste, even the smell of the food is evident in each recipe.' All the while, his eyes remained on me. I felt confused. Did he know it was I who had given the descriptions of the food?

Philippe grunted, mollified. 'Well, I'm glad you liked it,' he said gruffly, walking up to him. 'I didn't realize you were the one who produced the book. Binet, that clever old rascal, never told me. But that's the way of the world, isn't it, people taking credit for other people's work.' He laughed loudly, putting an arm around the man's shoulders. 'Perhaps you'd better stay for dinner after all. Leela loves to cook, she'd be disappointed if there was no one to eat her food.'

I felt suddenly ugly again. 'I . . . I have t-to see to the f-food,' I stammered and ran towards the kitchen.

When I returned, Philippe was showing off his latest acquisition, an art deco mirror that he had picked up in a chic but overpriced gallery in Brussels. I thought it was a fake.

'Do you like antiques?' I asked Despres when Philippe had finally run out of things to say.

'I do, but not to possess them, just to look at them.'

'That's lucky, you wouldn't be able to afford them anyway,' Philippe remarked, coming back to us at that moment.

'I love antiques because of the detail,' Despres replied. 'Knowing about antiques teaches you to look at things more closely, and to appreciate the finer points of craftsmanship.'

'Why bother to love something you can't possess?' Philippe scoffed.

'But sometimes one cannot help oneself,' Despres said.

'And knowing is possessing too,' I added, unable to resist.

'Of course.' He smiled at me delightedly. 'When you know something, you possess it forever.'

'Do you really think so?' I asked eagerly. 'Why?'

'Forever?' Philippe cut in. 'There's no such thing. We all die, and that's it, *point final.*'

He turned to Despres. 'Enough of small talk. Let us go into my study and discuss the project.'

Their footsteps retreated, and I heard the door close behind them.

They continued talking business over dinner. 'We have people copying us all over, in Lyons, Geneva, Tokyo. And do you know why this is so?' Philippe asked, looking hard at Despres.

The young man shifted nervously in his seat. 'Because it is such a success?'

'Yes. Because I reinvented food. I sold them food as sensual, food as aesthetic, food as seduction. I turned good eating into an obsession, something way beyond mere desire. That's why I became a symbol of success.'

Despres nodded his head smoothly, very much the acolyte, but said nothing.

Philippe continued, 'But my success has been my worst enemy. Once I created it, the idea was available to all the copycats, the third-world imitators, the thieves, to use. I invented it, but I don't get any author's copyright, like you do in the advertising business.'

My mind began to wander. I was bored with Philippe's bragging.

Hardly any of the food had been touched. The hot food slowly went cold, its smell ripening, slowly turning sour and unpleasant like stale cheese. I had worked so hard on it all too, sending the cook away and doing it all myself. But it would be eaten later, I knew, Philippe would demolish it once the guest had been disposed of. Despres had eaten very little, I noticed. My eyes travelled up to his face. And with a start, I realized he was staring at me. We both looked away guiltily. I forced myself to listen to what Philippe was saying.

'Since we can't sue the copycats, we have to change, to move on, to look for another umbrella under which we can sell.' He paused to catch his breath. 'That's why I need you. I want you to come up with something different, something that will once again set me apart.'

'Of course . . .' Despres nodded. 'I shall be honoured to.'

'So, any ideas?' Philippe shot back.

Despres blinked. 'I don't know,' he said at last, 'I have trouble thinking tonight. What does madame think?'

'Me?' I started forward in surprise. 'Maybe you could market these smells,' I said pointing to the food that lay untouched. 'That would be new.'

'Don't talk like an imbecile,' Philippe snapped, 'or Despres will think you're mad.'

'I'm sorry . . . it was a joke . . .' I began to apologize. I looked nervously at our guest. He was looking at me, an arrested look in his eyes.

'But wait. I think that's a wonderful idea,' he said, smiling at me warmly. 'Can you tell us more about it? How exactly would you go about doing it?'

'Oh. I . . . I don't know,' I said quickly, glancing at Philippe. 'It was silly of me. I meant the food's getting cold, you know. That's all I meant.'

'No, no. There's much more to it, I'm sure,' Despres brushed aside my excuses. 'You shouldn't denigrate yourself. You have a fresh, unspoiled perspective. You notice things we Occidentals never comprehend.' He turned excitedly to Philippe, 'Smell could be the third front, the undiscovered frontier of attack, a way to seep into people's subconscious without their even knowing it. More powerful than words and images, unknown, unexplored, different.'

Philippe interrupted his flow of adjectives. 'When you have finished humouring her, could we get down to some business? I'm a busy man and I don't have all night for bullshit.'

'This is not bullshit, monsieur,' Despres said quietly. 'It is the freshest idea I have ever heard. We only need to work out how it is to be done.'

Philippe's face grew black. 'Fresh? It stinks! The whole idea stinks. I have a business to protect, a business that is built on a reputation—for wholesomeness, for quality.'

I looked at Philippe in surprise. He was the one who never tired of the smell game.

'But won't people get scared of strong smells? And won't the smell then stop them from buying?' I asked Despres.

'Not if it's handled properly,' Despres replied energetically. 'We won't use scents that are too strong or too easily identifiable. We will make it a fantasy. After all, we want to use the idea of smell to sell.'

Suddenly I grew irritated. 'What do you mean—"the idea of smell"? A smell is not an idea. It's real. Everything has a smell, and the smell changes all the time depending on how it's treated. A smell is a world . . . it is memory too.'

But Despres brushed my words away lightly. 'It is the concept that is unique. The smells are immaterial, they can be light and pleasant, entirely forgettable. What is important is that we will become the first people to associate smell with the selling of a food, Bon Marché's food.'

I looked towards Philippe, expecting him to throw the man out. But to my astonishment, he had his bland business face on, his eyes like stones.

'How would we do it?' he said.

Despres's face went blank for an instant. He turned to me.

'Maybe in the magazines, like the advertisements they have of perfume,' I said mockingly.

We were no longer three people joined by food and conversation, but three different species of being, our thoughts spinning away from each other at a faster and faster pace. And still the talk continued.

'Food perfume! What a truly original idea! *Madame, je vous salute*,' he cried.

Philippe cut in dryly, 'All right, enough. How much money are we talking about?'

I began to laugh. I could not contain myself. It poured out of me, insane and without end, trying to fill the gaps between us, pouring like cement on the ruins of the dinner.

Finally Philippe slapped me, and it stopped. I put my hand to my cheek to stop the pain. I blinked rapidly. Then I turned to Despres, 'I'm sorry.'

I got up and began to clear away the dishes, each still bearing its burden of food. Despres got up to help me. But Philippe made him sit down again. 'Let her do it. We still have business to discuss.'

When I returned from the kitchen, they were gone. I could hear the young man still talking excitedly in the hall. Philippe's voice was a low bass rumble. I couldn't make out the words. Suddenly they both laughed. Men's laughter—short and to the point. Followed by a quick clearing of the throat.

I poured myself another glass of wine from the bottle, and drank it quickly. I reached to refill the glass but the bottle was empty. I picked up the guest's glass of wine, which was still three-quarters full, and drank that instead.

I heard the front door shut. I held my breath. A few minutes later, I heard Philippe's footsteps crossing the hall and moving away, out of earshot.

I quietly cleared away the remaining dishes. In the kitchen I threw the food into the garbage and stacked the plates in the sink. I looked at them for a moment. Then I turned on the tap and grabbed an apron. I let the sink fill with hot water as I tied the apron strings securely and pulled on the rubber washing gloves. The sound of the water calmed me.

When I finished, I pulled a bottle of white wine out of the refrigerator and, armed with two tall crystal glasses, went to find Philippe. The apartment was in darkness. I opened the bedroom door. The room was dark, except for the moonlight that poured in through the window. Philippe was stretched out on the bed, naked, his arm behind his head.

I went up to him. He did not turn his head. I placed the bottle and the glasses beside the bed.

'I brought you your favourite wine. Won't you have a little?'

He ignored me.

I poured a glass and slowly sipped at it. The wine tasted thin and green, like gooseberries and freshly mowed grass. I felt the liquid cutting through the layers of food in my mouth, erasing their memory from my palate. Soon it would enter my brain, erasing the memory of the evening from my mind.

'It was a strange evening, wasn't it?' I said tentatively. 'A funny man.'

At last Philippe spoke. 'A fool,' he spat. 'I can't understand why Binet keeps him.'

He took the glass of wine I was holding and sipped slowly. I began to undress.

'He must be very highly thought of by M Binet if he is the one in charge of the Bon Marché account.'

'He is an ass.'

'It wasn't such a bad idea though, making food perfumes for the new campaign,' I said lightly. 'You seemed to like it at the time.'

Philippe snorted. 'What? Using food smells to sell? It would never work. Smells are dirty, only sick minds can think of such things. I didn't want to embarrass you in front of the man by saying so. But he made me sick with his blatant flattery. It was disgusting to watch him drooling all over you. I want a man I work with to be a man, not a courtier. Food perfumes!'

I listened to him, appalled. Why did he keep me then, I wondered. 'But why? Why can't it work? You love to hear me talk about smell.'

He was silent for a few seconds. 'That's different.'

'How? How is it different?'

'It's private.'

'But you love it,' I insisted. 'I know you do.'

He looked at me wearily. 'Maybe I do. But that's because I'm different. Normal pleasures, the kind normal Europeans have, don't satisfy me anymore.'

'There's nothing abnormal about being sensitive to smells. It is natural,' I insisted.

'Smell is like dirt. Some people like it. They think it's natural. But dirt isn't desirable . . . and it doesn't make organic potatoes sell.'

'Smell is not like dirt,' I said angrily, standing up.

He pulled me back to him. 'Don't be a fool. Smell is dirty, unclean, unspoken, that's why it's exciting, erotic, savage, like you.' He rubbed my belly as he spoke, pulled down my underwear and dug his fingers into my buttocks. 'But you cannot change the order of things, my love. Or else there will be chaos.' He grabbed my hand and wrapped it around his penis. 'And people will think you are crazy, and put you into an asylum.' I felt myself slowly disappear until all that was left was a hand limply holding a soft slippery rock. Philippe wrapped his hand around mine, holding it firm while he rocked back and forth, until it became hard, talking all the while. 'The order of things cannot be threatened, some things have to remain in the dark.'

'Philippe!' I cried out, unable to bear his words anymore. 'Please, it can't be. Our pleasure is not dirty.' The darkness felt like a blanket, holding things in place. Underneath, my body was melting into a pool of filth.

He looked down at me for a long moment. Finally, he said, 'You, my sweet, are a little savage. And savages have no morals. That's why you still excite me, after all these years. You opened a door into a forbidden place. You live in there, in your little hovel of smells, sex, and decomposition. You revel in it. I don't understand what fuels your passion, it has to be a sickness or it could not last so long.'

My head began to throb, my eyes turned inward.

'No, no, no,' I began to moan. A terrible smell reared up from under my skin, a smell that came from a sewer in Nairobi where the dead dogs were left.

His hand touched my face tentatively. I shrank away from him. Suddenly his face hovered above mine, looking anxious.

'I didn't mean that. I love it that you prefer me to young punks like Despres,' he said, nuzzling my hair.

'Just leave it,' I replied sharply, turning my back to him and curling up on my side. He lay down beside me. I felt trapped.

I wondered bleakly how I would be able to continue to live with him. His finger traced a line down my back.

'Turn around now. I've forgiven you.' Forgiven me for what? I wondered confusedly.

'Turn around, I want to look at you,' he ordered, his voice shrill. He grabbed my hair and jerked my head back.

'Stop it. You're hurting me,' I screamed, clawing at his hand.

He let go suddenly. 'Now turn around,' he ordered quietly.

Slowly I turned around.

'That's better.' He smiled at me, his eyes raking my face. I tried to smile back but my cheeks felt frozen.

'Now tell me what I want to hear,' he said in a baby voice. I looked at his face. It was alight with anticipation.

'Tell you what?'

'You know what I want to hear,' he pouted.

Suddenly I understood. He wanted to play the smell game. He was waiting for me to begin it. I saw the game begin.

'I want to hear those words . . .' he licks his lips.

'What words?' I prompt him.

'Smell words,' he replies greedily. The ritual begins to wrap me in its embrace. Words stir in my brain.

'Words like . . .' he stops.

'Words like . . .' I mimic his baby voice, 'like your armpits have a sharp screaming smell that rings like metal on teeth. And shall I tell you how your breath smells like petrol poured over a body that is lighted by a match so that the flesh sizzles and the fat mixes with the petrol as it burns. And your . . .'

I stop. His eyes have a fixed glassy look. He is so lost in the magic of the game that he has not even noticed that I have changed the text.

'And my . . .' he prompts, running his hands across my buttocks.

I want to find a way to hurt him. 'I can't remember,' I say.

'What do you mean you can't remember? Do it. Say the words,' he roars.

'You have no special smell. You're like everyone else. I made it all up, every last bit of it.'

He looks at me as if he has never seen me before. His face becomes drawn. 'You're lying,' he whispers. 'You're lying, aren't you?'

'No. I'm not.'

'You can't do that. It's not possible.'

'It is. I did.'

His face looks as if it is breaking into pieces.

Slowly his hand pulls back. I know he is going to hit me, before the hand reaches my face. But he surprises me, and punches me in the stomach. I feel the breath leave me in a rush and pull my knees up in reflex. He hits me again and again. He climbs onto his knees and hits me in my stomach, on my ribs, on my face, on my ears, on my ribs and again in my stomach.

He hits my face with his fist now, once, twice, three times. My head swings left and right from the force of his blows. He is going to kill me, I think dully, wondering when my neck will snap, hoping it will happen quickly.

Then he stops. He buries his face in mine and starts to cry. I feel his tears running into my eyes, the water collecting in the hollows. His mouth dribbles saliva, and his hot meaty breath condenses on my skin.

His heavy body shakes and the tremors enter mine and are absorbed by it. I lie still till I am sure he is asleep. I wriggle out from under him and climb off the bed. I pick up my clothes and leave the room, quietly shutting the door behind me. As it closes, I hear him turn and mumble my name. I don't look back.

PART *four*

o n e

In the Gare du Nord, where the trains come in, there is a *terrasse de café* which betrays its name. For it is not really a *terrasse* because it is not open to the sky, but is locked in by criss-crossed bars of steel and sheets of tin and fibreglass that shelter the northbound trains. The roof is painted grey, and echoes the colour of the dour November sky. Below it, the trains and the people come and go at the command of a bored, sexless voice. Only for the announcement of the superfast TGVs does the voice betray any excitement, becoming loud and insistent like steam in a kettle.

Around me the empty fluorescent orange tables stand out sharply against the grey pavement and the smoky brown walls of the café behind us. Through the glass doors, I can see shadowy figures against the bar, their arms rising and falling in concert as they lift their glasses from the counter to their lips.

I have been coming to the café every day for the last two months, ever since I left Philippe, my thoughts going round and round, trapped in a circle of despair.

In the beginning I stayed away from him only to punish him. It wasn't the pain of what he had done to me that had hurt, but the idea that he could have cared so little for my pain. I knew he would never have beaten me if he hadn't taken me for a possession, a thing without will or life. But that had been my fault, I realized. Because, long before that last evening, I had ceased to feel needed, and I had stopped feeling alive. So for six days I lay on my bed in the tiny hotel room and waited for him to miss me.

On the seventh day, weak with hunger and with barely enough money for a Métro ticket, I went back. But Philippe wasn't there. He had left for Argentina, the stone-faced cook told me, barring my way with his square body.

'And when will he be back?' I asked.

'He didn't say,' he replied.

'Oh,' I said and tried to move past him. But he refused to budge.

Instead he took out a letter from his pocket, 'He left this for you, madame.'

I took the letter from his outstretched hand and tore it open. The letter, which was from his lawyer, M Albin, was short and to the point. It stated that M Lavalle did not wish to see Mlle Patel again. That she was to remove her personal belongings from his home within three days of receipt of the letter, otherwise they would be thrown away. And that a sum of fifty thousand francs had been deposited into her account as compensation for the inconvenience caused. In addition, if she were ever to try to contact M Lavalle again, her French residence permit would be revoked. I couldn't believe I had understood the French right. I reread it carefully, taking my time over each word. But the contents remained the same.

So I returned to the anonymous hotel. The bar downstairs was full of the same people, tradesmen, tourists, immigrants, and train people. None of them looked up when I walked in. At the reception, the same olive-skinned Italian sat talking into the telephone. He didn't speak to me as I handed him the money for another week. He didn't ask any questions as he gave me my keys. His eyes followed me indifferently as I climbed the stairs.

Alone in my room, I lay down upon the same grey bed and stared out of the window. For the first time, I noticed the view, railway tracks and across them an endless grey wall pockmarked by windows with bright African *bou-bou*'s fluttering outside them. Then I fell asleep.

I woke up in the middle of the night. The room was freezing. The window was open and moonlight streamed into the room in a great square right over the bed. I got up and went to the window to shut it. I counted the tracks. There were thirteen of them. They gleamed in the moonlight, an alien landscape, flat and symmetrical, without mystery or life.

The next day, I telephoned the house. I spoke to the now openly supercilious cook and gave him the address of the hotel. I hoped Philippe would call him and ask about me. Perhaps a week was too short, and it took longer to miss a person. I stared at the silent telephone on the table beside my bed and waited for it to ring. The pristine white walls glared at me. Suddenly I realized that Philippe's heart, too, was as cold as the walls. Only my need for him, for all that he signified, had made me blind. Now there was nothing.

I COME TO the café every day at quarter past eight. Every day I wear black. And I carry with me a black canvas bag with a a drawing of the Eiffel Tower on it. On the other side of the drawing are the words, 'I love Paris' written in flowing gold letters. It is a bag meant for tourists, produced for them, sold to them and bought by them or those with a tourist's imagination. I had bought the bag from a Sri Lankan—or perhaps an Indian—on the Métro platform a few feet underground. He smelt of scented hair oil and the Métro. I took the bag and dashed up the stairs. On the street, I wavered. The scent of the Epicerie Madras filled my nostrils, and I was torn between longing and shame and regret. Then I remembered the L-shaped back room.

I got no further that day, or the next or the next. And sometime in between I discovered the café. 'Are you in mourning?' the waitress with the raccoon eyes asked me on the third day. I noticed that she kept a healthy distance from me. Perhaps she smelled it. I shrugged. After a moment she nodded in satisfaction, thinking that this was one misfortune that had escaped her. 'There are many like you that come here.' She looked wisely at me, just like she would look at a TV screen. 'I knew it.' And she went away without taking my order. I stared after her silently. A month earlier I would have stood up and shouted at her, or just left. But now I remained where I was, unmoving, and waited.

She came back eventually to take my order. But only after she had gone to the bar and leaned over the counter to whisper something to the sad-looking bartender, her elbows greasing the silver top which he always kept so clean. I saw her looking sideways at me and shaking her head. The bartender didn't reply. He took off his cap and looked down, as if he had lost someone too, once upon a time. I noticed that he had a nice face. I wanted to tell him that it was only really painful the first time, when loss had the power of novelty. After that it became an episode in a serial, without remorse or memory. That's how I remember Philippe now. Neutral, like a number.

I make this daily trip to the Gare du Nord from my little hotel by the Gare de l'Est. I leave at exactly ten minutes to eight. It takes me twenty minutes. First I have to cross the tracks. Then I walk along forgotten streets till eventually I come to the bridge over the tracks leading to the station. I pause there before I go in, remembering my first sight of the great station. The silver tracks seemed to be suspended by miles of wire that stretched endlessly towards the north, offering me the possibility of escape. It never fails to thrill me. Perhaps that is the reason I return each day. Or maybe it is because, as my father would sometimes joke, we Gujaratis are a nomadic people. Our people built the railways in Africa. And before that they built ships.

My first journey on a train was the one I was born on, on the way down to Mombassa where my uncle the doctor lived. 'Always too eager,' my mother would say, 'she was in too much of a hurry to be born.' The trains in Kenya when I was a child were wooden and wobbled back and forth on the tracks, the carriages permanently off-balance from the many animals that had collided with them in the night. Mostly they were wildebeests, but once a baby rhino was killed and for nights on end, the country's most skilled white hunters sat upon the train, waiting for the mother to take her revenge. But she outwitted them all, staying just out of firing range. Night after night they waited for her to come closer. Then one day she disappeared. Maybe the pain went away. Or rhino memories are shorter than human memories. My parents and I would argue about it for hours until we fell asleep. In my dreams I'd see the head of the rhino with her horns breaking through the wood panelling of the compartment. Our father told us the story every year when we went down to Mombassa. We always went together as a family, for the school holidays. Except for the last year, when he decided to remain in Nairobi to oversee the renovations in the shop, and got killed for it. And my mother's memory had proved shorter than a rhino's. I laugh aloud, causing people to look up in alarm.

Just then the voice of the speaker announces the arrival of the train from Dunkerque.

Dunkerque? I look up. It sounds familiar, like a voice from the past. I like the sound of it and idly wonder where it might be. I imagine it lying in a cup of low hills. I say the name to myself, 'Dunkerque.' It sounds reassuring. I wonder suddenly if it is beside the sea.

'You can catch the boat from there,' the woman sitting opposite me says, her grey head bobbing up and down on her skinny neck as she speaks. I stare at her distantly. Her thin body looks dried up like a carrot stick and she is clad in some hairy material.

'What boat?' I ask dully.

'The boat from Dunkerque, of course. The one that goes to England.' She adds dreamily, 'My husband took me to England once.' The name sends a shiver through me as I remember my mother's empty promise to come and take me away. But my excitement dies down quickly. She won't want to see me. She has a new husband, a new life. 'My mother,' I say the words aloud. They feel unfamiliar now.

'What did you say?' the old woman asks irritably. 'You weren't speaking German, were you? I don't like Germans. They never stay in their own country, always want to go to someone else's.'

The waitress comes back bearing a tiny cup of black coffee, which she puts in front of the old woman.

'She's not German, is she?' the old woman asks her loudly, pointing to me.

'No. She's in mourning,' the waitress replies.

'What? Impossible. She's trying to fool you, make you feel sorry for her so she won't have to pay. Foreigners, huh.'

I watch the waitress retreating. Her hair is stiff with lacquer and her hips sway as her heavy muscular legs propel her forwards. 'Where's Dunkerque?' I shout after her.

'It is nothing special,' she shouts back over the roar of a train that is just pulling out. And adds something I can't catch; something that sounds like 'industrial.' The next word is also drowned out by the scream of the whistle. I strain forward to catch her words. At last the whistle stops. 'Driftwood'—the last word floats back in the sudden silence. What does she mean, I wonder. But she is already inside and whispering to the barman with the crumpled face before I can ask her.

Suddenly I want to see the sea again. I pull open my purse and pay my eleven francs. No tip for the waitress, I decide. I won't be coming here again. Then I grab my weekend bag and go in search of the departures board.

The train to Dunkerque is a TGV which goes via Lille. I feel surprised because the voice had not announced 'Lille' with its usual TGV lilt. I examine the train carefully. But there is no mistaking the orange-and-silver lines and the snub bullet-shaped face of the engine. There is one at either end, like a Chinese New Year dragon. I go in and find my seat. The train fills up with tired-looking passengers. The orange-and-silver seats leer at me. I try to catch someone's eye to reassure myself that I am not dreaming. But the other passengers all look at me as if I were transparent. A woman in an olive-green dress with a pinched face walks down the aisle, suitcase and bag in hand. She looks at her ticket and then at me. Her lips become even more compressed. It seems she has the seat next to mine. She puts her bags carefully in the overhead carrier. Then she sits down, her hands folded primly in her lap, her ankles crossed at exactly the right angle. She looks like a schoolteacher. Her tiny eyes watch me through their hard slits.

'Where is this train going?' I ask her.

She speaks to me without looking, through the side of her mouth. 'It goes to Dunkerque via Lille.' Her nose twitches as she says Lille.'

'Do you go to Lille or to Dunkerque?'

She sniffs.

The heating is on inside the compartment, but I clamp my arms to my side, and pull my coat around me more closely. Inside my coat I am even hotter. Slowly the moisture forms in my underarms, on my back. It prickles slightly. I rub my back against the seat. And my knees open wide, knocking against the lady beside me.

The woman's mouth tightens, and her nostrils flare angrily. But she says nothing.

I try again. 'Is it a nice place, Lille?'

She turns and looks me full in the face. Her face has come alive with angry colour. 'How did you know I live in Lille? Who are you?'

'I . . . I don't know,' I reply, 'I was just . . .'

But she is already standing and I am speaking to her wide soft hips.

She pulls her bag out of the overhead bin and moves to a seat three rows in front. She bends down and asks the person on the other seat if the one next to him is free. Then she smiles gratefully and with one last look at me, puts her bag in the overhead bin. As she sits down, she is already talking rapidly, her thin lips moving intimately.

The train has already left the station. It makes no sound and doesn't wobble like most trains do. My body remains still, as if I were in an aeroplane. Suddenly the houses end. And we are in the midst of fields. The speed of the train cannot be felt, only seen. In the silent stillness, I feel that I am not travelling, but sitting in a movie hall. The scenery changes like a cartoon, the trees, hedges, and houses blur, blending into each other seamlessly as the train gathers speed. My head begins to hurt with the effort of keeping them apart. When I can no longer bear the sight, I shut my eyes. Slowly, the anxiety inside me stills. I fall asleep.

When I wake up, the train is leaving Lille. I watch the station fall away from the train, and we are among fields again. The hues of evening soften the landscape. The train picks up speed and the colours blur once more. Pale cream melts into rose and both are consumed by blue, which gets stronger and stronger. I discover that it is possible to look outside if one stops looking for still lines or fixed shapes, and just concentrates on the colours.

A voice announces our arrival at Dunkerque. I must have fallen asleep again for I am woken up by the joy in the announcer's voice. It is the first happy sound I have heard in a long time. The train empties rapidly. I watch the passengers file out of the carriage, but remain in my seat, not knowing what to do with myself. It is the first time I am in a strange town alone. The attendant walks through the carriage one last time, waking up sleeping passengers and checking under the seats to make sure that no one has left any baggage behind.

He arrives at my seat. He stops before me and looks down, frowning. 'Come on. You must get down now.' I look at him blankly. He looks puzzled. 'Don't you have somewhere to go? Your friends must be expecting you.'

I get up and walk quickly to the door, but he senses my uncertainty and follows me, straightening seats and picking up garbage as he goes along.

From the doorway, I glance up at the low leaden sky of Dunkerque. It looks stern, but not unkind—like my grandfather's portrait which always hung opposite the entrance of the house in Parklands. Here and there, the sky is broken up by the tall necks of cranes, reaching up like skeletal hands between warehouses and factories with short fat furnaces—for melting iron and making steel—and long, slim chimneys. But there is no smoke coming out of the chimneys, and the factories are all quiet. The silence of the station is terrifying after the ceaseless but familiar din of the Gare du Nord. Against the vast expanse of sky above us, the little station looks no larger than a matchbox. Industrial driftwood, the waitress had said. I take a deep breath and pull the coat close around me.

The man helps me out of the train and begins to walk down the almost deserted platform towards the station house and the exit. I fall into step beside him.

'Do you live here, monsieur?' I ask him.

'No, I don't,' he replies abruptly. As we approach the station house, the attendant's face brightens. Suddenly he turns to me and smiles. 'I love Dunkerque. It reminds me of when I was a child, before the war. I used to pass all my vacations here. My family was from Lille.' His accent is as flat as the land we have passed through, but lilts a little at the end of each sentence.

'The land, it is so flat,' I say, 'and the sky is so big, it seems to have eaten all the land up.'

He smiles and nods, looking up at the sky. '*Et oui*,' he grunts.

I feel better. 'It's the first time I have come here,' I confide. 'What is there to see?'

He looked at me surprised. 'You're not a tourist!' he exclaims. 'Not in this season. Why, it's almost November.'

'I'm not really a tourist. I live in Paris.'

'Ah.' His expression becomes distant as he looks me over carefully, taking in the gold earrings, the cashmere coat and expensive Hermes scarf. 'I know you Iranians,' he says suddenly. 'You are the kind who prefer the beaches of the south.'

'No, I haven't been to the beach since I was a child. *Mon . . . mon mari n'aimait pas les plages,*' I lie. But only partially. It was true that Philippe disliked beaches, he was afraid of getting skin cancer. But it wasn't true that he didn't go to the south of France. He remained in the hotel most of the day, only going out to shop, eat gargantuan meals by the old harbour, and go to huge parties at night. I shiver at the thought of him.

The attendant begins to speak again, the words rushing out. '*Et oui,* the beaches of one's childhood. We always return to them you know.' He smiles sentimentally. 'I've plenty of colleagues who have retired here. It is not expensive, and the beaches here are the most beautiful of all France. I would happily do the same when my time comes but my wife, she doesn't like our northern beaches. Says there's too much wind here.'

'Wind?'

'Oh yes, there is always a wind here.'

All of a sudden I become aware of it. I notice that despite the factories, the air smells fresh and the stiff little breeze steals away my breath which in Paris would have been curling from my mouth like steam, for it is cold here. I stick my face into the wind and breathe deeply. I can smell the salt now and the rusting iron and the oily undertones of paint within it.

The attendant waves his hand towards the horizon. 'That's the harbour there. But there is nothing now except abandoned warehouses. In the old days they built the world's biggest ships in there.'

I follow his hand with my eyes and notice the missing pieces: the empty spaces for ships that went elsewhere, the abandoned windowless warehouses, the unmoving quays. The low keening of the wind blowing through wires adds music to the vista of industrial death.

We walk on towards the exit. At the gate he stops. 'The promenade is that way,' he waves his hat in the opposite direction from the abandoned factories. 'You can take a bus at the main gate which takes you into the town or walk on the promenade General de Gaulle until you get to the beach.' He pauses, staring at me reflectively, trying to guess what has brought me here. 'It's the tail-end of the season now, and there are very few tourists left. Most of the restaurants are closed. Try the Restaurant de la Gare—it's on the road that parallels the sea, second turning to your right, rue Palombine. And they have rooms at the Maison d'Agnes just a little farther down the road.'

I thank him and take the path by the sea. The promenade is a slim strip of grey cement, flanked by a low grey wall on the seaward side. I follow the little path past what look like welfare flats, small, square, and painted grey and brown. These slowly give way to small semi-detached stone houses painted in gay colours with tiny fragile gardens.

On the other side of the wall, the sea is distant and sluggish, a darker shade of grey than the sky. Between the sea and me the beach stretches wide and flat. The sand is grey-brown with streaks of olive. I am surprised at how different it is from the sea at Mombassa where my brothers and I would play. There are no palm trees here. In fact, there are no trees at all. No bright pink bougainvillea splash the sides of the buildings with colour. The feeling of endless empty space makes me feel like a survivor. I feel proud to be alive, and to be battling against the ever-present wind.

I push against it, and it pushes me. We struggle together. I become hot and break into a sweat under my coat and heavy sweater. I open the buttons of the coat and let the air blow though. For a fraction of a second I can smell my own sweat. Then the wind snatches it up and tears it apart with its teeth.

All at once the sky lightens. At the very western edge of the sea, the sun has broken free of the blanket of cloud and pauses before plunging into the sea. The beach changes colour, the silvery grey turning platinum white, and the brown turning golden bronze. The dark grey sand takes on a red hue. I am struck dumb by the delicate beauty of the change. In moments it is over. The sun dips below the horizon and the clouds take over once more.

The advancing darkness reminds me that it will soon be night, and that I have not eaten all day. I walk slowly, searching for rue Palombine.

By the time I find the café, there is a tempest raging in my stomach. I push open the door and am greeted by voices, some in slow-moving conversation, some raised in argument. The café is small and dark, and around the bar, people, mostly men, are massed. The dining area is empty except for a single diner sitting in a corner by the window. I am shown to the table next to his and order a Kir and a carafe of wine.

He is so close I can almost touch him. He is eating a sausage. I stare at it hungrily. It is encased in taut, transparent skin. The fork pierces the skin. The knife in the steady blue-veined hand slides through it neatly. The slice goes arrow-straight to an almost lipless mouth hidden in the shadow of a large overhanging nose.

The chewing sounds are loud. His long loose chin slaps against his neck, making a small intimate sound—*phat, phat, phat.*

I lean forward fascinated. Our elbows touch.

'I'm sorry,' I say and move back.

'My pleasure,' the old man smiles. 'Now I can talk to you.'

I look up at his face, surprised.

His smile widens, 'You see, it's all about human contact. You touched me and now we can talk.'

He reaches over and touches my cheek deliberately. 'It's wonderful to make contact with people, especially young people.' I pull back—surprised but also a bit alarmed. I don't want the burden of contact with this strange old man who doesn't mind talking to strangers.

'What were you thinking of when you touched me?' he asks conversationally.

The question takes me by surprise. 'I . . .' My mind goes blank. 'I forget . . .' I shake my head. 'It wasn't very important.'

'No, tell me, what was it?' he insists.

'What is your best memory?' I ask abruptly, changing the subject.

He sits back and thinks for a few seconds. 'Sleeping with my wife for one year before I married her.' He nods to himself, 'Yes, that was the best time.'

'And after you married her, what happened?'

'We started a restaurant. I cooked, she served and cleaned.' He looks around the restaurant. 'But it isn't good to stay always in one place. One must travel, change the air.' He stares at me, his eyes intense. I nod in encouragement. 'So I travel, I go to many different restaurants, big ones, small ones, bad ones, mediocre ones, and even great ones. I have three daughters. All good cooks. They encourage me to travel. In our little town in the Alps we go stale seeing nothing except the cows and ourselves. The people and the cows begin to resemble each other.'

'Where my family comes from, they trade them for wives,' I joke.

'Really?' He takes another bite of his sausage and chews on it. 'Human cows. Perhaps your people and mine, we aren't so different after all.' He laughs loudly at his joke and grabs his glass of wine. *'Santé!'* he toasts me, tipping the glass at me, before he drinks. I pick up my glass and do the same. Suddenly the Kir begins to taste better. I smile at him.

He watches me closely, a naughty smile on his lips. 'But I bet you don't have lonely cows,' he says, and cackles triumphantly.

'What do you mean?' My laughter has a slight edge of irritation to it. 'Lonely cows don't exist, they are always part of a herd.' I drink some more of the Kir.

'Human cows are always lonely,' he says sadly. 'It's a new breed. Maybe you don't have them yet.' He reaches for his carafe of wine. It is empty. I reach over and pour him a glass from mine. He thanks me and takes a long sip. Then he begins to speak again, his low voice now barely audible above the noise of the bar.

'Eventually the sameness becomes loneliness. And we wrap ourselves in it. Then with the loneliness comes the forgetting, and all is grey and more grey. There was a painter in our village. Every day he would mix one drop of white paint in a pool of black, and paint a picture. When he finished, he would stand in front of an old camera which sat by itself on a tripod and take a photograph of himself and his painting. This he did every day. Each day he would add an extra drop of white to the pool. At first the canvases stayed black. Then, they began to change. They became dark grey at first, and then ever so slowly the colour began to lighten and the painter was surrounded by shades of grey stretching into infinity.' He cuts himself another piece of sausage. I finish my Kir and start on the wine.

'And? What is the end of your story?' I ask impatiently.

'There is no end. He is still there painting the same thing every day,' the old man replies simply.

'Oh,' I am disappointed. 'So why did you tell me this story?' I ask sharply.

He looks at me blankly, 'Why?' Then he begins to cackle again. 'I don't know. I've forgotten.' He is stopped by a fit of coughing. When it is over, he wipes his forehead with the napkin that is tucked around his neck. He sighs, 'I forget easily now. But I have a way to beat it. I always keep the bills of the restaurants I go to in my right pocket and my train ticket in my left jacket pocket. My daughter Isabelle leaves me at the station in Martigny. There I have a kir at the Restaurant de la Gare opposite the station. That way I mark the starting point of my journey. From there on, I guard all my bills. And if the bill doesn't have the name of the restaurant, I make them write it down. That way I know where I am, where I have been, what I did today and yesterday.' He nods to himself. 'A most efficient system.'

I listen to him enviously. The old man is happier without his memories. Perhaps he knows that, which is why he can talk freely to others, because he will forget them, like he will forget me and only remember the name of the restaurant.

He finishes his meal without more words, lost in his timeless world. Then abruptly he gets up and leaves. His plate is wiped clean. The carafe of wine is empty. Between the two sits the bill, slightly soiled and still unpaid, the name of the restaurant clearly written on it. I grab the bill and I run out of the door. 'Monsieur,' I shout after him. But the wind snatches away my words. The old man is swallowed by the darkness.

* * *

THE NEXT MORNING, the promenade is transformed. The cafés have opened their striped awnings and the carousel goes round and round to the sound of an accordion. The sidewalk is filled with people. Not the fashionably-clad, confident men and women of Nice or Cannes, but people of all ages and sizes, old men with lined faces and plump women in dark clothes and headscarves. Only the young girls look beautiful. But their beauty feels transient here. It is the old men and women who seem to belong. Some sit on the low wall and look out at the sea, their faces neither sad nor happy. Others stand around and smoke their cigarettes, oblivious of their surroundings, but only because they are a part of them. On one side, a group of old men play boules. A little child cycles by, screaming with delight, followed by a small dog. Then comes the mother in a shabby black coat, pushing a broken-down pram.

The wind is less fierce this morning and only whispers its complaints. I look out at the sea across a wide expanse of honey-coloured sand. It looks dreamlike and faraway and blue. The huge, cloudless, pale-blue sky leans over the beach, shrinking the chimney stacks and cranes in the harbour to harmless little pinpoints.

The sand is very soft and slips away under my feet, so I take off my shoes and socks as I used to when I was a child in Mombassa. It feels warm, though the air is cold. I walk down the beach away from the town.

The people are the first to disappear, then the houses, as the beach narrows and cliffs block the sight of the land beyond. Wild grass, pale green and yellow, grows on the top, giving the beach a desolate air. The wind bends the grass. Its shushing voice drowns out the distant voice of the sea. The smell of rust and salt fills my nostrils.

I keep walking, no longer alien, no longer foreign. The cliffs give way to enormous sand dunes. The landscape is all softly rounded curves now.

At last, I turn back. The tide has risen, and the sea covers more than half the beach. Seagulls fly in and settle on the sand. There are few people out on the promenade now. The gaily-coloured umbrellas in the cafés have been folded. I sit on the parapet that divides the promenade from the beach and dust my feet off with my hands. They are ice-cold and numb. I rub them between my hands and slowly the blood returns to my toes. The tranquillity of the spot seeps gently into me. I sit still, afraid to move, lest the feeling were to go away.

It comes up to me so silently that until I hear the sound and smell the hot fresh urine, I don't even know it is there. I leap to the rescue of my bag, but it is too late. It is already soaked. I stare at it in disgust. Then I turn on the dog.

'Eh, what are you doing?' I shout at it. The dog stops peeing immediately and freezes, one leg still held stiffly in the air. It is the strangest looking creature I have ever seen. Short powerful hind legs with massive thighs of the kind that bulldogs have, are attached to an arched back and a fairylike waist. The tail is not curly but straight and shaggy, and held out stiffly like a sword. 'Shoo,' I say to the hind legs, torn between disgust and fear, but even to my ears I sound weak. But the dog understands. It puts its leg down, turns and looks at me apologetically out of long sad eyes. Its face is strange too. It has a wrinkled forehead and a squashed upturned nose, rather like that of a bulldog. But unlike bulldogs, its ears are large and flop forward.

The dog stares up at me, the worried frown on its face deepening. Then it starts moving slowly towards me, wagging its tail hesitantly. I freeze. It thrusts its head gently against my legs and then looks up at me, begging for my liking. I feel the strength in it as it leans against me. I look down at its head. The fur is short and looks clean. I reach out and touch it. It feels smooth and velvety. I begin to stroke it. The dog presses itself more firmly against me. Only then do I notice the other dogs.

Suddenly the space around me is swarming with browns, blacks and whites, as the motley collection chase each other around me. Some have elegant bodies but others are so odd-looking that I can hardly believe my eyes. In one of those little silences when the wind pauses to take a breath, I hear the rubbery whooshing sound of wheels on cement and pebbles. The sound grows louder. I look up and in the distance, moving quite fast, is a wheelchair. From it, a man is shouting furiously as he moves towards us, 'Blandine, Leo, Castel. *Qu'est-ce que vous faites*? How many times have I told you not to bother strangers?'

The dogs stop playing. They all turn anxiously towards the sound. Their tails stop wagging. My friend, the dog who urinated on my bag, gives me an apologetic look and slowly moves to the front of the pack.

The wheelchair comes to a halt before us. It is large and sturdy, with big thick wheels. In it is a powerfully-built man, with big shoulders and forearms, and a huge dome of a head. He addresses my friend, 'Leo, haven't I told you not to scare strangers? What has made you so naughty today?'

Leo walks up to him and puts his big heavy head in the man's lap. Immediately the man's hand goes to the dog's head and begins to scratch him behind the ears and then lower, around the neck and chest. I watch him carefully, a part of my mind commits to memory how a dog should be scratched.

The man's voice changes as he scratches the dog. He still scolds but now his voice is lower and has lost its stridency. The other dogs sense the change, rush up to him and jump all over his chair, fighting with each other to lick his hands. I feel alone again, and am almost jealous of the man in the wheelchair.

Then Leo remembers me. He turns to look at me, then turns back to his master. 'Leo, stay here,' the man calls warningly. Leo takes a step towards me.

'Leo,' I call tentatively, putting out my hand. He takes another step and his dog face seems to brighten. Then I hear the wheelchair moving. The man parks himself in between Leo and me. He looks at me angrily and says, 'So you're trying to steal him away from me, are you?'

'Of course not,' I reply, stung. 'He peed on my bag.'

'Peed on your bag, that's rich,' he snorts.

'It's true,' I insist. 'Look.' I hold up the bag.

He looks at it in silence. Then he says, 'Leo's a very expensive dog. Was your bag expensive? It doesn't look it.'

I look at the bag. It looks like a rag now. The other dogs have played with it too. 'Not terribly, but . . .'

'My dog's pee is probably worth a hundred times more than your bag,' he cuts me short, waving his arm grandly. 'Leo is unique.'

'That's not the point. That bag is the only one I have.'

His eyes narrow. 'So you're trying to claim that your bag is unique too? Bullshit.' He rolls himself forward and jabs a finger at me. 'I bred that dog, I created it. Leo is alive, you understand? A bag is a thing.'

I give in. 'You're right. He's a lovely creature. They all are.'

'You like them?' he asks. I nod. He is silent for a second. Then he begins to speak. 'I used to be a dog walker before I lost my legs.' He points at his thighs, covered in a light blue rug. 'I walked people's dogs. I didn't care for them, it was just a job. Sometimes I would take the blood of a female in heat and rub it on my legs. The male dogs would smell it and they'd follow me anywhere without a leash. I'd walk through the town with them at my heels, like the Pied Piper of Hamelin. How the people would stare! It was good for business. Then one day I walked them too near a mine, one of those the Germans had left behind. I saw it just as one of the dogs, a badly trained Afghan hound, ran over to it and pawed it playfully. Like a fool, instead of running away, I ran towards the dog, and the mine went off. I flew off the cliff and landed on the beach, the remains of my legs scattered around me. That's where they found me.'

I don't know what to say. 'Well, at least you were alive,' I murmur at last.

'Of course,' he says and laughs bitterly. 'It was the best thing that happened to me.' He jerks his head towards the dogs. 'I became a dog breeder. See. They are the living proof of my genius.' He looks up at me from his chair.

'Your genius? I don't see. They are all mongrels. Of what value are they?'

He explodes. 'They are not mongrels. They are my artistic creations. I visualize them and they come to life.'

'Of course,' I say sarcastically.

'I sell one puppy for more money than you can make in your life,' he claims angrily.

'How do you know what I can make?' I splutter. 'You don't know anything about me. And as for you, your dogs are all just . . .' I pause, searching for the right word, 'just mistakes.'

'Wh-what do you know of dog breeding?' he asks angrily.

'Not much, but I do know a story when I hear one.' I get up off the wall and straighten my clothes. Seeing me stand, Leo grabs my hand with his mouth.

'Tell your dog to let go.'

He laughs. 'I can't. You'll have to come back to the house with us.'

'Make him stop!'

'I can't. Leo has a mind of his own.'

'Please, can't you somehow persuade him then?' I beg.

He shrugs, 'Leo's not very persuadable when he's decided he likes someone.'

Reluctantly I agree.

We move away from the town in a grand parade along the promenade, the man in the wheelchair leading the group. Like the Pied Piper.

His house is in a grey social-housing building beside the promenade. It stands alone, its back to the town, facing the abandoned harbour and the sea.

He opens the door and rolls himself in. We follow, the dogs barking and yelping with excitement, Leo still holding onto my hand. I find myself in a large room, which serves as both kitchen and bedroom. Huge windows make the sea omnipresent.

As soon I enter I become aware of the dog smell that fills the house. A hot, concentrated odour that is different—warm, sweaty, meaty, and vinegary all at once. I wrinkle my nose, not sure if I like it, but unable to dislike it either because it feels so natural.

He pours me a glass of wine and brings it over.

'Sit on the bed,' he says. 'I so seldom have guests that I threw the furniture out. This way, the dogs have plenty of room.'

I look around the room at the dogs lying carelessly all over the floor with their tongues hanging out, and begin to laugh.

'It is for the dogs that I live here,' the man admits, laughing with me. 'They can make as much noise as they want without upsetting the neighbours. And of course the smell—in winter, it gets pretty smelly in here with twenty dogs. But that's why I like to be here, in the midst of the wind.' He looks at me, 'You don't mind the smell, do you? I can open a window if you like.'

'No, I'm fine. But it must be so lonely for you out here by yourself.'

'I'm not alone,' he says gruffly. 'I have the dogs.'

'But dogs can't replace people.'

'People? What people?' he chortles. 'When I had legs, I needed people. Now I realize I don't. That's another lie I have seen through. No one needs other people. You just need something to love.'

'But . . .' I protest. Leo comes up to me and licks my hand.

The dog man laughs. 'In a way you were right, these dogs were mistakes. I had a bitch who had a very fertile womb. She went into heat when I was ill. All the dogs knew, and they poured their seed into her. I didn't have the heart to stop them doing what I couldn't do. And these were the result.' He waves his hand at his oddly constructed dogs, his face tender. 'No one else would have them. So I kept them all.' Leo goes to him and licks his hand. He fondles Leo's ears and the dog shuts his eyes in delight. His joy is reflected in his owner's eyes.

'Are you happy with your life then?' I ask him.

'No, not happy, but I've learnt to be content with it.'

I look at him sitting in his wheelchair, Leo by his side, and smile.

He sees the smile and thinks I am laughing at him. 'You don't believe me, do you?' he says angrily. 'You think a man without legs has to be unhappy. That he exists only be pitied.' His face becomes contorted with rage, 'You're on the run, and you're happy. You think you've solved your problems. You're wrong. They're smarter than you. They follow you like bloodhounds, tracking you by your smell, they make you run and run till you are exhausted. But you cannot stop, you are full of the running sickness, and you must run till you die. Well, I died once already, so now I am wise.' He lowers his voice to a whisper, 'But every wise man needs a fool, so you must be my fool. Welcome.' He begins to laugh, a loud ugly sound.

I begin to cry silently. The dog man watches me with growing concern and finally wheels himself over.

'Forgive me, I didn't mean to upset you. I get carried away sometimes. It's nothing personal.'

'No, no. It's all right,' I assure him. 'It wasn't you that made me cry but myself.'

He says nothing. But his face says it for him. What can you possibly have had happen to you that can compare to what has happened to me?

I feel ashamed and the tears slowly dry up. At last I reach across and touch his shoulder. 'I'm glad I met you,' I say, looking into his eyes.

His cheeks and ears go red. 'Really. Why, because you never met a man without legs before?' he says gruffly.

'No. Because you have made me realize I can't run away anymore.'

two

I returned to Paris the next day. At the Gare du Nord, everything looked exactly as I had left it. The same greyness, the almost invisible layer of pollution softening the shadows, making the air smoky and dense like cotton wool. But it no longer affected me. I went to a café and dialed Olivier's number.

He picked up the phone on the fourth ring as he always did.

'Allo?' He sounded just the same.

'Olivier, it's me, Leela.'

'Leela?' his voice held surprise and a question.

'May I come over?'

There was a long silence. Finally, he spoke. 'Come at five.'

At a quarter to five, I stood in the street outside his building. The grey day was slowly transforming itself into a shadowless twilight, the heavy grey clouds hanging so low over the street that they seemed to be touching the tops of the narrow white buildings. A light rain had begun to fall.

I looked up. The curtains were pulled back and there was a light on in his living room. Soon I would be in that room again, warmed and welcomed.

As I climbed the wooden staircase to his apartment, I heard loud classical music. I gripped the banister tightly as memories, half-forgotten, sprang to life. I stood still, listening to the music, feeling Olivier's presence gather around me.

But the music was different, and as I listened, I grew uncomfortable. It was quite unlike anything Olivier had played for me in the past. There was hidden darkness, like the stench of unforgettable memories, that hung over the happy little melody, making it seem absurd. I climbed the last few steps to the landing and found myself staring once more at the lion-head knocker on the door. Olivier didn't like doorbells. They cut into the music, he said. I straightened my dress nervously. Without any warning, the music died away, leaving behind a terrible tension.

I picked up the knocker and rapped twice. But just at that moment, the music crashed out again—brass instruments, horns, strings, all joining to create a wall of sound. I wondered if I should knock again. But a softer melody had now begun and I was unwilling to interrupt it. I waited a little, and when I could only hear cellos and oboes, I knocked again. The music stopped abruptly. Footsteps came to the door. I heard the gears of the lock click and then the door opened.

Olivier stood squarely in the doorway, silhouetted against the warm yellow light. I felt overwhelmed at the sight of him. He looked taller and more substantial somehow. I waited for him to say something, unable to speak. He seemed equally dumbstruck, and stood where he was, staring at me. I looked at him uncertainly, trying to read his expression. But his face was in shadow and gave nothing away.

In the end, it was I who spoke first. 'Olivier. Thank you for seeing me.'

He shifted his position slightly but wouldn't leave the safety of the threshold. 'You don't have to thank me,' he said awkwardly. 'What is it you want?'

His response confused me. 'N-nothing.' I stared at him uncertainly. Then I remembered the box of pastries I had brought him. 'I brought you some almond croissants.' I knew they were his favourites.

He took the box from me gingerly. He did not invite me inside.

We stood there, staring at each other uncomfortably.

Finally Olivier spoke. 'Come inside,' he said coolly, stepping aside and opening the door wider.

I stepped inside the once-familiar room. Nothing seemed to have changed. The same blue-and-brown Turkish rugs lay scattered on the wooden floors. From the ceiling hung the same old-fashioned blue drop chandelier that I loved so much. The bookshelves were stuffed with books, and more books still stood in stacks on the floor. The cushions on the sofa were piled untidily in a corner, the way Olivier liked to have them when he took his afternoon nap. I inhaled the familiar smell, a mixture of tobacco and lemon and mint, that was such a part of the place. I looked shyly at Olivier.

'I was forgetting my manners. Would you like tea? Or would you prefer coffee?' he said.

The barely disguised contempt in his voice was like a whiplash. 'Don't talk like that! You sound like a stranger,' I cried.

He laughed dryly. 'You walk into my house after three years. You abandon your friends without a word. You live with a man who respects nothing, not even you. And you walk in here expecting . . .' He stopped suddenly, his face flushed. 'Oh forget it.'

'I came hoping to be listened to without judgement,' I said with dignity. 'But I suppose that was too much to ask for.' I began to move slowly towards the door.

As I reached for the door handle, his voice stopped me. 'You know, in a battle, one doesn't leave till one's enemy is dead. You can't go yet.'

A surge of hope went through me. I crossed the floor between us quickly. 'Olivier, I came to you because you were my friend.'

Olivier's face showed disbelief.

I continued, groping for words, 'I came to you today because when I was at the Baleines', this apartment was my refuge. You always welcomed me, you played me music and made me a part of your world. You never made fun of my ignorance, or laughed when the others made fun of me.'

'And you realized that yesterday so you came rushing here to tell me so,' he cut in, his voice tinged with scorn. 'How did it happen? In a dream?'

'I've come to you because I'm lost,' I said. 'You saw something in me that you cared for. What was it?'

Olivier's face melted. 'Oh, Leela, how could you be so stupid?' He pulled me into his arms. It felt like coming home.

I don't know how long we stood like that. I must have been half asleep when I felt the vibration of his voice murmuring something into the top of my head.

I looked up. I could only see his chin and his nose. 'What is it?' I asked.

He stepped back, looking a little embarrassed. 'Shall we have some tea now?'

I laughed. The knot of anxiety slowly dissolved. 'I would love some,' I replied happily.

We went into the kitchen together. I sat down at the tiny table and watched him move confidently around the tiny space, admiring the way he plucked the fresh mint leaves off their stems and dropped them into the plump Meissen teapot. The kitchen was neat and orderly. There was an intimacy to the way things had been placed—the herbs, the copper pans, the antique coffee grinder which spoke of Olivier's love of old things. But these didn't have the frosty touch-me-not look of antiques, they looked well-used and loved, the kind of ordinary things that gained beauty and value from use alone. I noticed these details now, perhaps for the first time seeing Olivier's life not just in the moment but as being connected to a deeply rich past. He poured the water into the teapot. The smell of mint filled the kitchen.

'I hope you don't mind herbal tea,' he said apologetically. 'I know you prefer black tea at this hour of the afternoon, but I've run out—I don't drink it myself.'

'But you used to drink black tea with me.'

He smiled a little sheepishly. 'That was for you,' he said, and then added hurriedly, 'to keep you company.'

'Of course,' I felt a shiver of awareness run through me. We smiled at each other.

Over the tea we talked of other things. He told me what he had been doing over the last few years.

'I give a class or two at my old Ecole de Commerce,' he told me shyly.

I felt stunned. 'You're a professor,' I said in awe.

'Not yet, just a lecturer. I'm studying for the Ph.D. now. Then one day maybe I'll become a professor. I am not yet sure I want to though.'

I was silent, imagining him in front of a roomful of students in the dingy lecture halls of Nairobi University that I had known, with their dirty benches, and the notes that flew across the classroom. I shook my head, he would not teach in a place like that. The place he taught in must be quite different—clean, beautiful, sunny. I looked up and found him watching my face closely.

'What were you thinking of just now?' he asked, looking concerned.

I paused. 'I was thinking how my father's death changed things for me.'

'Your father's dead!' he sounded shocked.

'Didn't I tell you that already?'

'Of course not. I thought you had run away from your family because they were trying to force you to marry someone against your will.'

I laughed harshly. His ears reddened.

He looked down at the teapot. Suddenly he glanced up, 'So what *did* happen to you? Tell me the truth then.'

'The truth?' Even as I said the words, I felt false. The truth only made sense in Olivier's world where everything remained the same. My world had been snatched away from me so many times. How could I know what the truth was? But as I looked at him, I felt I owed it to him to try. Maybe the truth would come out by itself, knowing instinctively that it had found the right ears into which to flow.

'All right,' I said. 'I'll try.'

I spoke haltingly at first. Then my words came faster and faster, I couldn't stop.

When I finished my story, the kitchen was in darkness. We sat in silence, with only the light from the other room to relieve it. I felt empty. But it wasn't unpleasant, it was a nice waiting feeling. As if I was finally ready to start again, to begin filling myself with good things, things that were of my own choosing this time. Olivier got up and switched on the overhead light.

'No, please. That is too bright,' I protested. He switched it off immediately.

'So what do you want to do now?' he asked gently.

Fear clutched at my heart again. 'What . . . what do you mean?'

'Would you like a drink? Or shall we continue with the tisane?' Olivier asked.

He was always such a perfect host, he couldn't help it. 'I'd love a glass of wine,' I answered, remembering our evenings spent drinking wine and listening to music. Then I remembered the music I had heard as I was coming up the stairs and felt a twinge of uneasiness.

'What was that music you had on just before I arrived, Olivier?'

He looked blank for a second. Then his face changed as he remembered. 'Oh, Prokofiev. The sixth symphony . . . the first movement.' He nodded to himself. 'A great composer, an original. The sixth was his last. It was performed just once in Russia in 1947, just before his music was banned.'

'Banned?' I asked. 'Why was he banned? And by whom?'

'By Stalin. Because his music was thought too difficult for the Soviet worker to enjoy.'

I was shocked and remained silent. My feelings must have been clearly visible in my eyes, for Olivier smiled suddenly in sympathy. 'Yes, it was terrible. You see, he had only returned to Russia a few years earlier, from Paris.'

'From Paris?' I was incredulous. How could someone want to leave Paris? 'Was he thrown out by immigration?'

'Of course not. He was a great composer. Everyone admired his work already.'

'Then why . . . ?'

'Because he could not forget his motherland, his home,' Olivier replied. 'He was a Russian.' He pulled out two long-stemmed crystal glasses and filled them with red wine.

I felt uncomfortable. Perhaps that was why his music was so disturbing. Maybe he both hated and loved his country, the way I did. But, in the end, he had gone back. I could never go back because Kenya didn't want me or my family.

Olivier took my silence for sympathy. 'Would you like to hear it again?'

I was about to refuse, but the eagerness in his face stopped me. I nodded silently. He smiled and handed me a glass of wine. He placed the other glass on the table and went to switch on the stereo.

The first bars of the music, loud brassy trumpet calls like the beginning of a hunt, broke the silence in the apartment. I felt a chill run down my back. Then a strong and beautiful melody began. It sounded like a song celebrating victory and I was immediately caught up in the triumph of the sound, which was then picked up more strongly by the horns. But there was something cruel in the melody, a feeling that got stronger as the second line drew to a close. I shivered.

Olivier came back. He stood for a moment in the doorway, a tall shadow framed by the light from the other room. I looked at him and was struck by how tall he was. Suddenly the trombones came in, taking up the first melody in a loud brassy military sort of way, and Olivier, transformed into my commander and I, his helplessly adoring soldier, were both swept away on a tide of bloodlust and uncertainty. The music became more frenzied. Olivier moved into the dark recesses of the kitchen. The melody was everywhere now, winding itself feverishly around me, carrying me forward into its centre. Then the sounds exploded outwards in a clash of discordant brass and woodwinds and strings and cymbals and timpani. The music slowly died down. I found I had been holding my breath, and slowly exhaled.

Olivier reappeared, his face caught in the glow of the candle he was carrying. Just then a second melody began. It was sweetly sad, and somehow comforting after the conflict in the previous section. I felt suddenly very light, empty of all feeling. I looked across at Olivier holding his wineglass and looking intently at me. We smiled, and I felt a rush of happiness at the rightness of the moment. Then his eyes went blank as his mind turned inward to the music. I watched him leave me sadly.

The first melody returned and began its assault again, bringing out the same strong and terrible emotions: fear, excitement, anger, cruelty, and desire. Suddenly I felt alone, caught in the maelstrom of my emotions, unable to get out. But even as the feelings became unbearable, echoes of the second melody came trickling back, relieving the growing tension inside me for just long enough to make me a slave of those other darker emotions again.

The music ended in a strange, emotionless way. I felt as if I had survived some terrible event and was still alive. I looked across at Olivier, sitting across the little table from me, and wondered what he heard in the music. His face was calm, absorbed but not distraught, the way I felt. But before I could ask him, the next movement began with a tremendous clash of instruments. I stole another look at him, remembering how it was at this very place in the music that I had picked up the knocker and banged at the door. How would my life have been if I had turned to Olivier for help in escaping from the Baleines instead of going straight to Philippe's bed? Could we have been old lovers by now? I felt overcome by sadness at what might have been and lowered my head so that Olivier would not see my face.

The music, too, had changed. It was gentler now. I listened, astonished by the sheer beauty of it, and the peace. But then that changed too. More instruments—horns, trombones—joined in, and the music grew darker and more despairing. The peace inside me went sour. I listened carefully, feeling more and more as if I were the spectator to some terrible tragedy that was engulfing me. I began to shiver. The feeling was one that I knew so well. And all I could do was stand still and watch it happen. I shut my eyes, feeling despair take possession of me. Suddenly I felt Olivier's warm hand over mine, holding it strongly. I opened my eyes, and his face trembled through the tears that filled my eyes.

'Shall I stop it?'

'No, let it play.' I looked at him and wondered again what made him like such music. What tragedy had he known in his life? He had everything.

The music ended and I felt better. The third movement began with a carefree innocent melody. I listened to it, feeling curiously detached, and when another melody came in that seemed to echo the cruel self-confidence of the early part of the music, I was not surprised.

The two melodies seemed to dance with each other, weaving in and out of each other's arms. Then the beautiful song of the second movement came back briefly. It disappeared again in the rising frenzy of the other more warlike sounds. I listened fascinated, no longer separate from the music nor trapped inside it. My feelings had vanished, and all there was was the music. But, framing the music, creating the space for it to exist, was Olivier, with his hand on mine at the candlelit table in the kitchen smelling of mint.

The music came to an abrupt and loud end. The stillness that followed was almost frightening. I could not move. Olivier, too, looked pensive. The candle guttered and went out. That broke the spell. He reached up and switched on the light. This time I made no protest. The light felt reassuring. He came back with the wine bottle and refilled our glasses. 'Shall we go into the other room?'

We moved into the living room. He lit the electric fire and came back to me, standing rather dazed in the middle of the room. I could feel the despair of the music still reverberating inside me.

'Would you like to listen to something else? Something a little more cheerful perhaps?' he asked, smiling self-deprecatingly.

'Why do you listen to that music? Do you really like it?' I asked brusquely, unable to contain myself. I was certain the answer was important.

He looked embarrassed and a flush slowly mounted from his neck up to his ears. I sat down on the sofa, pulling him down beside me. He sat awkwardly on the edge of the cushions, looking very self-conscious. I felt equally nervous but tried not to show it, arranging myself comfortably on the soft maroon upholstery, giving him time to answer. We carefully avoided looking at each other.

But when he still wouldn't speak, I tried to prompt him. 'It's so messy, so confusing, this Prokofiev. You never played him for me.'

He gazed at me steadily. 'Perhaps it was because when I was with you, I never felt the need.' He looked down, 'I don't remember. It was a long time ago.'

I knew he was lying. Because I remembered. I remembered all the music he had ever played. The names I may have forgotten, but I had never forgotten the music, how it made me feel.

He spoke again, quickly, as if he couldn't wait to get rid of the words, 'I put it on to calm myself. After your call, I couldn't work anymore.'

'How can it calm you? It is full of despair and such . . . such terrible aloneness.'

His face became painfully animated. 'Music makes feelings bearable by giving them form, beauty. And so inside one grows calm, no matter how sad or despairing the music. Surely you felt that, Leela? What do you think dried your tears?'

Instinctively I put a hand to my cheek. He was right. Olivier had, in a few words, told me the secret of the music. Admiration turned to gratitude as I realized just how much he had given me. 'But it was you, Olivier,' I blurted out, full of emotion. 'You made it possible for me to hear the music. You were the frame that held the music and the pain, and made peace possible.'

His face grew unimaginably bright and I wondered how I could ever have found it ugly. And then, although I wasn't aware of his having moved, his lips found mine.

Afterwards, he cradled my body against his and we half-sat, half-lay across the sofa without speaking. I felt wonderfully alive and yet utterly relaxed at the same time. It was a strange sensation, like having eaten the perfect food or listened to the most sublime music or having seen something flawlessly beautiful. As the feeling slowly ebbed, like bubbles leaving the surface of the water, I became aware of another deeper sensation, not so much a feeling, but the absence of one. It was the absence of fear.

Suddenly I spoke, 'You know, the last time I listened to classical music was three years ago.' I wanted him to know that a part of me had always been his, that I had never betrayed him. 'I never could listen to music with Philippe.'

'Shushh.' His arm tightened around me. 'Don't say his name. You're never to go back there.'

I turned to face him. 'Oh, never. I realized that in Dunkerque.'

He looked at me quizzically. 'Why Dunkerque? The beaches there are like graveyards. They tried to make it into a vacation town, but it never became fashionable. The water is cold it's windy, and the beaches are still full of bunkers and World War Two mines. Dunkerque can never escape its history.'

I stared at him silently, remembering the beach with the abandoned factories and poorly constructed houses. But I felt he was wrong. The beaches were sad maybe, grim certainly, but strong and alive too. 'Have you been to Dunkerque recently?'

He shook his head, his face grave. 'Never. It reminds me too much of the madness and folly of the war. Too many died on those beaches. I don't think I even want to see them.' He laughed grimly. 'It's what Prokofiev warns us about in his music.' Then his expression changed, grew more thoughtful. 'How appropriate, your Dunkerque, his music.'

'It was like the music,' I said quietly. 'The children were playing on the beaches, the old men were out and so were the women, the sun was shining, and the sky was so unbelievably clear. Yet behind all that, I could feel the weight of history hanging over the beach. But it was beautiful, Olivier,' I said eagerly. 'It gave the place a depth that other beaches lack. One can escape there from the pressure of always pretending happiness. One can be free. Like in the music.'

He said nothing and I began to get worried. Suddenly he kissed my forehead gently. 'Will you go to Dunkerque with me?' he asked, looking deep into my eyes. 'I'd like to see it with you beside me.'

I smiled but, womanlike, looked down, so he would not see the joy spilling out of my eyes. 'If you will tell me about its history, which you know so much about,' I replied, 'then I'd feel a part of it. Like you do.'

Three

Not long after my return to Paris, winter arrived in earnest. I discovered that my cheap hotel room near the Gare de l'Est was without regular hot water and had no proper heating. I refused to move in with Olivier. I was reluctant to repeat any of my old patterns of behaviour. I wanted everything to be new.

With Olivier's help, I found a more comfortable little room on the sixth floor of a nineteenth-century apartment building. I didn't know the people who occupied the other rooms on my floor. They seemed to be an amorphous group of students and waiters, all of whom were seldom in. For me, the only thing that mattered was that it was close to Olivier's apartment.

When I was with him, I felt I was at the centre of the world. The cold winter darkness remained outside his door, providing the frame for our happiness. We remained indoors, content with each other's company, not going out much or seeing other people, just listening to music and talking, simply sitting together reading or even watching television. The only person we allowed into our little world was Annelise. I was nervous about meeting her at first. But when she did come for dinner one night, she completed my happiness. Annelise, after all, was a part of our past, and it seemed fitting that she be the one to turn our togetherness into a fact.

I began to search for a job. But it proved to be much more difficult than I had imagined. In the beginning I had wanted to work with a chef but I was told I didn't have the necessary qualifications. I had gone to various supermarkets and clothing companies to be a buyer, but they wanted a business degree for that. Then I tried the suppliers of the Bon Marché, many of whom I knew in person, but they were categorical in their refusal to let me work for them. 'Start something on your own,' one of them had told me kindly. 'We are family businesses, we don't take outsiders.'

I joined the hordes of the unemployed hanging around the libraries and the newsstands, searching the newspapers for jobs. But those jobs, even the ones for receptionists, gave preference to French citizens. So I went back to the *petits annonces* boards in the supermarkets, working either as a baby-sitter or housecleaner every other week. The money was all right and there was no shortage of work until one day a baby-sitting job ended early and I decided to go to Olivier's for a cup of tea. He was out of Paris on a consultancy so I let myself in with my own key. As soon as I entered the flat, I smelled an alien perfume. I froze. As I was deciding what to do, the owner of the smell came out of the kitchen, a cup of tea in her hand.

She let out a small 'Ohhh' when she saw me.

Then she recovered and smiled at me. 'Ah, of course, you must be my brother's new cleaning lady. I must congratulate you, the house is looking much cleaner than it was the last time I came to Paris. I am Olivier's sister. Don't mind me, I'll keep out of your way while you clean.'

I stood where I was, unable to move. She looked straight at me then. Distance, and then embarrassment, crossed her face. 'Oh, you must be Leela! Olivier told me about you.'

I found I could not speak. I turned and ran out of the flat.

I BARRICADED MYSELF into my room after that. I drew the curtains and lay in bed, rank and sweating, refusing to even brush my teeth. Slowly I became aware of a strange heavy odour permeating the room. But I was too apathetic to move. All I could do was pile more bed-clothes on top of me in an effort to prevent it entering my body. When Olivier returned and tried to call me, I wouldn't answer. Finally, he came in person and banged on my door, threatening to call the police and break it open if he had to. So I gave in.

The moment he saw me, the smile on his face disappeared.

'And how is your search for the perfect job going?' he asked.

I looked away. 'I haven't found it yet. You distract me.'

'Good.' He laughed. 'At least you have your priorities right.'

'What do you mean, do you think I am not serious about it?'

Olivier looked at me strangely. 'You know having a job can be more wasteful to society than not having a job,' he said.

'What?' I was in no mood to be patronized.

'It's true. People who are on welfare for more than four years cost the state less than one full-time factory worker.'

'Really? So why aren't you on welfare then?' I challenged, still feeling annoyed.

'Because I don't need to be. My father invested wisely.'

'How wonderful to have such a generous family,' I said sarcastically, ignoring the self-deprecating irony in his words.

He caught me by the shoulders and shook me. 'Stop feeling sorry for yourself, Leela. It makes you ugly.'

I went still in shock. He let go of me gently. 'You know that I will always help you, Leela. Why don't you trust me?'

I didn't reply.

'If you want I could introduce you to some of my friends,' he offered hesitantly.

I clutched the table. 'No, I'm fine,' I replied.

After that I began going out again—but only to Olivier's. The outside world was too threatening. It divided the winners from the losers and I didn't want to lose Olivier. So I insisted we stay inside, making love to him desperately until we were both physically and emotionally exhausted. Olivier couldn't understand why I refused to go out, and although he inevitably gave in, I could see the weariness in his eyes.

Then in March my residence permit, the *carte de sejour* that Philippe had obtained for me, ran out. I didn't know how to tell Olivier, fearing the distance that would surely creep into his eyes, just as they had crept into his sister's. I lived in terror of being picked up from Olivier's apartment in the middle of the night by the police. The unexpected warmth of the spring sent all of Paris into the streets, and set the seal to my despair. Finally, I turned to Annelise for help.

She told me to meet her for lunch at the Café des Artistes beside the Louvre.

I arrived early and as I waited for Annelise, I thought about how she had changed. She was no longer the struggling freelance journalist who constantly bit her nails out of sheer nervousness. Now she was an assistant editor of *Elle* and had her own column. Her new self-confidence took the shape of an extra four inches around her hips that she carried with pride. But she still wore outrageously colourful clothes and long earrings. And she was always ready to complain loudly.

As if I had conjured her up, Annelise appeared.

We greeted each other and then she turned to the hovering maître d'hôtel.

'Raoul,' she cooed, 'I have reserved a table for lunch.'

We followed his stately back to a table set at the centre of the room. Almost immediately a young waiter came to take our orders.

'So, tell me, what is it that you wanted to see me about?' Annelise asked, leaning greedily across the table.

I felt nervous and couldn't meet her eyes. 'Annelise, I need a job.'

Her eyes narrowed. 'Why?' she said sharply. 'Are you not happy with Olivier? He's worth a hundred Philippes.' She almost spat out the last word. I wondered if she knew something about him that she was hiding and was tempted to ask her. But I decided against it. I wanted to forget about that part of my life.

'Annelise, do you think I don't know that? Olivier is the reason I want a job. I can't just go to his bed and expect to have him pay for the privilege for the rest of his life. How will he ever respect me ?'

Annelise shrugged. 'What has a job got to do with love? If everyone thought like you, no one in France would fall in love anymore. No one, not even a well-connected Frenchman like Olivier, can get a job easily today. There aren't any jobs to be had. Have you seen the lines of people trying for even a sales clerk's job?'

I nodded miserably.

She squeezed my hand. 'Don't make things difficult for yourself. Forget about a job—at least till you get married and become a citizen.'

'How can you be sure Olivier wants to marry me?' I burst out irritably, feeling trapped.

'Of course he will marry you if you want him to. He loves to help people on the margins.'

'What do you mean?' I asked, with a touch of foreboding.

'Why do you think he chooses us? A German immigrant and an Indian refugee?'

'What do you mean? He's Maeve's friend, and she is not marginal . . .'

'Maeve would be considered declassé by Olivier's relatives. He comes from one of the oldest families in Strasbourg, you know.'

I looked away, wishing I could make Annelise stop.

My attention was caught by a man who was approaching our table. He carried himself with a certain easy assurance that made me envy him—as if he knew everyone in the restaurant and they were all his friends. I assumed he was one of Annelise's acquaintance. I looked the other way and waited for him to speak to her.

But to my surprise it was me he was staring at. 'Didn't we meet at Philippe Lavalle's home last year?' he asked, confident that he had me correctly placed. I felt panic grip me and then recede as I remembered who he was. It was the young assistant to M Binet, Marc Despres, before whom Philippe had so humiliated me. With everything that had happened after he left that night, I had completely forgotten about him. Until now. I looked up uncertainly, my face flushing with embarrassment. 'Of course . . . I remember.'

'And how is M Lavalle? I'm sorry to have missed him.' He looked around, as if he expected Philippe to appear.

Annelise whirled about to face him. 'Oh, he won't be joining us today,' she laughed. 'And who are you?'

'Marc Despres,' he said, smiling charmingly.

Annelise stared at him hungrily. 'I'm Annelise Schwartz. I'm a journalist. And what do you do?'

He smiled even more widely and looked pointedly at the empty chair between us.

'Please sit down,' Annelise invited, 'and tell us about yourself.'

'With pleasure. I belong to the world of advertising,' he said, looking mock-rueful.

'And what's wrong with that? Without you people there would be no journalism. Tell me,'—she bent towards him and lowered her voice conspiratorially—'are you successful at what you do? If not, you'll have to leave, because I don't like failures.'

I cringed inwardly and gave him an anxious look. Our eyes met, and he winked slightly. I relaxed and watched him charm Annelise. Success had given a confident gloss to his boyish good looks. He was wearing an olive-coloured, flamboyantly cut suit with broad lapels and many pockets, and a salmon coloured shirt—a combination only a man who was very sure of his attractiveness to women would wear.

'I wouldn't be here, would I, my dear lady, if I was a failure? Shall I prove it by ordering you a bottle of champagne?'

Annelise looked quite taken aback. He smiled at her roguishly, 'But seriously, I have just begun my own media management company, so I am in fact quite delighted to meet you.'

Annelise laughed and flirted with her eyes. 'I'll have to get to know you better before I can decide whether I'm equally delighted to meet you.'

'In that case, let me get that champagne, and drink it with you. I have a client arriving shortly, but he's never on time.'

'You are no longer with M Binet?' I asked.

'No, I left him six months ago, just a little after I met you, and started my own public relations company with an old business school friend from Argentina.'

'It's wonderful to work for yourself,' I felt envious.

'What does it do exactly, your company?' Annelise cut in abruptly.

'We make sure a company that is just starting out in a country gets noticed—by the press, television, radio, anywhere it matters. Like you said, journalism makes things sell. We take journalists very seriously.' He looked intently at Annelise.

'Advertising is information, you're taking that idea to its very limit, aren't you?' I remarked sourly.

He turned to me, beaming. 'Exactly. That was precisely what I thought when I started this company.' He studied me with reward interest. 'And what are you doing now? Are you still working with M Lavalle?'

I felt suddenly cold, and as if I was under a spotlight. But before I could think of anything to say, Annelise had answered for me, eager to reclaim his attention.

'Leela's looking for a job. Do you know of one?'

He looked at me again, this time with speculation in his eyes. 'What kind of work did you have in mind?'

Again Annelise answered for me. 'Something in public relations would be just perfect.'

He became very still. 'Would you consider working for a very small struggling firm, with not even the smell of money within its offices?'

'Of course she would. Leela loves a challenge. Just look at how well she speaks French! Who would believe that she hasn't been speaking it all her life?'

The arrival of the waiter with our food created a welcome diversion. After he left, Annelise monopolized the conversation, talking inconsequentially about various fashionable events that had taken place over the last few months and about people they both knew in the media. It was a conversation that left no room for me. So I sat there, feeling more and more dejected, longing for the lunch to end.

At last a waiter came up and informed us that M Despres's guests had arrived.

He took the business card Annelise held out to him. Then he turned to me. I looked up, relieved, and pinned a polite smile of farewell onto my lips.

'We have just begun to negotiate with an American chef, the pioneer of nouvelle Indian cuisine in America. He wants to come to Europe and open a restaurant. You would be perfect. Would you like to work on that?'

I gripped my fork tightly, so that my hands would not shake. I didn't trust my voice, so I just nodded. My head was in a swirl.

He smiled, satisfied. 'And where could I contact you?'

I could hardly write, my hands were shaking so badly. But he pretended not to notice.

'*A bientôt!*'

We watched him weave his way through the tables until he reached the two men in dark business suits waiting for him. They looked ill at ease. But the moment he arrived, taking them by the elbows and leading them off, they began to smile and relax. The three sat down at a table in the sun.

Annelise turned to me. 'Well, you certainly know interesting men,' she laughed. 'He's quite a charmer. How did you meet him?'

'He was Philippe's advertising agent's assistant,' I mumbled ungraciously.

'Really? I'm not surprised. He knows how to get what he wants.' She nodded to herself, then looked sharply at me. 'You could learn a lot from a man like him. Just don't ever trust him.'

'What? I thought you liked him?'

'Marc Despres? He's like this *chèvre*,' she said, putting the last morsel of cheese in her mouth. 'Turn on the heat and he melts away. But when he wants something, I am sure he is very determined. And I think he wants you to work for him.'

I couldn't help laughing. 'Oh Annelise. You're unique.'

She looked pleased. 'No, you are,' she said gruffly. 'I am just weird.' She gulped down the last of her wine and reached for her purse. 'I have to go back to office, but you stay and have a coffee. You never know who you might meet in a place like this!'

She threw down a five-hundred-franc note and got up to leave.

'Annelise, that is too much,' I protested.

'Don't be silly. One cannot ask the jobless to pay for lunch.'

four

M̲arc waited eleven days to call. All the while I sat by the phone, torn between hope and disbelief.

'My dear, I've been thinking of you nonstop the past week. How are you?' he said effusively.

I clenched the receiver to stop my hand from shaking. 'F-fine. I'm just fine,' I stammered.

'Am I too late? Have you found something *qui te passionne* already?'

I gulped. 'Not yet. I've been busy with other things.'

'Oh, really? Like what? You aren't going away I hope?'

I laughed. He sounded genuinely worried. 'No. Just . . . things.'

'Well then, why don't you come to my office tomorrow afternoon.'

He gave me an address in the fashionable suburb of Neuilly. When I arrived, I was surprised to find myself in an old-fashioned nineteenth-century apartment. He caught my look and explained. 'I haven't found an office yet, so for the time being my parents have let me use their flat.'

'It's a beautiful place,' I said, admiring the expensive blue brocade furnishings and tasteful china scattered around the room. I wondered what his parents were like. Everything in the house looked so old and so sure of itself. Just like the man in front of me.

'I was going to go office hunting this afternoon,' he said in a rush, pushing his hair out of his eyes. 'Would you like to come with me? After all, you will come work with me, won't you?'

My heart leapt. Then it fell again. I knew I should tell him that my residence permit had run out.

I swallowed and looked at him. 'I would certainly like to,' I murmured.

In the lift on the way down I found him staring at me, a frown between his eyes. I felt certain he was going to ask me about my *carte de sejour*. My mouth went dry. 'What's wrong?' I managed to say.

'Your clothes.'

'Oh.' I felt relieved and then shy. I looked down at the severely tailored blue suit I was wearing. 'What's wrong with them?'

'I hope you don't mind my being frank,' he said at last. 'But it is a shame to see such a beautiful woman wearing last year's fashions.'

I felt naked. My skin burned with embarrassment.

'Would you . . . would you mind if I took you shopping sometime?'

Memories of Philippe came flooding back. 'Why?' I asked warily.

He smiled at me and suddenly I understood what had been bothering me about him. Unlike other Frenchmen, he smiled too much, showing an uncharacteristically straight, perfect set of white teeth. 'Please don't be offended. I think you are special. I want you to look special. Different. Unique.' He caressed each adjective as he spoke, making it sound like a promise. But I hardly noticed, feeling only relief that he still wanted me.

The lift stopped. We got out. He hustled me into a little café-restaurant at the end of the street. As soon as we were settled, I tried to tell him that my residence permit had expired two months ago. But he interrupted me as soon as the first hesitant word was out of my mouth, and began telling me instead about the project he wanted me to work on, a chain of restaurants serving fusion cuisine. His excitement was infectious, and I was only too susceptible. So I decided I'd tell him about the *carte de sejour* once I had made myself indispensable.

At last he stopped and stared at me expectantly. I felt guilty, so I looked away and said, 'You haven't yet told me what position you have in mind for me.'

He smiled. 'I already know what you did for le Bon Maraîcher. You would be a great asset to this project.'

'But what exactly do you think I can do for you?' I insisted.

'I want you to help me turn this man into a great chef. His food is all right, but the food I tasted that night at M Lavalle's was outstanding. I've never forgotten it.'

The memory of that terrible night swamped me. I shuddered and looked out at the street.

Marc took my silence for reluctance. 'I know it must seem small to you. But this is only the beginning, I promise. After this, you can find your own projects and work on them through my office. We could be . . .'—he took a deep breath—'partners.'

'Partners?' I stared at him in disbelief. 'Why would you do that?'

He blushed. 'Because I need you.'

'Me? Why would you need me?'

He looked uncomfortable and didn't answer. Then he said seriously, 'I have a problem, you see, no one notices me. I am just another Frenchman. Brown hair, brown eyes, pale skin. Boring. But you,'—he stared at me admiringly—'you are unforgettable. With your Indian beauty, your big mysterious brown eyes.' He paused. 'I want to make you the face of my company.'

PART *five*

one

~Marc certainly knew what he was doing. In a very short time I became the fusion food queen of Paris. I did not do the cooking of course, that was left to 'Bob', the humorless chef from New York. He was half Vietnamese, half white, and had been adopted by rich Swedish parents who lived in California to escape their own country's high taxes. Bob dropped out of school at sixteen and signed up as dishwasher on a cruise ship going across the Pacific to Japan. He learned to cook because he hated to wash dishes. When he returned to America four years later via India, he opened a restaurant in New York serving what he called fusion cuisine. That was where Marc found him. It did not take me long to see that Bob was at best a mediocre cook: He didn't know how to treat the spices. But for Marc that was no problem. Bob by himself was not beautiful or exotic enough. So Marc got us onto a cooking television program. Bob was to be as outrageous as he pleased, to lose his temper at least twice a show and throw the half-cooked food all over me, his clumsy assistant. But in the end, the food we produced looked utterly beautiful. I was put in charge of 'designing' Bob's plates of television food.

Thanks to the TV show, the fusion restaurants were a runaway success. And in a few short weeks Marc's company shot into fame, dubbed by Annelise in the press as 'one of the most successful little firms in Europe, specializing in "unusual" assignments'. Marc insisted on choosing my clothes and taking me everywhere, dressed like an exotic bird of paradise. Soon my face was once more being splashed across the society pages of magazines.

But the day came when I could no longer hide my *carte de sejour* problems from Marc.

The production company was clamouring to know where and how to make the payments.

'How could you be so stupid. Why didn't you tell me this before?' he exploded when I explained the situation.

'I tried, but then I got carried away by the work and . . . forgot. Couldn't you just get me a new one?'

'Are you crazy?' He stared at me in disgust, 'I can't possibly tell the immigration department that one of France's newest television stars is an illegal alien. I'll be put into jail.'

I was aghast. 'I never dreamed. Isn't there anything you can do?'

He looked at me coldly. 'No. It's too late now. Too many awkward questions will be asked.'

But he let me stay on with the company, getting the TV producer to make all my payments in the name of a friend of his. This friend then cashed the cheques and gave the money to Marc, who then gave it to me—minus a commission. Marc told me it was only reasonable that the 'friend' be paid for her services. Yet it was a risky business. The tax authorities were quick to notice discrepancies. He said I should be very grateful. And I was. Intensely grateful. I took over managing accounts and did the routine office work, too. Not content with that, I began to take on more and more of the research work as well.

Then Marc found a way for me to be even more useful. After the television series ended, our agency was no longer hot. Marc learned that the unusual or the exotic could only take you so far, and no further. He decided to approach the more established companies. He drew up a list of low-profile public enterprises and set about 'persuading' them to spend more money on publicity, using me as bait. The prospective clients, not very successful middle managers who had been relegated to public relations, were always flattered by my attentions. I made them feel important so they needed little encouragement to start talking about themselves. As they talked they would forget about me and lose themselves in their stories. Then when their stories became too painful to continue, they would turn to me gratefully. In the morning it was Marc who would squeeze out every last drop of their gratitude, while I retreated into the shadows.

I hated what I did. But even as I hated myself for it, the men's stories fascinated me. For while I listened, sharing those men's lives and emotions, I forgot I was basically an illegal alien.

Unable to bear it any longer, I tried to discuss it with Marc. But he just smiled charmingly at me and advised me to marry Olivier. 'Et voilà, you'll have your French passport and your problems will be over.' But where Olivier was concerned I was adamant. I would not use Olivier. Nothing could be allowed to taint our love, especially nothing as demeaning as this. In Nairobi, only secretaries, the kind that moonlighted as prostitutes in the cheaper hotels downtown, married white men for their passports. How could I become one of them? How could I live with the knowledge that Olivier would think I had married him for a passport? I tried to explain this to Marc. He shrugged elegantly. 'Such is life, *ma belle*, sometimes you have to compromise.'

And so I compromised.

Survival became everything to me. I ceased to think of a future. I lived from one project to the next, waiting for the day Marc grew tired of the charade and threw me out. I began watching his every move like a hawk, trying to read meanings into his every action.

Six months became nine and then it had been a year. I promised myself that I would leave soon. After one more party. Perhaps at the next one I would meet an important minister and I could ask him for a passport myself. But I stubbornly refused to share any of this with Olivier.

The strain of living a double life began to tell on me. I stopped cooking for Olivier. We even stopped going out to dinner together. I had no time for it. My evenings were full. A silence developed between us, a silence heavy with hurt. Only the music remained, a powerful thread that bound us together in a place beyond words.

I began to have nightmares.

two

~O~ne day I overslept and arrived at the office well after noon. It had been a long, tiring night in which I chased sleep unsuccessfully until I took a sleeping pill, and then frighteningly real dreams drew me back into a sluggish wakefulness. In my dream I was the rat again. I was running away from a train, and slipped down a dark hole. I fell endlessly until at last I landed on top of a multicoloured wooden globe spinning wildly on its axis. But I couldn't get a grip on the hard surface, so I kept running and slipping. Whenever I managed to get a toehold, the country under my feet lit up. But I couldn't hold on and so I'd slip to another spot, growing more and more tired each time. I'd had the dream many times. What woke me up was that this time I fell off.

The Spanish receptionist looked up as I walked into the office from the street. Her lips pursed disapprovingly. She looked at her watch. I pretended not to notice and headed upstairs to my office.

I reached the safety of my room. I shut the door quickly and leant against it, staring at the room with the eyes of a stranger. Everything was neat and orderly—papers in neat piles, pens and pencils in their respective boxes, my mail on the blotter before me, and the computer keyboard neatly aligned with the corners of the table.

I hung up my coat and switched on the computer. As I waited for it to boot, all the things that I had neglected to do yesterday came rushing at me. I reached for the telephone and called Marc, but the line was busy. I turned back to the computer and scrolled through the list of files, racking my brains for the title of the file he had wanted from me. But none of the names seemed even remotely familiar.

In my head, the meeting with the American client the evening before began to replay itself at infinitely slow speed. He worked for a company that manufactured equipment to keep restaurants odourless. But he wore a sweatshirt that said I LOVE GARLIC in big black letters. He was an engineer and described each piece of equipment he'd designed and sold in loving detail, from the special exhaust fans for kitchens to the material for the ovens. Throughout the evening he hadn't looked at me once. Finally Marc had signalled that I should leave, and so I had. Was he the one Marc was meeting with today? Was that why Marc had told me to take my time coming into the office? How could he make money from selling machinery that took the smell out of food? Who would want to eat odourless food? Suddenly I remembered the name of the file I was looking for.

I typed in the word *papaya* and the file came up on screen. Elaborately arranged multicoloured graphs, circular diagrams, flow charts, and densely packed columns of text made the document look like a textbook. I scrolled down to the end. The word 'Conclusions' with a blank space below it stared back at me. The office grew quieter, freezing into stillness as I strained every nerve to try and think. The ticking of the desk clock grew louder by degrees until it was hammering away like a timpani. I gave up. My head felt like the inside of an African drum, the rhythms of the drummer growing progressively wilder. I had to stop. Take a break.

I walked down the short corridor to Marc's office. His secretary stood up and planted her large body squarely in front of his door. 'He has some people with him,' she said severely, a touch of relish in her voice.

'What people?' I asked urgently. 'Why can't I go in?'

'He told me he was not to be disturbed—not even by you,' she replied firmly.

Suddenly the door opened, and four people, all talking at the same time, surged out of it. The three men with Marc were strangers. And yet, they seemed to know Marc well. They showed none of the hesitation and formality of prospective clients who were checking the place out. Marc saw me immediately but he pretended to be deep in conversation with the short bearded man beside him. They would have swept past me, and I started instinctively to fade into the background like Marc's secretary, but at the last moment, something made me step in front of them boldly.

'Hello, I was just coming to see you,' I said loudly.

'Lily!' Marc tried to act surprised. He kissed me gracefully on both cheeks. 'What a pleasure to see you. I didn't think you'd be available today,' he said. 'I was just taking my guests for lunch.'

He was lying. My suspicions burst into flame. I gave him my best smile. 'That's nice. I haven't eaten yet either,' I said, putting my hand onto his arm.

Marc looked confused. The others looked at him and then at me, intrigued. He disengaged his arm from my grasp. 'You must have a lot of work to do still on the Chailland project,' he said loudly, trying to sound authoritative, 'so I'll see you when we get back.'

'No, I've already done the survey you wanted,' I said. 'The secretary's printing it out for me. You've kept me working so hard, I haven't had time to eat,' I said, pouting prettily.

The short dark man beside Marc who had been watching me with interest spoke up. 'I do hope madame will be joining us for lunch. I, for one, will be delighted,' he said in a heavy Spanish accent. I looked him over carefully. He had salt-and-pepper hair, a dark brown moustache, and a neat little beard. The two encircled his mouth. Inside the dark circle, his lips looked very red. He turned back to Marc. 'Who is this beautiful woman? Why have you been hiding her?'

Marc's eyes narrowed. He looked from the man to me. A familiar look of calculation entered his eyes. He smiled meaningfully at me and turned to the client. 'I haven't been hiding her, I just didn't want to disturb her as we all work quite independently,' he said smoothly. 'Lily Patel. She is my right-hand person here.' I glared at his elegant wool-clad back as he left to hail two taxis, thinking of all the business I had brought him through Olivier's connections.

The client introduced himself as Alfredo Castellano, from Mexico. He was vice-president of Amber Productions Latin America. 'Call me Alfredo,' he said, winking at me. 'I hate to be formal with people I like.'

My eyes grew wide. Originally a Texas firm, Amber Productions was now the largest TV production house in the world. They made everything from music videos to news to talk shows, to soap operas. They also owned a chain of gourmet and women's magazines. The older man, an American with a patrician nose and shock of white hair, was Douglas Ambrey, executive vice-president marketing, Amber USA.

'How do you do?' We shook hands. He looked down at me out of impersonal, hazel-coloured eyes. Then he looked out at the road impatiently.

The last man, a good-looking American, introduced himself as Ray MacArthur, their public relations chief.

I smiled at him, but he didn't respond. He looked at his watch instead.

'Are we all ready to go then?' Marc came back into the foyer and hurried us into the waiting taxis.

He helped Mr Ambrey into one taxi. The PR man jumped into the passenger seat in front. Before he climbed in after the older man, Marc told me rapidly to follow in the second taxi with Alfredo Castellano and come to Talbeys at Place Clichy. In the taxi the Mexican spoke very little. But I could feel him looking at my breasts. And I couldn't avoid noticing how his thigh pressed warmly against mine. I stared out of the window at the rain and watched the streets slip by.

When we finally arrived at the restaurant, the maître d'hôtel was waiting to receive us at the entrance. He seemed slightly surprised to see an extra person, but quickly signalled to one of the waiters to place an extra chair at the table. He kept up an easy flow of small talk with Marc, who came to the restaurant often to eat oysters, and after a few minutes led us to a table standing empty at the centre of the restaurant. The restaurant was quite full. I felt the eyes of the other diners follow us.

At the table, Marc made a point of seating me next to the Mexican. The tight-lipped PR man, Ray MacArthur, was put on the other side. Marc, I noticed, had maneuvered himself into the seat beside Mr Ambrey.

I smiled across the table at him. 'Do you like seafood, Mr Ambrey?'

I enquired politely. 'They have the freshest shellfish in all of Paris here. The oysters especially are famous.'

Mr Ambrey replied drily, 'No, actually, I don't care for seafood. I don't like the smell of fish.'

I tried not to look surprised but failed. Then I looked at Marc. His face was flushed. It hadn't occurred to him to find out what kind of food his guests would like; he had simply booked his favorite restaurant. I felt like laughing. And so I did.

They all looked at me uncomfortably. But I couldn't stop. 'I'm . . . s-so s-sorry. I've been working too hard,' I apologized when at last I managed to stop. 'It's a pity that you dislike seafood, Mr Ambrey,' I said. 'You have good seafood in Florida.' I remarked, looking at his tan.

'But I live in Texas, and we prefer meat there,' he replied brusquely and went back to studying his menu. I felt piqued. From the attention Marc was paying him, he was the key man.

I tried again. 'We Parisians consider raw oysters with a dash of lemon the apogee of our culinary civilization,' I said loudly. 'It is a pleasure of the most refined kind—the taste of pain.' Around me, I felt the air thicken and cool. But I had Ambrey's attention now. 'You should try it. Some find it an aphrodisiac.'

'Never mind,' Marc cut in hurriedly, turning to Mr Ambrey. 'There are other things on the menu. The duck is very good—it's a *specialité de la maison*,' he said. I must have worried Marc greatly, I realised, to make him forget his English.

I turned to Ray MacArthur. He was studying the menu, a blank look on his face. I could tell that he didn't read French. I felt a rush of sympathy for him, remembering my own struggle with the language.

I placed my hand on his arm. 'Don't worry about the menu. When the waiter comes to get our order for drinks, I'll tell him to get you the English version.'

'Thanks.' He smiled gratefully at me. 'Do they have beer here?'

'I don't know, but I'll ask the waiter.'

'Don't bother,' he said quickly, still nervous. 'I'll just have what everyone else has.'

There was no sign of the waiter. The service in Talbeys, I knew from past experience, was slow. Slowness made Americans uneasy, and these men were no exception. I could see them growing visibly impatient.

'So what brings such a large company like yours to us?' I asked Ray.

He looked a little taken aback. I smiled at him encouragingly. He melted visibly. 'Well, your company was one of five firms short-listed by my department,' he said, smiling back.

'What, spilling the beans already, Ray?' Ambrey's cold, precise voice cut in.

Ray went red. 'Just telling Ms. Patel about our meeting this morning,' he muttered.

'I'm sure she has other things to look after,' Ambrey said.

I opened my mouth to speak, but the maître d' arrived.

'Let's order,' Ambrey suggested tersely. 'We don't have much time.'

I asked for oysters to begin with and salmon with a creamy mustard sauce as the main course. Marc and the Mexican echoed my order, Ambrey and Ray asked for salads and the *canard à l'orange*.

When the drinks arrived, I tried to question Ray some more. I wanted to know how long he had been in contact with Marc, how long Marc had been hiding this from me. But he avoided my questions this time.

'I can tell you're dying to know what we're planning,' the Mexican said in my ear. He had been sulking all this time, angry that I wasn't paying attention to him.

'Really?' I looked at him, somewhat sceptical. But his eyes were sharp and very sure.

'What kind of work does your company have in mind?' I asked.

'We're looking to launch our own channel in Russia. And we need someone to help us position ourselves. Your company has worked in Russia before, no?' He replied.

'Yes. A little,' I agreed. They had done their homework on us. 'But why did you choose us? We're so small.'

'Small is beautiful.' His face took on a look of animal greed, which he did not try to hide. 'Do you know that the profile of your breast is sublime? Just perfect. I am struck dumb by its beauty.'

I looked away, disgusted. Why should I bother to be polite to this man?

He read my thoughts. 'I am far more powerful than you think. Do you know how power is shared in Amber Productions?' he asked quietly.

'No,' I admitted, caught by the change sweeping across his face, as hunger sharpened his features. I glanced across the table at Marc. He was deep in conversation with Ambrey. I saw Marc's hands swing as if he were stroking a golf ball into a hole. I turned back to the Mexican.

'The company is a franchiser. I own the South American cable TV channel that runs Amber's stuff. We produce our own country-specific and language-specific shows, too, which we then sell back to Amber USA or to Amber franchisees in Japan, Australia, India, anywhere. Right now the largest number of programmes are made and sold out of Latin America, so we're the cash rich cow that will be funding the Russia venture.'

My eyes widened as I digested this information. He watched me confidently.

Just then the food arrived. The waiter placed an oval porcelain plate before me. This was filled with crushed ice crystals, and a covered silver dish was embedded in the ice. It steamed faintly, as the warm restaurant air came into contact with the cold of the ice. I closed my eyes in anticipation—looking forward to the moment when the waiter would remove the cover. He served the others.

The waiter lifted the lids ceremoniously. The Mexican squeezed my thigh. The smell of the oysters rose to meet me. I went rigid with shock.

'Wait,' I said sharply. The waiter paused even as he was lifting the cover off Marc's plate. He looked at me.

'These oysters are dead.'

The waiter's mouth fell open. For a few stunned seconds, no one spoke. Then the waiter said, 'But . . . but, madame. That is not possible.' I stared at him coldly, unmoved. He looked around for help. The others gazed at him blankly, and then at me. I left my chair and went around the table to face the waiter.

'These oysters are *dead.*'

'But . . . but the chef, he gets them himself everyday.' In utter confusion, the waiter let the cover slip from his hands. It landed on the floor with a clatter. He took a few steps back, his eyes searching for the maître d'hôtel, who appeared instantly beside us. 'Madame, is there something the matter here?' he said smoothly.

'Your oysters are dead,' I told him.

He looked shocked. Then he drew himself up stiffly, the epitome of outraged innocence.

'But that is not possible. We serve only the freshest of oysters here. We pride ourselves on their freshness. You are mistaken.'

For a second I wavered. Then I said firmly, '*Je suis desolé.* But I am never mistaken about food.'

'But you have not even touched a single oyster.'

'I don't need to taste them. I can smell them.'

'*C'est impossible.*' He was openly incredulous.

A shiver of relief went through the men at the table. I ignored it, focussing on the maître d'. It was him I had to convince. I ran in front of him and blocked his way. 'It's true. I smelt it and my nose doesn't lie.'

The maître d's mouth twisted into a sneer. His nose twitched. He turned away from me and towards the men at the table. He addressed Marc with exaggerated politeness, 'Monsieur Despres, you are a connoisseur, please taste the oysters and tell me what you think.'

'He doesn't think anything,' I cut in. 'He doesn't have my nose.'

'Leela, one moment. *Calme toi!*' Marc got up unhurriedly, smiled at the silent men, and joined us.

'Come now. Leela, we have to consider the feelings of Henri here. He is distressed.'

'Feelings? What about my feelings? This man is trying to make me out a liar,' I answered hotly, glaring at the maître d'hôtel, 'He gives us dead oysters and then tries to deny it. What does he think I am? A foreigner?' I turned to Marc, 'Tell him, Marc, tell him who I am.'

'Leela. *Détends toi*' Marc put his hands on my shoulder and began to draw me away gently from the table. 'Come, let us go outside and we will talk this over rationally.' He led me across the room towards the exit.

'Rational? But I am rational,' I spluttered. 'He is the irrational one if he thinks he can get away with this.' I glared at the maître d', who was following us out, still expostulating.

'All right, all right. But you mustn't make a scene here.' Marc whispered. 'Everyone is looking at you.' I looked around and saw that the whole restaurant was staring. I felt a moment of satisfaction. Let them all know how good my sense of smell is. But it quickly vanished before the realization that I was being inexorably led towards the door.

I stopped and turn around. 'You lie,' I spat. 'They were stinking stale. I should know. I have the best nose in the world.'

My arm was almost wrenched out of its socket as Marc dragged me away.

At last we were outside.

'I am sorry, Leela,' Marc said as soon as we were alone, 'but I had to get you out of there. You were making a scene.'

But I was not looking at him. I was looking with surprise at the sky. It was blue and sunny outside. The rain had stopped. Next door the terrace of the Val Nombreuse was filled to capacity. The street was crowded with people. 'I am not a child, you know,' I said finally. 'I'm perfectly aware I was making a scene. His oysters were bad. He deserved to have someone make a scene.'

I paused for breath and then continued before he could say anything, mimicking his careful tone. 'I was protecting our business. Do you think they would come to us if we let them get sick after we had taken them out to lunch? And you were talking to the wrong man. The real man is the Mexican, and I have him in my pocket.'

I looked at Marc triumphantly. But he couldn't have understood what I had just said because he didn't react at all.

'Marc, say something. Am I not clever?' I demanded.

It was as if he still hadn't heard what I had said. He was staring at me strangely. 'Are you all right?' he said finally.

'Of course I'm all right. Why shouldn't I be? Are you listening to what I've been saying? The Mexican man is the one we have to charm, not Ambrey. He is the one with the money for the Russian operation.'

Marc's eyes went blank and he stared at the street instead.

'What's the matter, Marc? What are you looking at?' I grabbed his arm. 'Why won't you listen to me?' Then I noticed that his nose was twitching. His nostrils were flaring and then becoming pinched as if he was searching for good air. A terrible anxiety took hold of me. I began to perspire. Marc pulled my hand off his arm and stepped away from me, into the shelter of the restaurant entrance. I watched him move away, defeated. Oysters and perfume. That's all I could think off, the smell of oysters and perfume. I gathered them to me and held on. I had a good nose, there was nothing wrong with it. Then I became aware that Marc was speaking to me, and the haze around me lifted a little.

'But you really must calm yourself,' he was saying. 'Your behavior . . . It's endangering the company. You have been far too aggressive lately.' His nostrils gave a final flare and stopped.

It was my smell. That's what he was trying to say. I knew it. It had come back. Only this time I couldn't smell it. Terror took told of me. I began to tremble.

'Is everything all right?' he asked. 'I mean, with Olivier.'

'Naturally. What gave you that idea?' I snapped. Why didn't Marc just say it, I smelled bad and that's why he wanted me to leave. Why did he have to hide behind his politeness?

'Fine. It's none of my business,' he said persuasively. 'But I'm concerned. I'd like to help.'

'And I'm trying to help you—even though I know you're trying to push me out.'

He looked at me awkwardly. I waited for the axe to fall.

Suddenly he said, 'Please excuse my frankness, but are you pregnant?'

I exploded into speech. 'Are you crazy, Marc? Do you think I would allow myself to become pregnant?' I was now certain he had smelt it. It was well known that pregnant women were out of control, subject to strange sweats, hot flushes, changes in body smells. Why else would he think me pregnant?

'Hush, don't be so loud.' He looked around, embarrassed.

'I won't, if you don't talk like a fool,' I said roughly. I decided to brazen it out, to pretend there was nothing wrong. 'Come. Let's go back inside.' I stepped towards the dark interior of the restaurant.

'No.' Marc held me. 'You cannot go back now. You've disgraced yourself.'

I stopped. The finality in his voice came as a relief.

'You know about it then?' I asked hoarsely, my eyes pleading. "It wasn't the oysters . . .'

'No.' He shook his head with infinite sadness. 'It wasn't the oysters.'

We stared at each other wordlessly. In his eyes, there was fear, and worse, distaste.

'I think you're right.' I said slowly. 'I have been feeling strange. I think I'll go home. Rest. This headache.' I covered my eyes with my hand. Through the chinks in my fingers I watched his face.

He looked glad. 'Yes. Take a break. You've been working too hard.'

'Make my apologies to them,' I said briskly, turning towards the street. 'And leave the Mexican's hotel phone number on my answering machine.'

'There's no need,' Marc said firmly. 'Just go home and forget about it. Take a rest.' He turned and walked inside.

I willed him to turn around. But he didn't.

Panic gripped me as the doors closed behind him. I watched him thread his way through the restaurant. His back sagged as he sat down. He seemed glad to forget about me, sweep me under the table.

Three

—Another world. Separated from me by a thin sheet of glass. My head is pressed against the glass. On the other side of it, an elderly couple stare at me. They look frightened. They whisper to the waiter and point. He turns and stares at me too. His eyes are empty and hard. I don't move. He shrugs and pulls out the chair of the distressed woman. Her husband, white haired and fragile, takes her arm protectively. They follow the waiter. The restaurant turns its face away from me and I am alone on the street. I turn and start walking. The street is awash with people. Africans, Indians, Arabs, Chinese, French, Tamils. It looks disorderly, the forms and colours and shapes of the foreign people wildly at variance with the old graceful buildings and secret courtyards. The bourgeoisie who still live in those courtyards have retreated behind fortified, wrought-iron doors. The streets belong now to the jobless, the hungry, the smelly, who fill them with their ceaseless, wordless needs. I don't belong with them. I belong inside, in a restaurant or a well-ordered apartment, where everything is arranged to evoke desire. I need to be in a quiet place filled with food and perfumes, and the subtle comfort of wool and smoke.

But they won't hide your smell, a small mean voice points out.

So I walk quickly down Avenue de Clichy. I walk purposefully, keeping a busy frown on my face. Others beside me have that same look, thin men in threadbare suits with imitation leather briefcases under their arms. I know their kind. They come to the office every day, their briefcases filled with résumés. Then they go to a bar and drink till nighttime. The bar smell trails them into the office, and when they leave, it stays behind mingling with the photocopying-machine smell that seeps out from their résumés.

I walk past sex shops where barrel-shaped men call to me, offer me money, anything if I will pose for them, let them touch me. They don't seem to notice my expensive suit. They only notice my smell. Like dogs scenting a bitch in heat, they reach out hungrily.

I begin to run. Past Place Pigalle with the giant red wheel of the Moulin Rouge, past bright restaurants filled with tourists with hungry, empty faces, clutching shopping bags, past holes in the wall with slowly sweating meat hanging in the window. I push past them, past the prams and babies, the men and the women, the pimps, the dealers, the fixers, the feelers. I move ahead because I am faster. The wind whips my hair. It pierces my clothes and cools my skin, turning my bones to glass. But still the smell follows me, keeps pace with me, betraying my every move.

I stumble forward, right, left, and right again onto another street. Slowly the noise of the boulevard recedes. The shops disappear. The street is quiet. The buildings are taller, prouder, grey and old. They know they have prevailed over time.

The pavement narrows. The people disappear. The houses curve back and forth like ribbons. I slow down to a walk again. I look up at the buildings. Wooden shutters on the first floor. Windows with curtains on the second. Plants on the fifth floor. Which one will take me in? A crack appears in the black steel gate and a man emerges. Cautiously he peers out, helmet in one hand, bag in the other. He lowers his foot carefully onto the pavement. I watch approvingly. He has chosen a spot that is free of dogshit, of rubbish, of involvement. The street is dangerous, his feet in their heavy soles tell me. His face is carefully sealed. Then fear comes into his eyes as he sees me watching him. He turns and carefully locks the door the door to his world. He tests it to make sure it is shut. His leather jacket shines in the late October light. He crosses the street gingerly. In a flash he is off, roaring down the street on rubber wings.

Suddenly I am besieged by a sense of familiarity. I know I have been here before. I walk on, turn the corner. Inside the barred courtyards there is a house with a garden and two children that I must go to. Children are savages. They don't mind strong smells. I must find it, the house of the whales. Then all I will have to do is to remember the code. And I will enter the iron gate and wipe out the past.

The buildings flatten out and unite behind their smooth white façades. The streets look the same, deceptive in their uniformity. A nanny walks past carrying her bagful of mistrust. Her nose twitches, and I go dark with shame. I turn around and walk the other way, endlessly. The streets become a backdrop against which my shadow moves. I no longer know where I am. The houses diminish and draw closer to each other.

I turn into an ugly street with small dark shops on the ground floors of the buildings. The windows are dimly lit and secretive, hiding the people and the goods they have. Some of them are boarded over. On others hang small washing lines heavy with brightly coloured garments in bold prints. Every few minutes a gust of air from the Métro pushes up through the vents and makes the clothes shiver. The smell of the Métro impregnates the air, giving to the place a feeling of movement and a promise of escape. A single light, a red neon sign, relieves the darkness of the street. I walk towards it. I must hide. I must rest.

I push open the door. The wooden walls are old and soak up the feeble yellow lamplight. The bar is almost empty. Four men stand by the counter, half-hidden in the gloom. They look up as I open the door but I cannot see their eyes. I see only the large bartender, in a white apron and black vest. He is wiping glasses and setting them on the rack above his head. The light shines through the glasses and spills onto his bald head. The silence is comfortable, broken only by the sound of glass hitting wood.

The bartender takes his time. First he serves the three workmen in yellow helmets on the other side of the bar.

Then he comes to me. 'What do you want ?' he says rudely.

'A cognac,' I reply.

'It's too early for cognac,' he says. The other men look up, scenting conflict.

'That's where you are wrong,' I reply calmly. 'In my world it's never too early.'

One of the men across the bar shouts out, 'Which world is that—the monkey kingdom?'

A flash of irritation, 'Shut up Jules, drink your whisky and mind your own business,' the bartender says over his shoulder. He hands me the cognac.

The fumes rise up and warm my face. Warm golden liquid slips down my throat, disinfecting the flesh as it travels downwards.

'Thank you.' I smile.

'De rien.'

'Please, why don't you sit with me, have a drink. I'll buy it.' Suddenly I feel like talking.

The hand that is wiping the counter stops.

'I told you she was looking for a man,' one of the yellow hats tells his companion.

'She didn't choose you, did she?' the other cackled.

'Ta gueule, tais toi,' the first one growls.

'I suppose you have a lot of people coming in here and bothering you with their stories, right?' I say. He turns around and folds his arms patiently over his chest. 'But I'm different, you know.'

'Do you want more?' he cuts in rudely.

'Do I want more what?'

'To drink.'

I look at the glass. It is empty. More disinfectant is needed for the patient.

'Here, take this.' He says, handing me wine this time. It is dense and black and smells medicinal. I gulp it down quickly and ask for more. He pours more wine into the glass. Before he removes his fingers from the glass I reach out and put mine on top of his. He pulls his hand away and the wine spills over my hand onto the counter. 'Watch it! Or I'll have to throw you out.'

The smell is stronger now, more demanding. It rears up from under my skirt. I thrust myself off the stool. 'I'm going to the bathroom,' I announce loudly. From the back of the room comes a roll of masculine laughter.

'No you don't.' The bartender comes striding around the counter. 'You pay before you go anywhere.'

'But I'm not going anywhere. I'm just going to the bathroom.'

'That's all right, but you still have to pay for your drink first.'

'All right.' I fumble in my bag for a hundred-franc note. At last I find it and hand it to him.

He takes it and counts out my change in silver pieces from the bag around his waist.

'You can keep it,' I say sulkily.

'You'll need two franc piece for the bathroom, or else you'll have to go to the men's,' he says, handing me a coin. More masculine laughter follows me down the stairs.

It is quite a while later that I come up the stairs. The bartender is again busy wiping glasses with a white towel. The drinkers have been replaced by diners. There are only two so far, sitting solemnly at opposite ends of the bar counter.

'Can I have another drink?' I say to the bartender, climbing onto a stool in the centre. My clothes still reek of the sour urine smell of the bathroom.

'*Dis donc, encore la?*' he laughs, 'I was thinking of sending one of our brave customers to search for you.'

I don't bother to reply. 'Now, where's my wine?' I say brusquely. The other diners don't seem to mind that I smell of the toilet, and neither does the bartender. I slump gratefully over the counter.

The bartender reaches under the counter for a glass. He pulls out an empty carafe and fills it with the same cheap dark wine. 'But we're serving dinner now, so you'll have to eat something as well. Besides,' he adds, 'I don't want you getting drunk too quickly.'

'I could have been the greatest chef in the world,' I tell him, 'so your food had better be good.'

But the bartender is already moving towards the kitchen door.

The man on my left asks me, 'Are you a chef, then?'

I look him over critically. His clothes, from the tan-coloured rain-coat, to the brown leather shoes, are of the kind that defy fashion. His eyes are small dark holes beneath a low heavy brow. His brown hair is receding, pulled into a tiny ponytail at the base of his neck. He has pronounced lines that run from his triangular nose to below his pale mouth. I tell him coldly, 'I could have been, but I'm not.'

'So what do you do then?' He smiles ingratiatingly.

'I'm in business,' I reply.

'Really? *Quelle coincidence,* so am I. Maybe you and I can do business together.'

He scoots over to the stool beside me. 'Mind if I join you for dinner?'

I shrug. *'Ca m'est egale.'*

The bartender dumps the two plates of food unceremoniously in front of us. 'What kind of service is this?' I demand angrily.

'I'm not here to service customers.' He moves to the other side of the bar.

The man beside me leans over. 'Don't pay any attention to him.' He smiles meaningfully at me.

I ignore him. I have to change my smell.

We eat in silence.

'So, what kind of business do you do?' he asks me suddenly.

'I sell things,' I say shortly.

'So do I. I have my own company in Auvergne. Central heating. Plastic flooring. Everybody wants it.'

'Tant mieux. It's nice to have what others want.'

'You're very sexy, you have what I want," the salesman whispers into my ear.

I pull back sharply. Can he not smell it?

I stare at him in amazement. Perhaps he is the cure, a little voice whispers.

I don't wait. 'Let's go to your hotel,' I say urgently.

He pushes himself off the stool. Fumbling in his wallet for the right change, his hands trembling, he pays our bill, his and mine.

In the street, the cars move silently, as in a dream. It is drizzling again, and steam curls out of my nose and his. He stops and faces me,

'My hotel is a few blocks up the road. But if you prefer to go somewhere else, I'm ready.'

'I don't care. Your hotel is fine.' I take his arm eagerly. We begin to walk up the road.

The rain falls softly on our skins. The headlights of the cars catch the tiny drops of rain as they fall, so that they seem to hang suspended in the light. I feel suspended myself, between fear and hope. I laugh and hug his arm. 'Will you tell me your story?' I ask. He stops.

'What do you mean?' he asks warily.

'I want to know all about you. Your problems, your life, that kind of thing. I'm a good listener. Men like to tell me things.'

He turns away. '*Merde*. What nut have I got this time,' he forces a smile to his lips. 'If this is your way of making me pay more, then I'll tell you now, it's impossible. I haven't sold an inch of flooring in years.'

'You're not a plastic-flooring salesman. Maybe you're an insurance salesman.' I begin to shake with laughter.

'Putain, of all the whores in Paris,'—he shakes his head, disgustedly—'*celle-la me rendra fou.*'

I hear *pu* and stop with a jerk. 'What did you say?'

He looks confused.

'You said I stink, didn't you?' I accuse him.

'Of course not. Why would I say that?' He begins to back away from me, looking guilty.

'Because I can see it on your face. You think I smell bad.'

He shakes his head in disbelief. 'You really are crazy. Just my luck.'

'What do you mean, your luck. It's my luck that's bad. I'm stuck with a psycho who thinks I smell.' I turn and shout to the passersby.

'Shh.' He puts his hand over my mouth. I bite it, and taste his blood. He pushes me and begins to walk away.

I run after him. 'Wait.' I grab his hand and pull it towards my breast, 'Look. I'm sorry. I . . . let me come with you. I'll try not to smell . . . and . . . and then after a while, you won't notice it anymore, I promise.' I am running to keep up with him.

'No. Let me go. You crazy witch.' He trips me. I fall down but cling onto his arm as my feet fly out from under me.

'Noo. Let me come with you. Let me come with you,' I wail.

He stops suddenly. 'Get up.' There is fear behind the imperative. I lie still.

'Will you get up?' he shouts.

'You'll let me come with you?'

He nods wearily. 'My hotel is right here, but I can't drag you into it.'

'And you like my smell? Because it's different?'

'Yes, because it's different.' He leans forward to pull me up.

'And because it's even a little bit exotic?'

'Certainly, very exotic,' he agrees.

I am on my knees. 'Irresistible,' I insist, laughing up at him.

'Of course.' He pulls me up and at last I am on my feet, staring happily into his face. Then his face fills with a savage pleasure. He raises his left hand and hits me hard on the side of the head.

'There. Take that, you bitch,' he mutters, and starts to run.

My legs give way and I fall into darkness.

four

—Bit by bit I become conscious of the sounds of the street. The hollow chuckling of water running swiftly through an underground gutter. The heavy drone and vibration of cars on the road. The whish of steam as it escapes from a sewer vent. There is a lump growing above my left temple, pushing up relentlessly from beneath my skin. It has a life of its own. Like everything else in this wet clinging climate, it grows with vegetable calm.

My smell surrounds me like a shroud, rotten and sweetly fermenting. My body smells worse than a garbage truck, I decide. Unlike the truck which is open to the sky, unlike the truck to which men cling every day, in my case the smell stays bottled up inside me, in a place without air or light, oozing out of my pores like a dreaded chemical waste, that no one will touch. I can feel the spiciness all around me, clinging heavily to the damp air. The rotten-food smell grows more and more pronounced as I breathe.

The buildings blend into the sky. There is only the sign. Red and pink, it flashes alternately, staining the sky. The rain is falling again. The drops swallow the light, fall heavily to the ground. I blink and the colours run together like a curtain. The colour dribbles into the hidden veins, forming labyrinths of streams beneath the city. Underground. It whispers to me. Go Underground. I stumble blindly in the direction of the Métro.

At last I am underground, in the safety of the station. The platform is crowded. But my smell bothers no one here. The train comes screaming into the station. The crowd pushes forward, taking me with them onto the train. At last the warning bell rings, the doors shut us in, and the train begins to move, gathering speed as it enters the darkness.

I stare at the door in front of me. The sticker on the door is the familiar one of the pink rabbit with its hand stuck in the door. From the spot where his hand is caught radiate thick black lines of pain. But the rabbit looks back over its shoulder smiling seductively. Separation is painful. But one must keep smiling. Perhaps it is natural to be parted from those whom one loves if one is to live a life of movement. Perhaps the choice is whether to love or to move. I think of Olivier. He must be waiting patiently for me for dinner. But I am trapped in a tunnel made for eternal movement. Goodbye, Olivier, I whisper sadly in my mind, I have fallen out of your world. Inside the carriage the false daylight smiles eternally.

The train rushes around a bend and slows as it enters another station. A puppeteer enters. I groan and look around the carriage. The others have turned their faces away also. The puppeteer doesn't seem to notice. He bends down, takes out a black velvet cloth and strings it up between the two poles of the carriage. Then he pulls out an old-fashioned home video camera and places it in middle of the corridor. He disappears behind the curtain.

From on top of the curtain a puppet appears, tunelessly humming a pop song. The passengers begin to mutter and shuffle their feet.

'Stop that noise,' a man shouts.

'You heard the man, Patrick.' A second puppet appears. He hits the first puppet on the head. 'Your singing is terrible.'

I look up in surprise.

'Aloua, Ahmed,' the first one replies. 'What else can I do? I have nothing else to do.'

The rest of his words are drowned out by the noise of a train as it passes us.

'What's that?' the second puppet asks.

'A train.'

'No. You're wrong. It isn't a train, it's the war.'

'And you're a fool,' Patrick snaps. 'There's no more war now. The U.S. protects us.'

Someone laughs.

'I can tell you I know the sound—it's war all right.'

'You're sure, huh? How do you know? God told you? He's your best friend?'

'I know because . . .' Another train goes by. The puppet jumps in frustration. '*Merde, putain de train, me fait chier*, I can't think.'

Some young girls giggle at the obscenities.

'What! Can you think?'

'Of course I can think.'

'What's the point? Anyone paying you to think?'

'Nooo. But I like it. I'm good at it.'

'Fool. You can't be good if no one's paying you. No one pays me to do anything.' Silence falls over the compartment. I can feel them listening to the puppeteer.

'Good. Then you're free to make money. D'you want to make money?'

Before the other puppet can answer, a heavy male voice snarls from behind me.

'Everyone wants to make money—but without working.' I turn around. It is a huge bear of a man, barrel-chested and grey-haired. Behind him is a gang of six men, all carrying the yellow hats of their trade.

'You know how to make money?' the first puppet asks.

'Of course.'

'Not possible. You're Arab.'

'What do you know? My people were traders before yours could count.'

'Bullshit, your people are all con men. Anyway, what's your plan?'

'My plan is so simple, it's elegant. We send an application to the government saying that since there aren't enough jobs, we want to create our own jobs, but we need capital. So what we propose to them is that they pay us a lump sum to start our own businesses.'

'Why would they do that?'

'Because then they won't have to pay any social security. You'll see, they'll be so pleased, they'll give us anything.'

Cynical laughter bubbles up inside me.

'But I like getting the monthly cheque. It makes me feel French,' the first puppet says.

The passengers laugh. But I am unable to join in.

'Don't be stupid. You can be independent. That's better than being French,' the second puppet says.

But to be independent one has to be French first, I think bitterly. I look at the faces around me. They wouldn't know that.

'Not possible,' Patrick says. 'I am stupid. That's why they kicked me out of school. I can't think of something no one else has thought of.'

The audience laughs again. I look at them and envy adds itself to my anger at the puppeteer.

'Don't worry,' the second puppet says proudly. 'I can help there. I have a brainful of ideas.' He faces us. '*Pour toi. Lavage-à-main*,' he pronounces.

There is a moment of silence and then the audience bursts into laughter. When the laughter ceases Patrick says, 'A laundry that washes clothes by hand? What good is that?'

'Some people prefer it to machine washing. It's more natural.'

'You're an ass. Get out.' He faces the front and begins to sing tunelessly again.

'You're wrong,' Ahmed insists. 'Believe me. I've studied the market.'

'You know nothing,' Patrick shouts, close to tears. 'You're just another good-for-nothing like me. You know what the rich pay my mother to do? To wash their beautiful expensive things for them in their houses.'

Ahmed jumps back. 'Why didn't you tell me what your mother does?' He pretends to think, hand under chin. 'But your mother, what does she do with her own dirty clothes after she's finished washing other people's dirty clothes?'

'She has a washing machine,' Patricks says smugly.

The audience breaks into laughter. In spite of myself, this time I join in.

'Why didn't you tell me your mother had a washing machine?' Ahmed demands.

'You never asked,' Patrick replies sulkily.

'All right. Let's not get personal here. You use her machine to start a real laundry.'

'I can't. I don't know how to use the washing machine. My mother always does it.'

Ahmed slaps his thigh in exasperation. 'Forget the machine then. Like your mother does for the rich people in Paris, you wash your neighbours' clothes by hand.'

'But . . . ?'

'No "buts",' Ahmed says firmly. 'We'll make people believe that you can do it better than they can. Better and cheaper, on a big sign board. They'll be lining up outside your door.'

'But people in my neighbourhood know me. That's why I'm hiding here,' Patrick whines.

Our laughter rolls out in concert. A grey-haired woman, her face lined with worry, catches my eye. We look at each other and smile.

'You a politician?' Patrick asks Ahmed. ' 'Cause if you are you'd better get out and leave me in peace. I don't vote.'

'I'm not a politician. I'm an *animateur des emplois*.'

Patrick looks confused. Then he chuckles derisively. 'What kind of a job is that? I've never heard of it before.'

Ahmed maintains his confident pose. 'Never mind,' he says arrogantly. 'I am the first in a long tradition that stretches into the future.' He raised his arm like a priest. 'I will create jobs for everyone.'

'You will?' someone in the audience shouts, snorting in disbelief. 'Even the government can't do that, nor the big enterprises.'

'That is because the big *chefs d'entreprises,* and the bureaucrats are so grand and important that they never bend far enough to look in the cracks.'

'For fear of being fucked from behind,' someone from the audience adds. Ahmed bends down slowly, keeping his hand splayed across his ass and looking back fearfully. The entire compartment claps wildly.

The train stops suddenly in the middle of the tunnel. A voice announces that something unforeseen has happened at the station ahead of us. The puppets discuss the possible cause for the delay. But I am no longer watching. I dream of a restaurant, my restaurant, swamped in the scents I create. The train begins to move. I am in Olivier's kitchen, our kitchen, warm with cooking, where my own smell has lost itself in the scent of our lovemaking.

With a sinking heart I return to the present. Our carriage is full of people again. They even stand in the aisles. I stare at the wall of bodies, feeling the temperature in the compartment rise and the air grow rank. A tunnel opens in the crowd and a little man appears, bent almost double. His lank greasy hair hangs low on his forehead, practically covering his face, and his eyes seem fixed on an invisible point three inches above the ground. He dangles his arms before him so that they move with a queer elastic will of their own that is at odds with the directionless shuffle of his feet and the apathy with which he sings his beggar's litany. A shadow falls over the compartment. The others stare at him and then turn away, looking uncomfortable or irritable. Only the group of construction men remain unaffected. They move out of his way, still talking.

I envy them for being able to ignore the beggar. I cannot. I watch the beggar's approach with superstitious dread, knowing he is my destiny. Now he is in front of some young boys who stare at him without expression. One of them puts a coin into his dangling hand. He moves on, past the three teenage girls. One of his arms accidentally brushes against one of the girls' stocking-clad legs. She screams, and the other girls look angrily at him. He turns around hurriedly, not meeting anyone's eyes, stupidly repeating *"Merci"* over and over again. In his confusion, he bumps into the construction workers. This time they notice him.

'*Fait attention, merde,*' the fat foreman explodes.

'*Vaurien,*' another man adds, scowling at the beggar. A third man, the smallest one in the group, with a face like a rat's, slaps away the beggar's hand, so that the few coins in it fly out and hit the floor. The beggar makes a sound and falls to his knees.

The foreman looks down at the beggar and then back at the black curtain where the puppets are. 'Why are you picking up that money?'

he says, bending down and grabbing the beggar by the hair. 'You've done nothing to earn it, you don't deserve to keep it.'

My chest grows tight with shock, and I have to force down the bile that rises in my throat. The beggar's face is clearly visible. His features are soft and wrinkled and look as though a mouse has eaten away at them. But worst of all are his eyes—set deep into his skull and ringed with dark circles they are blank and dead. They are fool's eyes—empty and inward gazing.

The foreman pulls the beggar relentlessly towards the puppeteer.

'Look,' he tells them. 'This thing here's a real unemployed person. You think he can find any job? No. He is unemployed for a reason. Because he is useless. So don't make excuses for your kind. Take your puppets and get out of here.'

I hold my breath. The compartment is utterly still.

'Are you talking about me?' Ahmed says in a high strangled voice. 'I'm not unemployed. I am the employer of the unemployed. One day you will come to me too. There are fewer and fewer jobs for pigs these days.'

'What!' the foreman roars. 'Are you calling me a pig?'

Ahmed pretends to cower in terror. His legs tremble wildly. 'Of course not, *monsieur*. Pigs are useful animals. They give us food.'

The girls begin to laugh, and then the others join in. The foreman's face, already a deep shade of red, goes purple. With a sound that ends in teeth grinding, he launches himself at the black curtain, grabbing for Ahmed's head.

Just then the train comes to a sharp halt. Thrown off balance, the foreman trips over the puppeteer's video camera and grips the black curtain. He falls heavily, bringing the curtain and the puppets down on top of him. The puppeteer looks down at him, and he leans down to help the older man up. But the foreman spits on him. I look at the other construction workers. There is murder in their faces. Instinctively I grab the puppeteer's arm and try to pull him into the aisle away from the construction gang. I hear a roar and the sound of something breaking as metal hits the floor.

I look back. The construction workers have rescued their furious leader and are revenging themselves upon the silent camera, which is still turning. The jump on it joyfully, pounding it to bits with their heavy boots.

'Hey, what the hell,' the puppeteer shouts. 'That's my video.'

'Right. We'll do this to you next,' says the foreman, and he takes Ahmed apart with his teeth. With a howl of anguish, the puppeteer rushes at him.

The huge foreman swats him off like a fly. The puppeteer falls to his knees. They surround him and begin to hit and kick him together, shouting encouragement to each other. I throw myself amongst them and crawl on top of the puppeteer. They kick us both. I feel the blows fall on my back, my head, the side of my face. Beneath me the puppeteer lies still. Then I hear someone shouting at them, telling them to stop, telling them not to hit a woman.

Suddenly the blows cease. I am pulled into a sitting position by a stranger. The other passengers stand in a protective ring around us. 'Here, let me help you,' a gruff voice says. 'Are you all right? Shall I take you to a hospital?' A large hand reaches down to me. I push it away and move slowly down the aisle, pulling the puppeteer behind me. He comes reluctantly, moaning softly, still struggling and fending off imaginary blows.

The train comes to a stop and the doors open. We jump off. He keeps moaning, '*Arrête*, my bag, my puppets.' I glance back through the crowds on the platform. The construction workers are milling around the door of the carriage, unsure whether to give chase or to remain inside. They stare at us through the windows, making threatening gestures. 'We'll find you again. Don't worry,' one of them mouths slowly. Finally the whistle blows, the doors shut and the train moves on, leaving us on the platform staring, as carriage after carriage thunders past.

At last the station is silent and we are alone, still holding on to each other. My body aches.

The puppeteer stares down the tunnel after the departed train. 'My video!'

I watch his face. 'At least you're safe.'

'And my bag, and all the other puppets. Gone too.'

'Except that one,' I say, pointing to Patrick, still held firmly against his chest.

'But what will I do with one?'

'Well, if you insist upon telling stories that make everyone angry, that's what's going to happen sooner or later,' I say impatiently. 'Why don't you stick to happy stories?'

He laughs bitterly. 'Happy stories. Mine was a happy story.' His eyes search my face. 'Or perhaps you didn't notice.'

Of course I didn't notice, I want to shout. How could I? My smell rises up and encloses me. I see the beggar standing before me, his empty eyes beckoning me to join him. 'It's your fault. Why do you make heroes of the *chomeurs*? They are the unemployed defeated men, people who have sold their self-respect,' I say.

His face closes up. He smells it too, I think. I know he is going to leave even before he says it.

I am alone with my despair.

Then, muffled and faraway, I hear him say. 'Maybe you can suggest a better story for me to tell?'

I shrug. 'You can tell them mine,' I say. 'It's even got a real beggar at the end.'

'What do you mean?'

I look up at him angrily and step close. 'Can you find a job for someone whose odour is as foul as mine?'

He takes a step back, surprise flaring in his eyes.

I go still closer, daring him to move away again.

At last his lips move. 'You don't smell,' he says.

'What?' I feel disgusted.

'You don't smell.'

'What would a Métro rat like you know about smell? You live in it,' I say nastily, wanting him to get away from me.

He doesn't answer.

'Go away. Leave me alone.' I turn away, pulling my coat more tightly around my body. Very gently, he turns me around to face him. He takes my chin and forces me to look up into his eyes. 'You smell just like anyone else.'

I go still. 'You don't know me, so maybe you cannot smell it yet,' I tell him sadly.

He puts his arm around me and gently pulls me onto a bench. 'Tell me about yourself then. I won't go away.'

Slowly, hesitantly, I begin to tell him about the smell. But, to my own surprise, I begin with my father's death. At the end I tell him about the oysters and how I knew the smell had come back again.

'Is that why you were hiding in the Métro today?' he interrupts gently.

I look at him, amazed. 'How could you know that?'

He smiles boyishly. 'I, too, love the smell of the Métro,' he confesses. 'It is anonymous—you can hide yourself in it and yet not be alone. For me, it is the smell of home.'

I look at him, speechless.

He stares at the tracks, lost in thought.

'You don't smell,' he says at last, 'It is only your fear talking. You want to think you smell, because then you do not have to struggle anymore. That way no one else will be able to hurt you, because you have already rejected yourself, you have already thrown away your self-respect.'

'How do you know?' I ask, torn between doubt and hope.

'Because my mother told me,' he answers simply.

'Your mother?'

'Yes. But it's a long story. And you should go home now.'

'I like long stories,' I say, clutching his arm.

'No, it will keep. We have already been through enough tonight.'

HAND IN HAND we leave the Métro and walk down the busy boulevard. At the end of it, we turn left into another brightly lit street. I enjoy staying close to him, like his shadow. His spicy smell envelops me and I feel safe. I notice how people look at him and move out of his way. We walk in silence.

The street begins to climb. The *trottoir* narrows and the uneven paving makes it difficult to walk. The buildings on either side revert to an old-fashioned two-story dinginess. But they are made mysteriously beautiful by the dim streetlights and multihued walls. At last we come to a tiny café at the top of a steep little *cul de sac*. It is called A go-go. Two tiny plastic tables sit on the pavement in front of it. The puppeteer pulls out a chair and invites me to sit down.

'Here?' I reply teasingly. 'I am afraid we will fall off the *trottoir*.

He laughs. 'We can't go in looking like this. We'll scare the customers.'

Just then a figure comes out of the door and strides towards us. Silhouetted against the light, her body bulges out of her dress at the hips and thighs, and from the centre of that great mass of flesh, her torso waves delicate and wandlike. She approaches quickly, shouting, 'It's closed now. You can't stay here.' She stops when she sees us, and her thick black eyebrows draw together. 'You two look like you crawled out of the sewers of Paris. What happened?'

Hers is a strange face—at once young and old, firm and withered. Her small dark eyes are made large with kohl under dirty blond hair piled high on her head.

'They destroyed Ahmed.'

'What? Again?' Anger illuminates her face, 'I can't keep up with this, those puppets are difficult to make. And I can't always find the materials, especially the wool for Ahmed's hair.'

'Yes, you can, Laure,' he replies. Then he adds, 'You're the only one who can.'

I stare at her in awe. She is the creator of the puppets!

'D'you think that's all I have to do in life? Make your puppets?' she grumbles, but already her voice has mellowed.

'And will you get us something to drink while we wait?' he adds, teasing.

She laughs, a deep belly sound. 'That's right. Just ask and you'll get. Is that what you think?'

'Of course. But give me a kiss first,' he says, pulling her to him. As she bends down, I catch a glimpse of her face. As if a light had been switched on somewhere inside her, it has become beautiful.

She moves back towards the bar. The men greet her with a burst of laughter. They lean into her like giant bats. She wags a finger in the nearest one's face, and says something.

I turn back to the puppeteer. 'How . . . how did you do that?'

'Do what?'

'Make her beautiful.'

He doesn't understand. 'You are the one who is beautiful,' he says.

'Me? No. Not now.' His face softens, and he kneels before me. 'Poor Leela. The smell was your only defence, your revolt against power-lessness. But it isn't real. It is no more real than your defencelessness.'

I remain silent for a long time. Then I tell him, 'Rats love the Métro too. I knew a rat once that collected cigarette butts and made little stacks of them. He was very elegant and had such delicate paws. He used to catch me watching him and look at me so proudly. I used to envy him.'

He begins to laugh. I watch him uncertainly.

At last he stops, '*Genus Rattus, Rattus Norvegicus*,' he tells me. 'They are also called sewer rats. A most successful immigrant species, very adaptive. They are at home everywhere. They came from India no one knows quite when, maybe five hundred years ago. They are great fighters, because they know how to use their environment. But unfortunately they suffer from agoraphobia and must remain in closed spaces. That's why they like the Métro.' He nods to himself, 'Oh yes, I know them well.'

WE CONTINUE TO talk through the night under the watchful gaze of Laure. She comes to the table once in a while and refills the carafe. At last the sky pales to progressively lighter and lighter shades of grey. On the opposite side of the street an open drain suddenly spews out water, grey and wrapped in foam. The kind that forms in manual washing machines. I watch the water silver its way over the cobblestones, making them shine, slipping into the cracks and slowly rolling downhill towards the traffic, gathering momentum as it flows.

Suddenly the puppeteer looks up at the sky. 'It's late. I have to go back and try to make some money.'

I look at him desperately. 'Can I see you sometimes? We could have a meal together, perhaps?'

He doesn't reply.

'Wh-where can I find you?' I ask breathlessly.

'You know where to find me already.'

'What do you mean? Here?'

'No. In the Métro.'

'In the Métro?' I repeat stupidly.

He nods.

'But, but, how will I know where you are?'

'By my smell,' he says, laughing.

I join him, and feel no bitterness.

He stands up. 'We will meet again, but it's time you went home.'

We leave the bar together. On the street he bends down and kisses me on the cheek. '*Au revoir.*' He walks away. I remain where I am, unwilling to leave. The street is peaceful. I look at the buildings that surround us. In one window there is a sign advertising a studio for sale. I look at it and smile, remembering the days at the Baleines when I roamed the city looking longingly at 'for sale' signs. I think of Olivier. He will be waiting for me. My heart fills with love, leaving no more room for fear. The sky lightens further and turns pale blue, and from the houses on either side, the sounds of people waking up emerge. I walk down the street in his footsteps. I am going home.